The rock was perfec...
blocks, rough to the...
this day there was no... ...ds were
filled with the falling s... ...ailing temperature and they
both knew that there was no retreat. To get down they
must first get up the last few hundred feet and find a
descent route on the south side.

As they moved upward the sound of the aircraft engine
increased, blotted out occasionally by rolling blasts of
thunder.

'He must be just on the other side of this ridge.'

'It almost sounds like he's below us. He must be trying
to fly down the valley below the cloud, he . . .'

The engine went berserk. From a few thousand rpm it
screamed up almost to the limit of hearing. Then nothing.
Silence.

The two men stared at each other. Alex struggled for
words. 'Jesus, I . . .'

Gordon Wilson said, 'It doesn't matter, Alex. Either he
made it or he didn't. It's not our problem yet. When we
get up this hill, then it can be our problem. Right now
we've just got to think about the next hundred feet.
Okay?'

DEADLY VORTEX

David Harris

SPHERE BOOKS LIMITED

To Art and Margaret Harris, for your faith and support

A Sphere Book

First published by Hodder & Stoughton Limited

This edition published in 1992 by Sphere Books Ltd

Typeset by J&L Composition Ltd, Filey, North Yorkshire
Printed and bound in Great Britain by
BPCC Hazell Books
Aylesbury, Bucks, England
Member of BPCC Ltd.

ISBN 0 7474 1044 5

Sphere Books Ltd
A Division of
Macdonald & Co (Publishers) Ltd
165 Great Dover Street
London SE1 4YA
A member of Maxwell Macmillan Publishing Corporation plc

1

GORDON

CHAPTER ONE

McChord Air Force Base, South of Seattle

THE ROOM was small and felt too tight. It was in the middle of the building and didn't have any windows and the jerks they had assigned to him both smoked. Holley hated cigarette smoke. It nauseated him and made him sweat, but every time he tried to go out for some air the thought that he might miss something reeled him back like a fish on a line.

Matheson had taken off from Prince Rupert, in B.C., at 9:00 a.m. that morning and headed west and then southwest. Around noon he had thrown Holley into a panic by landing at some town called Williams Lake, but the RCMP said that they had got a man to the airstrip before anyone left the plane. They said that both the pilot and the passenger used the washroom and then walked up and down the strip for a few minutes while the plane was being refuelled.

Just a pit stop, thought Holley. Just a chance to have a leak and stretch the legs. But he told them to search the washroom anyway.

Then the little Cessna was up again and pointed south and Holley forgot the cigarette smoke, forgot his nausea, and began pacing the room in excited anticipation.

Just one more hour, he thought, just one more hour. As soon as Matheson crossed the forty-ninth parallel the aerial surveillance would be taken over by the U.S. Air Force, and wherever Matheson landed, Holley would be about thirty seconds behind him.

He rolled a couple of quick fantasies of that scene, and

the one he liked best was the one in which Matheson tried
to resist arrest so that Holley could beat the shit out of him
with his bare hands.

This time, thought Holley, nothing can go wrong. There
was a storm building over the North Cascades and the
little aircraft would have to go around it to the east or
west, but either way, it had to come down somewhere,
and when it did ... Holley replayed the scene again in his
mind.

The jerk with the headphones interrupted his thoughts.
'He's starting to turn east.'

They had gone over all the possibilities as soon as the
clouds started to build, and the Air Force guys he'd talked
to all figured that if a real storm developed the pilot would
probably turn east as far as the edge of the weather,
coming into the U.S. somewhere over Okanagan county
in north central Washington.

Holley said nothing, and the radio operator lit another
cigarette and made notes in his logbook. Half a cigarette
later he said, 'It's definite, he's heading east. Sounds like
the weather is really turning rotten over the Cascades.'

Holley didn't care about the weather. All that mattered
was getting his hands on that bastard Matheson and if he
was heading east then Holley had to get moving now.

'Okay, I'm going to round up my team and get your
chopper pilot moving. You keep those phones glued to
your head and I'll be back here in about five minutes, just
before I take off. You got that?'

The radio operator stubbed out his cigarette and said,
'That's what they're paying me for.'

Holley fought down an urge to punch his lights out right
there, and headed for the door. He was halfway down the
long hall when the other operator started yelling after
him. 'Hey, come back. Come back. They've turned around.'
Then he was running, all thought of being cool in front of
the jerks gone. He charged into the room shouting, 'What
the fuck are you talking about?'

The chain smoker gave the headphones to the other

operator and said, 'They were headed east, just like I said, and then suddenly they turned real hard south and headed straight for the big clouds, and the RCMP pilot says he can't follow them and we can't get any radar on them from here because of the mountains.'

'You listen to me,' screamed Holley. 'You tell those assholes in the spotter to follow them. I don't care if they fly down a volcano, I want that spotter right behind them.'

He was yelling, but neither of them seemed to care. The chain smoker lit another cigarette and was almost smirking when he told Holley, 'You better see the Colonel about that. I don't give orders to no one around here, not even to Canadian cops.'

Holley slammed the door behind him in blind rage. Those bastards! Stinking useless coward bastards! Seven months setting this up just so some goddamned chicken-shit Mountie pilot could blow it for him.

And those half-wit fuckups in the radio room. He could hear them laughing through the door. They were probably both hypes themselves and had been secretly hoping Matheson would pull it off the whole time. What he wouldn't give for about five minutes in private with both of them.

He slammed out of the building into the grey Seattle drizzle, the heat of his anger boiling the raindrops off his black skin.

CHAPTER TWO

North Cascade Mountains

MT. REDOUBT (8956 ft.), N.E. Face. 1st. ascent F. Beckey and J. Rupley, 1971:
'... around rock divide between branches of the Redoubt

Glacier, then work west through crevasses to ascend glacier arm close to face on Redoubt. Above this, climb over schrund and up 600 ft. ice apron. Continue on steep snow and ice crest to final couloir leading to notch in summit ridge. Couloir itself or loose rock to right may be used. An exposed alpine climb; be prepared to bivouac.'

Alpine Guide to Southwestern British Columbia, by Dick Culbert.

Alex Townsend reached carefully upwards until he could grasp the karabiner with his left hand and unclipped it from the rope. He raised his right foot and kicked it into the loose snow a little higher up. Gradually he stood up on it until his weight was spread as evenly as possible between his feet, and waited to see if this new step would crumble out from under him.

When it seemed that it would hold for a while he began pawing at the snow around the karabiner with his mittened left hand, exposing a two and a half foot length of sling and an aluminium deadman. He was sure he could have had the deadman out with one sharp tug, but that would probably have been enough to collapse the snow under his feet.

This is insane, he thought. If I slip I'll pull Gord off and we'll both die.

He looked up the rope to where his partner was trying to plant another deadman a hundred and fifty feet above.

'Hey, Gord.' The figure above, clad shoulder to ankle in blue nylon, stopped burrowing and looked down. 'This is crazy. These deadmen aren't worth a damn. I'm going to untie.'

Somewhere beneath all this rotten garbage he knew there was a sheet of solid ice. Ice into which they could sink bombproof ice screws, but the act of digging down to find it would probably be more dangerous than continuing without protection. He looked up. About four hundred feet above them the face necked down into a short couloir and then opened again, hourglassing into another, smaller snow face. As far as he could remember from the guidebook description the original route went that way and then up a bit of rock to the right.

All in all, there must be over a thousand feet still to go to the summit, and if it was like this most of the way it wasn't going to be any fun at all. Looking down didn't help. If either of them came off while they were tied together, they'd both go for a last wild ride into the jumbled seracs of the big glacier below. The deadmen were just tokens.

Still, it was quite a view. Twenty-five hundred feet down to the hanging valley where they had bivouacked last night, and nothing but mountains in all directions.

A shout from above interrupted his wandering thoughts.

'Are you ready?'

'Yeah, I'm ready, I've untied.'

Slowly, patiently they began again, each feeling both more and less comfortable without the rope, and gradually the distance between them diminished as Alex was able to make use of the steps that his partner was so laboriously kicking, and, with about three hundred feet to go to the bottleneck above, Alex was only twenty feet behind.

'Hey, Gord, what do you think about the ice bulge over there to the right? I really wouldn't mind getting off this junk.'

'I don't blame you.'

'It's not much steeper, and at least it'll be solid. I'm going to traverse over and have a look.'

Slowly Alex Townsend began to ease rightwards toward a blue-grey bulge in the face, ice too steep for the snow to cling.

As he got closer, the face began to steepen and soon he realized that he wasn't going to be able to make it with just his ice axe for help. But, he reasoned, if the angle was increasing the snow should be getting shallower.

He transferred the axe to his left hand and started excavating with his right, all the movements small and controlled. He only had to go about eight inches. He cleared an area about one foot in diameter and then transferred the axe back to his right hand.

He brought the axe back about a foot and then swung it lightly forward. The pick embedded in the ice about one third of an inch and nothing cracked or shattered.

Reassured, he brought the axe back slowly to a point well behind his shoulder and then arced it forward and down in a smooth blur. The curved pick penetrated the ice over an inch and a half and there was very little cratering and cracking.

Perfect.

He clipped the axe sling to his harness, and with one hand on the axe head for balance, began kicking away at the snow with first his left, and then his right foot until he had the front points of both crampons securely into good ice.

Feeling comfortable for the first time in over an hour, Alex undid the chest and waist straps of his pack, eased his right arm out from the shoulder strap and brought the pack around to where he could reach his ice hammer, strapped along one side. It was awkward trying to stand in balance and untie the hammer. The axe looked good, would probably hold a fall, but he didn't want to find out for sure.

Finally the hammer was free. He slipped the pack back on, and began to clear the snow as high as he could above his head. As soon as a bit of ice showed through he planted the pick of his hammer with a single hard swing.

Fifteen minutes of careful clearing and climbing later he had completed his rising traverse to the foot of the ice bulge, with his partner Gordon Wilson only a few feet behind him. The face had steepened to just over seventy degrees and the ice was a fine condition, firm and dry, but not brittle.

'Shall we just keep going?' said Alex. 'Or do you want the rope?'

'No, let's do it. I'll just keep on trailing the rope behind me – there's nothing for it to hang up on and it'll be handy if we want it. Do you want a couple of screws?'

Gordon Wilson was still carrying all the ice and snow hardware except for the one deadman Alex had removed earlier. Now he took two slings from his shoulder and handed them across, followed by two ice screws passed carefully, one at a time.

'How do you feel about taking a break here first? Maybe have a drink and a chocolate bar?' asked Gordon.

'Sounds good to me. We've made good time so far so we might as well take a break.' Alex looked up at the clouds towering above the top of the face, 'Best not hang around too long though; it looks like the weather might not hold much longer.'

So they set about turning a few square feet of ice on this remote north face into a temporary rest stop. Two ice screws in right to the eye and joined by a long sling, ice hammers thunked in as deeply as possible, small steps chopped to take the strain off calf muscles, and finally their axes sunk into the ice overhead.

Each of them clipped in to three anchors; their packs hanging from the screws, they relaxed into their sit harnesses. Toes against the face, asses hanging out over empty air, they passed a water bottle back and forth and let their minds drift a little as they talked the lazy talk of men who have known each other for a long time.

Ten minutes and two Mars bars later Gordon Wilson began coiling the rope that was still hanging free from his harness. 'Might as well pack this rope away for now. If you carry it, I'll carry all the hardware.'

'I thought you were just going to trail it.'

'I was, but it'll be easier this way. I won't have to be careful about catching it in my crampons. Besides, you being so skinny and light, you'll be ahead of me and you can drop me a top rope if I need it.'

'Okay,' said Alex, 'but don't expect me to haul your two hundred pounds of lard up this thing by myself.'

'Not likely. And anyway I'm down to almost one ninety-nine. Here take this.' He handed Alex the rope and then continued. 'You know, it's a good thing I'm a climber, otherwise I bet I'd weigh three hundred pounds when I got old.'

Alex shrugged into his pack and began removing the ice screw he had been hanging from. 'You think climbing is going to keep you from getting a beer belly?'

'No, but I figure it'll keep me from getting old. Especially if I climb shit like that,' he pointed to the snow they had been on, 'in weather like this.'

Both men looked up. The grey sky had darkened and thickened and was beginning to descend.

'I hope the ceiling doesn't drop too low or we'll be finding our way back to the campsite by touch.'

'I think it'll hold off for a while, but we'd better get moving.'

They began the ice dance, the vertical ballet that combines cold precision with total freedom. Axe in. Hammer in. Kick in the right frontpoints and stand up on them. Kick in the left points. Then repeat the whole sequence again and again and again. Creativity in repetition. Climbing as the ultimate contradiction. Dance with death and learn to live.

As they gained height the distance between them grew, Alex pulling further and further ahead as Gordon had predicted. The weight difference had something to do with it; but Gordon Wilson knew that there was more to it than that.

He had been climbing as long as he could remember, since his parents had first taken him into the hills as a young boy almost thirty years ago, and he knew that Alex had less than five years' experience. But he also knew that Alex was a far better climber. A natural climber – fast, safe and smooth.

He looked up and thought to himself that if he tried to climb that fast it wouldn't be ten minutes before he missed a placement and fell to his death.

Gordon Wilson was a human fire plug. His body was thick and strong and his movements were easy and relaxed but not very graceful. He had a dense blond beard and moustache, and heavy blond hair hung to his shoulders.

He worked part time for a Vancouver printer, an

arrangement which suited both himself and the printer. This left him time to do a lot of climbing and skiing, and provided about half the money he needed to live the way he wanted to. To make up the difference he grew and sold a little dope.

After several hundred feet of steep-and-easy the angle eased off a little and they were forced once again to kick into a layer of rotten snow. Swirling mist now hung heavily around the summit and the sky was black above them. They looked with distaste at the upper snowfield.

Alex waited until Gordon had caught up. 'We could', he said, 'try the rock.'

The snowfield was bordered on the right by a rib of slabby rock. 'It doesn't look too hard, and it should be faster than this snow.'

'I hope so, 'cause I think we're going to get dumped on pretty soon.'

They climbed carefully right and soon found a way across the moat between snow and rock. Standing on a small ledge they surveyed the rock above them.

'This doesn't look too bad at all. Let's just leave the rope in your pack and go for it.'

'Okay with me.' Alex nodded in agreement. 'The rope would slow us down and I think I'd like to get a look at the descent route before we get socked in completely.'

'Me too. Still, it didn't sound that difficult,' said Gordon, sitting down on the ledge and undoing his crampon straps. 'But you never know – Alan was pretty drunk when he described it to me and you know what he's like when he's drunk.'

'Yeah, all the climbing he's ever done gets homogenized by the beer and pretty soon you can't tell whether he's talking about a snow plod or a death route.' Alex had his crampons off and was lashing them to the top of his pack. 'But I have to admit that he was right about this being a worthwhile route. And it would be even better after a dry winter. It would ... what?'

'Be quiet for a minute, I think I hear something.'

Then Alex heard it too. The sound of a small aeroplane approaching from the east. They looked at one another and Gordon spoke. 'I sure hope he knows what he's doing. He sounds awfully low.'

'He must be ...' Alex's reply and the sound of the engine were lost in a blast of thunder.

'Jesus Christ! That wasn't very far away. We'd better haul ass if we don't want to get fried.'

The rock was perfect – mountain granite shattered in big blocks, rough to the touch and solid underfoot – but on this day there was no joy in climbing it. Their minds were filled with the falling sky and falling temperature and they both knew that there was no retreat. To get down they must first get up the last few hundred feet and find a descent route on the south side.

As they moved upward the sound of the aircraft engine increased, blotted out occasionally by rolling blasts of thunder.

'He must be just on the other side of this ridge.'

'It almost sounds like he's below us. He must be trying to fly down the valley below the cloud, he ...'

The engine went berserk. From a few thousand rpm it screamed up almost to the limit of hearing. Then nothing. Silence.

The two men stared at each other. Alex struggled for words. 'Jesus, I ...'

Gordon Wilson said, 'It doesn't matter, Alex. Either he made it or he didn't. It's not our problem yet. When we get up this hill, then it can be our problem. Right now we've just got to think about the next hundred feet. Okay?'

'Okay. Sure. You're right, you're right. But I think he must have crashed, and we'll have to go looking. But you're right, let's get up first.'

With that he was away, and once again Gordon was left behind to marvel at the speed and grace with which Alex could move.

When he reached the ridge crest he could see Alex

about twenty-five feet away, at the top of a steep gully, uncoiling the rope. Fifteen hundred feet below on the broad south face of the mountain, a small yellow aircraft lay silent and broken in the snow, visible and then invisible through the ragged mist that blew around the peak.

'D'you think anybody's alive?'

'I don't know. It looks pretty bashed up to me, but I guess we better go and check.' Gordon shrugged out of his pack and began digging through it. 'I've got the second rope in here, I think we're going to need it – it looks like two long raps.' He got the rope out and started to uncoil it.

Alex took an end and tied the two ropes together. 'I guess we should figure out how to get from the plane over to the descent route. I think we can do it even if we get whited out, if we just make a slightly rising traverse east from the plane and above the rock bands there, and then contour straight across the face until we hit the east ridge.'

Gordon checked the anchors and was passing one of the ropes through the rappel slings. 'Looks about right to me. This is probably the descent gully Alan was talking about, and the summit's up there, another hundred feet or so.'

'Guess we're not going to see it this time.'

They each picked up a rope and threw the coils as far out as they could. Alex leaned out and looked down. 'Looks like they're okay.' He threaded the ropes through his karabiner brake and backed toward the edge.

'Alex.'

'Yeah?'

'Go slow. Alan said the gully was really loose, so find a sheltered spot for the next station and try not to kick too much debris down onto the ropes.'

'Okay, see you later.'

Two long rappels brought them to the top of the snowfield. They were out of the summit mists and had a clear view of the scene below.

'Look at that! You can see skid marks halfway across the face; and it looks like it's only got one wing.'

'Jeeees-us. It looks like he flipped into the air when he hit those rocks.'

'Poor bastard. I hope he bought it on the first hit.'

They stared downhill for a few moments more, then silently coiled and packed the ropes and unstrapped their axes.

Alex went first. Leaping the moat he landed on the snow and began a long swooping glissade toward the wreckage. Feet together, upper body facing the fall line and angulating from the hips he was a skier without skis, linking turns and taking advantage of every irregularity of the terrain to control his wild descent.

Then, at last, when it seemed that he must overshoot his target or else crash into it, he rocked back hard on his heels, sending up a spray of snow and skidding to a stop ten feet from where the wreckage lay in a slight hollow, one of the few low-angle areas on the face.

He looked up to see Gordon Wilson in full flight several hundred feet above, body upright and loose, knees taking the bumps. Three hundred feet ... two hundred ... long blond hair streaming behind, expressionless face belying intense concentration ... one hundred feet ... fifty feet, then back on his heels and a snowy halt two feet away.

Together they stared at what had once been a Cessna 182 four-seat aeroplane, now a crumpled monument to the force of inevitable gravity; and together they walked toward it and peered in through the hole where the pilot's door had torn away.

'Oh my God.' *

Both the wing and the door on the pilot's side had been torn off along with half the pilot. There was blood everywhere. The interior of the little aircraft and the clothing of the pilot and passenger were sodden. The two climbers stood staring, frozen in morbid fascination. Then:

'Jesus Christ, Alex, that other guy is still alive!'

They charged to the other side of the wreck, but could not force the door and in the end they had to move the body of the pilot out onto the snow before they could free the passenger from his seat belt and haul him, bloody and unconscious, back out the way they had entered.

'Do you think there's any chance that this thing might blow up, Gord?'

'No, I don't think so,' said Gordon. 'If it was going to burn it probably would have started already, or blown up when it landed.' He knelt beside the unconscious survivor and began wiping the blood from what had once been a handsome, middle-aged face.

Ten minutes later they had done all that they could. The man they had pulled from the wreckage seemed to have no broken bones – his only visible injury a ragged gash across his forehead. His clothes were bloodsoaked, but there was no way to tell how much had been his own and how much had come from the pilot.

When Alex had unbuttoned the bloodstained shirt to check for wounds on the chest and abdomen the cold air had woken the man briefly. His eyes opened and he groaned and mumbled incoherently for a few seconds before falling back into unconsciousness.

Gordon put what was left of the first aid kit back into his pack and stood up to gaze toward the summit they had almost reached, but it was now obscured by cloud and even this far down in the valley the wind was beginning to blow.

'I guess we have to drag this guy out.' He looked down at the still form. 'That's just going to be a real bitch.'

'I know, but with a storm coming on there's no way we can leave him here. It might be a week before anyone could get in with a chopper. We'll just have to wrap him up in our extra clothing and hope we can get him out.' Alex paused for a moment and then continued. 'What about the valley below us? Do you know where it comes out? Maybe we could take him out that way.'

Gordon looked west, the way Alex was pointing. 'I

know that it eventually joins up with a trail system that leads to the highway that goes to the Mt. Baker ski area, but we'd probably be bushwhacking for about two days just to get to the trail.' He turned and pointed back to the east ridge. 'I think our best bet is to go over the ridge and down the glacier, just like we would have done if this hadn't happened.'

He stripped off the thick pile jacket he was wearing and began to put it on the man they had pulled from the wreck. 'I'm not looking forward to getting him down the Depot Creek headwall, but I guess our first job is to get him over the ridge.'

'I've got my bivvy sack with me; maybe if we put him in that he'll slide easier on the snow.' Alex took a small stuff sack from his pack and pulled a bright yellow Gore-tex bivouac sack out of it.

'Here, lift his legs and I'll slide it up. Good. Now if you can lift his hips, I'll pull it right over him.'

They stood up and looked at each other. Both were covered in blood, and there were red patches in the snow and red smears on everything they had touched.

The nylon cocoon on the snow stirred and moaned, and a gust of wind whistled a response across the gaping hole in the wreck. The two men stared down at the sack, again still and silent, as a light rain began to fall.

'I wonder who he is. You didn't find a wallet or card case did you?'

'Huh? A wallet? No, I didn't even look.' Alex knelt once more and reached into the bivvy sack, groping for hip pockets.

'Here we go, it looks like he ... Holy shit! Has he ever got a stack of money here. There must be fifteen or twenty hundred dollar bills.'

Oblivious to the increasing rainfall Gordon Wilson reached out a hand. 'Thanks.' He too looked at the pack of hundreds, his forehead creasing in concentration above thick eyebrows as he counted. '... twenty-two, twenty-three hundreds and one ten. Now let's see who he is ...

uhn . . . here we are: his name is Walter F. Matheson, and he seems to be from San Francisco.

'Here, put this into one of the packs.' He handed the wallet back to Alex and started toward the gaping doorway. 'I think I'll have a look inside the plane.'

As Gordon clambered once again into the flightless bird, Alex Townsend pulled a 9mm rope from his pack and began uncoiling it. When it lay in a loose heap on the snow beside him, he pulled four slings from his pack and began untying them, cursing softly when he had to use his teeth on knots jammed too tight for his numb fingers.

Methodically, ignoring the rain, he began retying the slings in the form of a crude harness around the unresisting Walter Matheson.

'Alex.'

Gordon's voice was hoarse and soft and Alex did not hear it over the rising wind.

'Alex.' Still soft, but harsh and insistent this time. Alex turned to see Gordon crouched in the ruined aircraft kneeling on the seat with his head and shoulders sticking through the gaping wound in its side.

'Alex, I think you better come and look at this.' He lifted a small aluminium suitcase, obviously heavy, out of the plane and dropped it at his companion's feet.

It was not locked, and Alex lifted the lid and stared at the contents. Slowly he bent down and picked up a sealed plastic bag – one of over a dozen in the case. It weighed a little over two pounds and was full of lumpy, flaky powder, as white as the snow around them.

'Aaghh, fuck. What are we going to do now?'

CHAPTER THREE

North Cascade Mountains

HE AWOKE DRIFTING, floating on a tide of pain, but soon slipped away again to nowhere.

And awoke again. And more pain, to send him back.

And again.

And again.

Afterward he would forget most of the pain and remember other things. Things hazy and unclear – images unfocused by the pain through which he had observed them; but a few memories were etched sharp and permanent: cold hands on his chest and gut; much rain; fragments of conversation;

'. . . fucking hill go on forever?

'. . . turning to snow . . .'

'. . . easy, Alex, a few more minutes and it's all downhill . . .'

But clearest of all were the faces. Two faces which seemed to be peering at him whenever he awoke.

Long blond hair. Blond moustache flowing into long blond beard. All so yellow that everything else looked red. Red cheeks, red forehead, broad red nose and thick red lips. Warm concern in the blue eyes. Think of Santa Claus at thirty. Before the white hair, before the belly.

And the other face dark and saturnine. The short hair dark and curly, nose narrow and hooked. Thin lips and white teeth. And the eyes. No comfort or concern in those eyes. They were dark and still and every time he thought of them he remembered the pain.

CHAPTER FOUR

North Cascade Mountains

IN SOUTHWESTERN British Columbia, as in most mountainous regions, roads tend to follow river valleys. One such parallel road and river system starts in the remote North Cascade range, just north of the Canada-U.S.A. border where tiny Depot Creek runs beside a rutted dirt track. Growing water volume is matched by wider and smoother road surfaces. The dirt becomes gravel where Depot Creek enters Chilliwack Lake, and widens considerably where the lake is drained by the Chilliwack River.

As the river is swollen by its tributaries the road widens again and the gravel is replaced by good pavement until finally, not far from the spot where the Chilliwack joins the mighty Fraser River for the last sixty miles of its journey to the Pacific, the two lane blacktop joins the trans-Canada highway for the last sixty miles of *its* journey to Vancouver.

At 5:30 a.m. on that late August morning there was not much traffic on any of these roads, but along the shore of the Chilliwack River, about halfway between its headwaters and its confluence with the Fraser, an old and road-weary Volkswagen van chugged its way slowly into the breaking day. At the wheel, Alex Townsend fought off sleep and thought about the other occupants of the van.

He thought of Gord Wilson, his friend and regular climbing partner for over three years, now sleeping hunched against the passenger door. In the city Gordon was unremarkable. His powerful body did not show through the nondescript clothes that he wore, and the only thing that set him apart from the rest of Vancouver was his profusion of blond hair. But in the mountains he stood apart. His great physical strength and many years of experience made him a fine climber.

Somehow though, Alex mused, there was more to it than that. There were many good climbers and, technically, Alex himself was better than Gordon. But in the high mountains, where thin air and insidious cold sap the strength and numb the will, success and survival do not depend on technique alone, but on strength of character, intelligence and an ability to get along with others – qualities that ran deep in the man sleeping beside him.

But even more than that, thought Alex, Gord had a sense of humour, and that was something that was becoming increasingly rare these days. Many of the climbers that he met now didn't seem to be having much fun, and it reminded him of all the serious-faced young giants who had turned football from a good time into a heavy business.

At least Gord didn't make climbing into some kind of religion.

On that thought Alex fell asleep. He woke up when his head hit the steering wheel, and found that he had almost drifted off the left hand side of the road.

'Time for a break, Alex,' he said aloud.

He stopped the van and climbed wearily out the door. Leaning back against the van he fumbled with his fly and then arched a golden stream onto the road. The morning was pleasantly cold, and as Alex idly watched the steam rising from his warm urine, he thought of the other passenger, Mr. Walter Matheson.

It had taken almost eighteen hours to haul him and his shiny aluminium suitcase out to the road. When they had stopped for a snack at the foot of the ice bulge on the ascent, they had argued about the time it would take them to return to the van once they reached the summit. Alex had thought six hours, but Gordon had said they could do it in five if they pushed a bit.

Five hours! What a joke. It had taken them all of that just to pull the deadweight of Matheson and his suitcase

over the east ridge and down to the hanging valley below
the glacier. And the weather. Christ, what a storm. The
temperature had fallen rapidly and the rain soon turned to
sleet. The only good thing about the whole episode was
that they had been working so hard that they hadn't
noticed the cold. Not at first anyway.

Once they reached the ridge things had become easier
for a bit; the glacier hadn't been too badly crevassed and it
was all downhill until they reached the valley. But by then
it was dark and they were both beginning to feel the cold,
and there was no more snow on which to slide their
unconscious burden. Nothing for it but to take turns
carrying him through the bush. A horror show from
beginning to end.

They had tried everything from slinging him over their
shoulders like a sack of flour to making complicated
harnesses of rope and slings and strapping him on like a
great floppy one hundred and fifty pound pack.

They had no sure knowledge of the man's injuries and
they doubted that he would survive the rough journey out.
But they had left their sleeping bags in the van and they
knew that he would surely die if they left him behind while
they went for help. At least this way they would not have
to come back for the body.

When they finally reached the top of the Depot Creek
headwall they had again debated whether to leave him
and go for help or try to carry him out themselves.

'What do you think?'

'I don't know, how does he look?'

'Just a second, let me get my headlamp, it's too dark to
see much.'

'Well, he's still alive anyway. At least dragging him over
the snow wasn't too bumpy.'

'His head seems to have stopped bleeding, and he's
breathing okay.'

'How's his heartbeat?'

'It's still beating.'

In the end they had decided to carry on. They felt that if

he had sustained any severe internal injuries he would be dead already, and that the most important thing now was warmth. He had lost a lot of blood, and the sooner they got him into the van, with its powerful gasoline heater, the better. He would probably die on the way out, but he would certainly die if they left him.

Finally, just as the sky was beginning to lighten in the east, they had reached the road and the parked van. They stripped off his soggy clothes, wrapped him in a sleeping bag and laid him on a foam pad in the back of the van, beside his suitcase.

His wound was bleeding again, and Gordon rummaged through the van until he found a clean shirt which he tied around the bloody head.

'He's still breathing. I thought for sure he was going to die,' said Alex.

'Yeah, he sure lost enough blood. Did you see the inside of the bivvy sack when we took him out of it?'

'Where's the nearest hospital?'

'Probably in Chilliwack. You know that little city just where we turned off the freeway?'

'Right. Okay, I'll drive for a while if you want, and you can get some sleep.'

'You sure you're okay to drive?'

'Of course I'm not okay. I'm totally thrashed. But so are you, so you sleep for a bit, and then we can trade off.'

'Thanks.'

Now, an hour later, Alex was wondering if he should wake his friend and let Gordon drive. But the cool morning air felt good, and he decided to keep going. Besides, it was less than an hour to Chilliwack.

He climbed back into the van, checked on the man in the back, who actually seemed to be sleeping rather than unconscious now, and headed west.

He tried to think about this man named Walter Matheson and his fifteen kilos of white powder, and about a dead pilot lying in the bloody snow beside a crumpled aeroplane. He knew it was important to think but he just couldn't focus his mind for more than a few seconds at a time. All he could think of was how nice it would be to sleep. To be wrapped in a big, warm down-filled bag in a tent somewhere high in the mountains, drifting cosily away....

His face hit the steering wheel again, and this time his nose began to bleed. 'No problem,' he thought to himself, 'I'm already covered in other people's blood. Maybe the pain will keep me awake for a while.'

As he drove into the gradually brightening day his mind drifted back in time almost four years. He hadn't been living in Seattle for long and it had been less than a year since the divorce. Somebody – he didn't remember who – had told him of a two thousand foot granite wall just north of Vancouver.

It supposedly had some incredible routes and was only two minutes walk from the road. It had sounded too good to be true, but he had gone up to see for himself.

The rock, which was called the Chief, turned out to be even better than that. It was on the coast overlooking a beautiful inlet and a logging/mining town with the odd name of Squamish. It was on that trip that he first met Gordon Wilson.

This chance encounter had begun a climbing partnership still going strong after four years. They had climbed together up and down western North America. Weekends rock-climbing at Squamish in British Columbia and at Index and Leavenworth in Washington, or mountaineering and skiing in the North Cascades and in B.C.'s Coast Range. Two nine-day weeks in Yosemite. And three memorable expeditions to the big mountains of Alaska and the Yukon.

And through it all they had even managed to remain friends. Or maybe friends was the wrong word. Alex often wished that there was someone with whom he could be completely open, someone to go to when he felt small and alone; but after four years he was fairly sure that Gordon would never be that person.

Gord was strong and self-assured, and he maintained a closely guarded personal space which nothing penetrated. In either direction.

Nonetheless, Gordon Wilson was the closest thing to a friend that he had. Alex had never made friends easily, and starting life all over at the age of twenty-six had made it even harder. Now, at thirty-one, it still wasn't easy.

But it was getting better. The view from the top of Mt. Logan was a lot better than anything he had seen out the window of his office; and although he didn't make even a third as much money working at the garage as he had writing programmes in Silicon Valley, at least he didn't have to drink himself to sleep any more.

As the pendulum of his thoughts swung back into the present he tried again to think about the man lying behind.

What was in the suitcase?

Heroin?

Cocaine?

It had to be some drug. Slowly, into his fatigue-dulled mind came the realization that he had stumbled into the world of large-scale crime. The suitcase must be worth a fortune.

He thought of all the newspaper stories he had read, all the dozens of newscasts. . . .

'. . . *today announced the break-up of a major heroin trafficking ring . . .*'

'. . . *in a shoot-out when they tried to intercept a shipment of three kilograms of cocaine . . .*'

'. . . *believed to have been killed to prevent him from giving evidence . . .*'

Christ! There must be thirty or thirty-five pounds in the suitcase. Fifteen kilos. Fifteen kilos! How much was that worth in dollars? In human lives?

And then he thought of the bloody, dismembered corpse they had left by the aeroplane, and his whole body began to shake and he had to stop the van because he could hardly hold on to the steering wheel.

'Gord. C'mon Gord, wake up.'
'Hnnn?'
'Wake up!'
'Uhn, okay, I'm awake. What's happening?'
'I'm wasted, Gordie.'

CHAPTER FIVE

San Francisco

LIKE SOME malevolent black spider in its lair, William
Holley sat in his office and brooded. Nobody disturbed
him. His temper was legendary; everyone on the San
Francisco Police Department had heard about it, and
nobody, from the Chief to the greenest rookie, wanted
any part of it.

He brooded that way for two days after his return from
Seattle. On the third day he didn't show up until almost
eleven, and went straight to the office of the Chief of
Detectives. He didn't fool around with any bullshit about
Hello, or How are you, he just walked in and said, 'I want
off it.'

He pulled a file folder from his briefcase and said,
'Everything I know or suspect is in there. Give it to
someone else.' He tossed the folder on the Chief's desk.
'Or better still, drop the whole thing entirely.'

The Chief looked at Holley and sighed inwardly. How
do you supervise a volcano? 'Okay, Lieutenant, tell me
about it. I take it that last weekend's operation was a
failure?'

'It wasn't a failure, it was a fuckup. The RCMP fucked
up and now we're back to where we were a year ago,
which is exactly nowhere. You can read it all in there,'
Holley pointed to the file, 'but the bottom line is that

Tomlinson is going to go on supplying heroin to half of California and we are going to have to go on watching him do it.'

He stood up. 'The only hope we had was to nail this Matheson with a bagful and put the screws on him, but now that the Mounties have taken that away from us we're shit out of luck. Period. End of story.'

Holley was as black and hard as a piece of obsidian and the Chief of Detectives was a little afraid of him. He chose his words carefully. 'You've got other things to do, Lieutenant, so go ahead and do them. I'll read your report and think about the whole business and let you know what I've decided in a day or so, okay?'

'There's nothing to decide. The only way to stop him is to have him hit. Until we're prepared to do that we're wasting our time. He doesn't go anywhere near the shit personally, the money he makes is getting laundered somewhere else, and nothing anybody says about him is going to be worth a shit in court. We've been up one side of this and down the other a hundred times.' He started for the door but stopped and turned around just before he went through it. 'The one chance we had was with this Matheson and now he's probably dead. If you can't drop it then give it to somebody else.'

CHAPTER SIX

Vancouver

SLOWLY, AN INCH at a time, Alex surfaced from the depths of a bleak and empty sleep. He was being shaken and someone was calling his name.

'Wake up, Alex.'

'Wake up.'

'WAKE UP!!!'

'Oohhnnn?'

'Come on, we're home. Wake up. We've got work to do.'

'Huh? Where are we?'

'Alex, for Christ's sake wake up. Here, drink this.'

Obediently Alex took the offered bottle and came partially awake when warm beer foamed in his mouth and throat.

'Gah. That's awful.'

Still holding the bottle, he stumbled from the van and looked around him. Summer sunlight filtered through leaves still wet from the storm of the day before and illuminated the garbage cans of a residential alley.

'Where are we?'

'In the lane behind my house.' Gordon was opening the big side door of the van. 'Give me a hand and we'll get this guy inside. I don't think any of the neighbours are watching.'

Alex was confused. 'I thought ... What happened at the hospital?'

'Alex, I don't think a hospital would be a very good idea.'

'But we don't know what's wrong with him. He could have all sorts of internal injuries. He could die if we don't take him to a hospital.'

'Yeah, I suppose he could, but I think we're just going to have to take that chance. Look, help me get him inside, and we can talk about it, okay?'

Vague fear shook him again, but he was too tired and confused to argue, and he nodded and said 'Okay.'

They manoeuvred Walter Matheson out of the van. He was semi-conscious and they managed to stand him up between them, one of his arms across each of their backs, and half-walk, half-carry him into the yard and up a short flight of steps to the back door.

'I don't have the key for this door with me,' said

Gordon. 'Watch him for a minute while I go around to the front and open it from the inside.'

Alex stood silently, scowling at the inert form on the small porch until he heard the click of the lock being unset.

The house was dim after the bright sun and at first Alex could not see much. Gordon led the way into the bathroom, where they laid the injured man on the floor. Turning to Alex he asked, 'Are you awake now?'

'I think so, I'm pretty tired, but I'm awake.'

'That's good, 'cause we've got some heavy deciding to do.' Gordon plugged the bath and started filling it with warm water. 'But first let's get him cleaned up.'

'Why don't you want to take him to a hospital?' Gordon started to answer, then stopped and looked down at Walter Matheson on the floor. 'Come into the hall for a minute.' He led Alex out of the bathroom. 'I don't know how unconscious he really is.'

When they were well away from the bathroom door he stopped and faced Alex. 'Just how badly do you want your name connected to fifteen keys of cocaine?'

'What are you talking about?'

'If we take him to a hospital what are you going to tell them? Are you going to tell them about the drugs?'

Alex started to speak but Gordon cut him off. 'No, don't answer, just think about it. As soon as we mention that he had a suitcase full of coke we are suddenly going to be the only witnesses in a multi-million dollar narcotics case. *The only witnesses.*'

Alex felt the muscles clenching along his spine and a sour taste rose in the back of his throat as his friend continued.

'And if we don't tell them, if we just take him in and say we found him in the plane, what do you think he's going to do when they let him out? He's going to come looking for his suitcase is what he's going to do.'

'But there must be some way we can do it. Drop him

somewhere and then phone an ambulance without giving our names. Something like that.'

Gordon shrugged his thick shoulders. 'Maybe so. But we'd better think it over pretty carefully first. Anyway, he's lasted this long, so another hour or two won't make any difference. Let's give him a bath and put him to bed and then we can figure out what to do.'

He started toward the bathroom, but then turned and Alex could see a smile behind the bushy beard. 'Besides, there's God knows how many million dollars in that suitcase and the one thing I do know for sure is that if we give it to the police or flush it down the toilet not one cent of it is going to rub off on me.'

They put Walter Matheson in the tub and he seemed to wake up.

'Aaahh.' Eyes unfocused, leaning slightly forward, he brought his hands slowly up and cradled his face in them. He remained in that position for a long time, not speaking, the warm water lapping around him.

Gordon left to find some towels and Alex sat on the rim of the old tub and said nothing.

The voice, when it finally came, was weak and scratchy. 'It was raining.'

Alex could think of no response, so he continued to sit silent.

'Raining.' Walter Matheson raised bloodshot, gummy eyes and said quite distinctly, 'I think that it was raining.'

'That's right, it was raining, but you're all right now, we've brought you home.'

How inane, thought Alex; but what else was there to say? A thousand questions whirled and burned in his mind. He wanted to grab this man by his bloody hair and shake him and demand answers and explanations. . .

'Why couldn't you have crashed your fucking airplane somewhere else?'

'Why couldn't you have died in the crash?'

'Why don't you just die right now?'

But instead, he picked up a cloth and began gently wiping away the blood.

Gordon returned and they finished the bath. Walter Matheson did not seem to mind. Whenever they asked him to move, to learn forward or back, to turn his head or lift an arm, he responded like a slightly retarded child who is anxious to please. He often seemed confused and moved the wrong way, but he was generally cooperative and relaxed. He did not speak again.

Gordon pulled the plug and together they lifted him to his feet. What was left, with all the filth gone, was a medium-sized, fit looking man of about fifty. Loss of so much blood had given a pale, almost translucent quality to his skin, and blood again welled from the large wound on his forehead and dripped slowly down his right cheek.

The vertical position was too much for him and his knees slowly bent until the two younger men were supporting his full weight. Their bloodstained and dirty clothes made a strange contrast to his clean and still-wet body.

They sat him down on the toilet and began towelling him dry.

'That's good enough Alex, let's get a bandage on his head and get him into my bed.'

CHAPTER SEVEN

Vancouver

HIS THROAT was on fire.

For some unknown time that was all he knew. He had no conscious thought, no subconscious impulse, no sense of personal identity; only burning thirst.

Then his universe expanded and to the thirst was added

pain. Starting at the back of his skull and spreading down his spine into every muscle and bone, dull throbbing pain accompanied him on his journey to consciousness.

First came the realization of identity: once again there was an I. Where there is pain there is life. He knew he was Walter Matheson, and he was alive.

For a time that was enough, but eventually his universe expanded again. Faces and places floating randomly across his mind's eye added the flesh of personality to the skeleton of identity until eventually full consciousness returned.

What happened?

Where am I?

Shoving aside his thirst and ignoring the pain he struggled to a sitting position.

Dizziness and nausea.

Try again.

And again.

Finally, compromising, he got two pillows behind him and managed to maintain a semi-sitting position.

A brass bed. He could feel the cold metal against his shoulder. Curtain-filtered daylight in a small room. Sun outside and warm air fluttering the curtain. Hardwood floor, heavy oak dresser, open clothes closet and one closed door.

He wondered what was on the other side of that door?

Maybe he could get a drink.

Then voices. Two voices. He could hear them faintly through the door. One voice just ordinary, just like any other voice; the other somehow odd. Harsh consonants and shortened vowels. A Canadian.

And with the thought of Canada the gates of memory fell open, and once more he knew the insanity of thunder and lightning, and the terror and agony of the crash.

CHAPTER EIGHT

Vancouver

'ARE YOU SAYING that if we take him to a hospital we're eventually going to get killed?' asked Alex.

They were in the living room of Gordon Wilson's small house, weighing the consequences of Samaritanism. They were both clean and dressed in fresh clothing, each according to his custom. Gordon Wilson in blue jeans, a green T-shirt advertising Heineken beer, and leather sandals over thick grey socks; and Alex, who had shaved as well as showered, wore slacks of light grey wool, a slightly darker grey cotton shirt with very fine white pinstriping, grey socks and black moccasins.

'Yeah, probably.' Gordon was deep in an overstuffed armchair, a mug of tea balanced on one of the broad arms.

'So what do you suggest we do?' Alex was sitting on a straight-backed wooden chair that he had carried in from the kitchen. He was tense and unhappy.

'Well to start with I think we should go over all the alternatives we can think of and try to figure out what's likely to happen in each case. You used to write some pretty complex programmes so this should be a piece of cake. If *a*, then *b*, *c* and *q*; if *not a*, then either *x* or *y* but not both. That kind of thing.'

Alex was angry. How could Gord sit there complacently drinking tea and trying to be funny? He wanted to strike out with words, to lash his friend with abuse. He could feel increasing blood pressure, feel his skin begin to sweat and crawl. He fought for control and finally stood up and said, 'Give me a couple of minutes.'

He went out the front door and sat at the top of the steps, and stared at the trees and lawns of the quiet old neighbourhood.

Gordon was not surprised. He had seen this happen

before, though always when they were climbing. In the face of something difficult or dangerous, or after a near accident; whenever Alex felt emotion overriding self-control he would excuse himself with the same words, 'Give me a couple of minutes', walk a few feet away, sit down, and go into a trance.

It wasn't yoga, or T.M., or self-hypnosis, or bio-feedback or any other pop/psych technique, it was just Alex's way of dealing with emotional overload.

'Sorry, Gordie.' Alex returned and sat down again. 'Got a bit out of control there.' He was calmer now and he knew that Gordon was probably right. As usual. 'Let's go over it one thing at a time and see where we stand.'

'Okay, first things first. I checked the suitcase while you were in the shower, and I'm pretty sure it's coke. The only way to tell for sure would be to snort some but I'm not going to do that until I know for a fact that it's not some kind of experimental rat poison.'

'Could it be heroin?' Alex asked.

'I don't think so. I've only seen heroin a couple of times, and it was more powdery. But I've seen lots of coke and this sure looks like cocaine.' He paused, lost in thought. 'Fifteen kilos of cocaine. That's about . . .' His voice trailed off and his eyes lost their focus. 'I can't even count that high. Shit. Two million maybe. Dollars.'

He paused again and scratched through his beard along the line of his lower jaw. 'You know, I've never had two million dollars worth of cocaine in my house before.'

They were both tired. The climb the day before had been demanding, and hauling Walter Matheson and his suitcase out to the road had been worse. Gordon had had one hour's sleep and Alex just over two in the last thirty; but they were used to going short of sleep and working hard on long climbs, and they were familiar with the dangers of mental fatigue.

Slowly and carefully Gordon led Alex down the path he had been exploring almost from the instant he had discovered the suitcase in the blood-spattered aircraft.

If they took the injured man to a hospital they must
decide whether to report the suitcase. If they did, then
Matheson would eventually come to trial and as Gordon
put it, 'Sooner or later the word is going to get out that the
only thing connecting him to all that shit', he pointed
toward the suitcase which lay on the floor beside his chair,
'is our testimony.'

If they kept the suitcase and said nothing then Matheson
would undoubtedly come looking for them as soon as he
was out. Even if they could convince him that they were in
fact holding the suitcase for him until he recovered there
was a good chance that he (or someone) would have them
killed just for insurance.

'He would probably feel real bad about it; after all we
did save his life, but he might still do it.'

So, taking him to a hospital was out. Short of murdering
him and flushing his cocaine down the toilet the only safe
course was to do as Alex had suggested – dump him out
on a street corner somewhere and call an ambulance
anonymously.

'But that would still leave us with the problem of the
suitcase. We can flush the coke, or mail it to the police,
but Alex, I don't think I want to do that. That cocaine is
going to change hands four or five times, and generate
God knows how many million dollars before it disappears
up somebody's nose. If we're careful, and if we don't get
greedy, we can get some of those dollars for ourselves.'

For a while, maybe twenty seconds, Alex was silent.
Then he found his tongue. 'You mean steal it from him
and sell it ourselves?'

'NO, NO, NO! That is the one thing that would
absolutely, one hundred per cent for sure get us killed.
There is no way you want to get involved in selling this
much cocaine. That is a whole other world and you don't
even want to *know* about it, let alone get involved in it.'

Alex started to speak but Gordon cut him off. 'You
know that I sell a little dope now and then, right? Well
I've been doing that for about ten years now, and if there's

one thing I've learned about the drug business it's that I'm happy to stay small-time.'

He stopped for a moment and then went on quietly, 'Alex, the people who deal at this level are different from you and me. It's not that they're not nice people, although I guess some of them aren't, it's just that they're different. They play in a different league and by a whole different set of rules. You or me getting involved with them would be like a caterpillar trying to cross a freeway.'

'Well how can you make money out of it without getting involved?' asked Alex. 'If it's that dangerous why don't we just drop him somewhere near a hospital and flush everything down the toilet. I don't want to get killed.'

In a surprising gesture of warmth Gordon reached out and rested his hand on Alex's shoulder. 'Neither do I, believe me.' He withdrew his hand. 'But I've got an idea, and I think that there's a way in which we can do this guy Matheson a favour – something he'll appreciate a lot more than being taken to a hospital – with no danger to ourselves.'

Alex began to speak but once again he was cut off.

'Look, I know that you probably don't want to get involved in anything too illegal. That's fine, you don't have to if you don't want to, but listen to what I'm going to say and then after you've slept on it and thought about it for a while you can decide. Okay?'

Outside the house leaves and flowers bobbled in a light breeze and the noon sun warmed the city of Vancouver on a fine summer day. The air had been washed by the storm of the night before and the weather was perfect; clear and hot without being oppressive. Inside the house Alex Townsend grew cold and felt a droplet of nervous sweat run down his ribcage as Gordon continued.

'This guy Matheson was smuggling a shipment of cocaine into the U.S. At first I couldn't figure out what he was doing there, but the more I thought about it, the more sense it made. These mountains are by far the least-guarded way into the States, and getting drugs into

Canada is child's play. So even though it's a roundabout
route – South America to Canada to the U.S. – it's a lot
safer than going through Miami or San Diego.'

He stood up out of the armchair, stretching and yawn-
ing, then walked to the kitchen, speaking over his shoulder
as he went. 'And he's not some flunky courier. Do you
want some tea?'

'Tea? How do you know he's not? No, I don't want any
tea.'

'I looked in his wallet again. I spent some time in the
Bay Area in the late sixties and I know San Francisco a
bit. You don't get an address in Pacific Heights by being
somebody's errand boy. And he's got business cards for
something called Matheson Hydraulics with offices in San
Francisco and Portland.'

Gordon returned to the front room and sat down with a
fresh cup of tea.

'Anyway, just for the time being, let's say that he *is*
bringing cocaine into the U.S., and that he's more than
just somebody's pack mule.

'Now, try to look at this situation from his point of view.
What is he going to be thinking when he wakes up? He
doesn't know where he is, or how he got there. He hasn't
really seen us and he won't have any idea where his
suitcase is. He's going to be more than just a little bit
freaked, especially when he finds out that he's still in
Canada and has to find another way of getting across the
border.

'So, I'm going to make him an offer he can't refuse. I'm
going to tell him to fly back to San Francisco and leave the
suitcase with me. I'll deliver it to him in a few days . . . no,
no, wait a minute, let me finish. There's a way that we can
do this that gives absolute protection to both of us, so that
we can't get caught and he can't touch us afterward. When
he's gone back to California we'll just take the coke and
hike back up to Mt. Redoubt and then thrash our way
down that valley we looked at – the one you asked about,
but I said was too bushy to drag him out. It'll be a bit of a

grunt, but we won't have too much trouble if we keep our packs small, and after a day or so of bushwhacking we'll connect with the Mt. Baker trail system. From there we just drive down the highway to San Francisco and deliver it to him.

'There's no way it can go wrong. There's nothing, not one thing in the universe to connect us to this stuff. It was just blind cosmic chance that we were there when he came down, and we'd be crazy not to take advantage of it.'

Alex said nothing, but his mind was in a turmoil. Blind chance? Life as a cosmic crap shoot? Was God out there somewhere with His jacket over the back of His chair and His cuffs rolled up, hunched over His cupped hands crooning, 'Come on Little Joe, come on Little Joe'?

There had to be more to it than that. And yet Gordon was right, there *was* no chance of getting caught. They could haul *ten* suitcases full of cocaine across the border and never have to worry about trying to act nonchalant and honest in front of Customs, never feel the trickle of fearsweat in the hollow of the spine, never hear that voice behind the dark lenses asking, 'Anything to declare?'

Gordon was still speaking. '. . . and to protect ourselves from any sort of danger from Matheson we just have to make sure that he never sees you or your van. I'll be the only one he sees at either end, and I'll make sure he knows that I've got a partner who's been in from the beginning and will give his name to the police, the IRS, and every newspaper in the country if anything happens to me. Especially the IRS. He just *can't* want them checking his books.

Alex didn't know what to say. He was being forced toward a decision he was unprepared to make, and fragmented thoughts ricocheted through his tired mind. '. . . absolutely foolproof plan . . . Mafia . . . smuggling is glamorous . . . drugs kill . . . things go better with coke . . . how many years in jail . . . how much money . . .' Madness.

Gradually his mind cleared and he was able to isolate the essence of his problem from the crazy swirl. Gordon's

plan might not be perfect at it stood, but Alex was sure
that they could make it perfect; and there was no question
that he could use some extra money – who couldn't?

No, the basic question was very simple. Do you or do
you not want to be instrumental in introducing fifteen
kilograms of cocaine to the people of America?

So simple and yet so complex. He had once snorted a
couple of lines of cocaine at a party in L.A. and experienced
nothing more than a numb nose. As far as he knew it
wasn't addictive the way heroin was, or Valium or alcohol,
and he wasn't entirely sure what people saw in it.

But if the inherent rightness or wrongness of cocaine
traffic was open to debate, its legal status certainly wasn't.
Alex was happy to be a citizen of the United States of
America. He enjoyed living there and he mostly agreed
with what he thought America had done and stood for
over the years. He had no desire to break the law of his
country, but at the same time it was obvious that not all
laws were just. Any country that could make conscription
legal and cannabis illegal. . .

If only it had been something other than cocaine. It
would have been so easy to flush away bags of heroin. So
easy to help out if it had been hash, or diamonds.

'I don't know Gord. I just don't know. I could use some
extra money but I don't want to wind up bringing fifteen
kilos of misery into the world. Do you understand what
I'm saying?'

Gordon rose and walked to the front window. He stood
looking out, silhouetted against the summer sun. When he
spoke he didn't turn around and his voice was soft and his
words hard to catch.

'To the best of my knowledge, there's nothing evil
about cocaine, and I don't think that there are hundreds
of thousands of slavering coke-heads out there who are
ready to kill for their next fix. Shit, they used to put the
stuff in soft drinks.'

He turned around and the light rimmed his blond hair,
almost like a halo. 'Most of the misery that this will cause

will come from its money value. The same misery that you'd cause by smuggling gold or diamonds or rare stamps. And don't kid yourself, anything that's worth over two million dollars and can fit into a small suitcase is going to cause some misery. The only difference is that this stuff probably wasn't stolen from anybody the way gold or stamps would have been.'

'But the cocaine itself isn't addictive?'

'There are probably people who get addicted, but it's not like heroin or booze.' He paused, and then said, 'Look, the clearest way I can put it is to say that if I thought I was going to be spreading a lot of misery among innocent people I wouldn't get involved. You know me well enough to realize that.'

He walked back across the room and sat down on the arm of the big chair, facing Alex directly, and said, 'I don't have the wisdom of the Universe at my disposal, so I just go along and try to enjoy my life as much as I can without hurting anyone else. I sell a little pot to help with the mortgage. Does that make me a monster? You know it doesn't. There are people who howl about marijuana corrupting kids and leading to God-knows-what, but you've smoked enough dope to know that that's bullshit. The same people make a lot of noise about cocaine, but that's all it is, noise.

'I've done enough coke to be able to say that I'm never going to get addicted to it, and I believe that any harm that comes out of it comes from human greed, not from the cocaine itself. That's the best answer I can give you.'

Alex bent in the chair and worked his face with the heels of his hands. He needed sleep. He didn't want to think anymore, to answer this terrible question. Then, unexpectedly, he once again felt his friend's hand on his shoulder, and heard Gordon speaking.

'Do you remember when you were a kid, Alex? Thinking about what it was going to be like when you grew up? You never knew just how it was going to happen but you knew that someday you'd be grown up, and you'd know all the answers.'

He stood up once again and Alex, still hunched, heard him continue.

'You're grown up now, Alex, and so am I; but I never did find any of those answers. I always thought that one morning I'd wake up and find myself an adult, but it never happened, and now I realize that I've been "grown up" for a long time and just never knew it.

'It's probably the same with getting old. You expect that some day you'll wake up old, but it isn't going to happen that way. What'll happen is that one day you'll realize that you've been old for the last five years; and then, if cancer doesn't get you first, you're eventually just going to dry up and die.'

The words seemed to Alex as if they were coming from the far end of a long tunnel; reverberant and charged with hidden meaning.

'But what's going to happen to us? You and I aren't going to get any pension or monthly visit from our grandchildren. What's going to happen is that one of these days an avalanche is going to get you, or a belay is going to pull, or you'll break a leg someplace where you need two legs to get out.

'Maybe that's part of what keeps us climbing and keeps us digging being alive but there are still a few things left that I want to do and I think that it's going to be easier to do them if I can make twenty-five thousand dollars next week by delivering a suitcas full of cocaine to San Francisco.'

He stopped speaking and silence grew in the room. Alex rose and went to the window. He stood looking out, but his vision was turned inward and he saw nothing. After a long time he turned and said simply,

'Okay.'

Gordon heated a can of soup and took that, a pitcher of water, and a bowl, spoon and drinking glass in to the bedroom. He was out again very quickly and said to Alex, 'He's awake and eating the soup. I think he's going to be all right.'

He disappeared down the basement stairs and returned a minute later with two foam pads.

'I think we should get some sleep now, before he's up and about. Go ahead and crash right there on the couch, I'll sleep in front of the bedroom door. He won't be able to get out without waking me and I'll make sure he doesn't see you. We can talk about how to make the delivery foolproof later.'

Alex lay down on the couch, exhausted and ready for sleep, relieved that he did not have to think any more. But doubt and fear nagged him, and sleep was slow in coming. He rose and walked down the hallway to where Gordon was lying in front of the bedroom door.

'Gord.' He nudged at the body on the floor with his foot, then bent down to whisper when the eyes opened.

'Gord, what makes you so sure that he's going to go for your plan. Everything depends on him accepting your idea. What if he doesn't?'

Gordon slowly sat up and yawned, then said, 'He already did. I talked to him while you were in the shower this morning. He's only too pleased to have us carrying for him, going to pay us fifty thousand dollars. American dollars. Now go back to bed and get some sleep.'

CHAPTER NINE

U.S./Canada Border

THERE IS a certain inevitability about the speeches made when politicians from America and Canada gather, and the phrase 'the longest undefended border in the world'

usually figures prominently. But while this border makes
great fodder for speeches, it is an unending nightmare for
the DEA. Policing the approximately five thousand miles
which separate America from its northern neighbour is
impossible. Given sufficient men and equipment the water-
ways of the east and the open farmland of the prairies
could be covered, but how do you control five hundred
miles of uninhabited mountains?

There is no way. The only thing which keeps down the
volume of drugs crossing these mountains is the same
thing which makes them hard to police. The terrain is
steep and travel is difficult and dangerous, and most
importers are content to accept the stricter control of the
Mexican border and the major American sea and airports
in return for the relative physical ease of travel through
them.

But for those willing to make the effort, the mountains
remain the surest way of bringing illegal drugs into the
United States of America. It is true that this means that
the shipment must first be brought into Canada, but this is
laughably simple, and both the net cost and the net risk
can be reduced even though two borders must be crossed
instead of one.

If there is no rush, if a little extra time is no problem,
then the cheapest, most secure way is the oldest way of all:
hire someone to carry the goods through the mountains on
his back. Still, this is no easy task. The wide valleys of the
Rocky Mountains are policed and supervised, and the
more westerly ranges have a way of policing themselves.
They are steeper and more forbidding, glaciated and
avalanche prone, dangerous, even to an experienced
climber.

But climbers are natural smugglers. Many of them are
outsiders by nature and tend to think of the law as
something that applies to other people. They are used to
taking risks: and most important, they are used to careful
planning.

For Alex Townsend and Gordon Wilson, carrying fifteen

kilograms of cocaine through the mountains was a relatively simple and straightforward task; less dangerous, less strenuous and less complicated than their climb of the week before.

And yet, simple as it was, they spent the two days after Walter Matheson's departure scrutinizing every aspect of their plans, making certain that absolutely nothing would go wrong.

– What if we run out of gas? Or something equally stupid?

Buy extra jerry cans. Check the tool kits in each vehicle. Oil. Water. Battery. Spare tyre.

– What if the weather turns bad?

Take your Gore-tex and pile, we're not waiting for the weather on this one. Don't forget your bivvy sack.

Food. Maps. Compass. Headlamps, matches, stove, first aid.

Take a rope. Just a short one though, we don't need extra weight. Don't forget your prussiks.

Sunscreen. Insect repellent. Sunglasses, ice axe, water bottle.

And on. And on.

It was just a two-day hike. No technical climbing, just a walk in the mountains and a bit of glacier-bashing, but for twenty-five thousand dollars each they were willing to double-check the details.

The only hitch in their otherwise smooth preparation came when Alex phoned his employer to say that he would be a few days late getting back to Seattle.

As he said later to Gordon, 'I guess he just got tired of my three- and four-day weekends, and this was the overload that blew his fuse.'

'I never understood why you wanted to work in that garage anyway.'

'It wasn't that bad.'

'Good, bad or indifferent, you're going to make enough in the next few days to take the sting out of getting fired, so I wouldn't worry about it too much.'

'I guess. And things are starting to pick up now so I'll probably be able to find something else.'

It had been a strange two days. Walter Matheson stayed in the bedroom where Gordon brought him his meals. Alex parked his van several blocks away, and he and Gordon spent their time planning and bullshitting in a nervous and preoccupied way. Gordon took Matheson out on the second day to a clothing store to get something to wear and Alex went shopping to replace the sleeping bag that had been bloodied beyond salvation.

On the third morning Gordon drove Walter Matheson to the airport, and they realized that their preparations were complete. They had gone over everything many times, looked for anything that might go wrong, planned for every eventuality. Now it was time to act.

They put the suitcase in Gordon's closet and left Vancouver at midmorning the next day in separate vehicles and drove southeast along the TransCanada highway for about 45 miles. Here, where the highway is almost tangent to the forty-ninth parallel, they turned south and crossed the border at the tiny town of Sumas, Washington.

Alex went through customs first, with no problem. Gordon was right behind in his little brown Datsun, but customs wanted to talk. Alex waited about a mile down the road, until Gordon caught up about fifteen minutes later.

'What happened?'

'Ahh, that stupid fucker didn't like the colour of my car or something. Maybe he hates longhairs, I don't know. Maybe he was pissed that I could take the day off and he couldn't. Who knows. Anybody that works for customs has got to be a bit of an asshole to start with. They searched the car and gave me the red ass.' Then he grinned a huge grin and said, 'Good thing I changed my mind about bringing Walter's little bundles of joy along for the ride.'

'You're joking.'

'I thought about it for a while. They hardly ever check

anybody at this crossing, and it would have saved two or
three days of hard work, but in the end ... well, who
needs twenty years in jail.' He laughed. 'Anyway, I didn't
do it and there was nothing for them to find.'

The road wound south-east through a few miles of
farmland and then climbed up for three quarters of an
hour into the Mt. Baker National Forest. At the Nooksak
river, just past the Department of Highways maintenance
yard, they turned left onto a gravel road marked 'Hannegan
Campground'. A little less than five miles later this road
ended at a parking area and campground where there
were signs pointing to the beginning of a trail and a large
covered notice board carrying a map of the North Cascades trail system and a list of rules and the penalties for
their infraction.

The map did not show any trail leading into Canada,
nor was there any indication of the penalty for smuggling
narcotics through the area.

They left some canned food, a six-pack of Labatt's
Blue, and some clean clothes in Alex's van, locked it up
and left it there, parked beside three other dusty cars
whose owner were hiking somewhere nearby. Presum-
ably being careful to camp and move their bowels only in
approved locations.

Their return to Vancouver in Gordon's Datsun was
uneventful, Canadian customs merely asking if they had
anything to declare and waving them through when they
said they hadn't.

Alex was silent for most of the drive. The border crossings
had shaken him and the sharp corners of reality were
intruding into his acceptance of Gordon's plan. He had a
sudden urge to bail out right then, while he still could.

Just like a big alpine climb, he thought. You make
plans, go over all the details of the route, select your
equipment and make the approach. Then, at the base of
the climb, you get your last chance to back off, for you
know that somewhere on the climb you are going to cross
the line of no retreat.

He tried to analyze the source of his discomfort. What could possibly go wrong? Nothing. He knew that. They could not be caught and as long as they were careful about avalanche slopes and crevasses they couldn't get hurt. Nor could anything go wrong at the other end. Gordon's delivery arrangement was fireproof.

He finally identified his unease as a barely conscious revulsion at the idea of being associated with criminals. He didn't mind the thought of actually *being* a criminal – in fact there was something almost glamorous about smuggling cocaine – but to associate with criminals. . . .

'Sometimes I'm so middle class it's frightening.'

'What?'

'Nothing, just thinking out loud.'

It was late afternoon when they reached Vancouver. Gordon took the Grandview exit and soon they were westbound on East 12th Avenue where the rush hour traffic was going mostly the other way, hardly slowing them at all.

Even here, in a lower class residential area, the city was attractive and Alex suddenly realized that although he had visited Vancouver dozens of times he had never seen a slum or any kind of ghetto. Even the so-called Skid Row area around lower Main St. was clean and spacious compared to some of the districts he had seen in the large cities of California and the Northwest.

'Gord.'

'Yeah?'

'Let's eat somewhere really good tonight.'

'Sure. Why? You feeling rich already?'

'No, it's just that I've had a lot of good times around Vancouver and I don't know when I'm going to be here again.'

'What are you talking about? You can be back next week if you feel like it. This is only going to take us a few days – it's not as if you were off to Afghanistan or something.'

'I know, I know. But somehow I feel that . . . that . . .'

Alex paused and watched the city rolling by outside the window. 'I don't know exactly how I feel. Sort of strange, like I'm saying goodbye to something.'

He looked across at Gordon and said, 'I guess I sound like an idiot. But I'd still like to eat somewhere nice. Do you know someplace quiet, with good food and maybe a view of the city?'

Gordon thought for a short time. 'View of the city? Yeah I suppose so. There's a place on top of Grouse Mountain – you have to take a cable car to get there, and you look down on the city from about four thousand feet up. And there's the Salmon House in West Van. It's got a pretty good view and the food's okay but I've never liked it very much.'

He drove in silence for a while, then said, 'Wait a minute, wait a minute, I've got a much better idea. You want a real view of this place? Of what Vancouver is really about?'

The main dining room at the Cannery overhangs the water and from a window table Alex and Gordon watched the lowering sun expand and redden, dominating the harbour as it sank into the Pacific. Along the waterfront, monster loading cranes stood in sharp silhouette until the sun was gone and a million watts of artificial light outlined them in a new and even starker geometry.

The meal was as good as the view, and somewhere between the second bottle of wine and the café royales they decided to go to Yosemite when they finished their business in San Francisco.

'It's only two hundred miles, and it would be a shame to pass so close and not stop for a while.'

'And I guess that I don't have to worry about getting back to work on time.'

At ten-thirty the next morning, the thirtieth of August, Alex Townsend walked across the border slash with eight kilograms of cocaine in his pack. No bells rang and the

Lord did not strike him dead. He continued down the trail wondering what he had expected to happen and wondering if it was disappointment he felt when nothing did.

He finally decided that this kind of crime, like the border he had just crossed, was a matter of political definition, and that perhaps he had worried too much about it. The forest didn't change at the forty-ninth parallel, the big old firs were the same on one side of the border as the other. If they didn't care, why should he?

The trail they were following was the same one they had taken a week before when they had come to climb the north-east face of Mt. Redoubt. There are vague references to it in one or two climbers' guidebooks, but it appears on no map in either Canada or America and is not known to the government of either country. To reach it they had dodged potholes and logging trucks all the way up the Chilliwack River valley, turned south on rapidly deteriorating roads to the end of Chilliwack Lake, and then bumped along for a mile or two in the ruts above the marsh at the end of the lake until the Datsun would go no further. From there, a few hundred yards of walking had taken them into a jumble of old logging slash and the unmarked start of the trail less than a quarter mile north of the border.

The trail rambled several miles southwest through the ancient forest of the Depot Creek valley and then came to an apparent end at the base of the waterfall which sprawls in little leaps and jumps down the thousand foot headwall at the end of the valley. But the two men had been this way before; they walked through the spray at the base of the falls and climbed very carefully up twenty feet of slimy, mossy rock until they reached dry ground and the continuation of the trail.

'It must have been a pretty dry year when they cut this trail.'

'I guess so, but it sure feels good to cool off in the spray.' Gordon took off his pack and squatted down to drink from the creek. 'Do you want to stop here for some lunch?'

Alex considered the headwall above them and replied, 'No, if I stop to eat now I'll never force myself up that. Let's just have some gorp and a drink and then get it over with. We can stop and eat at the top.'

The Depot Creek headwall is not a technical climbing challenge. Rather, it is a quadricep-pumping, lung-bursting grunt up through steep forest and ankle-turning talus that suddenly ends in a hanging valley below the magnificent north face of Mount Redoubt. When they reached the top of the headwall they both collapsed. Alex was panting, guzzling from his water bottle and trying to talk, all at the same time. 'How did we ever manage to carry Matheson down that?'

'Yeah, and in the dark!'

After a lunch of peanut butter and honey sandwiches and Gatorade they crossed the valley and unpacked their crampons, rope and ice axes and ascended the small glacier that drops from Redoubt's west ridge. From the ridge crest they looked down into Bear Creek valley, a tangle of green with Bear Creek glinting silver and white at the bottom, and the North Face of Bear Mountain rising dark and ominous on the other side. Below and to their left, bright yellow against Redoubt's snowy white skirt, was the broken aircraft lying exactly as they had left it.

They looked at it and then at each other, but neither spoke.

They stayed high as long as they could, but eventually had to drop down and the heat of the late afternoon found them in hand-to-hand combat with the bush of the valley bottom. Devil's club tore at their clothes and skin and the slide alder was so thick and tangled that in places they could not keep their feet on the ground as they struggled through it.

'Can you imagine', asked Alex, wiping salty sweat from his eyes, 'what it would have been like trying to carry him out this way?'

'I don't even want to think about it. It would have taken days.'

They camped that evening in a small clearing beside the creek. Supper was more sandwiches, a can of salmon and tea.

'It ain't haute cuisine, but it's a lot better than that freeze-dried shit,' was Gordon's verdict.

They were tired, but neither was quite ready for sleep so they built a small fire to keep the mosquitoes at bay and sat, watching the flames. Alex finally broke the silence.

'What happened with you and Louise? I didn't see any sign of her at your place and you haven't mentioned her all week?'

'I guess we sort of split up.'

'She catch you in bed with the milkmaid?'

'No, nothing like that this time. In fact, that's the funny thing about it. I haven't even looked at anyone else in over a year, and let me tell you, that has sure as hell never happened before. And I think it was the same with her.'

Gordon threw more wood on the fire. When he resumed speaking there was something almost wistful in his voice, a trace of confusion. 'I liked her a lot, it was a real comfortable thing we had going, but she got an offer from an agency in Toronto. They liked her work and she said that she would have a lot more opportunities there than in Vancouver ...

'She wanted me to come with her.' His voice tailed off and he stared at the fire. 'Have you ever been in Toronto, Alex?'

'No.'

'It's the ass end of nowhere. I couldn't live there – it would be like you moving to Cleveland or some place like that.'

'I was in Cleveland once,' said Alex.

'Well Toronto's like that, only even more boring. There's about three million people there and most of them actually like it. In fact they're smug about it. But you know something? I even thought about doing it. I liked her that much. And I still miss her.'

Then he laughed. 'But I finally decided that I'm only

going to have this one life, and I'll be damned if I'm going to spend it in Toronto.'

He had been leaning back against his pack, and now he turned around and reached down into it.

'Here, try this.' He handed Alex a fifth of armagnac, the misshapen bottle looking strangely natural in this wild place.

They passed the bottle back and forth a few times in silence, then Gordon asked, 'What about you? Still waiting for Miss Wonderful to walk into your life?'

'I guess so. I don't know.' Alex could feel the brandy starting to work on him, a gentle amber fog billowing through his mind. 'Sometimes I wonder if I'll ever find anyone. It's so easy to get laid, and so hard to find someone to love. I get pretty frustrated sometimes.'

'Maybe you should just relax and enjoy getting laid now and again, and stop worrying about True Love.'

Alex could hear the capitals. 'I can't Gord. I've been married once and I know how good it can be. Maybe I'm too much of a romantic, but I'm willing to wait as long as I have to.'

'It's your life, I suppose, but just be careful you don't run out of patience and start building dream castles around someone. I've seen that happen to a few people and boy, can it ever get messy.' Gordon capped the bottle and put it back in his pack. 'Anyway, we've got a long day in front of us, so I'm going to crash.'

They woke just after sunrise and breakfasted on Granola with powdered milk and several cups of tea. Two hours later they broke out of the bush onto the North Cascades trail system which they followed for four sweaty hours up and over Hannegan pass and down to Alex's van.

They drank warm beer and ate smoked oysters out of the can with their fingers, and Gordon talked and sang nonstop all the way to Seattle.

'Just as ugly as ever.' Gordon was admiring the non-view from Alex's living room window. He turned and looked around the room. 'But at least it isn't so bad inside now. Goddamned if I know how you stood it here at first. It was about as homey as the men's room in a bus station.'

Alex lived in a decaying apartment in a small building on East Fir. It was the first vacancy he had looked at when he arrived in Seattle, and he had taken it without any thought. He furnished it with what was on sale in the bargain basement of the nearest department store and had lived in it that way for two years before he first imprinted it with something of his slowly developing personality. Then, gradually, he began to replace the instant furniture with solid, comfortable pieces until, in its present state, it was a pleasant enough residence for a single man.

It did not have the solidity and warmth of a real home, and there was still a temporary feeling in it. But Alex was not yet a solid person, and there was still something temporary about him too.

But he was working on it. He had arrived in Seattle empty, held together only by negatives; running from, rather than coming to. Now, four and a half years later, he was almost a whole man and had even begun to dream; not exactly about his future, but about the possibility that he might have a future worth dreaming about.

They both showered and changed. Alex put on light wool pants in medium brown, a white shirt with brown pinstripes, a coffee coloured pullover wool vest and brown socks and moccasins. Gordon wore his usual T-shirt and jeans. He asked, 'You hungry?'

'Yes, but I don't think there's much in the kitchen.'

'Good, you're a terrible cook anyway. Let's grab a beer and a sandwich somewhere and head straight back to pick up my car. We can camp right there if we're tired or drive back to Vancouver and stay at my place. Then in the morning we can pack up all my rock-climbing gear, come back here to get your gear and the coke, and then head for California.'

'Okay, but give me a few minutes. I'll postdate a couple of cheques for my slumlord, and I should probably phone Eleanor . . .'

'You deceitful swine!' shouted Gordon. 'You told me you didn't have anything going for you here. I can't trust anybody anymore. Does she have a sister?'

'She's *my* sister you horny clown. She came up here a few months ago to do a Masters in some kind of esoteric biology. I don't see her much but I always let her know when I'm going to be out of town for a while. If I don't keep in touch then my whole family gets worried and they come up here to make sure I'm okay.

'She's a genuine, right out of the mould, Townsend. You wouldn't like her, and even if you did, she sure as hell wouldn't like you.'

CHAPTER TEN

San Francisco

WALTER MATHESON had a slight headache. He had debated seeing his doctor about it, but then decided that a mild headache wasn't unreasonable considering that it was only a week since the crash. He would give it another week before he called the doctor. In the meantime, aspirins seemed to help, and a tumbler or two of whisky in the evening didn't hurt either. And when he thought about it, a sore head was a small price to pay for his freedom.

He poured a drink and made a silent toast to the memory of the pilot, Kiniski. If he hadn't spotted the other aircraft... But he had, and although it was too bad about the crash, at least Walter had been prepared for the police when they arrived.

Ever since he returned from Vancouver he'd been expecting to be questioned. Good luck to them. With the pilot dead and that climber, Wilson, carrying for him, there was no way he could be connected to anything. The plane crash was turning out to be an unbelievable piece of luck.

He had almost caught up at the office, and Marion accepted his story about a fall down a rocky hillside near the fishing lake and was taking 'extra special care of my poor husband'; and even that snotty black bastard from the Police Department hadn't been able to put a dent in his good humour.

He finished his whisky and laughed out loud. Let them try to charge him with anything. Let them tap his phone, audit his books, anything they wanted. He was so clean he squeaked, and after maybe two more shipments he would kiss the whole lot of them goodbye. Goodbye to stupid, fat Marion, goodbye to snotty suspicious cops, goodbye to the whole city and country. And he didn't even have to worry about the pilot anymore.

Now, if only that Wilson would phone, and his head would stop hurting. . . .

CHAPTER ELEVEN

San Francisco

ALEX TOWNSEND was nervous. He sat on the bed in his hotel room and looked at the entertainment guide on the bedside table. He turned the pages absently for half a minute then stood up and dropped the magazine on the bed behind him. He walked to the television and turned it on. He stood in front of it and changed slowly through about half the channels then angrily slapped the off switch. He looked at his watch, then crossed the room, opened the big sliding window and stepped out onto the balcony.

It was a warm summer morning and the city of San Francisco was spread out above, below and around him, but he didn't really see it. He looked at his watch again and then turned back into the room and stood staring at the telephone, willing it to ring.

Gordon had said he would call every half hour and now twenty-five minutes had passed since the last call. That call had been short and to the point. Alex had answered on the first ring and Gordon had simply said, 'It's all set. I'm meeting the man in a restaurant called the Bayview in a couple of minutes. It's right downtown, not that far from your hotel. There's plenty of people around and I can't see any way anything can go wrong. It's quarter to eleven now so I'll call you by eleven-fifteen. Okay?'

'Okay, just be careful.'

'Yeah.'

Alex paced the room and looked at his watch again. Twelve past. He wondered what to do if the telephone didn't ring. Leave immediately? Wait an extra few minutes? Their emergency plan was for Alex to leave immediately if Gord didn't call on time, and then to call Gordon's hotel every hour or so from a pay phone.

He had just decided that he would give Gordon five minutes' grace when the shrilling telephone startled him so badly that he dropped a magazine that he didn't remember picking up.

'Hello?'

'Everything's okay, Alex. I'm downstairs in the lobby, so pack up your pyjamas and toothbrush and meet me down here. I'll buy you lunch.' He giggled. 'I think I can afford it.'

They ate in the hotel dining room and Gordon described what had happened.

'I called Matheson this morning at his office. He said I should call another number and ask for Carl. So I did that, and this guy Carl said that I should meet him at the Bayview Restaurant. It's one of those plastic twenty-four-hour places, but it had a parking lot for customers only, which is probably why he picked it.'

'So what happened?' Alex was like a schoolboy trying to pry information from a friend who had just done something exciting and forbidden. He tried to sound casual, but he was burning with curiosity, and more admiration than he wanted to admit.

'Nothing much. Carl, if that's really his name, met me there right on time and we made the swap in the parking lot. He gave me this ...', Gordon pointed to a cheap-looking vinyl attaché case on the chair to his left, '... and I gave him the big suitcase. The whole thing took about three minutes.'

'But how did he know who you were? How did you know that there was the right amount of money in the case? How did he know that you weren't ripping him off?'

Gordon looked at his friend with amused curiosity. 'You've been watching too much television Alex. He knew what I looked like because I had told him on the telephone, and we each knew what was in the other guy's case because we opened them up and looked.'

'In the parking lot?' Alex's voice rose an octave and cracked on the last two words.

'Relax, relax. We sat in the car I rented and he looked in my suitcase and I looked in his. I didn't count the money down to the last dollar and he didn't weigh the coke, but we both checked that each case looked about right.' Gordon took a spoonful of soup, then said, 'And what the hell, Matheson knows where I live, and I know where hc lives, so nobody is going to be ripping anybody off. What would be the point? Anyway, the whole deal took about three minutes and nobody paid the least bit of attention to us, so relax and enjoy your lunch.'

Alex took a bite of his club sandwich then asked with his mouth full, 'What about this guy Carl?'

'What about him? He's a sort of medium-sized black guy who's had his face kicked in a few times. I don't even know if his name is really Carl. He's Matheson's bagman,

that's all I know about him. That's all I *want* to know
about him. He didn't talk much excpt to say that
Matheson wants me to give him a call sometime in
January or February if I want to do another carry.'

'Another?'

'Yeah, I guess he likes me.'

CHAPTER TWELVE

San Francisco

LIEUTENANT WILLIAM HOLLEY was furious. His anger
simmered just below the surface and some of the guys in
the drug squad had started a pool based on the hour and
day that he would finally explode. Even the secretaries
and the com-ops were getting their money down.

The last time he had been this way was when Judge
Partington had given a suspended sentence to a kid that
Holley had caught with almost half a kilo of smack. He
had sat at his desk brooding, not talking to anyone for
three days after that. On the fourth morning he had shown
up with a split lip, a badly puffed eye, and two fingers in
splints. But cheerful and ready to go back to work. When
somebody asked him, 'What does the other guy look
like?', he had just smiled and said, 'Which one?'

This time it was worse. He had taken Matheson's
escape from the RCMP as a personal insult and when he
heard that Matheson had appeared back in the city he had
hurled a telephone book across the room and stamped out
of his office.

Three days later he was still boiling. The pilot and the
aeroplane were gone – disappeared as though they had
never existed. And yet they couldn't have crashed because
here was Matheson alive and well in San Francisco with a

bullshit story about being marooned at some lake and
cutting his head on the way out. Did he expect Holley to
believe that?

Holley knew exactly what had happened. The airplane
had come through the storm and landed at some private
field in eastern Washington or Oregon. The airplane, and
the body of the pilot were in a deserted barn or garage and
probably wouldn't be found for ten years. It looked like
the pilot had got in one good lick before Matheson
murdered him, but that was the only satisfaction he could
find.

Then came the last straw. A strictly-from-hunger check
of incoming passenger lists showed that Matheson had
flown into San Francisco on a Canadian Pacific Airlines
737 from Vancouver. *Vancouver*! It didn't make any sense
at all. What the fuck was he doing in Vancouver?

The RCMP pilots might be idiots, but there was good
civilian and military radar all along the Fraser valley and
everybody agreed that the little Cessna hadn't come back
over the border.

Holley gave up trying to think. He went home, drank
most of a bottle of vodka and passed out before supper.

He awoke a little after midnight and made the first of
many trips to the bathroom. After a while he stopped
going back to bed between spasms and just lay on the cold
tiles where he eventually fell asleep just before dawn.

He got to his office in the middle of the next afternoon,
a little shaky but calmed right down, and started asking
around to see who knew anybody in the Vancouver Police
Department.

CHAPTER THIRTEEN

Vancouver

POLICE DETECTIVES almost always work in pairs. There are a lot of good reasons for this, but when one partner gets sick, the other is often unable to carry on alone with the job they were working on.

Andy Cutler and Doug Popov had been working a trio of real nasties. Dirtballs with a maim-for-money service and a seemingly inexhaustible supply of acid and speed. When Popov came down with a cold bad enough to keep him in bed, Cutler decided to give himself some time off from the case.

As he explained to his sergeant: 'Rico, these guys are not only stupid, they're mean. They're also bigger than me and I am not going anywhere near them alone. I'll shuffle paper and answer the telephone for a day or two until Doug is healthy again.'

The day passed uneventfully. Cutler caught up on his paperwork and spent a lot of time on the telephone. Most of the calls originated within the Department and were simply requests for information or requests to speak to a particular member of the drug squad. The few calls from the outside were equally dull. Complaints about kids smoking pot in a parking lot; or offers of information, like:

'Uh, listen, I know where these guys are going to be doing a deal on some hash, right? And I was thinking that it'd probably be worth something for me to tell you, right?'

The usual.

Then, late in the afternoon, just as he was about to call it a day, he caught one from the switchboard.

'Sir, San Francisco P.D. is on the line. It's a Lieutenant Holley, and he wants to talk to someone in Drugs.'

'Okay Ellen, put him through.'

'Yes sir. Hello sir, you're connected to Detective Cutler, go ahead please.'

'Detective Cutler? I am Lieutenant William Holley of the Narcotics Investigation Section of the San Francisco Police Department. I am investigating the actions of a man whom I suspect to be bringing large amounts of cocaine into this country through the Canadian province of British Columbia, and I believe that he may have spent some time in Vancouver in the last two weeks. I would like to ask for some help from your department, but before I do I would like you to verify that I am who I say I am.'

Cutler always felt uneasy with people who spoke formal English, and this guy was a positive steamroller. At least his meaning was clear. 'Okay. Hang up and I'll call you back.'

'Fine.'

Cutler broke the connection and rang the switchboard again. He got the same operator. 'Ellen, it's Andy Cutler in Drugs. Will you call San Francisco P.D. and see if they'll connect me to a Lieutenant William Holley in the Narcotics Investigation Section? Thanks.'

He hung up and lit a cigarette. This sounded more interesting than kids smoking pot in the parking lot.

Andy Cutler was a quiet man in his late thirties. He had a long body and a long, lined face under curly blond hair; and blue eyes that were still full of excitement even after eleven years of police work. He smoked too many cigarettes and felt guilty enough about it to run two or three miles every other day, but not guilty enough to quit smoking.

Most of the time he enjoyed police work and felt it important. He was not a redneck or a law 'n' order fanatic, just a man who believed that a policeman who did his job with intelligence and compassion was making an important contribution to the society in which he lived.

He had done well since joining the Vancouver force,

making Detective after only seven years, and he knew that he would get Sergeant in the spring. And through it all he had even managed to keep his sense of humour.

Now, as he went back to the last of his paperwork he wondered just what Lieutenant Holley wanted, and why anyone would be smuggling 'large amounts of cocaine' to the States via B.C. Why bother? It must be somebody doing it privately, an amateur who thought that getting fancy was the way to fool Customs and the police.

The telephone rang on his desk. 'Hello sir, I've got Lieutenant Holley on the line from San Francisco, shall I connect you?'

'Yes, please.'

'All right sir. Hello sir, I have Detective Cutler on the line, go ahead please.'

'Thank you. Detective Cutler?'

'Hello Lieutenant, how can I help you?'

'You can help by telling me what a man named Matheson was doing before he flew out of Vancouver on twenty-ninth August. I've written up a full report on this and I'll telex it up to you, but here's the general picture.' Holley's voice was still crisp and intense, but the formality was gone.

'I was working a guy named Carl Adams a couple of years ago. We knew he was riding shotgun on heroin deals for one of the big importers here, a concert promoter named Tomlinson, and we were pretty sure he had pulled the trigger a couple of times. One day we got a tip that there was a big deal going down and we staked him out. It turned out that there was no deal, he just had a meet with a guy and nothing changed hands. We had them covered with a blanket, I mean we had five guys watching and I *know* nothing changed hands. We followed them both away from the meet and got nothing except that this other guy went home to a very nice piece of real estate in Pacific Heights, which is not exactly the low rent district.'

Cutler was taking notes and wondering where this was going.

'We checked him out. His name is Walter Frederick Matheson and he's an engineer. He runs his own company and he's completely legit. He really is a full-time engineer – well thought of, very successful, no record, no extravagant lifestyle, nothing. So what the hell is he doing meeting with a piece of human trash like Carl Adams? I mean Adams really is the quintessential ratbag, and anybody he talks to has just *got* to be dirty.'

Cutler wrote 'quintessential ratbag' on the margin of his notepad and drew a circle around it.

'So I dug a little deeper on this Matheson, figuring that it was probably blackmail, but guess what I found?' Holley's voice sharpened, became even more intense. 'I found two things. One, he's got a brother in Peru; and two, he takes a week or two off every year, sometimes twice a year, and goes fishing in Canada. More specifically he goes salmon fishing out of a town called Prince Rupert, which is an isolated little place right on the coast and he ...'

'Smack city,' interrupted Cutler.

'What?'

'Prince Rupert. We used to call it smack city. It's actually a fairly busy seaport with a really big fishing fleet. A lot of heroin comes in through there.'

There was silence at the other end while Holley thought about this new piece of information. Cutler didn't say anything more, just stubbed out his cigarette and waited. Finally Holley said, 'Hm. I didn't know that. But I don't think there's any real connection between that and this Matheson business. I think he's strictly on his own. Let me explain. After I found out about the brother in Peru I leaned on a couple of people I know and they told me that the people that Carl Adams works for are in the coke business in a minor way. We thought they were strictly into heroin, but it seems that they also get a bit of cocaine now and then, maybe ten or fifteen keys, maybe twice a year. It gets stepped on of course, but the word is that it's pure as can be when they get it.

'So', Holley's voice bored on, 'it looks to me that the brothers Matheson have an import-export business going. The one in Peru either sends it or takes it up to Canada on a boat and Walter meets the boat and brings the shipment back into America from there. He then sells it to Adams' people and sends the money down to Peru. Does that scan okay for you?'

Cutler had been trying to think of a way to work the phrase 'quintessential ratbag' into his next conversation with Rico and the question caught him off guard. He reviewed the conversation quickly and then said, 'That seems reasonable to me, have you managed any hard evidence? Can you talk to Peru about the money end of it?'

Holley just snorted, 'Not fucking likely. What government wants to talk about drugs going out and money coming in? But I do have a certain amount of evidence.' He explained how he had set up a cooperative deal with the DEA and the RCMP and how everything had gone perfectly until somehow Matheson had discovered the RCMP surveillance and disappeared into the storm over the North Cascades.

'What does the pilot have to say?' asked Cutler.

'Well, that's where the evidence starts to get less hard. You see the pilot isn't anywhere to be found. Matheson flew into that storm in the afternoon of twenty-third August and showed up at the Vancouver airport to board Canadian Pacific Airlines flight 117 to San Francisco on the twenty-seventh. The pilot and the plane are still missing. The RCMP say he didn't come back to Canada, and he hasn't shown up anywhere here. What I think is that they got through the storm okay and landed at some private field in Washington, and that Matheson offed the pilot right there and hid the plane, probably in an old barn or garage. But what I *can't* figure out is what the hell is going on with this flight out of Vancouver. It just doesn't make any sense at all.'

'And I suppose you don't want to talk directly to

Matheson until you've got something hard enough to pull him in with?'

'No, there's no problem there, the fact that the plane went missing on a flight he chartered gave us all the excuse we needed to talk to him, but he had a bullshit story all ready for us, and even though I know he's lying, I don't see what I can do about it. I mean we can prove that he crossed the border in an airplane, but we can't prove that he brought in any coke.'

Cutler asked, 'Just what is his story?'

'He says he chartered the plane to take him fishing at some little lake the pilot knew about. He says the pilot put him down at the lake and never came back. He says that the lake is pretty remote, quite a few miles from the road and that after waiting for a couple of days with no food or camping equipment he thrashed his way out through the bush and hitchhiked to civilization. He's got a pretty good head wound which he says he got when he took a bad fall in some rocks on the way out from the lake, and things aren't too clear to him after that. He says he thinks he must have hitchhiked to Vancouver, or maybe taken a bus. He says he really doesn't remember much until he got back to San Francisco.

'Anyway, that's the problem: we know he's lying about being stranded at the lake, I mean there were two RCMP guys in the plane behind him all the way to the border. And I'm dead sure that he's bringing in regular shipments of cocaine; but there's not much we can do about it with what we've got. So, what I'd like to know is why he went back to Canada and what he did there until the twenty-seventh. Maybe I'm grabbing at nothing, but if there's any way you can help me on this I'd sure appreciate it.'

Cutler stretched and yawned, holding the receiver away from his head, then said, 'Okay, let's see if I've got this right? You suspect that a San Francisco engineer named Walter Matheson has an arrangement with his brother in Peru whereby the brother brings or sends ten to fifteen kilos of cocaine to Prince Rupert once or twice a year and that this Walter Matheson picks it up there and smuggles it into the U.S. by light plane. He then sells it to a big heroin dealer, named Tomlinson – who is the one you're really after – and then sends the profits back to Peru. On his last trip you had the RCMP follow him. They saw him take off from Prince Rupert and followed him non-stop to the Canada–U.S.A. border where he apparently became suspicious and flew into a storm. This was on twenty-third August. He showed up four days later on a flight from Vancouver to San Francisco, but the light plane and its pilot are still missing. Is that right?'

'That's right. I've been looking for a way to nail Tomlinson for about three years now but he keeps his hands completely clean. At least as far as his heroin business is concerned. Maybe he hasn't been so careful with this little side deal. Maybe Matheson knows something, and if I can give him the choice of talking to me or doing twenty years of hard time maybe he'll tell me something.

'Like I said, I may be grabbing at nothing, but I want Tomlinson pretty bad, and this is the only way I can think of to get at him. I've tried everything else. About ten times.' He sounded angry and disgusted.

'Okay.' Cutler made a quick note and then said, 'I've got a couple of questions.'

'Shoot.'

He looked down at his notepad, then asked, 'First, had the plane actually crossed the border, or was it just heading that way when the RCMP lost contact?'

'Very definitely across the border. They had good visibility on the Canadian side and they say he didn't come back out.'

'Okay, next question is whether the RCMP are working on this from the Prince Rupert end?'

'Yeah, they are, but ...', Holley paused, '... but mostly from the point of view of the missing airplane. I had a few harsh words for them after they blew the aerial surveillance and I don't think they're going to be putting a lot of energy into this on my behalf.'

'I see.' Cutler made an aimless doodle on his pad and then asked, 'Do you have any theory yourself about why he came back to Canada?'

'Mister Cutler, I don't have even the vaguest beginning of a theory as to why he would do a thing like that. It doesn't make any sense to me at all. As long as he's claiming that he spent the twenty-fourth and twenty-fifth at this lake, which, by the way, he claims not to know the name of, and that he hitchhiked or took a bus from there to Vancouver then he doesn't need any kind of alibi and there's no need for him to go back. So *anything* you can turn up for me might help.'

'What about this wound on his head: how bad was it, and how recent, and how do you figure it?'

'Pretty bad. He even took the bandages off to show me. It was at least four inches long, big enough to take maybe twenty-five stitches, but it hadn't been stitched. It was a kind of ragged cut that ran most of the way across his forehead just above the eyebrows. It still hadn't healed up when I saw it, but it must have been about a week old judging from the state of the scab and the shiners it had given him. My guess is that the pilot got in a good shot with a wrench or something before he was killed.'

Cutler thought for a long time and finally said, 'If the cut on his head was gory enough, I might be able to find someone at the airport who remembers him, but all that would prove is that he was at the airport, and you already know that. There's a chance that he might have given the airline a Vancouver address or telephone number, and I'll check that out; but what we really need is to find out if he did anything with his credit cards while he was here. If he was here a week ago the companies should be starting to get their copies about now. Can you check that out for me?'

'I've already started work on that, but the companies don't like to give that sort of information away.'

'Well, keep on it, because it's likely to be the only way I'll be able to find anything for you ... excuse me a minute, I'll be right back.'

A dark, heavyset man in a brown three-piece had left an office at the far end of the room and was walking toward the elevators. Cutler put his hand over the mouthpiece and stood up and called after him. 'Hey, Rico.' The man turned and Cutler said, 'Can you hang on here for a minute while I finish this call?'

The man said, 'Sure', and walked back toward Cutler's desk.

Cutler spoke into the telephone again. 'Sorry about that, but I wanted to catch my sergeant before he left for the day. Now, where was I? Oh yeah, I'll check on the airport and the airline for you, and anything else I can think of, and you work on the credit card thing. And you'll send up a telex on all this? And photos of Matheson? . . . Good, and in the meantime, can you give me a quick description?'

He wrote quickly as Holley described Matheson and then said, 'Okay, I've got it, but will you wire up some photos anyway?' He listened for a minute more and then said, 'Sure, no problem. Glad to help,' and hung up.

The afternoon shift was coming on and throughout the big room there was an exchange of How ya doin'?s and See you tomorrow's. Cutler filed the notes he had made into his desk and stood up. He was only two inches taller than the sergeant's five feet ten, but it looked like more, the difference exaggerated by their bodyshapes; he thin and the shorter man thick-shouldered and bearlike.

'Got time for a beer?' asked Cutler.

'Sure. As long as I'm home by six, Angie'll let me live. What's on your mind?'

'I just got a strange phone call. Let's go over to the club and I'll tell you about it.'

They left the station and crossed the street to the Union building, a six-storey structure of concrete and glass with a restaurant on the first floor, a credit union on the second, traffic courtrooms on the fourth, and mostly lawyers and accountants on three and five. It is owned by the Vancouver City Policeman's Union and the top floor is occupied by the Police Athletic Club, a members-only bar and night-club where the athletic events are dancing and elbow bending.

The bar was beginning to fill as the two men ordered beer and found a small table by a window.

'I caught a funny one on the telephone this afternoon, Rico.' The Sergeant's name was Richard Hofstadter. He had the well-dressed, jowly appearance of an old style hood and Cutler called him Don Rico. 'A guy from the San Francisco P.D., a drug squad Lieutenant named Holley, wants some information about . . .'

They drank their beer and Cutler repeated Holley's conversation. '. . . and he really sounded intense. He could have put the whole thing on the telex in about two paragraphs, but he seems to be taking this one personally.

'Anyway I'll see if anyone at the airport remembers this Matheson, or if there's anything still in the C.P. Air computers. I don't expect much, but I can see why Holley's interested. What would bring this guy back to Canada?'

'What about the obvious thing?' Hofstadter had a low coarse voice that matched his appearance.

'What obvious thing?'

'He flew up here as a tourist, went through customs, everything official and clean and okay, now he's back in the States but he hasn't officially crossed the border, so he sneaks back up and flies home. Maybe he just wants the cancelled airplane tickets as proof that he went and returned like five thousand other tourists.'

'I suppose that's possible,' Cutler didn't sound convinced. 'But Customs doesn't keep any records of who crosses that border and when they return. If anyone ever asks, all he needs to say is that he took a bus.' He finished his beer and asked, 'Another?'

'Sure, why not?'

Returning with two more bottles Cutler sat down and said, 'You're probably right, and the guy did get quite a crack on the head somewhere along the line, so maybe he wasn't thinking too carefully. Still, there's something that bothers me about all this, something in the back of my mind that I can't get at.'

'Hmph.' Hofstadter grunted and drank. 'You're probably not going to find out a damned thing, so it's all academic anyway. But you'll enjoy it more than actually doing useful work for this department, and it'll get you out of my hair for the day, so why not dig around and see what you come up with.'

They drank their beer slowly, talking idly and listening to the babble of conversation at the next table as a group of young patrolmen relaxed after a day on the streets.

'. . . weaving in and out of traffic all across the viaduct, and when we finally get him pulled over he turns out to be the world's biggest asshole. He's *not* drunk, and he's not going *anywhere* with any fucking cops. Not drunk! You should have seen him. He could hardly walk, and when we get him to the basement he's not going to take any breath test, and then he tries to pick a fight with Willy, and then, get this, he shits himself. Right there in his pants, deliberately. So we say fuck this, and book him, and the first thing he does when we get him upstairs is to pick a fight with the jail staff. They broke one of his teeth putting him away so you know what's going to happen.'

'Don't I just. He's going to scream assault, and everybody's going to forget that he was drunk out of his mind and driving through the city at a hundred kilometers an hour, and he'll get off.'

'Hah, you think that's bad. One night last week I was on with Duffy and we saw a guy who . . .'

Cutler and Hofstadter finished their drinks and got up. As they walked to the elevator Hofstadter said, 'Do you have anything planned for this Saturday?'

'I don't think so, what's up?'

'Nothing too much. Angie and I were wondering if you'd like to come over for the afternoon and join us for a couple of beers and then steaks on the barbecue. Interested?'

The elevator opened and when it had purged itself of a load of eager athletes the two men got in and started down.

'Who is she?' asked Cutler.

'Who?'

'Whoever it is that Angie has lined up for me.'

'What a suspicious mind you have.'

They left the building and walked toward the police garage. Cutler said, 'C'mon Rico, you know that Angie's goal in life is to see me married to someone she's picked. I can't even remember the last time I went to your place for dinner and didn't find some friend of Angie's there for me.'

'You complaining?'

'Complaining? Are you crazy? Your wife has got some raunchy friends. I'm just curious is all.'

'Well, drop by on Saturday afternoon and you'll be able to satisfy your curiosity.'

'Okay. See you tomorrow morning.'

They were walking toward their separate cars when suddenly Cutler stopped and turned around.

'Rico. Hey Rico.'

Hofstadter waited by his car as Cutler jogged over. 'Listen Rico, I just figured out what's been bugging me about this San Francisco thing.'

'So?'

'It's the wound on the guy's forehead. Straight across above the eyebrows and kind of ragged he said. You know what that sounds like to me? It sounds like dashboard is what it sounds like.' Cutler was excited. 'You remember what we used to pull out of MVA's, on the passenger side, before people started wearing chest straps?'

Hofstadter scratched his cheek and thought about it. Then he said, 'Yeah, a lot of people with horizontal gashes on their foreheads. The lap straps would hold them to the seat but they'd fold forward and prang their foreheads against the dash.' He continued scratching his cheek absently. He needed a shave. At five-thirty in the afternoon he would always need a shave. 'You don't see much of that anymore, with padded dashboards and full chest straps, so what do you think happened?'

'I think that a lot of small airplanes still have lapstraps and hard dashboards. I'll bet they crashed in that storm and Matheson walked away from it.'

'What about the plane and the pilot?'

'If they crashed in the mountains or in a forest the plane may never be found; and the pilot, well who knows. He could have been killed in the crash, or killed after the crash, or he could be lying on the beach at Puerta Vallarta with his share of the profits. No way to tell yet.'

'Sounds reasonable enough to me.'

'It sounds a lot more reasonable than the pilot giving him one in the head with a wrench,' said Cutler, 'but it still doesn't explain why Matheson came back here.'

CHAPTER FOURTEEN

Yosemite Valley

THE MOON was still three days away from full but it was bright enough to paint the dry hills pale silver and glint on the two-lane blacktop. Inside the van Alex leaned against the passenger door and watched the dark shapes of trees and occasional small buildings appear in the distance and then quickly rush by. The noise of the motor and the vibration of the van soothed him and settled him into a warm trance, suspending time as they rattled through the night.

The yellow light from the dashboard faintly outlined Gordon's features behind the wheel, a half smile just visible through his beard. He spoke.

'What did they pay you at that garage?'

'Ten-forty an hour, why?'

'No, I mean take home, per month.'

'A little over eleven hundred if I worked the whole month, but I usually took a few extra days off so it was under a thousand most months.'

'So in a year you were taking home about twelve thousand?'

'I guess so. About that.'

'This week you took home twenty-five thousand. That's more than you would have made in the next two years at the garage. Have you thought about that?'

'Yeah, a little bit.'

'So why aren't you smiling?'

Alex sat silent for a bit, watching the reflections of the white lines flash by on the inside curve of the windshield. Then he said, 'I'm glad to have the money, don't think I'm not. One day I want a little house in a small town in the mountains somewhere, maybe in Alaska, and this money puts me a lot nearer to that. And if we do more jobs for him that'll help too, but I'm not smiling for two reasons:

'The first is that something left over from my middle class childhood keeps whispering to me that I've done something I shouldn't have ... I know, I know, that's a silly attitude and I'll probably get over it, but right now it still bothers me.

'The second reason is that I just can't believe that there are no strings attached to this, that we're safe now. You have no idea how nervous I was waiting at the hotel. I really didn't expect to see you again. I was sure they'd kill you.'

It was Gordon's turn to be silent before answering. He thought about Alex's response for a minute or so and then said, 'The last thing in the world that Matheson wants is for something to happen to me. Even assuming that he could find out who you were he'd have to be completely crazy to have us killed. He was taking a big risk bringing the stuff in by plane, and he knows it. We're his guaranteed ticket to everything money can buy, there's just no way he wants anything bad to happen to us.

'As for you worrying about the morality of the whole thing, well in a sense that's a problem you're going to have to handle yourself, but I really think that you're making too much out of it. Cocaine just isn't that kind of problem.'

Alex was still watching the flashing reflections of the white line in the window, and didn't turn as he spoke. 'I'm sure you're right, and I know I'll be okay in a while, but I can't smile about it just yet. Give me a few more days and I'll be fine.'

But he was smiling even as he said the words and they both started to laugh. Then they turned the last corner into the valley and the south face of El Cap was blazing in the moonlight above them and they fell silent, staring up in awe.

CHAPTER FIFTEEN

Yosemite Valley

ALEX AND GORDON slept in the van that night and the next morning set up their tent in Sunnyside Campground, a walk-in tenting area on the north side of Yosemite Valley known to climbers from all over the world as 'Camp Four'.

Once the tent was up Gordon unzipped the semicircular cookhole in the floor near the door and gave a ceremonial burial to the fifty-thousand dollars.

'We won't be needing them until we head back into the real world, and they'll be safer under here than anywhere else.' He tamped the dirt back into place and zipped the cookhole shut. 'Now, let's go climbing.'

Millions of people pass through Yosemite National Park every summer. For many of them it is an opportunity to say, 'Ooohh! Wouldja lookit that', as they crane their necks to look up out of the windows of their cars and tour buses; for some it is an opportunity to do a bit of hiking and photography in one of the most beautiful places in the world, and for some it is a summer job selling food in a supermarket. But for the rock-climber, Yosemite Valley is as close to heaven as he will ever get. The quiet forests of the valley floor are walled for seven miles by huge monoliths of beautiful tan granite. Food is cheap, beer and dope are plentiful, and the sun almost always shines.

After a week of rock climbing in this granitic never-never land, Alex no longer thought much about what he had done to earn his twenty-five thousand. He hadn't forgotten, but it didn't seem to matter. All that mattered was the climbing.

And therein lies part of the magical attraction of this ridiculous activity. When a climber is stretched to his limit, high above his last protection, when all that separates him from a long fall to injury or death is the absolute concentration of his entire mental and physical power, then everything outside the immediate present disappears completely. It doesn't matter what political party is in power, or how many children are starving in Ethiopia. To the climber *in extremis*, politicians and starving children do not even exist. *Nothing* exists except the few square feet of rock immediately in front of his eyes. And if the climb has been hard enough, then the external world reasserts itself only slowly.

The post-climb mental state is a painless floating, dreamy and timeless like a post-coital trance, but better because it lasts longer and has no overtone of emptiness. Stripped of all the romance, climbing is just another mindwipe, another kind of junk.

Alex was climbing well. He climbed steadily through the first week, mostly with Gordon Wilson, but occasionally with others; climbers met in Camp Four or in the bar in the evening, or old acquaintances from the Vancouver and Seattle scenes. He started with some familiar classics: the east buttress of Middle, Nutcracker with the 5.9 start, the first five pitches of the Central Pillar of Frenzy. Nothing of more than moderate difficulty, but all good routes and all long enough to give a feeling of having done a climb rather than an exercise routine.

Then he began working on shorter routes of increasing difficulty, sharpening his technique and striving for the mind control needed on the long hard routes that embody the spirit of Yosemite climbing.

After a few days of this he felt ready to push it a little and talked Gordon into an attempt on Serenity Crack.

'I've heard that the bottom of the first pitch is pretty gross, but it's supposed to be nice above that, and I want to see if I can lead the thin crack at the top of the last pitch.'

Gordon wasn't particularly interested. He had climbed the first two pitches three years earlier, and hadn't enjoyed it a lot. His heavy body and large hands made thin cracks too much work for too little reward.

'Well it's not my favourite kind of climb, but I'll be happy to come along and belay as long as you don't mind leading the whole thing.'

'No, that's okay with me, but if you'd rather not do it I'll try to round up someone else.'

'Don't worry about it. Anything you can lead, I can jumar. I'll just take a six pack and my walkman and turn my mind off for the day, get a suntan.'

They started early the next morning, because Serenity crack lies on a concave face that becomes almost intolerably hot by midday. But early as they were they could hear voices above them as they scrambled up to the base of the climb. Female voices, and the metallic snapping of karabiners.

'Sounds like we've got a couple of ladies ahead of us.'

'I hope they're planning to do Maxine's Wall, not Serenity. I don't want to get stuck below them.'

'Alex, you're getting entirely too serious about this. Relax. If they're on Serenity then you can do Maxine's Wall, it's a good climb. Or we can sit on the ledge and watch them climb. There's worse things in the world than watching women climb.'

The women were getting ready to start Maxine's Wall. Gordon was quick to start a conversation, and Alex envied the affability that led so quickly to ease with strangers.

Anne-Marie was a knockout. She was French but looked like everyman's image of California. Blonde hair and blue eyes. Movie starlet body tanned golden brown and bursting out of bright yellow shorts and snug T-shirt. Lots of smiles and Gordon was doing his schoolboy French act for her.

'Ah. Tu es Française. Je suis Canadien.' And then having to switch back to English when he couldn't follow her response. Which was fine, because she spoke English as well as he did, if with an accent. She wanted to know about Quebec and the strength of the separatist movement, but Gordon could only shrug and say that he really didn't know much about it, but that he'd heard that there was some good climbing there, especially in the winter.

The other one seemed a few years older – maybe twenty-seven or twenty-eight. She had long, almost blonde hair tied low at the back so that it covered her ears, and slate grey eyes that took in a lot more than they gave out. Her body seemed lean and strong, but not much figure showed through the sweat pants and loose T-shirt that she wore. Her name was Linda and aside from the fact that she had a smooth alto voice, that was all that Alex found out about her.

Anne-Marie said that she was going to try the first pitch of Maxine's Wall, which started just to the right. It would be very hard for her but there were lots of bolts and a fall wouldn't be serious, and if she could manage the first pitch then she would rappel back down and spend the rest of the day swimming. Alex watched her trying first moves and decided that she would be lucky to get off the ground, let alone succeed on the harder section above.

He wanted to stay and talk to Linda whom he found

more attractive than her golden, jiggly companion, but he
was unsure of what to say, so he just finished tying in and
shouldered his rack.

'You ready, Gord?'

'All set.'

He turned to the woman. She was intent on watching
her partner but she seemed to sense him looking at her
and turned so that their eyes met briefly before she gave
her attention back to Anne-Marie. Over her shoulder she
said, 'Have a good climb.'

'Thanks. Same to you.'

She didn't reply and Alex turned to the rock cursing his
ineptitude. But that was soon forgotten as he came to
grips with the bombed-out pinscars that make up the first
forty feet of Serenity Crack. The most secure technique
seemed to be to curl his first two fingers behind his thumb
and insert them, with the thumb up, into the square holes
that were sometimes over an inch and a half on a side.
Incredible to think that this had once been a rurp and
knifeblade crack! Then he was twenty-five feet up and
trying to decide whether to try for some protection. There
was no way to get any kind of nut into these scars, but
maybe a Friend No. 1 would go. He finally decided to
forego any protection and just go for the bolt fifteen feet
above. People had climbed this forty feet unprotected for
years before the advent of Friends, and after all, it was
only 5.9.

He clamped the lid down on his mind and concentrated
on his fingers and toes. Thirty feet. Chalk up again. Thirty-
five. Too far to fall, but the bolt only a few moves away now.
Careful, careful. There, it's within reach. But no fast moves,
no grabbing. Clip a karabiner to the bolt. Now clip in the
rope. There. Take a deep breath. Look up. The crack above
widening, looking better. Not easier, but protectable.

Look down. Gord leaning against an old stump, talking
to the thin blonde and watching voluptuous Anne-Marie
who had finally made it to the first bolt on her route, about
fifteen feet off the ground.

'I've got a runner on, Gord, so you can think about giving me a belay.'

'You're on.'

He moved on. The crack was a real crack now and he could get solid fingerlocks. He put a nut in as soon as he could, to back up the bolt, and then moved up smoothly and was at the belay bolts in less than three minutes. Clip. Clip. Tie the rope off. Get in a nut to back up the bolts.

'Okay, Gord, I'm off. Come on up.'

'All right. I'll be up in a few minutes.'

The stance was much too steep to sit so he leaned back into his harness and let the morning sun work on him as he looked around. Even though he was only one pitch up the view was great. Especially over toward Sentinel and the Cathedrals. Down below, Gordon was just about ready to jug up and the French girl had managed about five more feet.

The rope went tight below the belay bolts as Gordon started up on his jumars. He had made about six feet and Alex had leaned back out and was staring up at the intersection of sky and valley-rim when there was a high-pitched shriek from below. He twisted around in time to see the last of Anne-Marie's short fall. She was hanging about five feet below the bolt and Alex's first thought was that the way she was climbing this would be just the first of many falls for her. Then he saw blood running down her leg, and she was yelling, and Gordon was back down on the ground and helping Linda lower her.

Alex began sorting out a rappel. He kept looking down and was suddenly amazed to see Gord yanking down the girl's yellow shorts and the white panties under them to reveal a small but bloody gash on her left buttock.

The scene below quickly resolved into the administration of minor first aid from Gordon's pack. Anne-Marie was laughing through her tears and patted Gordon's head as he knelt beside her, applying gauze and then taping it down with adhesive tape. Alex decided that the three of them had the situation under control and stayed where he was.

Gordon used his T-shirt to wipe most of the blood from her leg and then stepped back. She attempted to pull up her panties, but it apparently hurt her to bend and she asked Gordon to help. Alex wondered why she hadn't asked her friend Linda.

The three below had a brief conference and then Gordon called up. 'I'm going to help Anne-Marie down to the hospital. Can you manage to sort things out yourself? I'll leave the jumars and my rope here for you, okay?'

'Yeah, I'll manage.'

There was another conference below and Gordon's arm was around the injured girl's waist. Then: 'Alex, Linda says she'll come up if that's okay with you. I can get Anne-Marie down myself.'

I'll just bet you can, thought Alex. 'Sure, that's fine with me, and you can take your rope and jumars down with you then – we'll use their rope for the rappel. Just don't forget about the hospital, if she cut herself on the bolt she might need a tetanus shot.'

'Yes, Doctor. See you later.' And he was on his way, giving Anne-Marie more help than she appeared to need. But she didn't seem to mind. Then there was only the thin woman with the enigmatic eyes tying in to the end of his rope and getting ready to climb.

She clipped one end of the other rope to the back of her waist belt, then tucked the first aid kit back into the pack, shrugged into the shoulder straps and snugged them down. She looked up and shouted, 'Okay?'

Alex clipped the rope into one of the bolts above, pulled it up until it was tight between them, and slipped it round his back.

'Okay, you're on belay.'

She had some difficulty with the first section and her weight came on to the rope once, but when she reached the point at which the crack widened enough to admit her fingers she was fine. She was slower following it than Alex had been leading, but her movements were smooth and she didn't flail or thrash.

As she approached the belay Alex was able to take a more careful inventory of her features. Her face was slightly tanned and the skin was still tight over good bones. There were creases of course, no one in real life survives almost thirty years without some of those, but no sag. Her eyebrows were several shades darker than her hair and her nose had a definite, but not prominent bridge. As she got closer Alex could see that her eyes were not grey, but actually a pale, washed-out blue, and they glittered with concentration as she worked her way upward.

Her lips were a thin straight line, but when she reached the belay her concentration relaxed and she broke into a smile that showed a wide mouth and a very crooked lateral incisor on the upper left.

She tied herself in, clipped the pack and the second rope to one of the bolts and smiled again. 'Thanks for the belay. I hope you didn't mind.'

'No, not at all. In fact I'm glad you came up, it'll save me a lot of hassle getting down. How's your friend? Was she cut badly? I couldn't tell from up here.' Did he sound as stilted to her as he did to himself?

'Oh, I don't think you have to worry about her. She's not badly cut at all – she just scraped the bolt as she slid past. I don't even know if all that gauze and tape was necessary, a bandaid would probably have been fine, but they seemed to be enjoying themselves so I didn't want to say anything.'

They both laughed and Alex began to relax. 'Did you want to get back down right away? I was planning to do the whole climb, but if you want to check up on your friend we can rap out from here.'

'I'd really like to go on, if it's all right with you. Anne-Marie isn't my friend ... that is, I only met her two days ago. And I doubt if she wants checking up on right now anyway.' She looked up at the crack above then said, 'Does it get a lot harder? I don't think I can climb anything too much harder than what we just did.'

'I've never done it before, but only the last twenty feet of the last pitch is supposed to be really hard. There's some 10a on the next pitch and then some easier climbing, around 5.7, I think.' Alex thought over everything he had heard about the climb and then said, 'I don't think there'll be any problem. You didn't have any trouble with the crack below once you got past those weird pinscars, so you should be okay.'

He began reracking the pieces she had cleaned out of the first pitch, but stopped when he noticed her fidgeting beside him. She was using a wide, padded waist belt rather than a sit harness, and couldn't get comfortable on the steeply sloping stance.

'There's a set of aiders in the pack, why don't you use them. It'll take the strain off your waist.'

He helped her to rearrange herself in the aiders and she said, 'I never would have thought of that. I've never stood in aiders before.'

'Never?'

'No, I've done all my climbing in the east, it's been all free climbing.'

'Where?'

'Mostly in the Shawangunks. Have you been there? Just outside of New York?'

'No, I never have. I've talked to a few people who climb there, and it sounds like everything is either vertical or overhanging.'

She laughed. 'Everything *is* pretty much vertical or overhanging, but there are so many holds that there are routes every few feet all along the cliff.'

Alex was almost ready to go. 'Well, who knows, maybe I'll get there one day. Are you all set?'

She took up the slack and flipped the rope around her back giving him a belay as he unclipped himself from the bolts. Then he remembered the second rope. 'Why don't you clip the other rope to the back of my harness. You've got enough to carry with that pack.'

Then he was away and all thoughts of his new partner

vanished from his mind as he worked carefully up the second pitch. It was just a little harder than the first and he had no real trouble. He climbed a little less quickly, but still smoothly and under control, placing protection whenever he came to a decent rest spot, and was soon at the next belay.

Linda found it difficult, and it was obvious that she was at the limit of what she could climb with no falls. When she was secure, and had wiped the sweat from her eyes, she gave Alex another crooked-tooth smile and said, 'That was something else. Christ. I thought I was going to come off about six times. This is infinitely better than the Gunks. Why didn't I come here years ago?'

She was smiling and laughing, and talked enthusiastically while they made ready for the last pitch. Alex laid back and enjoyed her enthusiasm, let it recharge his emotional batteries. When he had reracked all the gear and was ready to start the last lead he said, 'I think this last pitch isn't as long as the others. It'll be pretty easy at first, but then it'll get quite hard, 10c I think, and I don't know if I'm going to be able to do it. I *should* be able to, I've done things that hard on short routes, and it's only really hard for about twenty feet; but it's hot, and I've already done two pitches.' He looked down. 'And I'll have a few hundred feet of air below me.'

'What you're trying to tell me', she interrupted, 'is that you might fall off, and that you want me to be paying close attention to my belaying. Right?'

'Right.'

'Don't worry. I might not know anything about aid climbing, but I've caught lots of falls.'

'Okay, see you later.'

And up he went, climbing quickly through the first fifty feet, and then coming to a complete stop. He got in a solid nut and took stock of the final section above him, trying to sort out in his mind the sequence of moves needed to get him up it.

It was a thin crack, barely big enough for fingertips, and

there didn't seem to be any footholds at all. He was hot and tired and thirsty and wondered if he would be able to do it at all. He stretched a tentative left hand high above and felt the first hold with his outstretched fingers. Not much there. Not much at all.

He backed down and thought about it a little more, scanning the rock above for anything that might work as a toehold until finally he thought he had it. Up with the right hand, not the left, and left foot way out there. Then left hand, right hand, and finally a foot just barely into the crack to take a little of the strain off his arms and give him a chance to fumble a number one Friend off the rack and ram it home above.

He was in the groove then, and the climbing became what climbing should be as instinct and intellect went into overdrive and he powered up the remaining ten feet until, with one last careful pull, he was on the ledge.

He set up a belay, pulled up the second rope and then took up the slack in the lead rope. 'Okay, you're on belay, come on up.'

Twenty-five minutes later she collapsed on the ledge beside him. For several minutes she just lay there staring at the sky and saying nothing, clenching and unclenching her hands in a slow rhythm. Then she sat up and looked down at what she had just climbed.

'I've never done anything that hard in my life. Look at my hands!' She offered them for Alex's inspection. They were dirty and covered with small cuts and tears, some of which oozed a little blood.

'How did you lead that? I must have fallen off fifteen times. I'm exhausted. And what's in this pack? It felt like somebody was putting another rock into it every five feet on this last part.'

Alex lifted the pack from her shoulders and loosened the top. He reached in and pulled out a large bundle wrapped in Gordon's pile jacket. 'What we have here', he said as he pulled the jacket open, 'is the secret piece of equipment that enables the famous Yosemite climbers to cling to smooth vertical walls, defying gravity and amazing the tourists below.' The jacket fell away to reveal six cans of Budweiser.

He separated one can and pulled off the tab. 'Would you care for a beer?'

'I don't believe it! Would I care for a beer?'

She took the can and tipped it up, draining almost half of it before putting it down again.

'Oh God, does that ever taste good!'

They sat looking around the valley and drinking beer in the hot sun.

'How is it that you've done all your climbing in the Gunks? You don't sound like you're from New York.'

'I'm not. I grew up in South Dakota, but I escaped to California as soon as I could. I think I was sixteen, and it was like being let out of prison. People talk about rednecks in Alabama and Mississippi; they should spend some time in South Dakota. Anyway I lived in California, and Oregon for a little while, until three years ago when I went to New York for a photo workshop. I somehow just wound up staying there. This is the first time I've been back. I guess it's kind of weird for a Californian to start her climbing in New York, but that's what I did.'

Then she asked, 'What about you? Have you been doing this all your life?'

He finished his beer and began sorting the gear and putting it away in the pack. 'No, only for about five years. Looking back on it now it seems funny that I could grow up in California and not start enjoying the outdoors until I was almost twenty-five; but my family lived in the Los Angeles area and for most of my life I didn't even know that there *was* an outdoors.'

He began setting up a rappel. 'Are you ready to go down?'

'Sure, if you want to. I could sit up here forever, it's just so beautiful.'

Alex thought that *she* was beautiful. She had a crooked tooth, her hands were torn and dirty, and after the hard climb she needed a bath and a change of clothes. Her eyebrows were too dark, she was too thin and wiry, and from where he stood he could see, down the neck of her loose T-shirt, that she had hardly any breasts at all. But he could not deny her beauty. It shone from her eyes and radiated from her smile. It vibrated from her healthy body and filled him with wonder.

Did he dare say anything? What *could* he say? And what would be the point? She probably had a husband and three children waiting at the campground. Still, nothing venture, nothing win.

'Have you seen the view from any of the lookouts on the valley rim?'

'No, I only arrived here three days ago and this is the best view I've had. And anyway, I don't think that I could do any of the climbs that lead to the top.'

'You don't have to climb at all. There are roads up there.' He pointed to the southern rim. 'And I was thinking ...' he braced himself '... that if you're interested, I could drive you up there tomorrow. That is, I don't know if you're here with anybody, or what your plans are, but ...' He let the sentence hang, and felt adolescent.

'Oh Alex, I'd love to.'

He floated down the rappel to the descent ledges, wondering why he bothered with the ropes at all. When they were back on the valley floor he said, 'Do you want to do another climb this afternoon?'

'I'd like to, but I don't think my hands could stand it. I think that I'll spend the afternoon walking, and try to get oriented. This place is so huge, and I almost feel lost in it. I don't even know where the roads go, let alone the trails.' She stopped and looked up at him and he realized that she was less than five and a half feet tall. Her slim body and erect posture had made her seem much taller. She carried on, almost shyly, 'If your friend is still occupied with Anne-Marie, and you can't find another partner ... I could fix up some lunch for us ... that is, you could be a tour guide for the afternoon. If you didn't mind?'

If he didn't mind.

They ate their lunch in El Cap meadows and between bites of avocado and tomato sandwich Alex tried to point out some of the big El Cap routes. 'There's over twenty separate routes from bottom to top now, and at least half a dozen major variations. And that's just the ones I've heard about; there may be four or five more in the last year or so.'

'Have you climbed any of them?'

'Not a one. Gordon and I are planning to do the Salathé in a couple of weeks.'

She wanted to know where the route lay and how hard it was and who had climbed it first, and when. He did his best to show her, but the southwest face is three thousand feet high and at least as broad and she couldn't follow his pointing arm at all.

He told her what he could remember about the first ascent in 1961 by Frost, Pratt and Robbins, and how Frost and Robbins had come back a year later to make the second ascent in only five days, and with no fixed rope.

'. . . and as to how hard, that's difficult to say. I think you can keep the free climbing down to 5.9, with maybe just a bit of 5.10, and the hardest aid is A3, but most of it has gone free now so you can make it just as hard as you want – right up to 5.12.'

'We'll just do as much as we can free and aid the rest. Neither of us is out to prove anything, we just want to enjoy the route as much as possible.'

They left the meadows and walked up to the foot of the Nose, the great south buttress of El Capitan, then uphill to the right along the base of the southeast face as far as the cavernous overhanging wall that marks the start of the Pacific Ocean Route, in its time the hardest aid climb in the world.

Then back down and across the meadows to the other side of the valley and up to the base of Middle Cathedral Rock.

Where El Cap had been monolithic, hot and intimidating, Middle seemed friendly and attractive. A place to climb just for the sheer kinetic joy of it.

'What brought you here? This is a long way from New York?'

She thought about the question for a long time before answering and Alex began to wonder if he should have asked. Then she said, 'I'm not sure I can pin it down exactly. It was a combination of things.' She was speaking quietly, testing her words before giving them away.

'I guess everyone who climbs dreams about a trip to Yosemite some day, but for me that was still a long way in the future. Then there's the fact that I hadn't been back to the west for three years. There were a lot of things that I liked about California, and I left some friends there when I moved to New York. But I probably wouldn't have come back for that just yet either.'

She stopped and thought carefully about what she would say next. 'But in the last few months I've had some major problems with the work I've been doing, and I finally decided to pull the plug.' She looked up at the two thousand feet of rock above her then sat down with her back to a tree. 'It just happened that my ... that a friend of mine was headed west on a combined holiday and business trip, so I tagged along for the ride, sort of on impulse.'

She suddenly smiled. 'And I thought, "What the hell, why not bring along my rope and EB's and hurl myself at the sheer walls of Yosemite."'

'And here you are.'

'That's right, here I am.'

In the late afternoon they stopped for a drink in the cool of the Mountain Room bar. There were a few tourists, and one table of British climbers celebrating their return from something that grew more difficult and dangerous with every round they ordered. Alex and Linda bought beer and retreated to the furthest corner.

'What made you stay in New York? You said you went

out there for a photo workshop, but it sounded like you had planned on coming right back.'

'I *had* intended to come back. All I took with me was one change of clothes; but one of the other people at the workshop had a line on a job that was too big for him and asked if I would help.'

The beer left a line of foam across her upper lip. She wiped it off with the back of her hand and suddenly Alex had a vision of Karen Allen as Marion in *Raiders of the Lost Ark*. They could be sisters. Linda's hair was blonde, but she had the same kind of angular beauty, the same slim figure and the same go-to-hell attitude.

When he returned to reality, Linda was saying '. . . just perfect. After so many years of useless, nowhere jobs, it was like, like . . . I don't know how to describe it. It was like a fairy had waved a magic wand just for me. To transform me from junior assistant nobody on the dullest paper in California to what seemed like a big glamour job as a New York City photographer.'

She drank some more, then laughed. 'There were a few worms in the big apple though. The guy who waved the wand actually *was* a fairy. Can you imagine how I felt? Spending most of my waking hours with the most exciting man I'd ever met and finding out that he was a committed gay?

'And then after we finished that job we pretty much starved for the next year, which wasn't very magical at all, but we stuck it out and by the beginning of this year we were doing pretty well. We had good jobs and they were getting better; but somehow the whole thing was beginning to lose its appeal. We'd been working really hard for almost three years and I finally realized that I just wasn't that dedicated. I love photography, I really do, but not with the absolute blind dedication that it would have taken to make it in any sort of major way.'

They finished their beer and went back out into the light and heat. 'Michael, my partner, had it. He lived for photography. And he's good enough to make it as big as he wants. But there were days when I just wanted to walk in the park, or take off to the Gunks to climb, or even just lie around my apartment and read, and I couldn't do that and still carry my share of the load.

'So I made myself a deal. I would work my ass off for three more months. Commit myself entirely, and see how I felt at the end of the time. If it felt all right, then fine, I'd go on with it and become rich and famous with Michael; if I was still unhappy with it then I'd take the next three months off completely. Not go anywhere near the studio.'

They began walking again and he asked, 'So what happened with the three months at hard labour?'

'It didn't work very well. I knew it wouldn't work, but I had promised myself three months so I stuck it out. Besides, it wouldn't have been fair to Michael to just walk away, so I told him what was happening and he had two and a half months to decide what to do.'

'So now you're on the second three-month plan? The three months where you don't go near the studio?'

'Not exactly. By then I knew for sure that I didn't have what it takes to be successful in New York, and I'd seen enough in three years to know that New York is definitely not the place in which to be unsuccessful, so I just sold Michael my share of the business and closed the door behind me.'

They walked until the sun went down and Sentinel Rock was lit with a rich purple alpenglow.

'Do you still want to go up on the rim tomorrow?' he asked.

'Yes, do you?'

'Yes, and I think we should go early. I haven't been up before eight since I got here, but it might be nice to be up there in the early morning.'

'Whatever time you think is fine with me.'

'Okay, I'll pick you up at your campsite at six-thirty. It'll be cold and dark and horrible, but that way we'll have as much of the day as we want.'

'Shall I pack some lunch?'

'That would be nice.' Then, while he stood, feeling awkward, trying desperately to force himself to touch her, to say goodnight without appearing foolish, she put her hands on his shoulders and stood on her toes to kiss him quickly on the lips.

'Thanks for the day, Alex.'

Then she was gone, melted away in the dusk, and Alex was left transfixed, with the smell of her lingering sharp around him and the cold burn of her lips on his.

The next morning found them looking down on the valley from Sentinel Dome and Glacier Point, then walking the trail to Nevada Falls. As they walked they spoke of the pasts which had led them to this place. So very different, yet so much the same. She, running from her middle-American family, through poverty and life on the streets of Los Angeles, to the long-dreamed-of success in New York; and he running from the desolating boredom of middle class professional and family life to the crystalline reality of the mountains and the dirt-under-the-nails reality of the garage.

'. . . and you're not the only one who's abandoned a job. I quit mine just before I came here.' They stepped aside to let a group of camera-slung Japanese go by and then Alex continued, 'I probably should have quit sooner, it was a hassle every time I wanted an extra day off, but for some reason I just hung on and hung on . . . partly I guess because I really do like working on engines, and partly because it was easier to go on than to quit, in some ways.'

That evening their kiss was longer and Alex held her close before saying goodnight. When she had gone he went to the meadow where he sat by himself and stared up at the huge granite walls around him. They shone cold in the pale starlight, but all he could see was the image of her, luminous in his mind, until finally the cold drove him shivering to his tent where he lay down and could not answer when Gordon asked what sort of day he'd had.

He climbed with her all the following day, and did not return to his own tent, but stayed the night in hers, where the heat of their passion pushed back the dark and consumed the world, leaving only two bodies writhing slowly in the light of a single candle; and two minds, locked more tightly than the bodies until climax sent them spinning to the far ends of the universe.

CHAPTER SIXTEEN

Vancouver

ANDY CUTLER'S partner was over his cold and back on the job. They were sitting in Sergeant Hofstadter's office drinking coffee and discussing the case they were working on. Cutler was speaking.

'We've already got good film of two of them selling about eight hundred dollars worth of speed to Doug here. It's enough for a conviction, but we want all three, and we want them put away for a while and selling a bit of speed isn't going to do that, so we'd like to set up an assault.'

Doug Popov was thirty and had only made Detective five months earlier. He took over the story. 'I know that they're doing that kind of thing on a semi-regular basis. The word's out that if the pay is right they'll do just about anything short of murder. Broken legs, disfigurement, rape, whatever you want; and I'd guess that it won't be long before they get to murder too.'

He was short and swarthy, a natural actor who could fit comfortably into any social dynamic. He had let his hair go greasy and his hands go dirty. The three suspects had accepted him without question.

'I've been complaining to them about the asshole foreman on the jobsite where I'm working. That he has it in for me, that he's trying to get me fired, and that I'd really like to beat the shit out of him but I can't because I need the job.'

Cutler broke in, 'They've already said that they'll do beaters on this foreman if Doug's willing to pay them for it, so there's no question of entrapment, and we want to set up a scene with me as the foreman; but it's kind of risky and I'm not going to do it without pretty substantial backup.'

'Hah!' snorted Hofstadter. 'I should fucking well hope not. Just what have you got in mind?'

'We've found a construction site that looks ideal. It's part of the new stadium that the city is building, and the area is deserted at night. Once they agree to work me over Doug will tell them that I work late sometimes and then give them a tip one night when I'm supposedly there alone. The site is perfect. There's only one way to get to the foreman's office and we can seal the place behind them, and there are rooms on either side with connecting doors where we can hide as many of our guys as we want. We can wire it for sound, no problem, and the light's good enough that we can get video too.'

'So how many men are you going to need?'

'Rico, these guys are animals. I think we're going to want at least five in addition to Doug and myself. Doug?'

'For sure, at least five. In fact maybe six or seven.'

Hofstadter thought for a bit and then said, 'Maybe I can set something up with E.R.T. If we can get half a dozen of the biggest guys on the Tac squad into the connecting rooms we might be able to pull if off with some degree of safety for you.'

He scratched his cheek and looked at Cutler. 'But under no circumstances are you guys going to proceed with this until I've personally seen your 'ideal' setup, and checked the entrapment angle with the legal department. Right?'

'Right,' said Popov.

'Don't worry, Rico. If anything goes wrong I'm going to be hamburger. I'm not going off half-cocked on this one.' Cutler looked at his watch. 'I'm expecting a call from San Francisco in about ten minutes; maybe when I'm done with that we can all go down for a look at the construction site, maybe even take someone from the E.R.T. if they're interested.'

'Suits me,' said Hofstadter. 'I think I saw Tom Forbes about twenty minutes ago. I'll see what he has to say about using his E.R.T. guys on this.'

The two detectives started to leave and stopped when Hofstadter spoke again. 'And Andy, about going off half-cocked. Angie was talking to her friend Margaret yesterday – the one you met at our barbecue the other night – and from what she tells me I don't think we have to worry about you going off *half*-cocked.'

Cutler coloured and left the office. He sat down at his desk in the Detectives' room, lit a cigarette and went to work on the endless stack of paper that is such a big part of every policeman's life. At 9:02 the phone on his desk rang and the switchboard connected him to Lieutenant Holley in San Francisco. They went right to business.

'I'm afraid I haven't got much for you, Lieutenant. I found a stewardess that remembered him on the flight. She says he slept most of the way and the only reason she remembers him at all is because of the bandages on his head. Canadian Pacific Airlines has him reserving the tickets in San Francisco two months ago, on the eighteenth of June, which means he may have come back here simply to use the tickets, to add weight to his story about the fishing trip. Did you get anywhere with the credit cards?'

'As a matter of fact, I did. I've got two purchases on American Express. One is from a men's clothing store and one from a restaurant. They're both dated twenty-sixth August, so he was in Vancouver at least one day before he flew out.'

'I probably won't get anything,' said Cutler, 'but if you give me the addresses I'll check them out for you.'

'I'd sure appreciate that. The restaurant is called The Butcher, at twenty-six seventy-six West Broadway, and the clothing store is Mark James Ltd, at twenty-nine forty-one West Broadway. At least I assume it's a clothing store, because the receipt is for a suit, a shirt, some shoes, and underwear and socks.'

Cutler noted the names and addresses and then sat silent, staring at the tip of his pen.

'Are you still there, Mister Cutler?'

'Andy. Call me Andy. Yeah, I'm here. I was just thinking that the restaurant and the clothing store are only a couple of blocks apart, but that neither of them is anywhere near a hotel. I wonder what he was doing out there.'

'Is that area pretty far off the beaten track?' asked Holley.

'Not really that far, and in fact those are pretty decent places to get a suit and a meal; they're just not the places you'd expect a stranger to show up.'

'Remember that he's probably been going through Vancouver for several years now on his fishing trips. He may have learned about them on a previous trip, or maybe a hacky took him there.'

'Well I'll check them out and let you know, but before you hang up I want to ask you something.'

'What?'

'Has there been any search made for the airplane, the one that flew into the storm?'

'Not really.' Holley sounded surprised. 'I mean where would we start looking? I sent a request to the State Police in Washington and Oregon to contact me if they get any reports of a Cessna 182, with or without those Canadian ID numbers, turning up in strange circumstances, but they're not going to be able to do much about searching for it.'

'No, no, that's not what I meant.' interrupted Cutler. He explained his feelings about the head wound. '. . . and I think it's possible that the plane, and maybe the pilot, are still up in the mountains somewhere. I don't know if you can persuade your search and rescue people, or the Air Force, or whoever, to have a look, but it can't hurt to fly over the area where it disappeared.'

Holley wasn't impressed. 'You mean you think Matheson walked away from an air crash?'

'It's just an idea.' said Cutler. 'People walk away from forced landings and minor crackups in small aircraft all the time, and it could certainly give him the head wound you saw.'

Holley still wasn't impressed. 'I suppose it's possible, but it doesn't seem too likely.' He stopped for a moment then said 'But, I suppose it fits the facts as well as my theory, so I'll see what I can do. And you'll check out the restaurant and the store?'

'No problem. In fact I think I can do it this afternoon and I'll let you know tomorrow what I find out.'

'Okay, Mister Cutler, thanks a lot.'

CHAPTER SEVENTEEN

Vancouver

THE RINGING TELEPHONE woke him from deep sleep. He rose from bed and stumbled through the familiar darkness to the living room and picked up the receiver.

'Uhn?'

'Mister Cutler?'

'Uhuh.'

'Mister Cutler, this is Lieutenant Holley in San Francisco. Sorry to bother you in the middle of the night like this, but something has come up that you might be interested in.'

'No?'

'Mister Cutler, are you awake?'

'Uh, I don't think so. Can you hang on a minute?'

'Yes, of course.'

He put the telephone down and switched on the lights. The room was identical to ten million others in highrise

North America. Department store furniture, console TV, 'component' stereo with dozens of controls and adjustments sitting in a book shelf with about twenty-five records, a collection of Book of the Month Club main selections and a dozen or so paperback best-sellers.

Cutler yawned, scratched himself absently and tried to remember why he was up.

'Oh, yeah,' he said half aloud. He walked to the bedroom, found his bathrobe, went to the kitchen and pulled a large bottle of Canada Dry from the refrigerator. Standing in the spill of light from the open refrigerator he unscrewed the cap and took a long drink straight from the bottle then went to the living room and picked up the telephone, a pad and pen, and returned to the kitchen.

He spoke as he walked. 'Hello Lieutenant, what can I do for you?'

'Not a thing, Mister Cutler. This time I might be able to do something for you.'

Cutler hit the kitchen light switch and sat down at the table. He took another drink from the bottle and said, 'What do you have in mind?'

'A little sightseeing tour.' Holley's voice was as crisp and efficient at 1:30 a.m. as it had been for their other conversations, and Cutler wondered if he was talking to a man or a machine. 'I'm sorry that I had to call at this time of night, but I've been out on a job and just found out about this myself.' He paused, but before Cutler could say anything he continued. 'They found the plane. Right where you said it would be, and I think they found the pilot too.'

Cutler smiled to the empty kitchen. 'How did they find it?'

'Exactly the way you said they could. By flying a search in the mountains. I didn't think there was a chance in hell that you were right about Matheson walking out of a crash, but it looks like you were. One of the search and rescue pilots spotted it late in the afternoon. The ID numbers on the wing match up and he said he thought there was a body lying beside it, but he couldn't tell for sure.

'Anyway, there wasn't enough light left for them to do anything so the site is still undisturbed and I talked them into letting me go in first, before the FCC get there and mess everything up, and I thought you might like to come along for the ride.'

'Come along for the ride?'

'Sure, we'll be flying out of Seattle and we can pick you up in Bellingham, which looks on the map to be only an hour or so from Vancouver. But it's all going to happen in about five hours, so that's why I'm calling now.'

Cutler said, 'Uh?'

'Look, I know this isn't actually your case, or even really a Vancouver case, but shit, it's a free ride in a helicopter, and the wreck is way the hell back in the Cascade Mountains and apparently the scenery is really something else. Snow, glaciers, the works. So I thought you might just like to tag along if you could take the time off.'

Cutler thought about it. 'Why not? I've got nothing on my plate that can't be put back another day, and God knows I've got lots of overtime banked. Where and when do we meet?'

The noise was overwhelming, and even with padded headphones Cutler had difficulty hearing.

'I can't put it down anywhere near here, Lieutenant. The best I can do is hold it over those boulders long enough for you to jump out.'

'All right, let us out and come back in an hour to pick us up.'

'Okay, one hour it is.'

The small chopper banked and dropped toward a group of large rocks sticking up out of the snow. The pilot said, 'I shouldn't be doing this. I want you guys ready to bail out the second I give the word. Get your belts off now and unlatch your doors.' He turned his head part way round and yelled to Cutler, 'Did you hear that?'

'Yeah, I'm set.'

The chopper settled slowly above the rocks. Down. Back up. Down again and back up. Finally the pilot said, 'Okay, I think I can manage. This time you go when I shout.'

Down again and 'GO!!'

The two men scrambled out and crouched as the blast from the rotors tore at their clothing and hair and the little helicopter with Washington State Police markings leapt back into the sky.

They were on a small rocky outcrop in the middle of the broad south face of Mt. Redoubt, about forty feet away from the wreckage of Kiniski's Cessna. High above them the morning sun lit the summit ramparts, and the glare from the snow was harsh even through their sunglasses. Several hundred feet below them the snow gave way to bouldery rubble, with the green tangle of the valley bottom another thousand feet below that. On the other side of the valley, dark and forbidding, was the two and a half thousand foot north face of Bear Mountain.

Cutler looked at Holley and decided that he looked almost as dark and forbidding as the mountain across the valley. He was the same height as Cutler, a little over six feet, but had broader shoulders and a leaner waist. He wore a beautifully tailored dark blue three-piece with a pale blue shirt and a dark blue tie. The clothes suited the man so well that they seemed designed for wear in just this place, and made Cutler feel inadequate in his old jeans and wool shirt.

But it was the face that held his attention. It was the handsomest face Cutler had ever seen. Holley was black, but his features were sharp and Cutler thought that some of his forebears must have been Arabic or Ethiopian.

He was about forty-five. His short hair was going grey and there were deep trenches running down from beside his nose past the corners of his mouth, but he had the timeless look of volcanic strength barely under control. He had introduced himself as William Holley, but Cutler, who wasn't normally much impressed with rank or procedure, could not call him by name.

'Well, Lieutenant, shall we go and have a look?'

'Might as well.'

The snow had softened enough in the sun to provide secure footing and by mountaineering standards the slope was not steep, but neither man felt secure and the forty feet to the aeroplane took almost two minutes. They stopped about five feet from the nose and Cutler said, 'Shall we circle it?'

'Yes. But we might as well have a look at the body first.'

They had seen the body from the air, lying on the snow below the wreck. It had appeared to be lying half on its side with one arm outflung, the other hidden underneath. Now they descended fifteen feet and traversed toward it for a closer look.

'Jesus.'

They saw that the body was lying face down, not on its side, and that the left arm wasn't tucked underneath, wasn't anywhere. The snow was red under the shoulder.

The helicopter was gone and their breathing was the only sound on the mountain. Cutler looked up at the wreck and down at the body. Without its wing the plane looked strange, not like an aircraft at all; but even without its arm the body was just a body. He bent down and carefully eased a wallet from the back pocket, then stood up and moved to where Holley could see as he went through its contents. He fanned out a thick stack of brown banknotes. Canadian hundreds. 'Whoever he is, he didn't die broke.'

He put the money back and flipped through the plastic windows of the card section, then handed the wallet to Holley and said, 'Gerald Kiniski. It looks like we've found the pilot, but I don't think he's going to answer any of the questions you wanted to ask him.'

Holley slipped the wallet into one of his own pockets and said, 'Let's finish our walk-around and then come back for a thorough look at this,' he pointed to the corpse with his toe, 'and then start on the plane.'

'Okay, but what about that big bloody patch by the tail?'

'One time around and then we check it out, okay?'

'Sure, okay.'

They were becoming used to the angle of the slope and made their circuit of the wrecked aircraft without too much trouble. There was a long shallow skid mark stretching away to the east, and nothing else.

'I suppose that if we followed the skid mark we'd eventually find that guy's arm and shoulder,' said Holley.

'I suppose. I wonder where the wing is. Funny we didn't see it from the air.'

'It could be a long way down the hill. As soon as we're through there'll be an inspection team from the FCC in for a look. They'll find it somewhere.'

They completed their circuit and stood by the body. Cutler said, 'Too bad we didn't find this sooner, before whatever tracks there were got melted away.'

Holley began stamping out a flat area in the snow. 'Don't worry too much about it. It's only thanks to you that we found it at all, and anyway, it crashed in a storm so the tracks probably got filled in right away. Look at the skid mark, it should be at least three feet deep, and it's barely visible at all.' He continued flattening the snow. 'Give me a hand rolling the body onto this flat area.'

The corpse gave them nothing more than the wallet they had already taken, and they were both thankful that the overnight weather had been cold at this altitude.

The bloody patch by the tail was slightly lower than the surrounding snow and there was a faint path between it and the hole where the pilot's door had been.

'What's this?'

Holley picked up a white loop that had been invisible on the white snow from farther away.

'Let me have a look.'

'It's some kind of webbing tied in a loop, but I've never seen anything exactly like it before. It feels like its woven of nylon or some synthetic.'

'Whatever it is, it's probably Matheson's, it's got a big black M written on this end.'

Neither man could identify it and Holley tossed it over beside the body.

'I guess it's time to check the plane.'

Inside the aircraft they found a lot of dried blood, a large leather suitcase, and a small plastic case full of folded maps. The interior was cramped and Cutler smudged his clothing reddish brown in several places. Holley emerged unmarked.

The suitcase had been embossed with the initials WFM. Inside it were clothes, toothbrush and paste, razor and shaving cream, cologne, towel, a paperback novel, and a plastic trash bag containing clothes that had very obviously been worn by a fisherman.

Holley repacked the suitcase, throwing in the loop they had found. 'What I would really like to know is how in hell Matheson got from here to Vancouver. Did you see the blood on the passenger side window and dashboard? How in hell could anyone live through a crash like that, let alone walk out of here? I mean, look at that wreck! How could anyone live through that?'

'I don't know. But then look at the automobile accidents that people walk away from.'

'I know, I know.' Holley closed and latched the suitcase and stood up. 'Anything else you can think of?'

'Not really. You've got the wallet?'

'In my pocket.'

'Who's going to bring the body out?'

'Probably the FCC.'

'We should make sure it gets printed and that we all, you, us and the RCMP, get a set of prints.'

Holley pulled a small leatherbound notebook from inside his jacket pocket and made a note with what looked like a gold pencil. 'Okay, I'll take care of that, and as soon as everyone here is satisfied I'll see that it gets shipped back to Prince Rupert.' He put the notebook away and said, 'Maybe you can notify the RCMP. Let them handle the family, if there is any.'

Cutler said, 'Okay, and I'll . . .' He stopped and cocked his head, listening. 'Sounds like our taxi is on his way.' He picked up the suitcase and started toward the rock outcrop where they had been dropped off, but then stopped and turned when Holley said:

'Let's get the pilot to fly us around the general area for a while. We probably won't see anything much, but I'd like to find out just where we are in relation to Vancouver, and where the nearest roads and towns are.'

Two hours later they walked into the Trawler, a seafood place on Bellingham's small waterfront. Cutler had changed into clean clothes: light grey pants, white shirt and light grey jacket, and a blue tie with red stripes. The clothes were fresh but Cutler, as always, looked rumpled. As they sat down he wondered how Holley had avoided smudging his suit in the aeroplane, and how it could still look like he had put it on just five minutes ago.

Their young waitress was looking at Holley with obvious lust and ignored Cutler. Holley ignored *her* and said to him, 'Order whatever you want, the city of San Francisco is paying for it.'

Cutler asked the waitress, 'What do you recommend?'

'Beg your pardon?' She dragged her eyes away from Holley.

Cutler gave up. 'I'll take steamed clams and a dark Heineken if you've got it.'

Holley ordered the same and the waitress pulled herself reluctantly away.

'So, Mister Cutler, what do you think?'

'I think that after we review everything we know about this we're going to be more confused than ever.' Cutler ran a hand through his curly hair. 'But first of all tell me how you see it now.'

Holley leaned back in his chair and stretched his long legs out in front of him. 'Okay. To start with, there's something you may not know, I can't remember if I put it in the report I sent you or not. Before Matheson took off from Prince Rupert he put two suitcases in the plane; a leather one, which we just found, and an aluminium one, the kind photographers use, which we didn't find. I think they're called Halliburtons.'

The waitress brought their beer, simpered at Holley, and left.

'Yes, I remember that. It was in your original telex.'

'Okay, then this is how it looks to me.' Holley drank some of his beer and paused to order his thoughts. 'Matheson picks up the coke in Prince Rupert, charters Kiniski to fly him across the border, and takes off. They approach the storm that's building over the Cascades and turn east to go around it, but somehow twig to the surveillance – maybe the RCMP pilot got careless with his radio, or came too close – so they decide to risk flying through the storm. But it's worse than they expect and they crash on Mt. Redoubt. The pilot buys it in the crash but Matheson is lucky and gets out of it with just the cut on his head.' He closed his eyes briefly and then continued. 'His door is stuck so he turfs out the body of the pilot, grabs the aluminium suitcase full of coke and staggers off down the mountain into the valley. He probably follows the stream until he gets to that trail that the chopper pilot pointed out to us and then follows that until he reaches the road. After that, nothing makes sense.'

Anger and frustration edged Holley's voice and he raised a fist, then let it fall softly onto the table. 'I talked to our pilot while you were changing, and from what he says it would be quite a feat to get from the crash site to the trail system. He says that the bush in these valleys is worse than jungle, that in places it's so thick that you can't get through at all, and that it would take a full day for a healthy man who knew what he was doing to get from the plane to the nearest road. And that's in *good* weather.

'That means that Matheson couldn't have reached the road any earlier than late on the twenty-fifth, and probably not until some time on the twenty-sixth.' He rapped his knuckles sharply on the table top. 'That road is here in

America. Yet we know he was in Vancouver on the twenty-sixth.

'All I can think of is that he hitched a ride with someone to Bellingham or Seattle – and God knows what kind of story he told them to account for the way he must have looked – then cleaned himself up and stashed the case somewhere and went to Vancouver so that he could catch the flight to San Francisco to make his fishing story look reasonable. Maybe a taxi driver turned him on to the restaurant and he just noticed the men's wear store in the next block and bought the clothes on impulse. Is clothing cheaper in Vancouver than here?'

'I don't think so. I think that it's still cheaper down here even with the devaluation of the Canadian dollar. But that's not why he bought them anyway.'

'What? How do you know that?'

Cutler looked up to see the waitress approaching with their meal. 'Just a minute. Here comes lunch.'

This time the waitress made a point of ignoring Holley completely. He didn't seem to notice that either. The clams were good and both men ate in silence for a few minutes. Then Cutler said, 'About the clothing. Did you get the message I left for you last Wednesday?'

'That you had checked out the restaurant and the store and that they remembered him and you'd send the details in a telex?'

'That's right, did you get the telex?'

'Nope. But I haven't checked my box since Thursday so it's probably there waiting for me.' Holley ate a clam and continued. 'It's been kind of busy these last few days.'

'Well you probably aren't going to like this, 'cause it pretty much blows the last part of your theory. I went to the restaurant and got nothing. Nobody remembers him, but at the men's wear store they remember him real well. He arrived there wearing an old denim shirt and a pair of blue jeans both of which were about two sizes too big for him. He had a big bandage on his head and a story about being in an accident in which he lost his luggage and

ruined the clothes he was wearing. He said that a good
Samaritan had loaned him the jeans and shirt until he
could buy some new clothes.

'Several people on the staff there noticed him and they
all identified him from the picture you sent up. They also
said that he was quite pale and seemed pretty weak. But
his credit card checked out okay and they had no reason to
believe that he was anything but an unfortunate tourist. I
think it's a pretty safe bet that if he'd gone to someplace
like Seattle or Bellingham he would have bought the good
clothes there so that he wouldn't have to cross the border
in bloody rags.'

'Shit!'

'Yeah. And there's something else that's pretty strange
too.'

'Do I want to hear it?'

'Probably not, but it's not in my telex so I might as well
tell you.' Cutler drained his beer and caught the attention
of the waitress. He ordered another beer and Holley
asked for some tea.

'I had some slack time on Friday,' said Cutler, 'so I ran
a check on all the hotels I could think of where a guy like
that might stay, and turned up nothing at all. Not a trace.
That doesn't rule out the possibility that he used a phoney
name, or that he stayed in some cheapo hotel, but that
doesn't seem likely to me.'

He ate the last clam on his plate. 'No, if he's the kind of
guy who spends almost eight hundred dollars just to get
something to wear on the flight home, then he probably
would have stayed in a decent hotel. If he stayed in a hotel
at all.'

Holley was about to speak but Cutler cut him off.
'There's one other thing, although this isn't for sure. If he
spent a day and a half fighting his way through bush that's
worse than jungle he probably would have been pretty
torn up. Scratches all over his face and hands. But nobody
at the clothing store said anything about that. They all
commented about the bandage on his head, and they

didn't say he *wasn't* scratched up, but I've got the feeling that they would have mentioned it if he had been. I'll check that out for you, but I'm pretty sure of what I'll find.'

The tea and beer arrived. The waitress had apparently given up on Holley, treating him like any other customer, and was startled when he thanked her for the tea.

Holley gently tapped one long black forefinger against the table top and looked around the restaurant. His eyes slid over the room vacantly and Cutler wondered if he was really seeing anything. Probably not. Then he spoke. 'Mister Cutler, it seems that I've got a problem.' His voice was soft, but Cutler could sense a strong undercurrent of anger. 'I had a perfect chance to put that bastard up against the wall with the choice of talking to me or doing twenty years, but it got blown and now that he knows we're on to him I'll never get another chance.'

He looked out the window at the ocean, flat and grey in the noon sun. 'I suppose that I'll keep digging away and hope that something new turns up, because I sure as hell can't make any sense of what we've got so far. I mean, the most reasonable explanation now is that he found Aladdin's lost lamp on that mountain and flew back to Vancouver on a rug.'

He took a sip of the tea and brought out his notebook and pencil. He spoke as he made notes to himself.

'I'll tell the Prince Rupert RCMP what we found and ask them to check Kiniski's background. Matheson probably used him before, and he may have talked to somebody.'

He scratched his upper lip with the pencil. 'What else? I suppose I should ask the FCC to be looking for a Halliburton suitcase full of cocaine, in case it got thrown out in the crash, and I'll have a look at the maps we found in the wreck, but they looked like standard aviation maps and they probably won't tell me anything new.'

He finished his tea and asked, 'Is there anything you can think of that I've missed? Any ideas at all?'

'Not really,' replied Cutler. 'There's that loop of

whatever it was that we found by the bloody area. You might see if anybody can tell you what it is. I can't think of anything else.' He finished his second beer and stood up. 'I'll ask around, see if anybody in our drug squad knows anything about Matheson. I don't think they will but who knows? Maybe he has some connection in Vancouver. After all, if he didn't stay in a hotel that night, where did he stay?'

Holley was about to put his notebook away but suddenly reopened it and made another note. 'I'll see if I can dig up any business connection for him in Vancouver. If he found himself stranded there he might have called up some business acquaintance and asked if he could stay overnight.'

He stood, and after tucking two dollars under his plate he walked to the cashier.

The sun dazzled them when they stepped from the dark of the restaurant. They stopped by Cutler's car, a twelve year old Chevy Bel Air that might once have been blue.

'Can I drive you back to the police station, Lieutenant?'

'No, I don't think so thanks. I'll have to go there eventually to pick up the suitcase and my pilot, but right now I'm going to take a walk and think this whole business over.'

'Good luck. If anything turns up in Vancouver I'll let you know, and I'd sure appreciate it if you'd let me know how it all turns out.'

'I'll do that, Mister Cutler, although it may turn out that I just decide to drop the whole thing. In any case thanks for all your help, you've gone out of your way for me and I appreciate that.'

'No problem, Lieutenant. Thanks for the invitation today.'

They shook hands and Holley walked slowly away with his hands clasped behind his back and no particular expression on his face.

CHAPTER EIGHTEEN

Yosemite Valley

THE DAYS grew to weeks and September turned to October. As if by unspoken agreement Alex and Linda did not analyze their affair or talk of the future. Each seemed to find in the other the piece that had been missing from his or her life, and each was content to enjoy the magic while it lasted.

For Alex it was as if windows had been thrown open on a musty corner of his mind, to let sunlight and sea breeze in to clean away the cobwebby dark. He had never met anyone like her. She was friendly without being pushy, honest without being offensive, beautiful (to his eyes), and her take it or leave it attitude forced him to be more open and honest with himself.

She saw in Alex everything that had been missing in the men she had met in New York. There, it had seemed that no matter how deeply she probed she encountered only guile and subterfuge, costume and design; whereas Alex was Alex all the way through. Solid without being dull, dependable yet somehow still mysterious, and (in her eyes) darkly handsome.

Gordon took the whole thing philosophically. During the first two weeks, while Alex and Linda were oblivious to the world around them, he climbed with others, enjoyed the multi-national kinetic frenzy of Camp Four, and finally borrowed Alex's van for a trip to Los Angeles, returning four days later with a dozen new tapes, two ounces of Sinsemilla and a medium-sized stuffed bear which he said he had picked up hitchhiking just south of Fresno.

He gave the bear to Linda, saying, 'I'm sure Alex is great in bed, but I thought you might like someone intelligent to talk to every once in a while.'

She took the bear and hugged Gordon. Then she started to cry. 'I'm going to go back to my tent and talk to my bear. Do you mind staying with Gordon tonight, Alex?'

'No, I don't mind.' He put an arm around her shoulders and asked, 'Is something wrong?'

More tears came, but she said, 'No, I'm okay. Honest. But I think I want to talk to this bear for a while.'

When she had gone Alex turned to Gordon and said, 'I wonder what that was all about?'

'Well Alex, you've been living with her, and you know her better than I do, or at least you should, but from what I gather she's had a fairly tough life, and I kind of doubt that very many people have given anything to her that didn't have a hook hidden in it somewhere.'

'But a teddy bear? I don't understand.'

Gordon sat down at the big picnic table that was kitchen and dining room for the nine who shared the tentsite. It was late afternoon and the denizens of Camp 4 were beginning to drift home after another day of climbing and climb-watching.

'I think it's time that I had a little father-to-son talk with you.' He stood up again. 'But not here. I see some of our sitemates returning from another day in the mines.'

Three young grimies were approaching, slung about with ropes and hardware and talking happily in German. They dropped their gear in front of their tent and came to the table. Two stood back slightly, but the third spoke in very slow English. 'Hello Gordon. It is good you are back again here.'

'I don't think I could have taken much more of L.A.'

'Yes? Is it not very good, the large city?'

'No, the city is very good. But I'm not so good as I used to be. Here, I brought you guys some presents.' He pulled six carefully rolled joints from his shirt pocket and passed them two each.

'Oh, thank you. Very nice.'

'Danke.'

'Danke.'

'Be careful with this stuff, Walter, it's pretty potent.'

'Po-tent?'

'Yeah, potent. Strong. Powerful.'

'Oh yes, strong. We are smoking hashish in Germany. That is very stronger.'

'No Walter, this shit is very stronger than your hashish.'

Walter translated to his companions who looked at Gordon curiously.

'Well don't say I didn't warn you. Oh, thanks.' One of the Germans had gone to his tent and returned with a six pack.

'So what did you guys climb today?'

'Today we are climbing on the Cookie cliff. It is very difficult and we are falling off, but after perhaps many attempts we are all climbing Outer Limits. It is very good now. After.'

'It's always very good after.'

Walter lit one of the joints, took a big hit and passed it around the table. As it started a second round Gordon turned to Alex and said, 'No more for you and me – we've still got to have that father-to-son chat.'

The German boys were on their third hit and one of them was getting out another joint. Gordon took it from him and put it back in the young man's pocket. 'Nein, nein.' He held up a hand with fingers spread, 'Fünf minuten, okay?' Then he turned to Walter and said, 'You tell Kurt that he should wait five minutes before he smokes any more.'

He took Alex's arm and said, 'Untrance yourself and come for a walk with me. See you guys later.'

Afterward Alex couldn't remember where they had walked but all of Gordon's words stayed with him.

'You really didn't understand what I was saying, did you?'

'No, not really.'

'Think about it. She ran away from some town on the prairie and went to Los Angeles when she was fifteen or sixteen, right?'

'Yes.'

'Do you have any idea what life is like for a sixteen year old runaway in that city? When you're sixteen you don't stay at the Holiday Inn until you find the right suburb to move into. You live on the street and take your comfort wherever you can find it; and you learn that the more suspicious you are and the less you trust anyone, the safer you're going to be.

'It's not an easy world to escape from, and even if you do get out you can never get rid of the scars.'

'Yes but . . .'

'And the only difference between the New York advertising world and the streets of L.A. is that the damage you get when you let your guard down is financial instead of physical.'

Gordon stopped walking and looked straight into his friend's eyes. 'So now do you understand why she's crying? She's crying because she's starting to realize that you're not just using her as a convenient fuck, or as a stepping stone to something else; that you like being with her because just being with her lights up your life a little bit.'

Alex moved in with Linda in the Upper Pines campground. She had a large, old-fashioned canvas tent with a lot of floor area and enough room to stand up in. It became unbearably hot in the afternoon sun but was otherwise very comfortable.

They climbed together about a third of the time. Alex wanted to continue climbing with Gordon in preparation for their attempt on the Salathé wall, and Linda enjoyed climbing with some of the other women she had met. She also learned how to use jumars and after that spent many days hanging beside hard climbs with a battered old Nikon F, photographing the new gladiators in their vertical arena.

They were well suited to one another. Their backgrounds were just similar enough to give them some common ground but different enough to prevent the insipidity which so pervades most man/woman relationships.

They made love often and in a few weeks taught each other more about giving and receiving pleasure than either had learned in a lifetime.

Finally the day came when Alex realized that he could not imagine any future for himself that did not include her. It went far beyond *we*. Certainly that was part of it – their closeness was generating that third, joint personality that so many people mistake for the manifestation of love – but more than that, Alex found that her presence changed his concept of *I*.

She had caused in him the emergence of a whole new level of self-awareness and self-respect. And with the self-awareness came a new awareness of others. An appreciation of them in their own right rather than as walk-ons in the drama of his own life.

He tried to explain it to her. 'It was as though other people existed only relative to me. As though when they disappeared from my sight they simply ceased to be, coming back into existence only when I next saw them. Their lives, that is their personal lives, were about as real to me as the lives of the characters in a soap opera.'

They were sitting in the shade of a big pine beside Tenaya Lake, several hours walk from the noise and crowds of the valley centre, and had only seen three other people all morning.

'But now it's different. Somehow being with you has opened my eyes to other people. I can see everyone around me caught up in life just like I am. It's really frightening to look back and realize that I could see other people in such inhuman terms, like cardboard cut-outs floating in and out of my life.'

'I can't imagine you ever mistreating anyone.' Linda stretched out so that her head was on his lap and her long legs, bare below ragged cutoffs, were in the sun. Alex stroked her hair and replied, 'I don't suppose I ever did mistreat anyone in any overt way. But I didn't treat them as real people either. Think of going to a restaurant and having a meal. Does the waiter exist solely to bring food to you? No way. He works there the same as I worked in my garage or you worked in your studio. He's got friends and a life of his own. Maybe his kid is sick. Maybe his girlfriend is leaving him. Maybe anything. And yet for all these years I never saw that. He was just a human-shaped food-serving machine that ceased to exist as soon as I left the restaurant.'

'What about me?' asked Linda. 'Am I just a human-shaped orgasm-serving machine programmed to thrash and moan artistically underneath you every night?'

'Sure, and everytime I close my eyes afterwards you wink out of existence.' He ran a thumbnail along the line of her jaw and said, 'Actually it's just the opposite. Every time I close my eyes, night or, day, you're there waiting for me. Not just an image, but an essence; as if your personality was imprinted in my mind.' He looked down at her. 'Can you understand what I'm trying to say?'

She lay still, with her eyes closed, for over a minute, then she looked at him and said, 'I think so. Because the same thing happens to me. The instant I stop concentrating on something else, there's old Alex, dominating my thoughts and making me feel warm and tingly all over. It's spooky. Spooky but nice.'

For a long time they sat in silence, thinking their separate thoughts. The sun gradually enveloped them completely and they were both content to let it work its lazy magic.

'Linda.'

'Mmmm.'

'Can we talk about what comes next?'

'Mmmm?'

'Are you awake?'

She put up a hand to shield her eyes from the sun and looked at him. 'I'm awake.'

'What I was talking about earlier, about coming to accept other people on their own terms. That's important to me, and somehow you made it possible. And this business of you being inside my mind and me in yours; I don't understand it, all I know is that I like it and I don't want it to stop.' His voice was quiet and very serious. 'Before long I'm going to want to leave the valley, I know that, but every time I try to think about it I come face to face with a big nothing, a blank. I can't imagine life without you now; and yet I can't quite imagine life with you either. We're living in a sort of time warp here, as if reality had been suspended for us.'

She took one of his hands and placed it so that it rested partly on her breast and partly on her ribcage. He could feel simultaneously the softness and the hardness of her, and underneath, the slow steady rhythm of her heart.

'Am I so unreal?' she asked.

'You're more than real. You've turned my life upside down and opened a hundred new doors for me. Being with you is a foretaste of paradise, and I can't imagine what it would be like to have to go back to a life without you.'

She sat up and faced him. 'Most of those things are true for me too, Alex. You've shown me that there are people in the world that I can like and trust. I feel that the world has become a better place since I met you, and I can't imagine what it would be like without *you*. But I'm not ready to talk about it yet.' She stood up and brushed herself off. 'Let's walk a bit.'

They walked slowly, hand in hand, along the lake shore. She spoke again. 'There are things that I still have to settle for myself, questions hanging on from what I left behind in New York.'

They walked on and she continued, 'I'm not trying to avoid your question. It's important to me too, and I know that we're going to have to talk about it soon.' She stopped and turned to face him. 'You and Gordon are planning to do the Salathé pretty soon aren't you?'

'We're going to start the day after tomorrow. We just decided yesterday.'

'How long do you think it will take you?'

'I imagine about four days. We're going to take food for three and water for four.'

'When you come down we'll talk. Okay?'

'Okay.'

CHAPTER NINETEEN

Scenes on a Wall

Day 1, 7:00 a.m.

Alex stood with his hands deep in the pockets of his pile jacket and shifted from one foot to the other, wishing that there was some way up the first pitch that didn't involve cold and pain and fear.

He checked his tie-in one last time, clipped the haul line to the back of his harness and began jogging on the spot, trying to generate some warmth and enthusiasm.

It was always like this. All worthwhile climbs seemed to start in the cold and dark, and for the thousandth time in five years he asked himself why he didn't take up some other, saner, recreation. But then he looked up at the colossal wall above him, dark and heavy at the bottom, lightening gradually as dawn worked its way down from the summit headwall three thousand feet above, and he knew that in an hour the morning light and warmth would have reached down to where he was testing himself in ways that no golfer ever could, catching the start of a four-day wave that no bowler would ever ride.

He put on a small daypack containing a water bottle, a pair of jumars and a set of aiders; shouldered the rack and turned to Linda who had driven them to the start of the El Cap trail and walked in to the base of the route with them.

'See you in a few days.'

'Have fun.'

He put his arms around her and pulled her in close.

'You'll think about what we were talking about?'

'Of course. Don't worry about it, Alex, just have a good climb. I'll be watching you every day from the meadows, and I'll be waiting for you when you come down.'

'I'll miss you while I'm up there.'

'No you won't. Now get going. The sooner you go, the sooner you'll be back.'

She broke free of his hardware-encumbered embrace and turned to Gordon.

'Take care of him for me, okay?'

'Don't worry, I need him to tow me up all the hard bits, so I'll be real careful with him.'

They kissed and Linda turned away and walked down the trail.

7:40 a.m.

'What's in this haul bag? It must weigh sixty pounds.'

'Just wait until the end of the day, it'll feel like a hundred and sixty.'

'I can hardly wait.'

They rearranged themselves, and Gordon prepared to lead the second pitch, a relatively short 5.8 crack.

'This looks more my style. It would have been aid for sure if I'd tried to lead the first pitch.'

'Your time's coming,' Alex replied.

They had planned the route for maximum enjoyment, each of them to lead those pitches best suited to his own capabilities; and with no preconceptions about acceptable 'style'. They would free climb what they felt like free climbing and aid what they felt like aiding.

11:30 a.m.

'Hungry?'

Gordon had taken a small food bag from the haul bag.

'A little. Mostly I'm thirsty.'

They were sitting on a ledge at the top of pitch six and

Alex was feeling good. The sun was on them but there was enough of a breeze to keep it from being oppressive; and the ground was satisfactorily far below.

'We could split a can of salmon.' .

'Sure.'

The can opener was on a string tied to the food bag and Gordon set to work with it. Soon they were passing the can back and forth, digging out bites of salmon and spooning up the salty broth.

'Not a bad start,' said Alex.

'At this rate we'll be on Hollow Flake by mid-afternoon.' Gordon finished the salmon and licked as much of the juice out of the can as he could. 'This is a hell of a climb, Alex, I'm glad I let you talk me into it.'

'Say that in four days and I'll believe it.'

Gordon had had some second thoughts about the climb and had even suggested giving it up and making a run for the Bugaboos, but Alex had argued that they were there, they were in shape, and that if they didn't do it now they'd regret it forever.

'Come on, Gord,' he had said, 'we've been climbing here for a month and a half. There isn't a pitch on the Salathé that we can't crank off with no sweat. Let's just go up and have a few days of vertical fun. Everybody I've ever talked to about it says that it's *the* classic pure rock-climb in the whole world. We can go to Alaska or the Bugaboos and do some real climbing next spring, but as long as we're here ...'

3:40 p.m.

This is bizarre, thought Alex. Gord was running, flat out, back and forth across the face above. The rope ran from his harness to a point about forty feet above him and he was galloping, body parallel to the ground eleven hundred feet below, straining at the end of each swing to reach the Hollow Flake crack, far out to the left. Finally, concentrating all his effort, crossing the face in great bounds, he lunged and sank first one precarious hand and then a foot and another hand into the wide crack.

'YEEEEEE HAH!'

4:20 p.m.
'Welcome to the Hollow Flake Hilton.'

Gordon was holding out an open water bottle as Alex pulled over the lip and surveyed the ledge.

'Thanks.' He took the bottle and tilted it up, leaning back on his jumars and gulping until it was empty. 'So this is home, huh?' He handed the bottle back, clipped himself in to the belay anchors, and sat down with his back to the wall and his feet stretched out in front of him.

They were on a broad, boulder strewn ledge with plenty of room for a comfortable night. 'Not a bad spot.' Alex stood up again and lengthened his tie-in, giving himself a twenty foot leash. 'I'm going to the men's room. If the waitress comes by while I'm in there, order me a beer will you?'

He checked his pocket for toilet paper and walked to the far end of the ledge where he arranged himself as comfortably as possible.

'Pretty airy shitter,' he said when he returned to the belay. 'Must be a three or four hundred foot free fall off the end of the ledge. Anybody climbing the wide cracks on Excalibur would be exposed to some unusual hazards.' He scrunched around, trying to find the best compromise between maximum comfort and maximum exposure to the sun.

'The waitress came by with your beer,' said Gordon, producing a sixteen ounce can of Budweiser from behind the haul bag.

'What!'

He popped the top and handed it to Alex.

'Is this for real?' Alex held the can at arm's length. 'Is this a beer I see before me, the open top toward my mouth? Come, let me drink thee.'

He swallowed once, twice, three times and passed the

half empty can back to Gordon. 'Did you sneak that into the haul bag when my back was turned?'

'This one and three others, one per day.' Gordon drained the can. 'I thought we might appreciate them.' He smashed the can to a disk and put it on the ledge beside him and looked up at the wall above. 'How are you feeling?'

'Not bad at all. About twice as good as I was before you gave me the beer.'

'Good. Let's fix a couple of pitches before supper then.'

'Are you serious?'

'Sure, why not? We've got over three hours of light left, we might as well do something with it.'

Alex was amazed. 'And you're the guy who wasn't even sure he wanted to do this climb . . .'

Day 2, 7:15 a.m.

'What's for breakfast?' Alex peered out of his bivvy sack to see Gordon rummaging in the haul bag.

'Same thing as was for supper last night. Same thing as we'll be having for supper and breakfast for the next three days. Salmon, gorp, dates, dried fruit and cheese.'

'Mmmmm, good.' He sat up and looked at his watch. 'What are you doing up so early? We don't need to be up before noon today.'

Gordon brought out the food bag and began mixing Gatorade powder into a water bottle. 'I've been up for half an hour.' He passed the bottle and a bag of mixed dried fruit to Alex. 'I've been looking at the topo and I think we should make a change in our plans. Look . . .' He squatted beside Alex and produced the topographic line diagram that was their route map on this vertical journey.

'First of all, how do you feel?'

Alex stretched and let his mind wander through his body. 'Pretty good actually.' He looked at his hands. 'Didn't even tear up my hands too badly.' The hands were curiously pink where he had taped them against the abrasion of the rock, and filthy elsewhere. Small tears and cuts had scabbed over during the night. He flexed his fingers one at a time and asked, 'So what's this new plan?'

'Well, look, I feel as good as you do, and the way we're going, with three pitches fixed, we'll be on El Cap Spire in less than four hours. If we started now, we could easily be there by noon, and if we push on instead of staying there, we'll be able to make it to the Block for tonight's bivvy.' He traced the line of the route with his finger. 'It's only four more pitches, and even if there is a lot of aid we should be able to do it in six hours or so – shit, it's all 5.9 and A1 except for one short section of A2 here, on pitch 23.'

Alex crawled out of his sleeping bag and bivvy sack and walked to the front of the ledge to relieve himself. He was wearing all his clothes as well as his harness, and like Gordon, he had slept tied to the belay anchors.

'I thought you wanted to bivvy on top of the spire.'

'I did. I still do in a way, but if we do that, then tomorrow night we'll have that shitty bivvy on Sous le Toit ledge and a hell of a long day the day after that. But look at the topo, if we make it to the Block tonight, then we can have a reasonable day tomorrow and make it to Long ledge without killing ourselves tomorrow night. And the day after will be easy. We can sleep in all we want and still get over the top and down to the valley in good time.'

Alex took the topo and stared at it for a while, then said, 'Sure, what the hell, let's go for it. We'll be on El Cap spire for lunch anyway, and we can decide what to do then.'

9:00 a.m.

'Holy shit!' They were below the Ear and Gordon was staring up at what he had to lead.

Alex said nothing, just looked into the great open mouth that yawned down at them and was silently thankful that it was not his lead.

Slowly and carefully Gordon worked his way across, chimneying horizontally, nothing but air for fifteen hundred feet between him and the ground. Then, ten feet out, he said, 'Hey Alex, this thing really *is* only 5.7.'

His voice was distorted by the rock and his words almost indistinguishable. At first Alex couldn't believe what he had heard. This was supposed to be the most frightening lead on the climb and Gordon sounded like he was enjoying it.

Fifteen minutes later Alex was following it and even with the top rope he was shitting bricks. Was Gord crazy?

'Are you crazy?' He had reached the belay, where Gordon was leaning back in his belay seat smiling gently and looking as if he'd just returned from a morning stroll. 'How could you possibly have enjoyed that? I was freaked out following it.'

Gordon's blue eyes shone in the morning sun. He said, 'I wouldn't say I enjoyed it. In fact I'd say I was scared shitless half the time, but I sure am pleased with myself now. Now that it's done that is; while I was doing it I just kept saying "two hundred people have done this before, and they all say it's only 5.7.". I just said that over and over, and after the first couple of moves I pretended that I was only five feet off the ground, doing some real easy boulder problem. And it worked.'

'Five feet off the ground?' Alex looked down from where they hung, at the sloping granite wall dropping down, down, down to the valley floor so far away that individual trees were hardly distinguishable in the forest. 'Man, you *are* crazy.'

11:45 a.m.

Lunch time on El Cap spire. The heat of the sun poured down on them and they soaked it up gratefully. After six weeks in the valley they were both tanned and used to the heat, glad to have it in mid-October.

Gordon sat, legs dangling over the edge of their island in the sky, slicing salami and cheese with a little red Swiss army knife.

'I can see why they say this is the finest bivvy in the

valley,' said Alex. He was lying on his back with his forearm shading his eyes.

'It's not bad,' responded Gordon. 'Here, take this.' He passed several slices of meat and cheese. 'It's not like a *real* summit bivvy, but it's definitely the class of *this* place.'

Alex sat up and began eating. 'I can't believe how well you're climbing. It's almost as if you've learned something in the past six weeks.'

'Yeah, well you haven't been too aware of what's going on around you lately.'

The thought of Linda suddenly filled his mind and Alex said, 'No I suppose not.'

'In fact, I'm surprised you didn't give up the idea of this climb yourself,' said Gordon.

'It's kind of strange I guess, but somehow with Linda it's not like that. In fact it's sort of the opposite. Being around her makes me want to do other things, do good climbs, meet other people.'

He checked his tie-in and then came and sat by his friend, legs hanging over the edge. 'I mean, I know I spend a lot of time with her, it's still pretty new and exciting, but even so, I feel a whole lot more open to the world than I used to. It probably doesn't show too much yet, but I really do feel that way inside.'

Gordon's smile flashed through his tangled beard. '*I* can see it. Somebody who didn't know you very well would probably think that you were completely wrapped up in her, but I can see the difference clearly enough.' He cleaned the blade of the knife on the thigh of his sweatpants and folded it up and put it away in the food bag. 'Ever since I met you I've figured that you would be a pretty nice guy if you ever came out of your shell, and I can see now that I was right.

'She's the best thing that could have happened to you. Shit, if she wasn't so skinny I'd push you off here and go down and let her be the best thing that ever happened to me.'

He scratched himself through his beard and went on, 'If

you stay with her another couple of months you might even be human enough to take out in public.'

'Gee, thanks.'

'*Are* you going to stay with her for another couple of months?'

'I don't know for sure. She's thinking that over while we're up here. I'll find out when we get down.'

'Ahah! She loves me, she loves me not.' Gordon stood up and adjusted his harness. 'I wouldn't worry about it if I were you. I can see the whole thing pretty clearly from the outside, and she's just as bent out of shape over you as you are over her.'

He closed the food bag. 'Do you want to top up your water bottle?'

'Might as well, it'll be that much less weight in the haul bag.' Alex got up. 'I can't believe this place.' He looked around at the absolutely flat, ten by fifteen foot top of the spire. 'I wonder why it's flat like this?'

Gordon didn't answer. He poured the last drops from a one gallon plastic jug into Alex's water bottle and put the empty jug back into the haul bag; then began sorting the gear he needed for the next pitch.

Day 3, 11:30 a.m.

'Are you telling me that they *freed* this?'

They were hanging in belay seats, tucked in the corner under the big roof. Gordon was looking down at the pitch he had just led. 'I don't believe it. How could anybody free that?'

'I don't know, Gord, but they did. I think in '79 or '80. Maybe '81. I'm not sure exactly when, but two guys did this whole route with only about two hundred feet of aid.'

'That's depressing. Maybe I should give this up and get into bowling or something.'

'If you think it's depressing that they did the last pitch free wait'll we get over this roof. They did most of the roof free and some of the headwall above.'

'That's not humanly possible.'

'I saw pictures of it in *Mountain* a while back.'

'Shit.'

'Think about it the other way round,' said Alex.

'What do you mean?'

'Instead of thinking about how much we had to aid compared to them, think about it compared to the first ascents. Robbins and Pratt and Frost were the best rock-climbers around then and they could only free about 30% of it.' Alex had racked up and was ready to start leading the roof. 'Even though we're probably going to have to aid everything from here to the top except for the last pitch and a half, we'll still have freed about 70% of it.'

He clipped his aiders into the first of many fixed pieces leading to the lip of the roof. 'Am I on belay?'

'You bet.'

He moved out right, hanging awkwardly in his aiders, and looked back. 'Anyway who cares? Are we having a good time, or are we having a good time?'

Gordon looked down twenty-five hundred feet and then shook his head slowly. 'We may be crazy, but we are definitely having a good time.'

11:45 a.m.

'Oh God, Gordie, it's beautiful up here. Wait until you get over the roof.'

2:30 p.m.

'One more pitch and we've got it in the bag, Alex.'

Gordon was hanging free, toes against the wall, leaning back in his belay seat, watching Alex clean the last placements from the pitch he had just led. Their ropes dangled below, well out from the overhanging wall.

'Aren't you glad we made it to the Block yesterday?'

Alex, still ten feet below, took time off from his cleaning and leaned back, suspended on his jumars.

'Yes,' he answered, 'you're ever so clever; but I want you to know that I've figured out *why* you wanted to do it this way.'

'Yeah?'

'Sure. You said you brought along four cans of beer, right?'

'Right.'

'We were going to be on the wall four full days and have one can per day, but this way, by getting to Long ledge today, we don't have to worry about the fourth day, and we can have a whole beer each tonight.'

He heaved up on his top jumar and made another foot of progress. 'If we get to Long ledge tonight we only have three pitches left for tomorrow, which means that we'll be back in the valley by late afternoon, well before the bar closes. Right?'

He made another foot and unclipped the rope from the piece above, swinging out into space when he let go. Another three heaves up on his jumars and the piece, a number one Friend, was at chest level and he freed it from the crack and hung it with about twenty-five other pieces on his rack.

'But I don't mind, cause the sooner we're down, the sooner I'll see Linda again.'

CHAPTER TWENTY

Yosemite Valley

'DINNER AT THE Four Seasons?'

'Sounds good to me.' They reached the road, and after a last look up at the monolith they had climbed, began trudging east. Alex continued. 'If we can make it that far. Carrying all this junk back is worse than anything on the climb. Too bad we haven't got keys to my van. That would make ev ... What are you doing?'

Gordon had shrugged out of the haul bag and was

dumping it out on the ground. 'We *have* got keys. I always keep mine in my first aid kit.' He snapped the top off a small tupperware box and pulled out a single key. 'Here we go. Shall we flip to see who goes to get it?'

Alex took the key and said, 'It's okay. I'll go. You've carried down the heaviest load. Watch the gear, I'll be back in about twenty minutes.'

He walked and jogged alternately and in fifteen minutes reached the Camp Four parking lot. He thought about going to the tent for a clean T-shirt but decided that until he washed his body there wasn't much point in putting on clean clothes. Besides, his clothes were all in Linda's tent in the Upper Pines campground anyway.

Five minutes later he was helping Gordon throw their gear into the back of the van.

'Do you mind if I drive over to Linda's campsite before we go back to Camp Four?' asked Alex. 'I'll just let her know that we're back and see if she wants to come to supper with us.'

'Sure, fine by me.'

They drove in silence for a few minutes and then Alex said, 'I'm starting to float.'

'I've had a buzz on since halfway down,' said Gordon, 'and it just keeps getting better.'

'Yeah, what a route. What a far out climb.' Alex was rolling. 'What did you think of the Ear? I'm sure glad that was your lead and not mine.'

'Hah. I was trying to figure out some way to get you to lead it. That's the most ridiculous thing I've ever done.'

They babbled on as they drove the one-way loop that led to the Upper Pines campground, the big-wall buzz getting them higher and higher. Then they were at the campground and Alex drove slowly toward Linda's campsite.

'What's going on?' asked Gordon.

'Huh? What do you mean?'

'You must be really flying, you've driven us to the wrong campsite.'

'You're right. I must have turned down the wrong row. I thought that was our site there, the one with that camper trailer on it.'

He stopped and began to turn the van around. 'Hey. Wait a minute. This is the right row. Look, seventy-seven, seventy-nine ... We're in eighty-three, where that trailer is. What's going on? Where's the tent?' Alex jumped out of the van, leaving it blocking the road, and ran to site eighty-three.

A middle-aged couple with matching blue track suits looked up in shock from their picnic table as Alex raced up to them and shouted, 'Have you seen Linda ... How long have you been here?'

The man stood up and said, 'Who are you? What do you want here?'

Alex fought for control. 'Four days ago, there was a woman named Linda Cunningham staying on this site. Do you know where she is?'

'We arrived yesterday and I haven't any idea where any woman you're looking for might be.' The man clamped his jaw shut and tried to pull in his stomach. 'And I think you should leave or I'll report you to the Ranger.'

'Ranger? What are you talking about?' Alex didn't understand. 'I'm looking for someone who was staying here. Did she leave a message for me?'

The older man backed up a step and said, 'I don't know what you're talking about. Leave us alone.'

Alex's whole body slumped in defeat. She was gone. He turned and stumbled blindly toward the van. The couple watched him in fearful curiosity. 'I've never seen anything so disgusting. What kind of clothes was he wearing? He was filthy. Filthy!'

'Maybe he was a punk rocker.'

'Well whatever he was, he'd better not come back here.'

Alex reached the van, but did not get in. He stood by the passenger door saying nothing until Gordon got out and helped him in.

'Just sit down, Alex. I'll drive us back to Camp Four.'

Alex sat with his face in his hands as Gordon pulled the van away. Then he looked up and said, 'I wanted her to come back to Seattle with me. Or maybe the two of us to go to Alaska. She said she'd have to think about it, but that she'd give me an answer when we got back from the climb.'

Gordon made no reply and Alex buried his face in his hands again. When they arrived at the Camp Four parking lot Alex said, 'I think I'm going to get drunk tonight, Gordie. Can you kind of make sure that I don't do anything too stupid?'

'Sure, don't worry. Here, carry this pack back to the tent.' He handed Alex the small pack and shouldered the haul bag himself. 'C'mon, lets get this stuff dumped off and then we can grab a shower and get some food. If I'm going to be up all night taking care of you I'm going to need some calories.'

'Okay.' Alex walked down the familiar path to Gordon's tent. He stared at the ground and saw nothing around him. His feeling of loss was so strong that it was actually physical. It twisted his stomach and knotted all the muscles in his forearms. He tried to blank his mind, but the thought of her was overpowering. 'Don't think,' he said to himself. 'Just keep putting one foot down, and then the other. A month from now it will be all right. Concentrate on that and it won't be so bad now.' But he couldn't do it. Couldn't keep her out of his mind. Desolation overwhelmed him and he could feel tears burning on his face.

And then she was calling his name, walking toward him. He stopped, understanding nothing as her arms went around him. He let himself go and cried openly, tears of joy and grief mixing on his cheeks.

She stepped back from him. 'Alex. What's wrong?'

But he couldn't speak. Could only reach out and pull her back to him, oblivious to the stares of the people around them. Finally he said, 'We went to your campsite. And I thought that . . . I thought . . .'

She began crying too. 'Alex, you idiot. How could you think that?'

She saw Gordon and broke away from Alex to give him a hug and a kiss. 'I thought I told you to take care of him.'

'Yeah, well I thought I *had* taken care of him. I got him up and down again in one piece, but then I let my guard down, and zingo, look what happened.'

She grabbed Alex by the hand again and hugged them both. Then she stepped back and said, 'You guys smell awful. I'm going to take you both to supper, but first you shower, right?'

Alex was still not sure what was happening. 'But what about your tent. Did you find a spot here in Camp 4? And what happened to your face? You've got a big bruise on your cheek. Did you fall?'

'Not exactly. Look, sit down for a minute and I'll try to explain. And you sit down too,' she said to Gordon, who had started to walk tactfully away. 'You'll hear about it all eventually anyway.' Then she turned to Alex and said, 'Do you remember that I told you about a friend who was coming out here on business and who gave me a ride? Well it wasn't exactly just a friend. It was a guy that I've been seeing a lot for the past year or so. He had about a month's worth of work to do in the west, and he dropped me here and was going to pick me up when he was done. He wasn't interested in climbing and when he was finished with his business we were going to take the scenic route home. Reno, Vegas, New Orleans.'

The sound of her voice receded and his vision began to tunnel. She was setting him up for a goodbye. He knew it.

'He came to pick me up last night and . . .' It *was* going to be goodbye. Alex dropped his head into his hands. '. . . and I told him I wasn't going.'

She put her hands on Alex's shoulders and he looked up at her. She said, 'And here I am.'

Alex put his arms around her waist and hid his face

against her stomach. His voice was muffled. 'Where's your
tent and all your stuff?'

'It was all his. Tent, sleeping bag, stove, everything
except my climbing equipment. He took it all away with
him.'

Alex stood and took her chin in his hand and tilted her
face so that the left cheek was toward the light. The bruise
on her cheekbone had begun to colour. 'He hit you, didn't
he?'

'Yes, he hit me, but I think I probably had it coming.'
She gave them a big crooked smile and said, 'Besides, I
gave him a pretty good kick in the balls. He'll be feeling
that longer than I feel this.'

'Anyway, that's the whole soap opera, and here I am if
you want me.'

'If I want you?' Alex was stunned. He wanted her more
than anything else. More than *everything* else. He tried to
speak, but could find no words.

Gordon spoke for him. 'The man's in shellshock, Linda.
He's had too many ups and downs for one day.' He turned
to Alex. 'Listen. She just told you that she wants to stay
with you. She's given up home and hearth for you. What
she really wants to say, but is too much of a coward to
admit even to herself, is that she's fallen in love with you.'
Then he said to Linda, 'And as for him, he's pretty strung
out from the climb and from finding you gone, but when
he gets himself under control he'll tell you that he loves
you too.'

He ducked into his tent and came out with clean
clothes, a towel, soap and shampoo; and said to them,
'Once you've both done that we can get down to the
important thing, which is supper. I'm going to have a
shower.' He turned to Linda, 'When the boy wonder
comes back to earth send him for one too. I'll meet you
back here in about half an hour.'

Supper was an exuberant celebration. Alex got back on
his high and was soon reliving the climb with Gordon.

They each ate two orders of spaghetti with meatsauce and drank gallons of beer to wash it down. Linda ordered a small steak and let the two men do most of the talking, knowing that they had shared something important, but not minding.

Around them was the swirl of humanity on holiday. Quiet, well dressed tourists from Japan and the Midwest. Noisy, carelessly dressed tourists from everywhere else. Hikers, nature lovers, photographers, climbers. The usual mixture of people enjoying autumn in the park, all contributing to the cheerful, slightly drunken ambience of the restaurant.

They finished eating just after nine and ordered coffee. Linda asked for a Remy Martin, but their young waiter didn't know what that was.

'It's cognac,' she said. 'If you haven't got any, just ask the barman for three snifters of the best brandy he has, okay?'

'Okay.'

She was wearing a loose-weave white wool sweater with a high roll collar. The light of the candle on the table gleamed on her tanned skin and Alex was torn between his conversation with Gordon, and the need to stare at her in awe and wonder.

The restaurant was beginning to empty and the atmosphere was changing from noisy cheerfulness to relaxed intimacy as the remaining diners lingered over last drinks. Alex and Gordon were still high from the climb. Linda sipped her brandy and listened to them talk. She was tired and happy and riding a high of her own. She had never felt for anyone what she felt for Alex. No one had ever affected her this way. She eased her chair back from the table and pulled her feet up onto it so that she was sitting with her chin resting on her knees and her hands clasped round her ankles. The brandy was beginning to take her and she let herself drift while the two men talked.

Alex dominated her thoughts and she tried to analyze his effect on her. He gave her a feeling of emotional security. Not physical or financial security, but emotional. With Alex she felt no need to keep her guard up, no need to analyze his every word and action looking for hidden meanings and motives. Around him she felt free. She loved him, and she needed his love, but there was no pressure to try to please him for fear of losing it.

She took a small sip of her brandy and kept the liquid in her mouth, letting it run only slowly down her throat. Alex and Gordon were still a million miles away and she went back to her own thoughts. Any love affair she had seen or been a part of had been based on some form of emotional blackmail and she wondered now if she had simply been living among unhappy, insecure people, or whether what she and Alex had was something unique.

She looked at him. He was turned toward Gordon and in full right profile to her. The four days on the wall had burned away all traces of subcutaneous fat and now, in the candlelight, he was piratically handsome. His dark, slightly curly hair, aquiline nose and darkly tanned skin gave him a Levantine appearance, and the physical effect on her was strong. Watching him gave her a shivery sensation like she used to get on the first days of spring when, as a child in South Dakota, she would find a spot out of the wind and let the sun wash the winter from her body. She could never quite escape the wind though, and its occasional cool touch would raise goosebumps on her skin. But the sun would be warm enough that it didn't matter and the sensation had been strongly erotic.

Now, as she looked at Alex, the same shivery contractions rippled the surface of her skin and she realized that she was massaging herself through the fabric of her pants. She put her feet down and reached for her brandy glass to distract herself.

Alex and Gordon were in high gear. Talking fast, interrupting each other, and using a lot of arm and body motion as they relived moves from the climb.

'. . . and what about the middle of that pitch above the

spire. You know, where you stem off those tiny little edges and then make that long reach to ...'

'Yeah, yeah. That was great. I thought for sure you were going to fall off.'

'*You* thought I was going to fall? How do you think I felt?'

Linda listened for a few more minutes and then interrupted. 'Has anybody given any thought to tonight's sleeping arrangements? I don't have a tent anymore, remember?'

'Uh, no, not really,' said Gordon. 'We can all fit into my tent, but it will be a pretty tight squeeze.' He looked at Linda and then at Alex. 'I suppose since you've been separated for so long you'll want some privacy though, so why don't I just crash in the van and you two can have the tent to yourselves. I've got a two inch foam pad on the floor which you may appreciate.'

'Well ...' said Alex.

'I suppose we might.' Linda was smiling. 'On the other hand it looks like you two are going to be up all night with this post-game analysis.' She turned to Alex and continued, 'I'm going to call it a night. It's been a pretty wild day for me, and I think I'll just crawl off to the tent. When your libido gets down off the wall come and wake me up. If you're sober enough to do anything, that is.'

'I ...' Alex was obviously torn.

'Oh, don't worry. I'll survive another few hours without you. I know you're still two thousand feet high so just stay here. I'll settle the bill and ...'

The two men began to protest but she cut them short and said, '... I will so. This is on me and I'm not going to listen to any more bullshit from either of you.'

She signalled the waiter for the bill and stood up when he arrived with it.

'I'm going to get some sleep.' She stood behind Alex with her hands on his shoulders, preventing him from getting up. She leaned over and nibbled the lobe of his right ear. Gordon smiled and the young waiter blushed.

'You stay up as long as you want. We've got lots of nights together to look forward to, but you two are never going to have the night after this climb again, so enjoy it while you can.'

Gordon had risen and she hugged him, kissed him once, hard, and said, 'This time, take better care of him, okay?'

And she was gone.

For a minute neither of them spoke. Then Gordon, still standing, picked up his brandy, raised it to the door through which she had gone, and drank it down. 'Do you have any idea how lucky you are?'

'Yes.'

'I hope so.' He sat down and said, 'If only she had a sister. With maybe a little more meat on her.'

The waiter, who seemed almost too young to be serving drinks, returned to the table with two more snifters. 'The lady asked me to bring these for you.'

When he had gone, Alex said, 'I do know how lucky I am. This is the best thing that ever happened to me.' He tasted the drink, and when he spoke again it was as much to himself as to his friend. 'You know, when I was first married I was only twenty and it was all kind of unreal, but after a while I started to realize that I was into something good.

'Even when we split up we didn't quarrel or argue and I think our feeling for one another was as strong as ever; we just realized that we had some completely incompatible needs and would be better off apart.

'It took me a long time to get over that. I knew that I'd eventually find someone else, but I never expected or hoped for anything very much different.'

His eyes refocused on the present and he looked directly at Gordon. 'But this, what I've got with Linda, goes so far beyond that, so far beyond anything I've ever experienced before, that I sometimes wonder whether I was even alive for the last thirty years.'

'So what are you going to do?'

'Do?'

'I mean what are your plans? Honeymoon on Mars? White House in '96? You seem to have found the key to universal happiness, and I'm just curious to know what you're going to do with it.'

'I really haven't any idea. Maybe open a combination garage and photo studio in Talkeetna.'

'Will it have a guest bedroom?'

'You bet.' Alex held his snifter so that the brandy was lit by the candle on the table. He stared into it for a few moments then said, 'I really don't know what we'll do. Probably go back to Seattle for a while and see how it works out, living together in the real world. We haven't talked about that yet, so I don't really know.

'But no matter where we wind up, I think that we'll probably want to leave here quite soon. Within a few days.'

'I've been thinking pretty much the same thing myself,' said Gordon. 'I've enjoyed the last month, but I think I've had about enough. The Salathé ... well there's nothing like it I guess, but still, it's time to get back to the mountains to do some real climbing. So if you two go to Seattle in the next few days I'll catch a ride with you and then spend a couple of months in Vancouver working. Maybe after Christmas I'll go to the Rockies for a month or so and then sometime in February we can get in touch with Matheson and see if he's ready for another shipment. Taking it across in the middle of winter should be interesting.'

They sat silent for a while, and then Alex said, 'I guess I'm going to have to figure out how to tell Linda about that. Do you want me to keep you out of it?'

'No, I don't care. I don't think she'll mind.' He laughed. 'But that's enough talking about the future. Let's adjourn this meeting to the bar and ... uh oh.' He was looking over Alex's shoulder and his smile was gone.

Alex turned to see a thin black man approaching the table. He was of middle age and middle height and wore the kind of clothes that used to be called casual. Dark slacks, open-necked blue and white print shirt and a light jacket with both buttons done up. As he got closer Alex saw that his face was badly scarred and that his nose was bent to the right.

Gordon's description of Carl, the bagman, came back to him: '. . . a sort of medium sized black guy who's had his face kicked in a few times . . .' The fearsweat began to trickle down his sides.

The man sat down in the chair that Linda had used and said, 'I've got a message for you.' His voice was high and coarse and his brown eyes seemed empty as they flicked back and forth between the two younger men.

Gordon said to Alex, 'Look, I've got some business to talk over here, would you mind if I asked you to leave? I'll get in touch with you tomorrow.' But Alex knew that Carl, if that really was his name, had been addressing them both. He started to speak, but Carl cut him off.

'Forget it. Mr. Matheson wants to see you both. He said I should tell you he's got a job for you.' He turned to Alex and stuck out his hand. 'I'm Carl. You're Alex Townsend.'

Alex took the hand automatically. It was bony and thin, like the rest of the man.

'Mr. Matheson is waiting, so if you're finished supper I'll take you to him right now.'

Alex couldn't speak. How had they found out about him? How had Carl known they were in this restaurant? He couldn't think, could only grip the arms of his chair and hold on tightly.

But then he calmed down. There was no danger. He repeated that to himself. Carl seemed friendly enough, and he was just passing a message. He was too small and too old to be any kind of threat.

Gordon said, 'Where is he staying? It would probably be better for us to see him tomorrow morning.'

'Nah. You hafta do it tonight.' Flick, flick, flick. The brown eyes danced back and forth. 'He just drove out here this afternoon and he's gotta go back tonight. We

been looking all over to find you.' Flick. Flick. 'Mr.
Matheson isn't gonna be here tomorrow morning.'

Silence. Alex and Gordon looked at one another and
then at the little bagman. Gordon spoke. 'Do you mind if
we talk in private for a minute here?'

'Sure. You go ahead. I'll just go get myself some
cigarettes.' He stood up and walked toward the cashier's
counter.

'How did they find out about us? How'd they know we
were here? What d'you think he wants?' Alex's questions
tumbled out in a mad confused torrent, but Gordon cut
him off sharply.

'Shut up. None of that matters. We've got about one
minute before Carl comes back so just listen to me and do
exactly what I say.'

Alex fell silent and grabbed a long breath. 'Give me just
a few seconds.' He turned his chair around and sat with his
elbows on his knees and his chin resting on his closed
hands. He shut his eyes and drew two more slow breaths
then turned around again.

'Okay.'

'All right, I'll go to this meeting, but you're not going
to. As soon as we leave here, you go to the van and drive
away. Don't go home to Seattle, and don't go to any place
you've stayed before. Just take Linda and camp somewhere, or go to a motel for a couple of days. Then rent a
car and come back here. If everything is all right, which it
probably will be, I'll be waiting in Camp 4, but don't come
walking in there to find me. Just find somebody we both
know and ask him to take a message to me. Okay?'

Alex ran it through his mind again and said, 'Okay.'

'Good, now Carl's coming back, so let's just take it
easy.'

Carl sat down and peeled the cellophane from a package of cigarettes and lit up, then stowed the package
inside his jacket. He blew smoke and said, 'So?'

'So we're ready to go, but there's one thing,' said
Gordon.

'What's that?'

'Only one of us is going.'

'Whacha mean, only one?'

'Come on, you know what I mean. You take me to see Matheson. No problem there, I *want* to see him. But Alex stays away. That way we all know that everything is going to be smooth and easy, right?'

'Hey, nothin' heavy's going down here. The only thing heavy is what happens to me if I don't bring you both back. Mr. Matheson told me he wants to see you both. You wanna get me in trouble?'

'Come on, Carl, there's nothing you can do about it right? So let's you and me get going and leave Alex to finish his drink.'

Carl sucked on his cigarette and blew more smoke. He looked at it and said, 'Fuckin' low-tars. No satisfaction. I should stick to Luckies. Yeah, sure, I know whacha mean. So let's go.' He stood up, leaving his cigarette burning in the ashtray.

Gordon stood up with him. Standing beside the small black man he looked like a muscular Viking, and Alex felt some comfort coming back. Gord could take care of himself.

'Okay, see you later.'

He watched them leave and then signalled the waiter.

'Do we still owe anything?'

'No sir, the lady paid for everything.'

Alex handed him a five and said, 'Well, take this anyway.'

The young man took the money. 'Thanks.' Then he said, 'Uh, I hope you don't mind, but I heard you and your friend talking about the climb you just did. It sounded like it was the Salathé.'

'That's right.'

'I thought so. I started climbing this year and I'm planning to do it some day too. What did you think of it. I've heard that it goes almost all free now.'

Alex did not want to talk. He felt as though he had been

wrung out and left in the wind to dry. 'Well, it might if you can climb overhanging 5.12, but for us there was still a fair bit of aid.'

He wanted desperately to get away, to be with Linda, to touch her and know that the universe was still unfolding as it should. He said, 'Look, I really can't talk about it now, I've got to get going. My ladyfriend and I are leaving the valley as soon as I get out of here, but you can talk to Gord – the guy with the long hair that we had supper with. He's in Camp 4 and he'll be around for a few more days.'

'Oh. Okay. Thanks anyway.'

Relief. Now he could go. 'No problem. I wish I could stay and talk with you.' He stood up from the table. 'His name is Gord Wilson and he's on site fourteen.'

He went to the coat rack by the entrance, put on the sweater and parka that he had left there, and then walked slowly toward the door. He felt drained. Physically and emotionally. He had never had a day anything like this and he wanted only to lie down and let the heat from Linda's body ease him into deep dreamless sleep. But he knew Gord was right and that he should get away. He would let Linda drive and find somewhere out of the park to pull the van off the road for the night. Or better still they could go to Modesto and get a hotel room. It was only a couple of hours drive, and then he could spend a day or two there, sitting in the sun, with no more excitement, no surprises and no ups or downs.

He pushed through the inner doors, into the dark foyer and was suddenly looking into a scarred black face. 'Wha ... gghhh!' Something slammed into his stomach and he doubled over in pain unable to speak or breathe. He could see dark slacks and small black loafers. The feet walked out of his vision and he knew that they had moved behind him. He tried to straighten up, tried to turn around but something struck the back of his head and the whole universe imploded softly inside him.

Blackness and blinding flashes of light chased around his mind. Vertigo and nausea seized him and all sense of time and space vanished. All that remained was a voice, barely understandable.

'Okay, Alex baby, let's walk. C'mon now, walk, let's go.'

Part of his mind came back. He was staggering across dark pavement. A parking lot. He stumbled and something held him up. Somebody. Someone was helping him walk across a parking lot. Then he was beside a car, a big dark car, maybe green, or blue; and whoever was helping him walk opened the door and helped him get in. He clung to the steering wheel as the door closed. He was dimly aware that there were other people in the car, in the back seat, and then the passenger door opened and a man got in and looked at him out of empty brown eyes in a scarred face, and everything came back.

Carl was pointing a gun at him and saying in his high, rough voice, 'Look in the back, Alex baby.'

Alex turned. Gordon was slumped in the corner behind him, eyes open but unmoving, breathing loudly through his mouth. On the other side was a big man with another gun. Alex couldn't see him very well but he seemed to have dark hair cut short and spiky, and looked quite young. He was wearing black clothes.

'Okay, Alex baby, start her up, but don't put her in gear.'

Alex did as he was told. The car was an old Chev but the engine caught immediately. He released the key and once more clutched the steering wheel with both hands. He was shaking with fear and nausea and knew that if he looked at Carl he would lose control completely.

'Awright, pal, I'm gonna tell you some things and you listen to me, 'cause they're real important.' The voice was like a rusty nail being driven into his mind. 'The first thing is that you keep your hands on the wheel and do exactly what you're told. No stupid tricks with jamming on the brakes or blinking the lights or any of that kind of shit, cause the first thing you do, Big Robbie breaks both your arms and I do the driving. D'you understand?'

Alex was paralysed. Mindless. But he understood. Finally he looked up and said, 'I understand.'

'That's good. Now the next thing is that as long as you do what you're told, there's no more rough stuff. You got that? You just cooperate and nothin's gonna happen to you. I hadda teach you a lesson, show you who's in charge, but now you just do what I tell you and everything's copesettic.' He took out a cigarette with one hand and lit it with a Bic lighter. 'Now, back out of here, and when you get to the road, turn left.'

As he drove the nausea left him and his mind began to clear, but the fear remained and he could think of nothing to do.

'Hey, Carl.' The big youth in the back seat had a quiet voice. 'I think the hippy is waking up.'

'Okay, Alex baby, pull the car off to the side. Slow and easy.' When the car was almost stopped Carl said, 'Just a little further ahead, so the moon gives us a little light.'

Alex let the car slide forward out of the shadow of a big pine and into the pale light of the waning moon.

As the car stopped Gordon hunched forward and mumbled, 'Going to be sick.'

Carl said to his partner, 'Round the other side and take care of him Robbie.' Then to Alex, 'Hands through the wheel and on the dashboard. *Right now.*' Alex did as he was told.

It was awkward and he knew he could never untangle himself in time to do anything. Carl's gun was halfway between him and Gordon and his eyes were flick, flick, flicking from one to the other. Then Big Robbie was opening Gordon's door from the outside and holding the back of his coat as he leaned out and threw up loudly.

When he was done he sat up by himself and stared stupidly around the car, wiping his mouth and chin on the sleeve of his jacket. The door slammed shut beside him and seconds later Robbie was back in the other side and had his gun out again.

Carl said, 'Can you hear me, hippy?'

'Yeah.' Gordon's voice was thick.

'Good. Listen real close while I tell you what's happening. We're gonna drive down the road and meet the man. You do what I say and nothing happens. You fuck up and we blow you apart. You got that?'

'I said you got that?'

'Yeah, I unnerstand.' Gordon's words were slurred. 'Jus don' drive fast or I get sick.'

Carl laughed and said to Alex, 'You heard your buddy. No fast driving or he's gonna barf, so just put your hands back on the wheel and take us out of here, nice and easy.'

Alex drove. And tried desperately to think of some way out, but all that came to him was jamming on the brake. That might bounce Carl into the windshield, but the big man in the back would probably kill them both. He did not believe that Matheson was waiting for them. Matheson had somehow found out who Gordon was using as a backup and had simply ordered their execution. Alex felt lonely and helpless and the weight of his mortality began to crush him.

Headlights came at him out of the darkness and flew by, but they only reinforced his loneliness.

'Okay, slow down, we're almost there.' Carl's voice was showing excitement and Alex decided that as soon as he was out of the car he would run. He would not stand and let this man slaughter him like a helpless steer.

'See that road on the right? Turn in there and drive along it slowly.'

Alex turned onto a narrow paved road and drove up it about a quarter mile until it ended at a concrete building with a small floodlit parking area.

'Drive into the parking lot and turn the car around.'

He did as he was told. Gordon groaned as the car went through the one hundred and eighty degrees.

'Now drive back out onto the road and park on the shoulder.'

When that was done Carl said, 'Now, keep your left hand on the wheel and put her in park with your right, but don't shut her off . . . now turn off the lights and put your arms back through the wheel with your hands on the dash.'

Alex hunched forward and put his hands on the dash. He knew nothing about guns, but the ones these men were holding seemed enormous and the fear of death was blotting out all thought.

'Where is Matheson?' he heard himself saying.

Carl giggled. 'Well I guess I must have forgotten to tell him about our little party tonight, Alex, 'cause I don't see him at all.' The brown eyes no longer seemed empty, but glittered with a kind of excitement that was more frightening than the guns.

'Now listen to me and I'll tell you what's gonna happen here. I gave your pal in the back seat a briefcase full of money a while back. I counted it and I know there was fifty big ones in it. Big Robbie followed him back to the hotel where you were staying and then followed you almost all the way out here. But he ran out of gas just near the park entrance. We know you didn't put the money into any bank before you came here and we did some checking around and we know you been here ever since, so you still have that case full of money somewhere.

'So, what's gonna happen now is that you are gonna tell me where it is and then the two of us are gonna go and get it while Big Robbie waits here with your hippy pal.' Carl's eyes were practically jumping out of his head. His face was not clearly visible in the dark car, but Alex could see the whites of his eyes dancing crazily.

'Now, Alex, sweetheart, where is it?'

Alex's mouth worked spastically as the overwhelming desire to speak, to do as he was told, crashed head on against the almost sure knowledge that by speaking he would sentence himself to death. And Linda. Oh God. Linda was asleep in the tent, right on top of the money. The thought of bringing this animal to where she lay was more than he could stand, and he clamped his mouth shut.

Carl's voice stabbed into him again. 'Don't want to tell

me? Well then let me tell you something. You *better* tell
me, cause if you don't then we haul you both out of the car
and Big Robbie goes to work. We'll see if watching your
friend get his knees smashed makes you talk better.'

Alex was physically shaking, his arms knocking against
the inside of the steering wheel. He was balanced on the
very edge of sanity. If he told Carl what he wanted to
know, then they would all be killed. First Linda, then him,
and then Gordon. There was no way that Carl was going
to let them live. But if he didn't tell, then Gordon would
be tortured and killed and then the same thing would
happen to him.

He tried to speak. He tried to keep himself from
speaking.

'Okay, Alex baby, I warned you.' The eyes flicked to
the back. 'I'll cover them, you go round to the other side
and haul the hippy out of the car and then I'll bring this
one out. And Robbie . . .'

'Yeah.'

'Don't hurt him yet. Let's get them over into the light
where Alex here can get a real good view of what happens
to his friend.' The high pitched voice was full of excited
anticipation.

He must escape. He must.

Big Robbie was dragging Gordon out and he and Carl
were alone in the car. He reached a decision. If Carl
ordered him out the driver's door he would make a run for
it. Big Robbie would be watching Gordon and he might be
able to reach the forest. If Carl got out first and ordered
him to come out the passenger door then as soon as his
hands were out of the steering wheel he would throw the
car into gear and floor it.

He knew he probably wouldn't make it, but at least it
was better than letting them lead him to his death like a
helpless cow in a slaughterhouse.

'Okay, pal, the emergency brake is by your left foot.
Step on it good and hard and then we're going to get out
my side.'

All hope left him. He could not hope to get the brake off before Carl shot him. He did as he was told, stamping down on the brake and then coming out the passenger side.

'Okay, sweety, around the car and watch your friend go for his last walk.'

He saw Gord sagged against the car, right hand clutched to his abdomen, left hand hanging onto the door post, obviously still groggy and in pain from the beating he had received while Alex sat in the restaurant telling himself that everything was all right.

Big Robbie, in his new-wave clothes and haircut, was standing beside him, waiting patiently, looking bored. In the light from the parking lot Alex could see that he was hardly more than a boy, no more than eighteen or nineteen. But enormous.

'You know, Robbie, I think there's enough light here, so why don't you just go ahead.'

'Okay.'

The big youth put his gun away and Carl said to Alex, 'Too bad your friend is only half awake, he'll miss the best part of the show.'

As Big Robbie stepped toward him Gordon slowly lifted his head. It was the first movement he had made and the others all looked at his face as it came into the light and no one saw his right arm fly up until it was too late.

Big Robbie screamed in agony and fell to his knees clutching spasmodically at the red plastic handle of the pocket knife protruding from his chest and Gordon was already in the air as Carl brought his gun around. He crashed into the smaller man as the sound of a shot exploded in the night. They fell heavily to the ground and the gun bounced under the car.

Big Robbie had let go of the knife handle and was trying awkwardly to pull his gun from its holster as Alex began to react to what was happening around him. He leaped at the youth and tackled him clumsily, knocking him from his kneeling position. Alex had not been in a fight since his childhood and had no idea what to do. He scrambled to his knees and swung his fist blindly. He felt it hit something and then his breath was choked off as huge hands clamped down on this throat. He tried to pry at the fingers as black spots began to dance in his vision.

The hands were like steel clamps and he could not move them, but suddenly the pressure relaxed and Big Robbie was clutching at the knife again. Alex saw the handle of the gun and grabbed it from the holster as Robbie's body convulsed and he was thrown to one side.

He looked up to see Carl scrambling for the car. He pointed the gun and pulled the trigger. The explosion jarred his arm all the way to the shoulder and the rear window shattered as Carl let off the emergency brake and slammed the transmission into drive. He fired and missed again as the car rocketed away with tyres screaming, out of sight around a bend in the road.

'Are you okay, Gord?'

'Gord?'

He went down on one knee and touched Gordon's shoulder. 'Are you hurt Gordie?'

But there was no response, and when Alex finally took his eyes from Big Robbie and looked down he saw the large bloodstain that had spread across his friend's back. He pulled up the bloody jacket and shirt to find the middle part of the left side a mass of blood, bone, and strange pieces of flesh and tissue.

'*Gordie*!' he screamed.

Alex sat on the ground with Gordon's head in his lap. He made small unintelligible sounds and several times ran the tips of his fingers through the long blond hair. Otherwise he was motionless, staring into the forest across the road, seeing nothing, tears seeping slowly out of the inside corners of his eyes and running down his face onto his shirtfront.

After a time he stood up and walked dazedly to the other body. The big youth lay on his back, eyes open to the night sky, his chest soaked with blood that looked almost black in the dim light. He too was dead.

Alex put the pistol he was holding into one of the pockets of his jacket and bent down to pick up Gordon's little Swiss Army pocket knife from where it lay beside Big Robbie's right hand. As he folded it closed he could see Gordon, sitting on El Cap spire with his legs dangling over two thousand feet of air, smiling as he served up pieces of cheese and salami cut with this same knife.

He tried to close his mind to the image, but he could not, and once again tears filled his eyes.

Still in a daze he picked up Carl's gun from where it had fallen and then started back toward the body of his friend, but before he had taken two steps he was stabbed by the sudden thought of Carl taking a last desperate gamble and searching the tent. Finding Linda there, asleep.

'*NO.*'

He was running down the dark road toward the highway, unmindful of the heavy pistol in his pocket slapping against him as he ran; unaware of the other pistol still in his hand, or of his voice yelling madly, 'NO, NO, NO!'

Gradually the madness receded and he realized that he had two or three miles to go. He desperately wanted to run, to race to Linda as fast as he could, but he knew that it was too far and that full-speed running would just exhaust him.

So he jogged, and the rhythm of his pounding feet held back the huge wave of fear and shock that he knew would inundate him as soon as he let his guard down. He concentrated on one thing, and repeated over and over to himself, in time with his strides, 'She's all right, she's all right, she's all right . . .'

As he reached the main road, headlights lit the trees ahead and without thinking he dived into the forest and lay panting with the gun pointed out in front of him, but the car was a white Volvo which whipped by without slowing down. He stood up slowly and put the gun into the remaining empty pocket of his jacket and began jogging again.

A few more cars passed him each way, but he could see their headlights coming and took shelter in the forest while they passed. None of them was an old blue Chev.

Twenty minutes of steady jogging and he reached El Cap meadows. The traffic was heavier and there were people out walking. He was close to Linda and more than ever he wanted to break into an all out run, but he held himself back, forced himself to slow to a walk, to be just one more tourist out for an evening stroll before bed.

His mind was racing out of control again and furiously he clamped a lid on it. Carl was probably halfway to San Francisco. He would not risk coming here. Linda was all right. Asleep in the tent.

As he approached Camp 4 his terror alternately waxed and waned. What if Carl *had* taken a last chance and tried to search the tent? Surely he would have killed Linda. But if he had done that, the whole place would be in an uproar now and since all was quiet then she was surely all right.

But what if . . .

He was among the tents now. A few people sat around scattered campfires, but most of the camp was asleep and no one took any notice of him. He reached his own site and knelt in front of the door of Gordon's tent. His pulse hammered in his ears as he unzipped the door and crawled in. He could feel her legs through her sleeping bag. He reached for her shoulder and shook her lightly.

She moved.

2

ALEX

CHAPTER TWENTY-ONE

Yosemite Valley

SHE HALF WOKE to the touch of his hand on her shoulder. 'Mmmm?'

She levered herself up onto one elbow and opened her eyes. The tent was dark and she could see nothing. 'Alex?'

'Linda, I ... I ...' His voice was choked and he was having trouble speaking.

She sat up. The door was open and through it she could see the campsite in the moonlight. She was wearing only a T-shirt and it was cold outside the sleeping bag. She threw her arms around his neck and tried to pull him over on top of her but he resisted and she could feel his body tremble.

Fully awake now, she said, 'Alex, what's the matter? You're shaking all over.'

'I ... It's Gordie. They've killed Gordie.'

'WHAT??!'

'They killed him and ... and ... oh God, I was afraid that they'd killed you.' He collapsed against her, sobbing.

She wanted to hold him, to hold his head against her breasts and comfort him, and at the same time she was shocked and wanted to cry out, 'Who killed him? What happened? WHAT IS HAPPENING?' But everything she had learned on the street came back as if the last five years had never been. She scrambled out of her sleeping bag and, shoving Alex to one side, she ran out the door. The moonlight gleamed on her bare legs and buttocks as she scanned the area for any sign of danger.

The scene was peaceful. Quiet conversations around distant campfires. No menace. Inside the tent Alex was as she had left him, kneeling in the dark, saying nothing. She found her pants by touch and as she struggled into them she demanded, 'What happened?'

Alex drew a great ragged breath and let it out slowly, then, speaking in a dead, emotionless voice said, 'Before we came to the valley, Gord and I smuggled fifteen kilos of cocaine into the country. It wasn't ours, we just carried it for a guy and he paid us fifty thousand dollars. Two other guys from San Francisco found out we had the money. They found us in the restaurant after you left. They beat us up and said they'd kill us if we didn't give it to them. We fought them and they killed Gordie. I've got their guns but one of them got away.'

He didn't move as he spoke, but knelt in one position and let the words roll tonelessly into the darkness.

'The money is under the tent. They would have killed you. They were going to torture Gord to make us tell. The one that drove away is called Carl. He's a snake. He *wanted* to kill us. I think at the end he didn't even care about the money anymore.'

She had finished dressing, and ran outside again. Nothing. Back in. Alex had bunched the foamy into the rear of the tent and unzipped the cookhole by the door and was digging at the earth with his fingers. Before she could speak he said, 'Linda, listen to me.' His voice had regained some life but it was still full of strain. 'Right now I'm barely under control. I just saw my best friend get killed and ... and ...' He fought for control. 'And I feel like I'm coming apart inside. We've got to get away from here, and I don't know if I can drive. You might not want anything more to do with me after this, but ...' his voice broke and he shuddered once, '... but can you drive me to San Francisco? Please?'

In the dim light coming through the open front of the tent she could just see his face and the shining tears that ran slowly down it. She put her hands on his shoulders and bent forward to kiss him gently.

'No moré foolish talk, Alex. I love you, and I'll do

whatever I can to help you ... to help us.' She let him go and pulled her sleeping bag and a small pack from the end of the tent where Alex had pushed them. 'Everything else of ours is in your van and we can go anytime, but first you'd better tell me a little more. Even if it hurts you to talk about it, you've got to tell me so that we don't do anything stupid. Where did this happen? In the restaurant?'

'They caught us in the parking lot and took us to a place in the forest, past El Cap. Nobody saw any of it.'

He dug again and then with both hands pulled the vinyl briefcase out of its hole. 'Take this and wait outside.' He handed her the case and hastily scooped as much dirt as he could back into the hole and zipped it up. He pulled the foamy back into place and shook Gordon's sleeping bag out on top of it and crawled out of the tent, zipping it shut behind him.

'The man who shot Gord is named Carl. He's black, with a scarred-up face, maybe forty-five or fifty with real short hair. I've got his gun so he probably won't be back, but he knows my van, and if he's got another gun ...'

Linda finished stuffing her sleeping bag into her pack and walked to where he was standing. She looked up at him and he could see the half-moon reflected in the pupils of her eyes. 'Do you have the gun?'

'I've got both their guns.' But he made no move to produce them, as if somehow by not bringing them out he could erase what they had done.

'Do you know anything about guns, Alex?'

'No.'

She took his hand and said, 'Give them to me.'

One at a time, reluctantly, he took the two weapons from his pockets and gave them to her. He was starting to tremble again and he sat down at the picnic table and gripped its rough edge as tightly as he could. Linda checked the loads in the two pieces, then tucked one into the pocket of her own jacket and put the other on the table in front of him.

'Alex, this one is ready to fire. All you have to do is pull

the trigger. You're probably not going to hit anything, but
you'll scare the shit out of anyone who attacks you.'

'How do you know about guns?' He hadn't touched the
weapon on the table and his voice was a dull monotone.

'I grew up in South Dakota. Now put it in your pocket
and let's go.'

But his muscles were full of sand and he could not
move. He sat staring at the pistol on the table, the weight
of what had happened pressing him further and further
down.

'Alex.' He barely heard her.

'Alex!' He looked up slowly and caught the palm of her
right hand across his face. All of her strength had gone
into the blow and it staggered him off the bench and sent a
shockwave of pain and surprise surging through him.

Her voice came at him in a harsh whisper, and her
words shocked him even more than the blow. 'Wake up,
you stupid son of a bitch.' She had grabbed the front of his
jacket in both hands and was shaking him as hard as she
could, her voice hissing at him from only inches away.
'Gordon's been killed? Well get fucking mad about it! If
the bastards that did it are still around here then you had
goddamn well better be ready for them. You can cry
about it later. Right now you've got to get mad, you've got
to hate, Alex, hate. Do you understand?'

His strength returned under her onslaught. He took her
wrists and broke her grip on his jacket.

'Linda, I need about a minute to myself. I'm okay, I'll
be all right, but I just need a minute.' He let go of her and
sat down on the bench with his back to her. He blanked
his mind and concentrated on his breathing until some
calmness came back to him.

While he sat, Linda slipped the pack onto her back and
then moved into the shadow of the big pine that grew at
the edge of their site. She stood silently, looking slowly
around into the night.

It was about a minute and a half before Alex stirred. He
stood up, slipped the gun into his pocket, picked up the

case full of money and walked to where Linda stood under the tree. His step was purposeful and when he spoke there was some strength in his voice. 'I'll be okay.'

He cupped the back of her head with his hand, his fingers through her hair, and kissed her. 'When we get to San Francisco I'll try to explain everything and you can decide what you want to do then, but what happened tonight is this: the two guys from San Francisco took us to a deserted parking lot at some kind of power substation just a couple of miles from here. They were going to break Gord's legs but he got his knife out somehow and managed to stab one of them and then jumped on the other one, the little black guy called Carl. I don't know just what happened because I was fighting with the one Gord had stabbed but there was a shot and then Carl was running for the car. I managed to get the first guy's gun and shot at Carl, but I missed and he drove away.

'Gordon was dead. Carl had shot him. And the other guy was dead too, from the knife wound. I found Carl's gun on the ground. Gord must have knocked it away from him somehow, so I took the knife and both guns and then came here.'

He thought back over what had happened. 'Nobody saw it happen and I would guess that Carl is on his way back to San Francisco; or maybe he'll try to hide out somewhere, because he was working for the guy we carried the cocaine for. A guy named Walter Matheson. He's the reason that I've got to go to San Francisco.'

'He set this up?'

'No. I think Carl was doing this on his own, screwing his boss around. I don't want to see Matheson, but it's the only way I can think of to protect myself.'

'I guess maybe I got the wrong impression, Alex. I'm sorry I hit you.'

'It's okay. You got me back under control and I *am* mad. But I'm also frightened half out of my mind, and upset about Gordie. I'm not in complete control of myself, I can tell, but I'll be okay for a while.'

He pulled her close to him and held her tightly. 'Now let's go to San Francisco and get a hotel for the night.'

There were few people still up in Camp 4 and they met no one they knew. They approached the van from opposite sides, but saw no sign of Carl, and soon they were on the road.

The van was the old style, with a full bench seat in the front and once they were clear of the park gate Linda pulled Alex down so that he was lying stretched out across the seat with his head in her lap. He fell immediately into a deep and dreamless sleep and woke only briefly when she stopped to stretch her legs and empty her bladder just west of Modesto.

He slept all the way to the coast and woke again only when she parked the van and shook him.

'Uhnn?'

'Wake up Alex, we've arrived.' She shifted him into a sitting position.

'Uhn, where are we?'

'We're in the underground parking lot of the Hyatt Regency Hotel and I need to turn on the interior light but I can't figure out how.'

'The switch is kind of hidden. Just a minute.' Still half asleep, Alex reached under the dash for the switch he had installed there. The interior light came on, and dim as it was, the mess on his clothes was obvious.

'Do you have any clean clothes?' asked Linda.

'In the back somewhere, what about you?' Some of the bloodstains on his jacket had smeared onto her.

'I've got a suitcase back there too.'

The back of the van was cluttered and messy but they both found clean clothes and changed into them. He had never seen her in anything but jeans and T-shirt or plain blouse and sweater, and when she stepped out of the Van into the light of the parking lot he was stunned. She was wearing a matching skirt and jacket in rough wool, mostly grey-green, but with hints of brown and rusty orange; and a blouse of heavy apricot silk with a loose scarf-style collar. Her hair, which she normally tied back in a simple pony tail was coiled behind her head and pinned with a small leather and wood barrette.

'I wish this were some other time.'

She understood, and said, 'Thank you, Alex.'

She pulled a small suitcase from the van, locked the doors, and took his arm. 'I wish it was some other time myself,' she said, and led him toward the entrance.

When they were secure in their room, she took him to bed and made slow, gentle love to him, and afterwards held him till he was once again asleep.

CHAPTER TWENTY-TWO

San Francisco

'GOOD AFTERNOON, Matheson Hydraulics.'

'Hello, I'd like to speak to Walter Matheson please.'

'Who's calling please?'

'Uhn, tell him it's Gordon Wilson.'

'Thank you Mr. Wilson, hang on please.'

There was about a minute of silence, then,

'Mr. Wilson?'

'Yes?'

'Mr. Matheson is busy at the moment. If you leave your number he will call you back in a short time.'

'Uhn, no, I . . . I'm afraid I can't do that. Look, this is extremely important to Mr. Matheson personally, and it'll only take a couple of minutes. Could you please check with him one more time?'

'All right. Hang on please.'

Another minute of silence, then a male voice,

'Wilson? I don't think that this is appropriate.'

'Uhn, I'm not actually Wilson. You may not remember

me very well, but we did meet when you first met him, and I've got to talk to you.'

'I see . . . I'm not sure that there's anything useful for us to talk about at the moment. Perhaps I'll get in touch with Wilson in the spring.'

'Mr. Matheson, your man Carl found us last night, and Gord isn't going to be dealing with you anymore. Or with anyone. I think we should talk.'

'Where is Carl?'

'I don't know. He left in a hurry and he might be looking for you.'

'When and where can we meet?'

'Anywhere, as long as it's soon.'

'All right, how about the bar in the St. Francis Hotel at three. That's about half an hour.'

'Is that near your office?'

'It's not far, why?'

'I'm not far from there, but I don't know the city, so let's make it quarter past three okay?'

'All right. How will I recognize you?'

'Believe me Mr. Matheson, *I* will recognize *you*.'

Walter Matheson hung up the phone and reached for the bottle of Anacin that he kept in the top right hand drawer of his desk. What was going on? Was this some kind of trick? He spilled two tablets into his hand and walked to the small bathroom adjoining his office.

What kind of trick could it be? The only thing he could think of was blackmail, Wilson or his partner saying 'Give me money or I'll tell the world.' Well he could handle that. He only had to buy himself a few more months, and he didn't really believe that it was blackmail anyway. No, it was probably exactly what his caller had said; that bastard Carl trying to work some deal of his own.

And who was the caller? Alex something. He remembered dark features in a lean face. And dark eyes.

He swallowed the tablets with a glass of water and wondered for the thousandth time what to do about the headaches. Any sort of crisis and *wham*, someone started working on his skull with a jackhammer. Maybe he should see a different doctor. He returned to his office and put on his jacket.

If it was true that Carl had somehow gone into business for himself then this could be Carl trying to lure him into a trap. But that was stupid. If Carl wanted to kill him, he'd come for him at home, not in the middle of the day in the city.

He looked in on his secretary. 'Dianna, something's come up and I'm going to have to go to a meeting. I don't know if I'll be back today or not. If anything comes up for me just take messages and I'll deal with it tomorrow.'

'Okay, Mr. Matheson.'

He left by his private door and was soon riding the elevator down the seventeen floors to ground level. He was going to phone John Tomlinson, and he wanted to make the call from some place where he could see who went into the St. Francis.

But first he needed a drink.

CHAPTER TWENTY-THREE

San Francisco

When Alex left the St. Francis he did what Linda had told him to do. He walked into the nearest department store and mixed with the crowd of shoppers as best he could. He left by a different entrance and caught the first bus that came by, rode it for a few blocks and then got off and walked until he found a taxi. He had the driver let him off two blocks from the Hyatt Regency.

Five minutes later he let himself into their room. It was empty, as he had known it would be, but there was a bottle of Remy Martin on the table by the window and he

knew it was Linda's way of saying, 'Everything is going to
be fine. Sit down and have a drink and just relax until I
call.' Beside the bottle was a single glass. Not a hotel glass
but a real snifter of good crystal. He wondered how she
had managed that.

However she had done it, he felt better. Less alone.
And there were flowers. He walked to the low table and
bent to pick up a small pewter vase in the shape of a
pitcher with two roses in it. One red and one white.

As he replaced the vase on the table the telephone rang
on its stand by the bed.

'Hello.'

'Alex? Is everything all right?'

'Everything is fine. Where are you?'

'Downstairs.'

'Okay, come on up.'

'No, not yet. You wait there for a few more minutes.
Have a drink or something and then come down and go to
the Wicker Works. It's a bar just across the street from the
hotel. Just wait there for a few minutes and I'll come in as
soon as I'm sure no one is watching you.'

He felt panic starting to lap again at the edges of his
reason. 'What's going on? Did you see someone follow me
here?'

'No, I didn't see anything, but let's give it a few more
minutes just to be sure. Let's not take any chances. Now
have that drink and relax. Think about how much I love
you.'

Her voice, and the thought of her love, calmed him and
he said. 'You're right. I guess I'm a bit edgy, but you're
right about not taking any chances. I'll see you in ten or
fifteen minutes. And thanks for the flowers . . . they help.'

'You're welcome. See you soon.'

He didn't want to stay in the room by himself. He
wanted to go downstairs as fast as he could, forget the
elevator, race down the five flights of stairs and find her,
hold her. But she was right, it was better to wait just a
little longer.

He poured a drink and took it out onto the balcony. The room was not high enough to give any view and the traffic noise from the streets below soon drove him back inside. He turned on the television and went slowly around the dial, but nothing he saw made any sense to him. His reality had been reduced to gunfire in the night, irrevocable death, and burning love. What he saw on the screen offered him neither consolation nor escape.

He shut it off and drained his glass. Surely more than five minutes had passed? He rinsed the glass in the bathroom, dried it on one of the hotel towels and put it back on the table.

Out the door. Wait for the elevator as forty-five seconds pass like forty-five minutes. Down and into the lobby. Don't look around. Hands in pockets. Be nonchalant. Out into the street where sunlight and traffic were both starting to wane. Down to the corner and wait for the light with everybody else, then across the street and back up to the Wicker Works.

Inside, it was all ferns and rattan and well-dressed secretaries washing away the nothingness of another day in their office towers.

He ordered rye and water out of habit and then wished he hadn't, for the thought of drinking rye whiskey made him think of the parties that Gordon held every November. Although parties was not quite the right word. Gatherings. Evenings when a large but loosely knit group of friends consolidated the memory of another year in the mountains with stories, slides and films. An evening of beer and smoke and rye whiskey. Good food and good friends and a technicolour tour of the high places of the world. The Rockies, Yosemite, the Canadian Coast Range, Alaska, the Eastern Arctic, the Alps, the Andean Ranges and the high Himalaya.

But Gordon would host no more such evenings. Alex finished his drink and ordered another. Maybe if he got drunk he would be able to keep the nostalgia flowing, to think of Gordon as he had been, to accept the fact of his death slowly, a little at a time.

Linda arrived before the second drink. Alex, lost in his thought, was not aware of her until she sat down opposite him and said, 'So?'

He lurched back to the present and was once again riveted by the sight of her. She was wearing the same suit she had put on in the van the night before, her hair again coiled behind her head. Her beauty was the beauty of intelligence and strength, the crooked tooth in her wide smile adding warmth and humanity but no softness.

He told her of his meeting with Walter Matheson, '... and I think we don't have to worry any more. I told him what had happened and I think he believed me. And I told him that I didn't want anything more to do with this business.'

The waitress brought his drink and took Linda's order for a brandy and soda.

'Anyway, I didn't tell him my name and he seemed to accept that I wanted out, but it was really weird ...' He tasted the new drink. '... it was like he wasn't all there. Or that he wasn't there all the time.'

'What do you mean?'

'Well it just seemed that every once in a while he'd space out, get lost in the ozone for a few seconds and then make a real effort to snap back to what was going on. And once he even started mumbling to himself about head-aches, almost as if I wasn't there.'

'What about that animal Carl, the one that killed Gordon?'

'Yeah, well, I think they're going to kill him.'

Alex shivered and finished his drink in a gulp. 'Gord once told me that the people involved in this kind of thing were different from ordinary people. I didn't really believe him then, but now I think he was right. This guy Matheson talked about Carl as if he were already dead.'

He put his empty glass back on the table and said, 'That was the most frightening thing I've done. Walking in to meet him, and wondering if he would decide to have me killed. Or if he had already decided.'

'Did you tell him that you'd arranged protection for yourself? That if he tried for you he'd get burned?'

'No, I didn't have to. He just seemed to be totally unconcerned about me. He wanted to know what had happened and then he asked if I was interested in taking over for Gord. When I said I wasn't, that was it, he just seemed to lose interest. It was strange, he sort of retreated into himself – like his mind had suddenly teleported to Venus or something.'

Alex sat and thought about it, replaying the scene in his mind. 'I wonder if he got his brain a bit scrambled in the plane crash. He sure as hell cut his head open ... anyway, whatever his problem is, it's his problem and the only thing left for me to do is to go back to the valley tomorrow and pretend that I don't know anything.'

The muscles along his spine contracted slowly at the thought of going back, and unconsciously he gripped the table edge.

'Alex, your knuckles are white.'

'Sorry, I was just thinking about going back. I'm probably going to have to talk to the police, maybe identify Gord's body ... I don't know how I'm going to handle that ...' He looked across the table at her. 'I think I'm probably going to drink too much tonight. I hope you don't mind.'

'No, it's all right. I'll do my best to take care of you.' She looked around the room. 'But not here, okay?' If you want to get numb that's fine with me, but let's do it somewhere less trendy.'

Alex had had a drink in the hotel and two drinks in the bar all in less than an hour and he was starting to float.

'What about the bottle in our room? Let's go there and if I get stupid, or maudlin, it won't matter. And anyway I don't feel like meeting the public tonight.'

They stood up just as the waitress arrived with Linda's drink. 'Excuse me, did you forget about your drink?'

Linda took a five from her purse and laid it on the waitress's tray and said, 'Have it yourself or give it to someone else, we're leaving.' She took Alex's arm and led him to the street.

'I really dislike places like that.' She still had her arm through Alex's and now she pulled him along. 'C'mon, let's walk for a while. I need to burn off some energy.'

Alex hung back and she stopped and faced him. 'Alex, I'm not asking you to be happy. I know that you're sad about Gordon, and frightened about what might happen, and that you need support; but you're forgetting that Gordon was *my* friend too, that *I'm* sad about his death, that *I'm* frightened about the future, that *I* need support too. Now walk with me up and down these streets and hold my hand so tight that it hurts me.'

CHAPTER TWENTY-FOUR

Yosemite Valley

GORDON HAD DIED on Thursday night, and now, Saturday afternoon, Alex and Linda were rolling through the dry hills and forests on their way back to Yosemite Valley to confront that death again.

They had discussed it over and over until Alex felt that he could face whatever questions the police might have for him. He still felt only partially under control but the knowledge that Linda needed his support as much as he needed hers had strengthened him and he knew that somehow he would be able to get through the next few days.

When they reached Camp 4 they found Gordon's tent gone and the ground underneath it dug up in a circle of almost six foot radius. Groups of climbers milled around the site and Walter, the young German, saw them before anyone else. He stepped away from the group and took them aside.

'Walter, what's going on? Where's the tent? Where's Gord?'

'Alex, you must listen. There is much sadness about Gordon. He is found yesterday killed from the pistol, and the police have take the tent and equipments.' He put his hand on Alex's arm and said, 'I know he is your friend. I sorry to tell you.'

'What are you talking about? Where is he?' Alex's knees were shaking and the muscles of his abdomen contracted spasmodically. He did not have to fake anything. Linda took his other arm and she and Walter guided him to a bench.

'Yesterday they are finding the body and the Ranger is seeing the wounds of climbing on the hands and is coming here to ask for informations. It is your friend Gordon, but he not killed by the falling, he is killed by the pistol, by the gun.'

'Where is he?'

'Maybe I think in the hospital. Or they are taking him away. I do not know.'

Alex stood and looked at Linda, and the tears in his eyes were real. 'Take me to the hospital. Please.'

CHAPTER TWENTY-FIVE

Vancouver

ANDY CUTLER hung up his telephone and lit a cigarette. He wanted to stand by the window and look out at the city, which he knew would be all sharp edges and clean black shadows in the October light; but until he made sergeant he wouldn't have an office with a window, so he left his desk and walked across the big detectives' room to visit Rick Hofstadter who *was* a Sergeant and had one of the best windows in the building.

He entered without knocking and said, 'Got the coffee on, Rico?'

Hofstadter wouldn't drink the coffee in the cafeteria and kept a kettle and filters in his office. 'Sure, pour yourself a cup. I'll trade you for a smoke.'

They made the exchange and Hofstadter lit up. 'So what's happening?'

'You remember I told you about William Holley? That Lieutenant on the San Francisco force that phoned me about the coke importer – the one that was flying the stuff in from Prince Rupert?'

'Yeah, I remember. His airplane flew into a storm and then he turned up in San Francisco a week later with a story about being stranded on a fishing trip. You went for a look at the wreck a couple of months ago. Guy's name was Mathews or something like that.'

'Matheson. That was back in August. Apparently this guy Matheson is pretty smooth. We found his suitcase in the wreck in the mountains just over the border south of Chilliwack Lake, and Holley was going to spring that on him, but Matheson beat him to it – phoned him up and said he'd been trying to get in touch with the pilot because he'd left his suitcase aboard, and asked if Holley knew whether it had been found.'

Cutler walked to the window with his coffee. The mid-morning sun played in his blond hair and threw the bags under his eyes into sharp relief.

'Any chance of checking his bank accounts? Maybe getting some cooperation from the tax people?' Hofstadter asked. 'If this guy is actually smuggling in planeloads of cocaine it's gotta show up on his balance sheet some-where. Unless he's giving the stuff away.'

'Not likely. He's got a brother who's a mining engineer in Peru, which is probably where he gets the stuff, and the two of them have quite a few legitimate businesses down there. That's probably where the money goes. It probably gets laundered through about six different companies and stays in Peru.'

'And your friend Holley hasn't got a chance of finding anything out down there, right?'

'Right.' Cutler tried to scrunch himself up onto the window sill, his back against one side of the frame and his feet against the other, but the sill wasn't quite wide enough and he almost fell off. 'I wouldn't exactly call Holley my friend either. He's too intense for me. In fact I wouldn't be surprised if he wears his badge to bed. But he's interesting – sort of a study in applied fanaticism. And I think he's pretty good. He sure hasn't missed much on the Matheson thing. He put it all together by himself from just a few bits of information, and if that RCMP spotter hadn't screwed up he probably would have put Matheson into the bag with a plane load of coke.'

Hofstadter scratched his nose and said, 'The RCMP actually saw this guy get into the plane and followed it down to the border? No chance he's telling the truth about the fishing lake and hitchhiking down here?'

'I wondered about that, so I looked into it myself. I know a few guys with the RCMP and I asked them to check it out. They said that it was solid. Matheson got on the plane with two suitcases in Prince Rupert, a regular one and one of the shiny aluminium cases photographers use, and they followed him right to the storm.'

Cutler returned to the desk. 'So it sounds to me as though Holley's right, but for the time being there's not much he can do about it except eat his liver.' He took a cigarette and threw the pack back at the desktop. 'But that's not what I wanted to see you about.'

'No?'

He walked to the window again and smoked in silence, ordering his mind and going over the telephone call he had just received. Then he asked, 'Does the name Gordon Wilson mean anything to you?'

Hofstadter thought for a short time and then replied, 'No, I don't think so. Should it?'

'I don't know.' Cutler had his back to the room, holding his coffee cup with both hands, the cigarette dangling from his lips. 'I got a call a few minutes ago from Holley in San Francisco. Apparently two bodies were found on Saturday in the forest in Yosemite National Park in California, about two hundred miles east of San Francisco. One shot, one stabbed, both male.

'Holley found out about it because one of the dead guys was from the Bay area. It was some low grade thug who worked for another guy named Carl ... Carl ...' Cutler put his coffee down on the windowsill, pulled out his notebook and flipped through the notes he had made during the telephone call.

'... named Carl Adams who does a lot of odd jobs for one of the big importers down there.'

Cutler looked up from his notes and added, 'Adams was once seen meeting with this Matheson, which is what got Holley going on this whole thing in the first place.'

Hofstadter thought about this for a minute and then said, 'Okay, I get it. I imagine you're going to tell me that the other corpse was Gordon Wilson, and since Holley called you about it, and since you're asking me about it, he must be from around here somewhere. Right?'

Cutler was amazed. How could anybody who looked and dressed like an extra in an old gangster film be as good as Hofstadter? 'Rico, when they make you Superintendent of Detectives you won't forget who gave you all those cigarettes will you?'

Hofstadter laughed. 'You'll owe me so much for coffee by then that I'll have to promote you just so you can afford to pay me.' Then, seriously, 'But unfortunately I don't think I know anything about Gordon Wilson. Do they know anything down there?'

'Not a damn thing. They didn't even know his name until some acquaintances of his identified the body. It seems that he was a mountain climber and he and a friend were in this Yosemite Park because there are some big rock walls there.

'But you're right about him being from Vancouver. This friend, who's an American by the way, doesn't seem to know too much. Apparently he was having dinner in a restaurant with Wilson and then Wilson went away somewhere with a middle-aged black guy he called Carl. There's a waiter in the restaurant who confirms all this and the descriptions of this Carl match up with Carl Adams, the one that led Holley into all this in the first place.

'Now this Carl has disappeared, and the Sheriff's people in Modesto, who've got jurisdiction in this, haven't got any ideas at all. Holley says he's going to go and talk to them and he asked if I could look at it from this end.

'The dead guy's friend gave the Sheriff's man an address and said that this Wilson was single and worked part time for a printing company called Ambledon printing.'

Cutler looked at his notes again and read aloud. 'The body was a white male, about thirty years of age. Shoulder length blond hair, thick blond beard and moustache. Five feet eleven inches, one hundred and ninety-five pounds. No needle marks or signs of regular drug use. He was muscular and seemed to be in excellent health except that both hands as far up as the wrists were covered in very fresh scabs, some quite large.'

He looked up again. 'The park Rangers say that the scabs are very common with rock climbers. They get them from jamming their hands into cracks in the rock faces when they climb, and the friend confirms that he and Wilson had just done a very hard climb the day before the killing.'

'What's this friend's name?' interrupted Hofstadter.

Cutler checked his notes. 'Alexander Townsend. Lives in Seattle.'

'And Wilson, what's his address?'

'Thirty-two sixty West Fourteenth. I checked with the city, it's a private home and Wilson was the sole owner.'

Hofstadter snorted. 'A thirty year old long hair with a part-time job and he owns a house in Kitsilano?'

'Yeah, that's what I thought, but it seems he bought it about ten years ago. It's a small place and he got a good mortgage.'

'It'd have to be pretty good if he could afford it when he was twenty and only has to work part time to pay it off.'

'Well, who knows? Maybe he inherited. On the other hand maybe he's involved in this cocaine thing in a major way.'

Cutler emptied his coffee cup. 'Anyway, whatever the story is on this guy, I figure it's worth having a look at the house. So if it's okay with you I'll go and do that now.'

Hofstadter snorted again. 'If it's okay with me! What a crock. Since when has me being your sergeant made the slightest bit of difference to what you do? Here, don't forget these.' He tossed the cigarette pack across the room. 'Let me know what you find out, and make me a copy of the description of this Wilson. I'll see if anyone around here knows anything about him.'

Cutler was almost out the door when Hofstadter called after him, 'What were you pretending to be at work on when you got that telephone call?'

'Nothing that can't wait. It was those bikers out in district three, the ones with the laboratory in the basement. Their court date was postponed again, so this'll give me something to do to keep me from drinking up the rest of your coffee.'

'Okay, have fun. And if I'm around when you get back let me know what you found.'

The thirty-two-hundred block on West Fourteenth Avenue is quietly residential. Huge old poplars shade the street, small and medium sized houses sit well back on neatly clipped lawns. Small orderly hedges and large disorderly flowers are everywhere.

Most of the houses were built in the thirties and forties and many are still occupied by their original owners. 3260 was small and well kept. With stucco walls and green asphalt shingles it looked like almost all the other houses on the block.

A large pear tree dominated the front yard and Cutler thought he could see a weeping willow behind the house. He didn't stop in front of it but drove on and parked at a corner two blocks away.

'Two-two.'

'Go ahead two-two.'

'I'm in the thirty-two hundred block on West Fourteenth. Have you got a patrol car nearby?'

'I've got several units within a few minutes of that area, shall I send one to meet you?'

'I'd prefer a one-man unit if that's possible.'

'Um, just a minute two-two.'

Cutler leaned back against the headrest and smoked patiently. He let his mind ramble unchecked, facts, fantasies and images tumbling over one another like water rushing down a stream.

Every detective has a different method of working. Some jot ideas down on paper, some bounce ideas off other detectives, or off their wives; Cutler liked to stack up all the information and all the facts at his disposal, shuffle them thoroughly and then toss them randomly through his mind.

It didn't always help, but it never hurt and he knew from long experience that it had a calming effect on him and made him more alert in the following hours. Even a minute or two helped.

'Two-two?'

'Two-two.'

'I've only got one one-man unit in a marked vehicle in your district. That unit is ten-sixty-two right now, how urgent is this?'

'No rush, just tell me where he's eating and I'll meet him there.'

'It's the White Spot, Broadway and Vine.'

'Thanks.' Cutler stubbed out his cigarette and was

about to sign off, then he added, 'Who is it? I mean which P.C. is in that unit?'

'Two-eight-two, two-two.'

Fucking numbers. The badge number meant nothing to him. He had wanted a name and suspected that the dispatcher knew it. Patience.

'Can you give me a name to go with that number please?'

'That's Constable MacGregor, two-two.'

'Thank you, ten-four.'

Cutler didn't know MacGregor. In fact he'd never heard of MacGregor. Sometimes he toyed with the idea of transferring to the police force in a small city or town. Somewhere he could get to know everyone on the force and a good percentage of the citizens. But he knew it was something he could never really do. He needed the city. Needed to walk its streets and feel the ever-accelerating pulse of its life. Andrew Cutler was a quiet man, but he drew his sustenance, spiritual, emotional and intellectual, from the current of anonymous human electricity that flows so strongly in a big city.

Pushing open the heavy double doors of the White Spot he looked around and soon spotted the only police uniform in the restaurant. Constable MacGregor was short for a police officer, had medium-length brown hair, brown eyes, and a clean, tanned complexion carefully set off with just a hint of green eyeliner and a rich burgundy lipstick.

There are some things, thought Cutler, that aren't that bad about a big city police force.

She looked up from the newspaper she was reading and gave him an efficient once-over. He could see the card file flipping over behind her eyes, see her fast glance past him and to both sides, analyzing the geometry of confrontation as he approached. Then he saw her relax a bit and knew that she had tagged him as a fellow cop.

'I'm Detective Cutler. Andy Cutler. May I join you while you finish lunch?'

She looked at him absently for a few seconds, her face and eyes giving nothing away, and then said, 'Please do.'

Her voice was pleasant but emotionally neutral. Cutler sat down opposite her and said, 'Sorry to interrupt your break. I wanted a one-man unit and the dispatcher said that the only one-man unit was having lunch here so I thought I'd just drop in and order a coffee and brief you while you ate. If that was all right with you.'

Her face and eyes relaxed as he spoke and her response was warmer. 'Yes, that's all right with me. Actually I'm finished anyway', she gestured at the debris on the table in front of her, 'and I was just about to go back to work.'

'Did you have anything coming up this afternoon?'

'No, I'm just on patrol.'

'Well, I'm afraid this isn't likely to prove too exciting.' Cutler remembered how he, like all constables, had been excited whenever he got a chance to work with the detectives. 'I'm going to search a house in the thirty-two-hundred block on West Fourteenth. Do you know that area?'

'It's mostly residential isn't it?' She thought a bit and then said, 'You know, I've been in district four for three years now, and I can't remember a thing about that block, so it must be pretty quiet.'

She swallowed the last of her coffee and grimaced. 'God. I don't know why I drink this slop. So you want a uniformed officer and a blue and white along so that the neighbours don't call the police when you enter the house?'

She's just like Rico, thought Cutler, knows what I'm going to say before I can say it.

'That's right. The house belongs, or belonged, to a guy named Gordon Wilson who was killed in the States over the weekend, and who *may* be involved in a big drug deal . . .'

As he spoke he puzzled over her reaction to him. Why had she been so remote at first and then only partially thawed out? The timing was all wrong. Her first reaction

had been understandable, it was the reaction of any
policeman when approached by a stranger, but when she
tagged him as another cop she only relaxed part way. It
wasn't until he started explaining why he wanted her that
she dropped the pose of cool politeness.

'... so anyway when I drove through the neighbourhood I realized that I was going to need uniformed backup
to keep the 911 phone from ringing off the wall, and since
there was no need to take two guys off patrol I asked for a
one-man unit. You're the only single on this shift so here I
am.'

He stopped speaking for a moment and then added, 'By
the way, what's your first name?'

She had been listening carefully to his story and
answered the question before she was aware of it.

'Valerie.'

But even as she spoke the impersonal mask came back
into place and the brown eyes hardened.

He had it now. He held up both hands, palms toward
her, and said, 'Easy, easy, I've been on this police force
for eleven years. In all that time I haven't made a single
pass at a policewoman. Not one. This is business and I'll
call you Constable MacGregor if that makes you happier.'

She looked at him for a little longer. She could see
nothing but honest good humour in the drooping lids and
light blue eyes. She relaxed again.

'No, please, call me Valerie. It's just that half the guys
on the force seem to think that the PWs are there for their
own personal amusement. It gets pretty tiring.'

'I suppose it must.' Cutler stood up. 'If you're finished
lunch we might as well get moving.'

Constable Valerie MacGregor rose from behind her
side of the table. She may have been short for a police
officer but she was tall for a woman. Slim without being
thin, and her arms were as tanned as her face. Her
uniform didn't give much away about her figure except
that she had a small waist.

Cutler said, 'Will you phone in and tell your Corporal

that you'll be working with me for a few hours? Don't use that thing.' He pointed to the tranceiver she had just picked up from the table. 'We don't need any spectators or helpers. I'll head over there now and wait for you. It's a small stucco house on the south side of Fourteenth between Blenheim and Trutch. About the fourth one from the corner of Trutch.'

As he drove Cutler thought about the policewoman he had just met. She reminded him of Hofstadter. Which was pretty funny considering the physical differences, but she had the same quick mind and the same straightforward nature.

He turned on to Fourteenth and parked in front of the little house and pretended not to watch the elderly neighbours pretending not to watch him. After two or three minutes the patrol car pulled in behind him and the neighbours stopped pretending.

They locked their cars and stood together on the sidewalk, she looking at the house and he looking at her. The autumn sunlight threw her features into topographic relief without being harsh. She had a strong face with high cheekbones. A straight nose fell from real eyebrows to a real mouth. No cuteness or artifice. It was, Cutler thought, a face made for expressing real emotion. Her eyes had looked brown in the artificial light of the restaurant but here in the sun he could see that they were a mixture of browns and greens. Hazel.

He brought himself back to reality and hoped she hadn't minded him staring. 'We might as well knock on the door before we do too much skulking around.'

The front door was in a small covered porch six steps up. Their knocking was answered only by empty silence and the door was securely locked.

They walked around the house clockwise. The lot was a standard city lot, thirty-three feet by one fifty, but it seemed large because the house was small. The front yard was grassed and continuous with the lawns of the houses on either side, the rear was enclosed on one side and the

back by a low wooden fence and on the other side by a
tall, dense hedge. A back gate opened to a wooden stand
with two empty garbage cans in a gravelled lane.

An old weeping willow dominated the backyard and
beneath it was a heavy picnic table with attached benches.
Six steps led up to a small deck and the back door. Under
the steps were dozens of cases of empty beer bottles.

They continued round the house until they were back at
the front door. The house appeared empty – there were
curtains drawn across the basement windows and the main
floor windows were too high to let them see in.

'Do you know anything about picking locks?'

'Just the kind where you can work on the tongue with a
knifeblade,' she replied. 'The front door looked like a
good quality deadbolt to me.'

'Well maybe the back door won't be as tough. You walk
around that way and check all the windows you can reach,
and I'll go this way.'

Just over a minute later they met in the back yard.

'Nothing?'

'Nothing.'

'Okay, let's have a look at this door.'

The back door lock was as good as the front, and the
door itself didn't budge or rattle when Cutler threw a
tentative hip into it.

He sighed. 'Oh well. Now you get to watch how a shit-
hot detective finesses his way past a locked door.'

He looked into the one neighbouring back yard that he
could see to make sure no one was watching then drew his
revolver and smashed the small pane of glass set into the
centre of the door near the top. He knocked out as many
of the fragments as he could and then reached up and
through the broken window. But it was too high and even
on tiptoe he couldn't reach down to the lock.

He sighed again, took off his jacket and handed it to the
policewoman. 'I'll kneel down so you can stand on my
back. Put my jacket on so you don't cut yourself on the
glass.'

He knelt down on all fours so that his back offered a level platform about two and a half feet above the deck. Craning his neck to look up at her he added, 'And you might take off your shoes.'

She stepped up on his back, one foot on his shoulders, one foot over his hips. He tried to hold steady as he felt her lean and stretch. There were metal on metal noises and a muffled 'Damn'. More noises and then she stepped lightly down.

As he rose she wiped her forehead with her left hand and said, 'I think I got it.'

She had been bracing her left hand high above the door, just under the eaves, and now there was a smear of dirt where she had touched herself. His coat hung halfway to her knees and the sleeves were well past her fingertips. With her shoeless feet and smudged face she looked like a Gasoline Alley urchin. And very desirable.

He took the coat from her and removed a handkerchief from one of its inside pockets.

'Hold still.' He cupped the back of her head in one hand and cleaned the grime from her forehead. Looking into her eyes he knew that she would accept when he asked her to dinner – and that she knew he would ask.

But duty first.

'Wipe your hand on this.' He gave her the handkerchief and turned the doorknob.

She slipped on her shoes and stepped in behind him.

They were in a small hallway looking into a pleasant sunlit kitchen/breakfast nook.

'What are you looking for?'

'Nothing.'

'Nothing?'

'Nothing specific. Nothing and everything. The guy who lived here was found dead in California, in some national park. Apparently he was a mountain climber and there are some rock faces in that park. He'd been shot in the chest and there was another body beside him that had been stabbed. The other body was some no-mind heavy

on the San Francisco drug scene. Dumb. Just a kid, but
lots of arrests – assaults, B and E's, possession, that kind
of thing. The guy I've been working with on this says that
the stab victim usually worked for another guy named
Carl Adams who was seen with Wilson shortly before the
killings, and who had been seen with a man named Walter
Matheson who is suspected of smuggling cocaine into the
States from up here.'

He paused and then went on, 'So it's all pretty tenuous,
it could be anything. Wilson, the guy who lived here,
might have been an innocent bystander or he might have
been masterminding a huge coke operation.' He paused
again. 'He only worked part time and he had to make his
house payments somehow.

'So I don't really know what I'm looking for. Fifty kilos
of cocaine in the cupboard under the sink? Dead bodies in
the basement?'

'A huge collection of Old Masters in the attic?' said
Valerie, getting into the spirit of the conversation. 'A
secret transmitter under the floorboards with a codebook
in Albanian?'

'That's right, subtle clues which might lead us to believe
that the deceased had fallen in with evil men.'

Valerie drew herself up to full height and adopted the
pinched, nasal voice and clenched-cheeks walk of one of
Vancouver's more obnoxious trial lawyers. 'So as you can
see Your Honour, my client is essentially an honest young
man, and only ran this multinational narcotics cartel to
support his widowed mother.'

She turned her back for a second and then turned once
more to face Cutler from behind an imaginary judge's
bench. She peered nearsightedly out over imaginary reading glasses and in a deep, pompous voice said, 'Uh, no
shit, eh?'

Cutler had recognized the caricatures and they were
both laughing. Gradually the laughter stopped and they
simply looked at one another. Finally he said, 'First things
first, okay?'

'Okay.'

They moved into the kitchen. 'I really *don't* know what I'm looking for. Right now I'm just looking. For anything. Let's just wander around separately and see what we see. Touch all the doorknobs and light switches you want, but be careful of everything else.'

Andy Cutler was a good cop. He put Constable MacGregor out of his mind and began working. He hung up his coat and walked slowly through the house. It was a small house and he didn't open any cupboards or check the basement, so his tour only took a few minutes. He stood in the middle of each room and looked slowly around three hundred and sixty degrees, then went on to the next.

When he had seen each room he walked to the living room and sat down in a large overstuffed armchair and closed his eyes.

Valerie MacGregor had watched and taken part in several house searches in her four years on the force but she had never seen one like this. For almost a minute she stood watching Cutler in the chair, then she shrugged her shoulders and started for the top of the stairs leading to the basement but stopped again when Cutler stood up.

He turned to her and said, 'Tell me about the guy who lived here.'

The question took her completely by surprise. Everything this man did surprised her. 'I ... I can't really say ... I mean we haven't really had a good look at anything. I ...'

'I know all that. Try anyway.'

'Okay, if you want me to. But just let me think for a minute.' She looked slowly around the room. Fireplace with three-quarter-full wood box. Solid wooden bookshelves jammed with books. Hardwood floor with a good rug. Two armchairs and a couch all in the overstuffed style of the forties. Old but solid, with good upholstery. Low coffee table – solid, like the bookshelves. Fairly new console television.

What else? A couple of old-fashioned upright lamps with heavy cloth shades. Large window area looking over the front yard. A fairly large room. Light and spacious enough that the heavy furniture was not oppressive.

What else? A pair of framed prints on one wall, colour photographs, one of a mountain with snow blowing off the top and the other of somebody climbing steep ice. And a framed reproduction of Breughel's 'Peasant's Wedding' over the mantelpiece.

What else? Complex and expensive-looking audio components and what looked to be several hundred records shelved with the books. Two very large speakers near the front of the room. The sound system bothered her, but she wasn't sure why.

She sat down in one of the chairs and asked herself, Who lived here?

'You said that he was a climber, but if you hadn't told me that I would have said that he was pretty much like most of the other people on the block. A sort of quiet old man who took good care of his house. He probably wasn't rich, but he made enough to buy this little house and some solid furniture – maybe twenty-five years ago.

'He was probably retired, maybe a widower or a bachelor since there doesn't seem to be any feminine feel to the place.'

She had been speaking quietly, thoughtfully; now she stood up and in a more normal voice said, 'Something about the stereo bothers me though. But I'm not sure what it is.'

'Probably the fact that not many "retired widowers" have multi-thousand dollar component stereos,' said Cutler. 'This is a funny kind of job. A man was murdered in California. He might or might not be involved in heavy crime. There might or might not be something here that's significant. We might or might not recognize it.

'The guy has no record, not even a parking ticket, and neither Rick Hofstadter nor I have ever heard of him. We'll ask around, check with the neighbours, find out

what we can; but this part, this house search, is different.
We're probably not going to find any stash of cocaine in
the basement, or any hidden code books; whatever clues
there are are probably small and easy to miss. That's why I
gave the place a quick walk-through, just to form a
general impression so that anything unusual will have a
chance of standing out a little more clearly.'

He stood up. 'Now, let's shake the place down.'

For a while there was nothing much. Cutlery and
utensils and some canned food in the kitchen drawers and
cupboards, but nothing perishable. The refrigerator was
unplugged and the garbage container was empty. The
sugar, salt, flour and baking powder containers contained
sugar, salt, flour and baking powder.

The bedroom was clean and tidy. Large brass bed nicely
made with a thick down comforter folded at the foot.
Department store clothing in the closet. Blue jeans and
Levi shirts mostly, no suits and no ties. Nondescript
collection of T-shirts, socks and underwear in the dresser
along with several well made but not stylish wool sweaters.
No jewellery anywhere and nothing under the bed.

Cutler removed the comforter and peeled the bed one
layer at a time. Near the foot of the bottom sheet were
several large reddish-brown stains, faint but quite
noticeable.

'What the hell?'

'Maybe he has hairy feet and cut himself shaving,' said
Valerie, then giggled.

He peeled the last sheet and looked at the mattress.
Clean.

'Help me turn this over.'

On the other side of the mattress were more stains, near
the head of the bed. Together they shook out the bottom
sheet and put it back on, reversed top to bottom. The
stains on the sheet matched those on the mattress. The
pillowcase was clean, but the pillow itself was prominently
stained.

The living room yielded nothing of interest except a

carved wooden box with a tight fitting lid sitting on the bookshelves. In it was one plastic bag containing about half an ounce of marijuana and another containing a few grams of black hash. Lying loose in the box were a small wooden hash pipe, three boxes of wooden matches, a half empty package of pipe cleaners and two spare screens for the pipe.

The bathroom was just a bathroom. Drano and cleansers under the sink along with spare toilet paper and a large plastic basin. Aspirin, bandaids and scissors in the medicine cabinet. Soap and shampoo on the ledge of the tub.

Valerie MacGregor turned back to the sink and medicine cabinet. 'It's strange, there's no toothbrush or toothpaste, no shaving equipment, no deodorants . . .'

Cutler said, 'Yeah, but not that strange. He probably took the toothbrush and paste with him, the description I got said he had a thick beard so he probably didn't shave, and there are a lot of people who don't use deodorants or aftershaves.' He paused. 'In a way it goes with the clothes and the dope and the long hair. He probably bathed regularly and figured he didn't need any chemicals on his skin.'

The basement was unfinished except for a small room, about eight by twelve, that had been built in one corner. There was a furnace in the opposite corner, a freezer along one wall, a lawn mower and a rake and a workbench with a moderate collection of tools along another; but what first caught their interest was a large three-level industrial shelving unit against the remaining wall. It was stacked with multicoloured equipment and clothing, both loose and in boxes.

Cutler walked closer and stared. 'What *is* all this shit?' He picked up a smooth rope of blue and gold threads. It was coiled neatly in two and a half foot loops. 'This is some kind of rope, but what is all this other stuff? Did you ever see anything like *this*? It looks like something out of a medieval war.'

'It's an ice hammer.'

He stared at her.

'All this stuff is for climbing.' She began pointing at things. 'That one in your hand is an ice hammer, these are crampons, these are karabiners, here are some pitons, these loops of flat material are slings, these are ... '

'Do you actually climb mountains?' He sounded horrified.

'No, but I had a friend who did. I tried it a few times and didn't like it much, but I learned a bit about it.'

Cutler picked up a white sling from the pile on the shelf and said, 'Tell me more about this.'

'What do you mean?'

'What is it made of? What is it used for?' He peered at the tag ends of nylon protruding from the knot. 'And what am I going to order when Holley buys me the best dinner in San Francisco?'

'What are you talking about?'

'See this?' He showed her the black ink on one end. 'It's a W isn't it? Wilson just marked it with his initial. Holley and I found one by a plane wreck which I'll tell you about in a few minutes and we assumed that it was an M, for Matheson. Hah! I *knew* that nobody walked out of there alone, I just knew it. Now, what is this thing.'

'It's called a sling. It's just a piece of one inch nylon webbing about five feet long. The two ends are tied together with a special knot that won't slip. Climbers use them for all kinds of things. Hanging things on, connecting ropes to pitons; they're just sort of general purpose things that people carry with them when they go climbing.'

'I see.' He told her how they had found the other sling and not known what it was. 'Now let's have a look at the rest of this stuff while I think about that dinner Holley is going to buy me.'

One by one they emptied and repacked the boxes. They contained clothing, sleeping bags, tents and camping equipment, ice-climbing equipment and odds and ends of rock-climbing gear.

'Nothing for us there. I wonder what's in that room?'
Cutler walked across the basement and tried the door. It
opened and he peered into the darkness, groped inside
and found a light switch.

'Well, well, well. Now we know how he paid the rent.'

It was a growing room. Wire mesh, pumps, plastic
plumbing, gravel beds, rows of lamps that could be raised
or lowered and a shelf at the far end that held jars of
fertilizers, jars of seeds, and a large germinating tray.

Behind him Valerie said, 'I don't understand.'

'It's a growing room with all the latest equipment for
the grow-your-own pot gardener.'

'He grew his own pot in here?'

Cutler snorted. 'His own? Do you know anything about
wet gravel hydroponics?'

'No.'

'Well if you know what you're doing you can get half a
pound from each plant. At least half a pound. And if you
know what you're doing you can duplicate just anything –
Columbian, Hawaiian, Californian Sinsemilla, anything at
all. If this guy was even moderately successful he could
have pulled five pounds out of here three or four or even
five times a year. That's as much as twenty-five pounds a
year and even if it wasn't great he'd be getting a minimum
of a thousand a pound for it. That's twenty-five grand a
year and no taxes. Minimum. And possibly over a hundred
thou if it was really first class.'

Fifteen minutes later he was on the telephone, holding
it carefully by the earpiece.

'Hi Rico, it's Andy. I'm at Wilson's house on West
Fourteenth. We need Ident down here ... No, no jack-
pot, but plenty just the same – bloodstains in the bedroom, a pot farm in the basement ... Yeah, that's right,
and about five pounds of pot in the deep freeze ... No
they're not fresh, but Holley told me that Matheson had a
bad cut on his head and most of the stains are on the
pillow and around the head area; *and* I've got something
that puts this guy Wilson at the site of the plane wreck ...

Right, if he wasn't dead, Holley would want to talk to him
real bad ... Yeah, I'll be here ... Okay, thanks, see you
tomorrow.'

He hung up the telephone and sat in the big armchair
hunched forward with his elbows on his knees and his face
in his hands. After almost a minute he looked up and said,
'What shift are you on?'

'Six to four.' She looked at her watch. 'In fact I'm due
off in about half an hour.'

'Christ, I don't know how you can handle those ten-
hour days.'

'Three-day weekends help a lot.'

'I suppose so.' He paused then said, 'I was going to
suggest supper, but if you've got to be at work by six in the
morning ...' He let the question hang.

She looked down at him. 'My next three day weekend
starts in twenty-five minutes.' There was heat in her eyes
and in her voice. 'What do you like to eat?'

CHAPTER TWENTY-SIX

San Francisco

HIS HEAD HURT. The headaches had almost disappeared
when Wilson's friend dropped the roof in on him. Now
they were back and getting worse. Maybe it was just
the tension getting to him, and when he resolved this
immediate problem the headaches would go away. He
decided to give it one more week and then see about
getting some serious medical attention.

At least Carl wouldn't bother him again. It had been a
distinct pleasure to arrange that. Walter Matheson was
not an exceptionally violent man, but the thought of Carl's
corpse floating in the bay gave him more relief from the

pain in his head than aspirin, and a pleasant sensation — kind of tingly — all over.

He didn't even need to justify it to himself. Carl was treacherous scum and had gotten exactly what he deserved.

He poured himself another drink and looked around the room. It was the only room in the house that was really his and his alone; and he had decorated it to his own taste. He liked everything about it from the rough cedar panelling on the walls to the view out the window, but nonetheless he was looking forward to the day when he could leave it, and the house, and the whole life he lived here, for the last time.

Two more shipments ... maybe even one really big one. ... If only Wilson hadn't gotten himself killed. ... Maybe Wilson's friend would change his mind if Walter explained how important this was ...

CHAPTER TWENTY-SEVEN

Vancouver

WHEN ANDY CUTLER got to work the next morning he found a large scrap of white paper on his desk with the words 'SEE ME' scrawled on it in bold black felt pen. The note was unsigned but he knew where it had come from.

'You wanted to see me, Rico?'

'Uhuh. Pour yourself a coffee and sit down, I've got big news for you. But first you tell me whether this Gordon Wilson business is something we're going to have to deal with here; and if it is, can you handle it yourself or will you need Popov?'

Cutler tasted his coffee and then sat down and lit a cigarette. 'I think we're probably going to have to do something about it. I'm not sure that it's going to get us much, but we should do *some* work; and no, I won't need Doug. Why? Is he sick?'

Hofstadter plundered Cutler's cigarette pack. 'No, he's fine, it's you that's sick.'

'Me?'

'Yup. You're about to come down with the same disease I've got.'

'Cerebral flatulence? Terminal insipidity? Middle-age spread?'

'Nah, those are just the symptoms. The disease is responsibility.'

'Responsibility?'

'Yeah. They're going to give you sergeant in a couple of weeks. I'm not supposed to tell you about it, but since it's obviously going to affect assignments for you and Popov you might as well know now. Just try to look surprised when you get the official word.'

'Will that mean I won't have to call you Sir and salute you anymore?'

'Hah!' Hofstadter snorted and lit his cigarette. 'What it means is that you'll have to start working for your paycheques again. However, the next two weeks will be something of a holiday – even by your standards – because I can't assign you to anything new, so you'll get to answer the telephone and sort a lot of paper.'

He dragged on the cigarette and continued, 'Now tell me about yesterday.'

'Wait a minute,' said Cutler. 'What's the story on this sergeant thing? Why now? I wasn't supposed to get bumped until sometime next year.' He had forgotten his coffee and smoke. '*I* know how good I am, and what a valuable contribution I make, but what woke them up upstairs? Why the sudden rush?'

'Because Al Ericson is resigning effective Christmas, and Stumpf, in Fraud, was in a bad MVA last week and is going to be off duty for at least six months, and we were already short two sergeants anyway, and the Board, with its limited vision, has decided that you are the one to take up the slack. Now tell me about yesterday. What did you find in that house and what do we have to do about it?'

They were well into their second cup of coffee when Cutler finished, '... so what I think is that Wilson probably helped Matheson out of the mountains and let him stay in the house on West Fourteenth – which, by the way, is only a couple of blocks from where Matheson did a lot of shopping on his credit cards. Anyway, Wilson may or may not have helped get the coke to San Francisco, I don't know about that, and then he went off on his holiday. Maybe he tried to blackmail Matheson, or maybe Matheson just decided to have him hit for insurance, but the main thing, from our point of view anyway, is that prior to all this he probably wasn't involved in anything more serious than growing and selling a little pot.'

Cutler finished the coffee and leaned back in his chair. 'But that's only probably, so we'll have to do a bit of work on this – talk to the neighbours, his employer, maybe track down some of his friends and see if anybody has any idea why he was in the area where the plane went down.'

'Any chance he could have been there to meet the plane?'

'Rico, you didn't see where that plane went down. No way an airplane could land anywhere near there. Even the helicopter couldn't land. We had to jump out while he hovered.'

Hofstadter pulled fresh cigarettes for both of them, but then put them back in the pack and rooted around in his desk. He produced a package of cigars and said, 'If you're going to get promoted we might as well celebrate.'

Once the cigars were drawing well Hofstadter said, 'So you think that this Wilson's being at the wreck was just coincidence?'

'I think so, but I'm not sure. He was a mountain climber and there are lots of mountains there, but on the other hand they may have been planning to drop the stuff to him and then fly back to Prince Rupert,' said Cutler. He drew on the cigar and exhaled a cloud of blue smoke. 'You know, I think I might even enjoy being a sergeant.' He puffed contentedly for a while and then said, 'I don't know much about mountain climbing, but I've heard that mountain climbers always go in pairs. If that's true then there may have been someone else there. If we can find out who it was then we may find the answers to all of these questions.'

'If whoever it was hasn't already been killed too.'

'Yes, there's that.'

'So what are you going to do about it?'

'Right now? Right now I'm going to go and talk to old Fred in Personnel to see if there's anyone on this police force who knows enough about mountain climbing to point me to someone who might know something about Wilson.'

Cutler stood up. 'So I'll get to work on that. Thanks for the cigar, and thanks for telling me about the promotion. If I'm finished at a reasonable hour I'll buy you a drink.'

'You mean you'll buy me a *couple* of drinks and try to pump me about your new assignment.'

'Yes,' said Cutler, and started for the door.

'And one other thing, Andy.'

'Yes?'

'This could be the last of the good weather and Angie and I will probably try and get one more barbecue in before the monsoons. Do you want to come over Saturday?'

'That would be nice.'

'Okay. Now, do I tell Angie to find a friend for you or will you bring Constable MacGregor?'

Andy Cutler blushed bright red and almost dropped his cigar. 'How did you know about that?'

'Sergeants know everything. You'll find out for yourself in two weeks. Now go and find a mountain climber who knows all about drug smuggling and murder.'

Constable Jamie Barr, when Cutler finally reached him on the telephone, said that he was strictly an amateur who liked to get out into the mountains whenever he could.

'Nothing too technical, just a snow plod now and then.'

'So you don't know anything about this Gordon Wilson?'

'No. If he's climbing in Yosemite valley then he's way out of my league, but I know someone who can probably help you. Got a pen handy?'

'Shoot.'

'Okay, the name is Goossens. G-O-O-S-S-E-N-S. Paul Goossens. He lives at three twenty-five East Twenty-third Avenue, and his number is 873-2509. He rents the top floor of a house there. He's a really good climber and he seems to know everybody in the climbing scene around here.'

'He's a friend of yours?'

'Yes, he is. He's too good for me to climb with, but we ski a lot together in the winter.'

'Do you know where he works? Or where I can reach him during the day?'

'As a matter of fact you can probably get him at home. I was talking to him last night and he said he was going to spend the day working on his house. I think he's trying to build a balcony outside his bedroom window.'

'He doesn't work?'

'Oh, now and again. He's a carpenter and general construction labourer when he feels like it. A lot of climbers are like that.'

'Well thanks for the information. I'll give him a call and see if I can drop over for a visit.'

'Okay, see you around.'

Cutler hung up and dialled Goossens' number. He let it ring a dozen times and then dialled again. Still no answer. He decided to go anyway. If this Goossens really was working on a balcony he might be outside, or off picking up some nails or whatever. Besides, he didn't have any other ideas and if Goossens wasn't there he could leave a message for him taped to the door.

Three twenty-five East Twenty-third was a big old three-storey frame house and Cutler could see someone on a ladder working outside a third floor window as he drove up. As he got closer he could see that it was a young man with a droopy moustache and brown hair flowing halfway down his back.

He parked the car and got out. Goossens, if that was who it was, paid no attention, did not seem to have noticed his arrival, and carried on hammering.

'Hello.'

No answer.

'Hello!' Louder. 'Paul Goossens?'

Still no answer. Was he deaf? Cutler put a tentative hand on the ladder. He hated ladders, but the young man seemed unable to hear, so . . .

As soon as he put his weight on the bottom rung the hammering stopped and curious eyes were staring down at him from behind medium thick lenses.

'Mr. Goossens?'

The young man removed a set of headphones that had been hidden in the long hair and said, 'Sorry, don't hear much of anything with these on. What did you say?'

'I'm looking for Paul Goossens.'

'Why?'

'I need some information about mountain climbing, and Jamie Barr said you might be able to help me.'

The morning sun glinted off the lenses of Goossens' wire frame glasses as he thought about what Cutler had said. 'You a friend of Jamie's?'

'Not really. I'm a co-worker.'

'You're with the police?'

'That's right.'

'And you want to get into climbing?'

'Not a chance. I don't even like stairs. But I want to talk about it if you can spare me a little time.'

'Okay. Just hang on a minute.' He disappeared through the window and a minute later emerged through the front door of the house, closing it behind him. He walked down the steps and offered Cutler a hand. 'I'm Paul Goossens.'

'Andy Cutler'. Goossens was just below middle height and dressed in faded, patched jeans and a faded blue T-shirt. The brown eyes behind the wire frames were openly curious as they looked Cutler over carefully. Goossens was in his mid-twenties and looked to Cutler as if he had just materialized from 1967 – a thin, muscular hippy.

'So you want to talk about climbing?'

'Mostly I want to find out about a man named Gordon Wilson. I understand that he was a mountain climber, and Jamie Barr said that you knew most of the mountain climbers around here.'

'Hmmmm. Have you got some ID?'

Cutler showed him his badge.

'You mind telling me what this is about?'

Cutler thought about that. Goossens had likely been a friend of Wilson's and probably knew all about the basement room. He would want to be protective and give as little to the police as possible. So . . .

'I want to find out why he was murdered.'

'WHAT??'

'He was found dead, shot in the chest, on Saturday morning. I want to find out who killed him.'

Goossens was stunned. The spring had gone out of his posture and he stood slumped, a beanbag man about to submit to gravity.

Cutler bored on. 'His murder is related to the fact that he's a mountain climber, and if I don't get some help from you there's a good chance that another mountain climber will be murdered.'

Goossens sat down on the front steps and said nothing. Cutler looked down at him for a while, then knelt so that their eyes were on the same level. 'Look at me, Paul.'

Goossens looked up and Cutler said, 'I'm a cop. I know all about the pot farm in your friend's basement, but I don't give a shit about that. For all I know you've got a pot farm in *your* basement, but I don't give a shit about that either. What I care about is that there may be somebody, maybe another friend of yours, who is going to be murdered very soon unless I get some help and information.'

The eyes behind the glasses were far away. 'I thought he was in the Valley.'

'Where?'

'Yosemite. In California.'

'That's where he was found, in a deserted parking lot by a power substation.'

'Oh Christ.' Paul Goossens stood up. 'How can I help?'

'The Lancelot?'

'C'mon Rico, if I'm buying, then I get to pick the bar.'

'But why a cesspool like the Lancelot?'

'Because I've got some business to do there later tonight and I want to check the place out.'

'Oh, all right, all right.'

The Hotel Lancelot is on Main Street, just north of the Canadian National Railway station and on the fringes of Vancouver's Skid Row. It is small and poorly cared for. End of the line shelter for end of the line people.

'The mountain climbing club meets here? In this dump?'

'It's not really a club and they don't actually call themselves *mountain* climbers, just climbers.'

'Fascinating.'

'Now Rico, relax. We don't have to stay here, I just wanted to get a look at the place.'

'Great. So now you've seen it and we can go somewhere civilized.' Hofstadter looked around. 'Unless you want to check around a bit more and make sure that this is really the bar – that we haven't wandered in to the men's room by mistake.'

They left, but Cutler was back at 8:30 p.m. that evening. He was dressed in jeans and a loose wool sweater over an old work shirt. Goossens had told him that there were half a dozen regulars, climbers who showed up virtually every Wednesday, and another dozen or so irregulars, any of whom might show up on a given night.

'Most of them know Gord, and somebody's bound to know who he was down there with. Just don't expect to see anyone much before 9:30 p.m.'

He took a table near the corner where Goossens told him they usually sat, and stretched a glass of beer and a newspaper over half an hour. The bar was quiet. A few old men nursing beer and memories, and four greasy pool players shooting hi-low for drinks. Not a woman in the place and ninety percent of the tables vacant.

The climbers began drifting in just after 9:00 p.m. and by 9:45 p.m. there were eight of them around three small tables pulled together. They ranged in age from just over twenty to just over forty and most of them wore blue jeans and old shirts with either wool sweaters or zip-front jackets in some kind of furry pile. They laughed a lot without seeming to drink very much, and they all looked healthy and fit.

Their conversations were fast and lively and, aside from a bit of talk about the economy, not much of it made sense to Cutler, eavesdropping from behind his newspaper.

'... crampons? No we didn't have any, just EBs and one tool each and it had hardened up pretty good overnight, but it was suncupped so we managed okay till we got to the foot of the buttress ... What? No, mine is the Molson's, I wouldn't drink what they've got on tap here. Anyway, we soloed up a few hundred feet of easy fifth and then it got steep so we got out the rope and after that it was great; mostly five-eight, five-nine with a bit of ten and a *great* bivvy ledge half way up ...'

Or:

'... but it's all psychological – no one really needs it up here.'

'Oh yeah? Go and hang out on Crime of the Century on a hot day. See if your hands don't sweat.'

'Maybe, but it's still psychological. I mean maybe it's true that there are some routes that won't go on some days without chalk, but the people who use it use it all the time.

Look at John there. He even chalks up to belay. He probably chalks up to piss . . .'

Or:

'. . . so what's left for us? The frontier, the cutting edge, is over in the fuckin' Himalaya, and who can afford to go there? Sure there's lots of new routes to do here, but they're just more of the same. What can we do here that wasn't done in Europe twenty years ago?'

'Waterfalls. We've got waterfalls here like nowhere else. Nobody in Europe or the States is doing anything like Polar Circus. Not unless they come here that is. And what about Slipstream and Aggressive Treatment? Or what about anything in Alaska in the winter?'

'Yeah, I suppose. Paul was up there last winter. He didn't climb anything technical, just skied for three weeks and checked out a lot of possibilities. He said he was going to go back this winter in February to try something, but I'm not sure exactly what.'

'Hey, speak of the Devil. There's Paul now.'

'So it is. Doesn't look too stable though, does he.'

Paul Goossens was walking slowly toward the group at the tables. He was unsteady on his feet and Cutler thought he had probably hit the bottle fairly hard that afternoon. He stopped beside Cutler's table and said, 'Guess I might as well introduce you, huh?'

Cutler stood up and followed the younger man.

'This is Andy.' Everyone was looking up at them. Goossens was obviously drunk. 'This is Eric, Bernie, John, Doug, other John, Al and Peter.' His arm waved vaguely around the circle as he gave the names. Then he pointed to a skinny youth of about twenty-one on the far side of the table. 'And I don't know who that is.' He fell into an empty chair and said to no one in particular, 'Andy wants to talk to us.'

'Hello?'

'Hello Lieutenant, it's Andy Cutler calling from Vancouver.'

'Ah, Mister Cutler. Nice to hear from you.'

'Yeah, well, I'm sorry to bother you at this time of night but I've got something that you're probably going to want to move on right away.'

'And what might that be?'

'You got a pen and paper handy?'

'Yes.'

'Okay. You remember the name Alex Townsend?'

There was silence for a few seconds, then Holley said, 'He was the friend of Wilson's who had been climbing with him before he was killed.'

'That's right. You want him real bad.'

'Why is that?'

'Because he either killed Wilson, or he's about to be killed himself.' Cutler paused for a moment as a new thought struck him. 'Or possibly both. In any case I think he knows all about Walter Matheson.'

'That would be nice.'

'But he also seems to have been Wilson's closest friend and the two of them may have carried the cocaine across for Matheson, so he may not be cooperative.'

'Perhaps not at first.'

There was silence on the wire after that, then Holley spoke again. 'What exactly have you got?'

'I'll tell you in a minute, but first have you still got that white loop that we found in the snow by the wreck?'

'Not here in my bedroom, but yes, I've got it downtown.'

'Well you hang on to it, Lieutenant, because it's the sling in which you are going to hang Matheson's ass.'

'Mister Cutler, are you sober?'

'No, Lieutenant, I'm not. I just made sergeant today, and I think I'm falling in love, so no, I'm not sober.'

'Congratulations.'

'Thanks. Actually, I've been in love before, in fact I fall in love pretty often, but I've never been promoted to sergeant before, so I thought I might celebrate. Anyway, you'll only have to listen to me babble for a couple of minutes. I'll telex all this stuff down to you in the morning, but here's what I've got ...'

Later that night, as he was on the edge of sleep, he suddenly remembered that Hofstadter had evaded his question.

'Val.'

'Mmmm.'

'How did Rico know about us?'

'Who?'

'Us. You and me.'

'No, who knew?'

'Rico. He invited us to a barbecue this weekend. I only met you yesterday and he knew about it this morning.'

'Who's Rico.'

'Hofstadter. Rick Hofstadter. My sergeant.'

'Oh, him. Isn't he nice? He's so cute sometimes.'

'No. No he isn't. But even if he is, how did he know?'

'He talked to me on the phone this morning.'

'He phoned you? How did he know you were here?'

'He didn't. Actually he wanted to talk to you but you were already gone. He just recognized my voice.'

'He just recognized your voice?'

'Sure. I worked for him for a couple of months about two years ago.'

'In Drugs?'

'Sure. I mostly just hung around in bars and listened to people talk. It wasn't as exciting as it is on TV.'

'So why didn't I meet you?'

'Were you hanging around in bars a lot?'

'No. Well sometimes. Are you sure it wasn't just over three years ago?'

'No.'

'No, it wasn't; or no, you're not sure?'

'No, I don't want to talk about it any more.'

'It's just that if it was three years ago I did a six-month shift in Major Crimes, so that would mmmmm. Ah. Yes. I think I rrrghhhh ...'

CHAPTER TWENTY-EIGHT

Interstate-5

LINDA WAS DRIVING – had been driving all day as they cruised steadily north on I-5. Alex had bought a bottle of Christian Brothers brandy in some town they passed through before noon and now it was two thirds gone.

'Where'r we?'

'About thirty or forty miles from Eugene.'

''S'great town. Ec'logical cap'tal 'f the world.'

'What?'

'Great town. Compulsory gelding f'r cars 'n' trucks, 'n' everybody runs five miles 'fore breakfas'.'

'Alex, what are you talking about?'

'Eu-gene, Ore. Kids grow up big 'n' strong 'cause they all get four ounces 'f milk 'n' a bowl of sugar-free eco-pops f'r breakfast.' He stopped talking and held the brandy bottle up so that he could look through it at the road ahead, but he didn't drink.

'Wanna see some llamas?'

'What?'

'Llamas. Beautiful animals. Turn right at Eugene 'n' drive over the mountains. 'S about, a hunnerd miles.'

'Alex, the only llamas round here are in that bottle.'

'Nope. Whole herd of llamas. Whole fuckin' llama ranch jus' over the mountains. At Sisters.'

'Sisters?'

'Town call Sisters. Stupid name. We c'n camp at the pass. Nice campsite there, 'n' you can take llama pictures.'

By the time they reached Eugene Alex had fallen asleep. Linda looked at the map, and found that there was a town called Sisters just over a hundred miles east. Did she really want to photograph llamas? *Were* there any llamas? Then something on the map caught her attention. Lava beds. The llamas probably existed only in Alex's mind, but the McKenzie lava beds sounded interesting, and if it took them out of their way, well, what difference?

God knew she could use a day or two in limbo, and it wouldn't hurt Alex to spend a day or two drying out and getting his mind clear before they reached Seattle. She knew that eventually the police were going to want to talk to them again, and that they had better have their story straight when the man came knocking at their door.

CHAPTER TWENTY-NINE

Vancouver

WHEN THE SWITCHBOARD told him that Lieutenant Holley was calling from San Francisco P.D. Cutler thought about answering the phone with, 'I thought I told you never to call me at work', but decided Holley wouldn't be amused; so he settled for 'Hello Lieutenant.'

Holley didn't even say hello, just went straight to it. 'Mr. Cutler, I'm going to see Alex Townsend in Seattle tomorrow and I'd like you to be there.'

Cutler was glad that he hadn't tried to be funny. He said, 'What have you got?'

'Right now I've got the square root of sweet fuck all, and I'm not very pleased about it. I talked to the trooper who ran the investigation in Yosemite and do you know what he told me?' Holley's voice was rising. 'He told me there was, "No way this Townsend could be involved". Not only was he on the way to San Francisco when it happened, he actually cried about his buddy's death – "Saw it with my own eyes, he was really broken up" – what a bunch of shit. If that moron was on this force I'd see that he got traffic control and rock concerts for the rest of his life.'

'You check any of this for yourself?' asked Cutler.

'Of course I did. Wilson, Townsend and some woman had supper in a restaurant in the park. The waiter is some kind of climbing groupie and he remembers them very clearly. The woman, who seems to be Townsend's girl-friend, left about 9 o'clock and Carl Adams – the short prick that I saw meeting Matheson last spring – came in a little while later.

'He talked to Wilson and Townsend for a few minutes and then he and Wilson left. Townsend left a couple of minutes later. This waiter wanted to talk to him, but Townsend said he and his girlfriend were leaving the park right away.

'They showed up at a hotel here in San Francisco about 4:30 a.m. the next morning; and that, and some tears, is why Townsend couldn't *possibly* have been involved. Jesus.' Holley's voice was filled with disgust.

'Where did the killings take place, and how long does it take to drive from this park to San Francisco?'

'The bodies were found about three and a half miles from the restaurant and the drive only takes five hours. Less if you push it a bit.'

Cutler did a bit of arithmetic and then asked 'Do you have any idea of the time of the deaths?'

'Sure. Sometime between the last time they were seen alive and the first time they were seen dead.'

'One of those, eh?'

'One of those,' Holley answered, and then said, 'And if I didn't get much there, I got even less when I went out to the park and tried to talk to some of the climbers there. Nobody knows anything.'

'Nobody *knows* anything, or nobody's *saying* anything?'

'Nobody knows.'

'You're sure of that?'

Holley's reply was angry and loud. 'Nobody lies to me. Nobody.' Then he calmed down and said, 'I mean, everybody lies, but nobody fools me about it.' He stopped again, then continued, 'I don't think anybody did know

anything. Wilson and Townsend and Townsend's woman
were there for a little over a month. Quite a few people
knew them, but the problem is that these climbers have a
pretty transient, day-to-day life there, and nobody seems
to have known them very *well* . . .'

'What's the story on this girlfriend?' interrupted Cutler.

'Her name is Linda Cunningham, she's white, in her
late twenties, is kind of thin, and has blondish hair. In
other words, I don't know anything more about her than I
do about anything else, so I'm just going to have to have a
little face to face chat with Alex Townsend.'

Cutler reached for a cigarette but found his pack empty.
He tucked the telephone against his shoulder and began
searching his desktop and then all the drawers. He spoke
as he hunted. 'You've had him picked up in Seattle?'

'Not picked up, no,' replied Holley 'I got on to Seattle
this morning and I've just heard back from them now.
Townsend is at his home address and the Seattle Police
are willing to watch him until we get there. They'll haul
him in if he tries to leave town but otherwise just watch
him. I want to come on to him cold so he doesn't have any
time to set up.'

Cutler's search was unproductive and he said, 'Can you
hang on, Lieutenant? I'll be back in a minute or so.'

'Sure. Or do you want me to call back?'

'No, this'll only take a minute.' He had seen a cigarette
pack on a vacant desk nearby and he walked over and
looked into it. There were three left and he took them all,
lighting one on the way back to his own desk.

'So, you want me in on this?'

'If you can make it.' Holley paused, and Cutler was
about to ask why when Holley spoke again. 'There are
several reasons for that. One is that you people are
working on this anyway and you may have some questions
you'd like to ask him yourself; the second is that I'll want
somebody along both as a witness and as a backup. I could
probably get a Seattle uniform for that, but I'd rather have
someone who knows something about this business and

you're the only one who does; and third, well, the third thing is that you may be able to get something out of him that I can't.'

Cutler couldn't imagine anyone withholding something that Holley really wanted. 'I doubt that, Lieutenant.'

'No, I'm serious. I had our people do some checking on this Townsend. Before he moved to Seattle he was pulling over a hundred thousand a year as a consulting systems analyst *and* he had family connections good enough that he could pretty well have written his own ticket. Then one day he divorced his wife and gave her every cent he had, and a month later he was working in a garage in Seattle. I don't know the story behind all this, but the bottom line is that he's probably smart enough to yell for a lawyer the minute I lean on him, and with the family he's got that would likely be the last time I see him. Sure, sure, if he's involved we'll get to him eventually, but not until long after the people I really want have had time to either cover themselves or disappear.'

Cutler didn't understand. 'And you think I'd do any better than you? I've got zero authority in Seattle. He doesn't even need a lawyer to tell *me* to get stuffed; and as for backing you up, I don't have the right to carry a gun outside the city of Vancouver, let alone in another country.'

'Don't worry about that, I'll get that fixed; but that's not too important anyway, the important thing is that you are a sympathetic and reasonable sort of person and I'm not. I've got a temper you wouldn't believe and I can't afford to screw this one up. Townsend is just about the only lead I've got left and if it turns out that sympathy and under-standing is the way to get him talking ... well, I'm not very good at that.'

Cutler put his cigarette down and said, 'And you think I am?'

'Yes. And you're also a whole lot brighter than you appear, which may be an advantage here; and you're white, which may also be important. Now, will you do it?'

CHAPTER THIRTY

San Francisco

WERE THE HEADACHES getting worse? Sometimes he thought they were, and sometimes he wasn't sure; but he was sure now that he wasn't going to go to any more doctors about it. The last one had wanted to do a CAT scan. To hell with that. Nobody was going to look inside *his* head. Besides, the headaches would stop as soon as he was out of the country. That was obvious, but he couldn't tell them that.

He poured another glass of Scotch and leaned back in his chair. Damn that Wilson for dying. Damn, damn, damnation. One more big shipment would do it. Just one more, and now Wilson was dead.

Kiniski dead, Wilson dead, Carl dead. The world around him was full of dead people who would have helped him if they were alive. Except Carl. Good riddance to Carl.

But at least they couldn't get him into trouble if they were dead. That was one good thing. But it would have been better if Wilson could have made one more carry before getting himself shot. Instead of leaving him with the biggest shipment of his life all ready to go and no way to bring it in.

Shit.

He would have brought it in himself if that black bastard policeman hadn't caught on. That would have been the best way to end it, bringing in the last lot himself. Look the border guard straight in the eye and just *will* him to pass the car unchecked. It was just a matter of having the right kind of dominant personality. But not with them watching his every move.

He drank off the whisky and poured a refill.

Sometimes he thought he knew who was watching him

but it was hard to be sure. There were a lot of blacks in the Bay Area and he couldn't always tell which of them was working for that arrogant bastard that had been so snotty with him. Right in his own house.

He drank some more and stared angrily around the room. It was his favourite place, this room, but he didn't like it any more. The sooner he was in Lima the better.

Why couldn't it have been that cop instead of Wilson? For that matter why couldn't Wilson's friend have been shot instead of Wilson? Wilson would have helped, but he had been shot; his friend wouldn't help and he got away. Where was the justice in that?

Still, the friend hadn't seemed too bad a fellow. Maybe if it was explained to him just how important this shipment was he would realize that he should do his share of the work.

Walter Matheson finished his drink and smiled slowly at the panelled walls of his study. That's what he would do. The friend's name was Alex something, and he lived in Seattle – he had overheard that much when they thought he was unconscious. It shouldn't be too hard to find him. His name might even be in the newspaper coverage of the murders in Yosemite. And once he knew where to find friend Alex he would just have to slip away from all the blacks who were watching him and take a quick flight to Seattle.

CHAPTER THIRTY-ONE

Seattle

THEY AWOKE SLOWLY, a little at a time, snuggling into each other's arms and in no hurry to leave the warmth of the bed. After a while Linda spoke.

'You're a nice man, Alex, but you've got shitty taste in housing.'

'It is pretty ugly isn't it?'

'It's worse than ugly. How did you manage to live here so long?'

'I don't know.' Linda rolled onto her side, facing away and Alex nestled behind her, spoon fashion. 'I guess I never noticed how bad it was.' His hand was on her breast and he could feel her nipple stiffening as he rolled it between thumb and forefinger. 'I'm glad we're moving,' he said. 'It's actually kind of exciting – the thought of going house hunting with you.'

'Exciting is it? Is that why you're poking into me?' She reached back between them to where Alex's erection was fighting for room to grow. 'I was hoping that it was just me that was exciting you.'

Alex let his hand slide down over her abdomen and onto her pubic mound, tangling his fingers in the coarse hair. She pushed against his hand and parted her legs slightly, letting first one and then two fingers slip into her vagina, and then back out to massage her gently. He nibbled at her earlobe and whispered, 'The spirit is more than willing, but the flesh has to pee.'

He disentangled himself from her and from the bedding and as he left the room he heard her mutter, 'Men!'

As he stood in front of the toilet waiting to detumesce he thought of one of Gordon's favourite jokes: 'The epitome of torque is waking up with an erection so intense that when you push it down to piss, your heels lift.'

The thought of Gordon had come unbidden into his mind and he was surprised to realize that while he was still sad about his friend's death, and frightened by the memory of that night, that at least he was able to maintain control, to think of the now and the future, as well as the then. Perhaps time *would* heal his wounds.

If he was given any time.

Later, as he and Linda floated in post-coital trance she

said, 'Alex, I think we should look for a new place this morning.'

'Mmm?'

'The sooner we're out of here the safer we'll be.'

'I suppose so, but I really don't think anyone's going to come looking for us. Matheson just didn't seem interested in me at all. And besides, he doesn't even know my name; how would he find me?'

'How did that Carl person find you?' Linda rolled him off and sat up, letting the covers fall to her waist. 'If he wants to find you he'll find you. Enough people know your name and know that you're from Seattle that it wouldn't take that much work for him to track you down; but if we get a new place in my name, and not in Seattle, or at least not in Seattle proper, then we'll be a lot safer.'

She looked down at him lying on his back with his eyes half shut. 'Are you listening?'

'Yes.' His eyes opened and he stared at the ceiling. The plaster was cracked and stained and needed painting. 'Yes, I'm listening. You don't have to convince me again, I'm just as interested in being safe as you are. And this place is such a dump that I'd want to move anyway.' The whole apartment was cracked and stained and in need of paint. How *could* he have lived here? 'But we don't have to go looking for a few minutes yet.' He reached up for her.

'Nope.' She threw the covers off and jumped around so that she was straddling him; half kneeling, half sitting on his stomach. 'Up and at 'em, soldier. We've got a lot to do today.' A cascade of blonde hair engulfed him as she leaned down for a kiss. 'Why don't you start some coffee while I go to the bathroom and then we ...'

Four sharp knocks resounded from the door. 'Who can that be? It's not even nine o'clock.'

Alex lifted her off and rolled out of bed. 'I don't know. There's a guy downstairs who sometimes comes up for coffee in the morning, it's probably him.' He was pulling on sweatpants and T-shirt. 'Get dressed as fast as you can

. . . ,' he threw yesterday's clothes from the dresser where she had left them, '. . . then open the window and get ready to jump. It's only about eight feet to the ground.' There was more knocking at the door. 'I'll look through the peephole and if it's anybody I don't know I think we should run for it.'

He walked as softly as he could across the living room and put an eye to the spyglass, then straightened up and unlocked the door and opened it to the two inches that the safety chain allowed. 'Yes?'

When he returned to the bedroom Linda was standing to one side of the open window. He said to her, 'It's all right, it's the police. They say they want to talk about Gordon's murder.'

He stripped off his sweatsuit and put on grey wool pants, a white shirt with a very faint pattern of small blue squares, grey socks and black slip-ons. As he buckled a narrow black belt Linda whispered, 'What kind of police are they?'

'What do you mean?'

'Are they wearing uniforms? Are they detectives? Are they Seattle police?'

'There's one in a Seattle uniform and two in suits. One of them is from San Francisco and the other from Vancouver. I guess they're detectives.'

'Well, we knew this was going to happen.' Linda began undressing. 'I'm going to put on clean clothes and go to the bathroom and then I'll join you.' She kissed him and then turned to her suitcase.

CHAPTER THIRTY-TWO

Seattle

IT STARTED OFF in a very low key. The uniformed Seattle patrolman accepted Linda's offer of coffee and sat quietly by himself in the living room. The other two both said 'No thank you' and sat at the table in the kitchen/dining room which was really the only place in the apartment that four people could sit in face to face conversation. The big black in the three-piece suit started off by introducing the other man, 'This is Sergeant Cutler of the Vancouver Police.'

The rumpled blond man with an engaging smile nodded to Linda and offered a hand to Alex across the table, but didn't say anything. Alex thought he looked tired, as if the trip to Seattle had taken him three days rather than three hours.

Holley turned to Linda and continued, 'And I am Lieutenant Holley from the San Francisco police. As I explained to Mister Townsend, Sergeant Cutler and I are both working on the murder of Gordon Wilson in Yosemite Park last week and we'd like to ask you a few questions.'

Linda looked at Alex, then back at the policeman and said, 'Yes of course, anything we can do to help.'

'Good,' said Holley. 'Now as I understand it you people knew Wilson for about four or five years, is that correct?'

Alex answered, 'I've known him for that long, but Linda only met him this summer, just before he was ... before the murder.' He could feel his heartbeat starting to pick up and the first drops of sweat forming in his armpits, but his voice sounded steady.

Holley pulled out a leatherbound notebook and a gold pen and made a quick note, then said to Alex, 'How well did you know him?'

'Pretty well, I guess. He lived in Vancouver and I didn't

see him every day or anything like that, but I knew him fairly well.'

'About how often *did* you see him?'

Alex thought about that. 'It varied. I'd go climbing with him for two or three days and then maybe not see him for a month. I suppose that on average I saw him for maybe three days a month – more often in the summer but less in the winter.' He thought about it. How often *had* he seen Gordon? He'd never kept track. Looking back over the last few years it seemed that they had spent a lot of time together, but it was almost always climbing and that magnified it out of proportion.

'But this summer you spent two months with him in California?'

'Sorry?' Alex had been lost in the past and didn't catch the question.

'You said that you would spend two or three days together once in a while, but the officer who interviewed you in Yosemite Park says that you told him that you had both been there for two months. Had you ever spent a long period with him before?'

'Oh, I see. Sure. We went to Alaska a couple of times, and to the Yukon Territory in Canada once – those were all for over a month. And we went to the valley, to Yosemite that is, last year and the year before for about ten days each time.'

Holley digested this information and then said, 'These trips were what? Holidays? Business?'

'They were climbing trips. We climbed mountains together.'

'Just the two of you?'

'Sometimes we'd go by ourselves but a lot of times we'd go with a few other people.'

Nobody spoke for a while, then Holley said, 'Tell me about Wilson.'

'What about him?'

'What was he like? You probably knew him as well as anyone.'

'He was really nice. A nice guy, everybody who knew
him liked him. He wasn't anything special, I mean he
wasn't ever going to be Mayor of Vancouver, or a TV star
or anything, he just worked and lived like everybody else;
but he was ... he was ...'

Alex was starting to lose control. He had never realized
what Gordon meant to him until after his death. He
squeezed his hands into fists beneath the table and tried to
carry on: '... He was just a good person. He was pleasant,
bright, good to talk to ... you know what I mean.'

Holley looked at him coldly. 'I know what you're trying
to say, and Sergeant Cutler has talked to a few people who
knew him in Vancouver and they all say the same thing –
that Wilson was just an ordinary guy, that everybody liked
him, that he was a really fine fellow. But ...' He tapped
the table with his forefinger for emphasis and repeated,
'BUT, either they're all wrong or I'm misunderstanding
something.'

He tapped the table again. 'You see, from where I
stand, this Wilson doesn't look anything like ordinary.
Ordinary guys have jobs that they go to every day, and
Wilson seems to have spent most of his time climbing
mountains, and yet he could somehow afford the mortgage on a nice little house. Ordinary guys don't look like
leftover hippies. Ordinary guys don't spend four days
hanging on rockfaces. Ordinary guys don't have pot farms
in their basements. Ordinary guys don't have business
arrangements with criminal scum like Carl Adams; and
finally, ordinary guys aren't found dead alongside sadistic
young trash like Robbie Hepburn.'

Holley's voice was rising and the words stung like
whips. Alex could feel the sweat soaking his shirt. He
didn't know what to do or say. Holley stared at him and
said very quietly, 'Let's get something straight here.
Gordon Wilson was no ordinary guy. He was involved
with some really ugly people, doing ugly things, and he
paid for it with his life. Now, tell me about him.'

Alex couldn't speak. He was wringing his hands together

under the table and his heart was hammering in his chest.
Hammering so hard it hurt him. He brought his arms up
and rested his elbows on the table, but couldn't stay still,
and had to put them down in his lap again. Holley's eyes
burned into him and he felt an overwhelming desire to
either run away from the house or tell everything he
knew.

'I think you *are* misunderstanding something, Lieutenant.' All their heads turned in surprise when Linda spoke.
'I don't know anything about these criminals you say
Gordon was dealing with. I'm sure that that's some kind
of horrible mistake – they must have thought he was
someone else – I just don't believe that he would be
involved with people like that, he was too nice a person.'

'But all those other things, the things you were talking
about, that no ordinary person would be like that; well
that's just because you probably don't know anything
about climbers. I didn't either until a couple of years ago,
but a lot of them are like that. They work part time and
they go off for weeks or months on their climbs. I've come
to know some fairly well and they aren't *really* very
different. It just seems that way if you aren't involved in
climbing yourself. I mean, look at Alex here – he's been
working full time at the same place for several years and
when he wants to go on a long climbing trip he just
arranges to take some time off without pay.'

She put her hand over Alex's and said, 'I went to
Yosemite more as a tourist than anything else and met
Alex and Gordon there. They took me climbing and
introduced me to some of their climbing friends and, well
it *is* a different kind of life, but they're not criminals just
because they don't have a nine-to-five job like you do.'

She sounded sincere and slightly angry and Alex was
thankful for her interruption. He cleared his throat and
brought Holley's attention back to him. He spoke, and
hoped that his voice would not give him away. 'Gordon
told me that he sold some marijuana that he grew. I don't
know if that makes him a criminal in Canada or not, but I

just don't believe that any of the other things you're
implying are true. The only thing I can think of is that
maybe the man who came to the restaurant wanted to buy
some marijuana from him, or sell some to him, but why
would they kill him for that?'

'You'd never seen him before?'

'No, never.' That, at least, was the truth.

'And you don't know where they were going?'

'No.'

'Okay, let's just go through it one step at a time. You
first met Wilson when?' Holley and the detective from
Vancouver both had their notebooks on the table and
their pens poised.

'About five years ago.'

'How did you meet him?'

Alex was back on comfortable ground and he answered
without hesitation. 'I had been climbing for a couple of
years and I heard that there was a good place to climb just
north of Vancouver, so I went up there for a look and just
ran into him.'

'Okay, and after that you started to go mountain
climbing with him at irregular intervals. Sometimes just
for a day or two and sometimes for more than a month, is
that right?'

'Yes.'

'And when did you find out he was a drug dealer?'

'I didn't ... That is I ... He ...'

Alex was starting to come apart again when Linda
interrupted, 'Just what are you trying to do here?' Holley
swung around to her and opened his mouth to reply but
she cut him off, 'Are you looking for whoever killed
Gordon or are you just here to badger us about not
reporting something that for all we know isn't even a
crime in Canada?'

Holley looked like he was going to explode, but the
Canadian detective spoke first. 'We're looking for whoever killed your friend, but we've got a problem.' His tone
was mild. 'You see almost all murders are committed by

family or friends. But Wilson didn't seem to have any close family, or none that we could find, he didn't have any current lover or girlfriend, and everyone who knew him says he was the world's nicest guy, and that he never quarrelled with anyone.'

He looked from Alex to Linda and back again. 'So if it wasn't family or friends, what was it? Virtually all other murders are either holdups, kidnappings or rapes that get out of hand; or just random psychotic violence. That doesn't seem to be the case here either, though, and that leaves only one possibility. The few murders that don't fit either of those categories almost all involve people in highly organized crime, and on the evidence we have it's fairly clear that your friend's death falls into that category.'

He sounded sincere and almost sympathetic, with none of the primitive animal power that radiated from Holley. 'Alex, you yourself told the officer who interviewed you in the park that Wilson recognized Carl Adams, the man who came into the restaurant. You said something to the effect that Wilson told you that he had some business to talk over with Adams, and believe me, Adams is a well-known part of the criminal underworld in San Francisco; and the man whose body was found with Wilson's was also a known criminal and an associate of Adams. They both dealt in drugs and so did your friend ...'

Cutler spread his hands and shrugged, as if to say, 'what else *can* we think?'

Lieutenant Holley had calmed down enough to speak in a normal tone and he took up his interrogation once again.

'Let's just talk about what happened before the murder then.' He looked at Alex. 'You and Wilson had been in Yosemite how long?'

'Uh, about a month and a half I think, maybe two months.' Alex had calmed down too and he felt some of his self-control returning.

'You arrived there when?'

'I don't know the exact day. It was at the end of August.

There was a full moon that night so you could look at a calendar and find out for sure, but it was sometime around the twenty-ninth or thirtieth.'

Both officers made a note and Holley continued. 'And between then and the night of the killings you didn't see Carl Adams at all?'

'The only time I *ever* saw him was in the restaurant. He came in and sat down, and Gord said that they should go somewhere else. I never saw him before that.'

'Wilson didn't introduce you? Didn't say where they were going? Or why?'

'No.' Alex was sweating again.

'Don't you think that's strange? If you're having dinner with a friend and someone you know comes to the table do you just walk away with no explanations at all?' Holley was relentless.

'No. I mean ...' Alex was in trouble. 'I mean no I wouldn't do that, but I just assumed Gord was going to buy some pot from him.'

They had known that question would be asked and they had agreed that a minor dope deal was the best answer. 'I don't *know* that that's what it was, it just seemed ... well, what else could it be?'

The two policemen looked at each other and then back at Alex. Holley spoke. 'That's what we'd like you to tell us.'

They waited. Implacable, patient, exuding inevitability. Alex was helpless. Squirming.

'Is there anything else you'd like to ask us?' Linda came to his rescue. 'We were planning to go out for breakfast this morning and ...' She let that statement dangle and Holley looked at her with some irritation.

'Okay, let me ask *you* a couple of things. How did you meet Wilson?'

'I already told you that. I came to California on a holiday. I met Alex', she nodded toward him, 'by chance. He was rock-climbing, I was rock-climbing, and we just ran into one another. We spent a lot of time together after that and I met Gordon through Alex.'

'And you never had any idea that he might have been involved in anything more serious than selling the odd bag of dope, right?' The sarcasm was heavy and obvious.

'Lieutenant, I didn't even know he did *that*, and I don't like the tone of your questions. If you can't conduct yourself any better than you have so far ...' She was looking straight at him and she stood up from the table as she spoke, '... then I think you'd better leave.'

Her face had darkened and her voice was rising. Holley started to reply but she shouted him down. 'Our friend was killed and all you've done so far is sit there and accuse him of being some kind of criminal.' Her voice came back down. 'Well that's a bunch of shit. If you want to ask questions that are going to help find whoever killed him, fine; but we've already told you about three times that we don't believe he was doing anything wrong.'

She stood with her fists on her hips, glaring at him.

Holley put his hands up in surrender and said, 'Okay, okay, I'm sorry if I offended you. Just simmer down and I'll try again. Okay?'

For a moment she said nothing, just kept on staring at him, and Alex thought that she was going to lose her temper completely.

'Miss Cunningham?' It was Cutler, his voice calm and quiet. 'I know this isn't easy for you, for either of you, but we'd like to ask just a few more questions. It won't take long, and then you can go and get some breakfast.'

He looked at her enquiringly, and finally she sat down and said, 'All right, but if there's any more of that "How long did you know he was a drug dealer" bullshit then you can ask the rest of your questions to our lawyer.'

They were all silent for a time, then Cutler turned to Alex and said, 'According to the trooper who talked to you in Yosemite, you and your friend had been on a long rock-climb for a couple of days, is that right?'

'Yes. For about four days.'

'And when you finished that you met Miss Cunningham and the three of you went for supper at the restaurant.

Why don't you just tell us about that evening in your own words. If we have any questions, we can ask them when you're done, all right?'

Sergeant Cutler seemed friendly and relaxed and Alex felt much more comfortable talking to him than to Lieutenant Holley. 'There's really nothing to tell you. We climbed a route on El Capitan. It took us about three and a half days and when we got down we met Linda at our campsite. Gord and I had a shower and then we all went to the Four Seasons for supper.'

'What time would that have been?' asked Cutler.

'I don't know exactly, probably around seven or so.' Alex looked to Linda, 'About seven?'

'Something like that.'

'Anyway, it was sometime around seven. We had supper, and sometime around eight-thirty or nine Linda said that she was going to go back to the tent. We had decided to go to San Francisco for a few days and she was going to get everything packed.'

Alex looked quickly at Holley to see how this lie was being received, but Holley just looked back at him expressionlessly.

'I stayed in the restaurant with Gord for another drink and to talk some more about the climb, and about twenty minutes or half an hour later – just as we were about to leave – the man you call Carl Adams came in.'

He was trying to stay calm, and he found that as long as he didn't look at Holley he felt much better. He shifted in his chair so that he was facing more toward the Sergeant from Vancouver and carried on with his lie.

'I really don't remember what he said. We'd had quite a lot to drink and I was still really high from the climb. All I remember is that he was a sort of middle-size, middle-age black man with a scarred up face; and that Gord said that they had some business to do.'

He looked at Holley and said, 'We were about to leave anyway, so it didn't seem very strange that Gord would go somewhere with somebody else.' He turned back to

Cutler. 'They left, and I sat there for another couple of minutes. I would have left right away except that the waiter wanted to talk to me about climbing. But I was only in the restaurant for a few minutes and then I went back to the tent and Linda and I left for San Francisco.'

Silence. Broken finally by Linda who said, 'I drove. Alex slept most of the way. In fact somewhere along the way I pulled off the road, I think somewhere near Modesto, and slept for a couple of hours too, so we didn't get to San Francisco until about three or four in the morning.'

She reached out and took Alex's hand. 'We went back to Yosemite a couple of days later to pick Gordon up and come back here, but someone had killed him.'

More silence.

Finally Holley said, 'Okay, there's just one more thing we want to ask you about.'

Alex wished he didn't have to look into those hard brown eyes, but as long as Holley was speaking, he couldn't help himself. He gripped Linda's hand tightly and tried to stay calm.

'Just before you and Wilson went to Yosemite Park you climbed a mountain here in Washington called Mt. Redoubt, is that right?'

'No.' How had they known about that? 'We were planning to, but Gord decided that he wanted to do it solo.' Thank God he and Linda had had time to plan this.

He continued to lie. 'We were all set to do it, packed up and ready to go, but then Gord changed his mind. He said he had had some problems with his girlfriend – she had moved to the east – and he wanted to be alone to think about it for a few days. So I came back here and waited for him. He took three or four days to climb it and then we went to Yosemite.'

Holley's black skin had become a mottled purple as he listened to Alex's answer and when he spoke he was obviously angry. 'And of course you don't know anything about who he met up there in the mountains, do you? Or anything about smuggling cocaine, do you? And you don't know anything about your friend's murder either do you?'

He rose up out of his chair and leaned over the table, keeping both hands pressed down on it as though in an effort to keep himself from doing violence. 'Do you think I believe one word you've said here? Do you think that? Do you think I'm stupid? Do you?'

He was almost roaring. Alex was terrified and began to answer, involuntarily, unable to stop himself. But before he had said more than two words Linda rose and leaned over the table until her face was only inches away from Holley's.

'Get out of here!' Her voice was low and full of power. It stopped Holley cold, as if she had slapped him, and it seemed to wake something in Alex, for he sat upright and looked at Holley without flinching.

For a few seconds no one moved or spoke as each of the four searched for the word or action that would end the impasse in his or her favour. In the end it was Alex who spoke. He stood up and put a hand on Linda's shoulder, easing her back gently from her confrontation with Holley, and said, 'I think you'd better leave now, Lieutenant.'

All the insecurity that he had felt while answering the questions was gone. He had lied to the police and he knew he had lied badly, but it was done and now he was in control again.

Holley looked from Alex to Linda and back to Alex. Without a word he picked up his pen and notebook, turned from the table and walked out.

Sergeant Cutler, who was still sitting, started to speak but changed his mind. He put his notebook and pen into the inside breast pocket of his jacket and stood up slowly, as if he were tired, and standing took most of his energy.

'I'm sorry . . .' He shrugged his shoulders and left the kitchen. He spoke briefly to the uniformed patrolman and followed Holley out the door.

'Thanks for the coffee, Miss Cunningham.' The patrolman put his empty cup on the kitchen table. 'Lieutenant

Holley asked me to ask both of you to please notify him if you change your address or if you plan to leave Seattle for more than two or three days.'

They both just looked at him.

'You can tell Lieutenant Holley to shove it up his ass.' Linda's eyes were bright and her face was still flushed. She stood with her fists on her hips, glaring, until the young cop backed down and turned and left the apartment.

CHAPTER THIRTY-THREE

Seattle

FOR A TIME, over a minute, they just sat on the couch in the living room. Alex felt the used-up and thrown-away emptiness that too much adrenalin leaves behind as it ebbs from blood and brain. But there was relief too. Relief that he had come safely through a difficult ordeal.

Gordon was dead and nothing that he did or said now would bring him back to life. That was true and absolute and final, and the lies he had just told were the first step toward acceptance of that finality, and toward the carrying on of his own life.

As that realization, and the thought that the interview with the police, a thing he had been dreading, was now over began to penetrate his consciousness the feelings of relief became a flood that washed through him with orgasmic intensity; and he sank back into the cushions of the old sofa limp and exhausted.

When he opened his eyes half a minute later it was as though the millenium had come and gone. The room was still the same shabby amalgam of cracked plaster and dusty furniture, and the view out the window was as dismal as it had been for the last four years, but Linda's radiant beauty illuminated the room and filled the future with golden promise.

He reached out and took her hand. 'Let's go out and get some breakfast. We can buy a paper and look through the rental listings while we eat.'

'Okay.' She stood up without releasing his hand and then pulled him to his feet. 'But if you're going to wear nice clothes like these you'll have to get rid of this.' She scraped the back of her free hand against the grain of his beard.

'Yes, boss.' He kissed her and began walking toward the bathroom, but stopped halfway there when someone knocked at the door.

Directing Linda toward the bedroom with a gesture he walked quickly into the entranceway and looked through the spyglass to see the detective from Vancouver standing in the hall. He looked weary, as though he had had to carry a heavy load on his trip back up the stairs.

Alex opened the door and said, 'Did you forget something?'

'No, not really.' The detective took a small leather case from his jacket pocket and removed a business card from it, then replaced the case and took a pen from the same pocket and wrote briefly on the card before handing it to Alex.

'I want you to take this and hang on to it. It's got my home number as well as the number of my office at the Vancouver Police Department.'

In the dim light of the hallway he looked somehow both old and young at once.

'I know you were with your friend when he found the wreck and that you helped him get Matheson back to Vancouver ...'

Alex was stunned. He slumped against the doorframe.

'... Somehow you've managed to convince yourself that lying to us is the right thing to do, and, for the moment at least, there's not much we can do about it ...'

The tired eyes looked right into his soul and Alex had to fight to keep from telling everything.

'. . . but I want to give you a piece of advice. You've stumbled into something that's a hundred times more evil and dangerous than you think. It's killed your friend . . .'

The words were like knives, flaying him alive.

'. . . and eventually it's going to kill you . . .'

He felt exposed and helpless and it took all of his will to remain silent.

'. . . If you want to talk to me before that happens, you can get me at either of those numbers. I've got no authority down here and you can talk to me without compromising yourself or the lady. It won't bring your friend back but it might stop the same thing from happening to you or to someone else.'

And then he was gone and Alex had barely enough strength to close the door and stumble back to the couch.

CHAPTER THIRTY-FOUR

Seattle

HOLLEY AND CUTLER rode in silence, staring out into the cold rain as Quinn, the patrolman, drove. The Sundance Tavern, which Quinn said was the best place he knew of for lunch, was not far away. It was on the corner of Eleventh and Pike in an area of discount stores and low-income housing, and from the outside it looked as shabby as the rest of the neighbourhood. Inside there were three pool tables, a lot of very old wood, some old photographs and beer advertisements, and a sound system good enough to pump muscular rock into two rooms without making conversation difficult.

Quinn said he wasn't hungry and sat down with the

sports section of the *Post-Intelligencer*. Cutler and Holley walked to the bar and studied the menu chalked overhead. Holley looked dark and forbidding, with thunderclouds gathered over him, and no one made any jokes when he ordered the quiche of the day and a cup of tea. Cutler decided on the barbecued beef in a bun and a bottle of Budweiser. He waited for the beer and then sat down with Holley, who looked at him stonily and said, 'So?'

Cutler took a tentative drink from his beer glass. 'Waste of time, Lieutenant. I told him that we knew he was lying, that sooner or later he was going to be killed, but he didn't buy it.'

Cutler took another sip and wished that he had ordered something other than beer. 'He halfway wanted to tell me, I know that, but something was holding him back and the only thing I can think of is that he believes he's in more danger if he talks to us than if he doesn't.'

Holley's fist hit the table.

'GODDAMN IT!'

Heads turned, but Holley didn't care.

'If that Goddamned woman hadn't been there I would have wrung him dry. He would have talked to me until there weren't any more words left in him.' With visible effort he calmed himself and carried on. 'All right Mister Cutler, let's walk through this one more time. Listen to me and tell me if you spot anything we might have missed.

'Matheson picked up a suitcase full of blow in Prince Rupert and flew south to the Canadian-American border. We know that because the RCMP followed him all the way. We can't prove it was cocaine, but I've talked to Matheson and I *know* it was. Right?'

'Right.' said Cutler.

'Okay. Then the pilot twigs to the surveillance and flies into the storm but he crashes on the south side of Mt. Redoubt and buys it in the crash. We know that because we saw the wreck and found his body, and we know that it happened during the storm because the skid marks and all

the tracks had filled in, and that was the only storm
between the time he flew into the cloud and the time we
found him. Right?'

'Right.'

'Wilson and Townsend found the wreckage and helped
Matheson, who had survived the crash, back to Vancouver.
We know that Wilson was there because we found his
climbing sling by the wreck and we know that ...'

Holley stopped talking as the bartender came to the
table with their food. Cutler's barbecued beef came in a
huge bun dripping with sauce along with a green salad and
a big side of home fries. He picked up the bun and bit into
it, leaning over the plate to keep the sauce off his clothing.
The meat was tender and delicious and the sauce was the
best he had ever tasted. Slightly hot, with a piquancy that
awoke his smoke-abused taste buds and let the flavour of
the meat come through unmasked.

Holley ignored his food and continued from where he
had left off.

'So we know Wilson was there because we found his
sling and we know Townsend was there because he can't
lie worth shit.'

'True enough,' said Cutler around a mouthful of fries,
'but I don't see any way we can knock his story apart as
long as he sticks to it.'

Holley lifted a spoonful of soup but stopped halfway to
his mouth. 'Unless we can show that it wouldn't be
possible to climb that mountain alone.' He put the spoon
back in the bowl. 'Did any of the climbers you talked to
say anything about that?'

Cutler shook his head and said, 'No. Nobody said
anything about that one way or another, but I'll ask
around when I get back.'

Neither man spoke for a few moments. Holley tried his
soup, then said, 'Assuming we don't get anywhere with
that, and we probably won't, that leaves us knowing
that Wilson and Townsend helped Matheson back to
Vancouver but unable to prove it. We also know that they

helped smuggle the shit across the line, again because Townsend is such a poor liar. Two months later Wilson is murdered by people who work with Matheson and talking about that makes Townsend *really* sweat. He's obviously lying about what happened that night, but once again there's not a single fucking thing we can do about it as long as he sticks to his story and his girlfriend backs him up.'

Cutler drained his beer and signalled the bartender for another.

'So', Holley bored on, 'we know that he's involved in this right up to his neck, we know that he's going to get offed unless he comes to us – and no matter how much trouble we can cause for him it's got to be better than being shot, so why isn't he talking to us?' Holley's voice was full of anger. 'What does he know that makes him think he's safe? What could possibly make him believe that?'

'I've been asking myself that question for the last half hour,' said Cutler, 'and the only thing I can think of is that he's got something on these people that he thinks will keep them off his back. You know, something like "If anything happens to me, a letter will be sent to . . .". But I just don't believe he's that stupid.' He drank some of his second beer and looked around the tavern, then wiped his lips with a napkin and pushed his plate toward the end of the table. 'Other than that, I'm afraid I don't have any ideas at all.'

Holley was silent for a long time. He too looked round the tavern without really seeing anything. Finally, with difficulty, he clamped the lid down on his anger and frustration and said, 'I was hoping to be able to go back to San Francisco with everything I needed to offer Matheson the choice of cooperating with me or going to jail, but I blew it, and now I'm back at square one.'

He stood up. 'Mister Cutler, there's two things I'd like to ask you to do for me . . .'

Cutler rose and said, 'Sure, anything I can do to help.'

'Thank you. The first is to talk to your climbers again and find out if it's possible that Wilson could have climbed Mt. Redoubt by himself, and the second is to run Townsend's girlfriend, Cunningham, through your computers and let me know what turns up.'

'You think she's got a record?'

'I don't know what I think about her.' Holley put some money on the table. 'Did you get the feeling that she was lying to us at all?'

Cutler thought back over the interview. 'No, I don't think so. She got fairly pissed off with you, and she was certainly doing her best to keep you off Townsend, but I didn't feel that she was actually lying about anything.'

Holley looked at him for a while. 'Think about it. She verified his story about that night; so either she's lying too and neither of us picked it up, or else Townsend was telling the truth, which he most definitely fucking wasn't.'

'I'll be damned.'

'Exactly. Nobody gets that good at lying to the police without a fair amount of practice, so let's check her out.'

CHAPTER THIRTY-FIVE

CONTENTS OF A TELEX from Andy Cutler to William Holley

1: A solo climb of Mt. Redoubt would have been dangerous but possible for a climber of Gordon Wilson's ability and experience.

2: Linda Cunningham does not appear in any file to which I have access.

3: Good luck.

CHAPTER THIRTY-SIX

Tacoma

FOR ALEX the following days were a slow climb from Hell. The interview with the police, and especially the encore with Sergeant Cutler, had almost broken his resolve. He walked mechanically through the remainder of the day contributing nothing to Linda's search for a new house, and slept badly that night. The next day started similarly with Alex, morose and unhelpful, letting Linda drag him along on her search for a new home.

The second place they looked at was the top floor of an old three-storey house in Tacoma, about twenty-five minutes south of Seattle on I-5. It was taller than any of the nearby houses, the rooms were large, the ceilings high, and there were just enough windows to provide a feeling of space and light without being cold or glassy.

Without furniture it was bare and lifeless, but even through his neurotic lethargy Alex began to feel the potential of the place; and, if he didn't pirouette through the arch between kitchen and dining area, or waltz with an imaginary lover in front of the fireplace as Linda did, he at least felt a lightening of his load and a desire to join her in turning these empty rooms into a home.

By mid-afternoon the next day they had moved everything they wanted from Alex's old apartment – mostly his tools and climbing equipment – and four days later the new place was decorated and furnished to their, or at least to Linda's, satisfaction.

At ten-thirty on that grey Wednesday morning they carried the last chair up the two steep flights of stairs and dropped it in the middle of the living room.

'That's it. I resign.' Alex wiped the sweat out of his eyes. 'If you want any more furniture moved you'll have to find a new man.'

Linda dragged the heavy chair into the corner below a standing lamp. 'That's okay. I don't think we need anything more until we decide what to do about all my stuff in New York.'

'You mean we're finished? You're not going to drag me to any more junk stores and pawn shops?'

'That's right.'

'No more antique stores? No more garage sales?'

'None.'

'All right!' Alex whooped and tried to turn a cartwheel, but the room wasn't big enough and he finished up sprawled half on a large couch and half on the floor. 'Let's celebrate,' he said from this position.

'You need a bath. And anyway, where were you planning to celebrate at 10:30 a.m.?'

He stood up and said, 'The bedroom will do just fine for a start.'

'After you have a bath, big boy. I'm not ... Alex, what are ... ALEX! ... Put me down, you animal ...'

But even upside down over his shoulder she still had most of his shirt buttons undone by the time they reached the bed.

All things pass. Alex Townsend and Linda Cunningham soon found the immediacy of their fear receding and the poignancy of their loss blunted. They were still afraid, and they still missed Gordon, but their lives went on. Moving to the new house helped.

They began to see some of Alex's old friends and acquaintances and two weeks after the move Alex found work.

'Trucks?'

'Not just.'

'What do you mean "Not just"?' She had been on the floor of the spare bedroom with a tape measure and pen and paper, trying to decide how to arrange her darkroom when Alex walked in with the news.

'I mean not just trucks. Cascade Timber is huge.

They've got company cars and all kinds of heavy machinery. Skidders, graders, cats, spar trees; and they're always breaking down.'

'But why you? What do you know about that kind of machinery? I thought you just worked on cars?' She recorded the measurements and pocketed the tape.

'Well, yeah, mostly. I've done *some* heavy-duty work, but the main thing was that I just happened to show up at the right time.'

Linda stood, then bent slowly from the waist until her palms were flat on the floor, and her hamstrings fully stretched. She looked up and said, 'You just happened to show up at the right time?' She stood upright again and arched the other way, stretching quadriceps and abdominals.

'Yeah, I had coffee this morning with a couple of guys I know, mechanics that I used to work with, and one of them said that he knew that a couple of guys had just quit at Cascade; so I thought what the hell, why not give it a try? I've got enough saved that I don't really *have* to go back to work for a while yet, but this sounded like the sort of job I'd like; and I'd have had to start looking eventually, so I just went out to see what I could see; and they offered me a job.'

He had wandered into the kitchen, and now called back, 'How come there's no coffee waiting for me? If I'm going to be a proper heavy-duty mechanic, you'll have to learn to have coffee ready when I get home. And bring me supper in front of the football game, right?'

'Piss off.'

'Oh. Well in that case, why don't I make you a cup of coffee.'

'That's more like it. And you might as well learn to bring me brandy in the darkroom.' She came into the kitchen and clasped her arms around him from behind. 'Will you have grease under your fingernails all the time?'

He measured coffee into the filter as best he could with her hanging on to him. 'Under my fingernails, over my fingernails, up my arms to the elbow, all over my face and thoroughly matted into my hair.'

'I'm sure I'll love it.'

'Especially when you see my coarse, grease-blackened, workman's hands sliding down the satiny white skin of your loins.'

'My loins is okay. You can have your coarse, animal way with my body, but if you ever get grease on any of my lenses I'll castrate you on the spot.' She let him go and hit him lightly on the shoulder. 'Capisce, Townsend?'

Alex sprinkled a few grains of salt onto the coffee and then poured boiling water over it. 'Speaking of your lenses, it looks like I'm not going to start this job until next week so why don't you pack up your camera and your long underwear and come skiing with me for a few days?'

'Skiing? I've only skied about three times in my life. I don't have any skis. I don't even have any long underwear.'

She pulled him over to the window and pointed out into the drizzle. 'And besides, that doesn't look like snow to me.'

He poured coffee for both of them. 'Don't worry about any of that. It's not even noon yet. We can get you skis and boots and all the winter clothing and equipment you need this afternoon and leave tomorrow. There'll be tons of snow in the mountains and we might as well put it to some use.'

It wasn't until two hours later when Alex was actually pulling a pair of metal-edged cross-country skis off the rack that she realized he wasn't talking about any kind of skiing that she had ever heard of.

CHAPTER THIRTY-SEVEN

Coast Range Mountains

THEY ROSE EARLY and were northbound on I-5 by 6:00 a.m., across the border without incident before 8:00 a.m. and passing through Vancouver at 8:30 a.m. Light rain was falling from low cloud, and the population was on its way to work.

'Not much to see now, but if there's time on the way back we should spend a day here. It's quite a beautiful city,' said Alex.

'Looks like any other city to me.'

'If the sun's out when we get back here you'll see what I mean.'

Linda twisted on the seat so that she was facing him. 'Maybe it would look better right now if I weren't so hungry. We didn't really have much of a breakfast ...'

'Okay, let's find a restaurant and get something to eat. I'm hungry too.'

After breakfast they drove north, first along a fjord, and then through a range of mountains of which Linda caught only the vaguest glimpses through the heavy dull cloud. The surface of the fjord was the same shiny grey as the surface of the wet road, the only colour relief coming from the slightly lighter grey of the rock by the roadside and the greenish grey of the forest.

After two hours Alex pulled into a small parking lot below the Blackcomb Mountain Ski area. The sky was still low and grey and light rain was still falling on the sodden rocks and trees around them.

'Alex?'

'Mmm?' He was in the back of the van putting food, clothing and equipment into their packs.

'Is this it?'

'This is it.'

'Alex, there's no snow. How do we ski without snow? And the lifts aren't even running. I don't think this place is open.'

He came to the front and pointed out the window. 'If it weren't clouded up like this you would see a vista of snowy peaks gleaming white in the sunshine, their every summit beckoning, and your heart would gladden with thoughts of floating down through clouds of fluffy white powder, your skis flashing in the crisp morning light as you . . .'

'Horseshit.' She punched him in the shoulder.

'Well, the diction maybe; but we really are surrounded by big mountains, and higher up they really are covered with snow on which we will be skiing for the next few days.' He grinned. 'Actually, for the first day or so I'll be skiing and you'll be falling over a lot, but you'll get it under control before long.'

He passed her an armful of clothing. 'But we've got a bit of a walk in the rain first, so let's get dressed and get going.'

With skis strapped to their packs they hiked steadily upwards for almost two hours, first on an abandoned mining road and then on a well-maintained trail in a misty pine hemlock forest. As they walked Alex described their route and destination. 'We're travelling up the south side of Fitzsimmons Creek valley. There are two big commercial ski areas, with all the hotels, restaurants, bars and nightclubs anyone could ever want, on Whistler Mountain and Blackcomb Mountain at the mouth of the valley.

'There are ridges of mountains running east from both Whistler and Blackcomb, and this valley lies between them. We go up to the end of the valley, cross a pass to the north called Singing Pass, and drop down just a short way on the other side to a hut beside a little lake called Russet Lake. The mountains above the hut are the eastern end of the chain that starts with Blackcomb. They're high enough to keep snow all year round and I'm not going to tell you how beautiful they are because you'd just think I was exaggerating.'

They climbed gradually and soon patches of snow began to appear. By the time they left the mining road for the trail the drizzle had turned to snow and snow completely covered the ground. Not enough to ski on, but a sign of what was to come. Half an hour later Alex stopped and said, 'The snow's getting deep enough that it'll be just as easy to ski as walk, so let's have a bit of lunch and then start doing what we came to do.'

Skiing uphill on gentle trails is easy and Linda managed the next two and a half hours without much difficulty. The snow deepened and the forest thinned out as they gained altitude and the trail became less and less distinct until Linda could no longer see it at all. In the cloudy, snowy weather all directions were the same, each cluster of small trees indistinguishable from the next.

'You realize Alex, that if anything happens to you, I'll never find my way back.'

'As far as we're going to get today you could just turn around and follow our tracks, and tonight I'll show you how to use a map and compass, so don't worry about that.'

The snow was soft and fresh and for Alex, in front, breaking trail became increasingly laborious. Finally he stopped and dropped his pack in a clearing in the centre of a clump of stunted trees.

'Let's stop here. It'll take a while to set up camp but there should be enough light to get in an hour or so of skiing on the slopes above us.'

For Linda it was like learning life's basic skills all over again. Winter changed everything. Setting up a tent, cooking, eating and drinking, even something as ordinary as sitting down to rest – all seemed infinitely more complicated and difficult in the bottomless, soft snow. But the new clothing Alex had chosen for her kept her warm and dry and she soon began to enjoy herself.

And the skiing. On the trail up it had seemed easy, not very different from walking, but downhill . . .

At first it was impossible. She could not turn the long

narrow skis, and could not go further than a few yards without falling over. But the falls were painless in the deep soft snow and gradually some of the things Alex showed her began to make sense. By the end of an hour she was tired and sore, but she could do a reasonable facsimile of a telemark turn as long as the slope was gentle, and she was looking forward to the days to come.

After supper they crawled into zipped-together sleeping bags and Linda surprised herself by sleeping through eleven hours in complete warmth and comfort.

It wasn't actually snowing when they woke at seven, but it had snowed heavily overnight and the trees around their tent wore huge white mantles which collapsed at the slightest touch.

They spent most of the morning skiing on the perfect powdery snow on the gentle slopes above the camp. Linda learned quickly and by the time they stopped for lunch she was even able to put together an occasional set of two or three linked turns.

Lunch was cheese, sausage, crackers and lots of soup. They ate sitting on their packs in front of the tent and Linda stared up at the slope they had been skiing and the cloud that hid its top.

'Alex, why is nobody else here?'

'What do you mean?'

'This is absolutely incredible. Even with all the cloud it's beautiful, and the skiing is fantastic. I don't understand why there aren't hordes of people here.'

Alex munched a salami-covered cracker and thought about it. 'I don't know. There's a hut just a couple of hours further on and later in the winter it gets crowded on weekends, and there's sometimes a few people there during the week, but as long as you stay clear of the hut you'll hardly ever see anyone. And at this time of year, November, even the hut is empty most of the time.' He ate another cracker. 'I guess the weather is just so dismal in Vancouver and Seattle that nobody's willing to get out in it. Nobody believes that there's good skiing until sometime in mid-December.'

He laughed, then said, 'And this is one of the most popular areas. If you go to any one of a thousand other places you won't see another person, even during the Christmas holiday.'

'But it's so beautiful ...'

They took the tent down after lunch and loaded their packs for the ski to the hut. The crest of the pass, where they stopped two hours later to remove the climbing skins from their skis, was above tree line, but with the heavy snowfall of the night before it appeared soft and round, rather than rocky and harsh. The cloud cover was beginning to thin but was still low enough to hide all but the bases of the mountains around them. Down below, about a third of a mile ahead, the hut was a strange orange and blue shape against the snow.

The slope down was gentle but Alex warned Linda that 'skiing downhill with a pack on is not the same thing as skiing without a pack. You're going to fall over about fifty times in the next fifteen minutes. Try to keep your sense of humour.'

The hut, when they reached it, turned out to be a steeply curved A-frame about twenty feet long and twelve feet from floor to roof peak. Inside were wooden sleeping platforms on two levels and two long tables against opposite walls with two benches between them.

Linda found it charmless and felt colder inside than out.

'Alex?'

'Yes.'

'Were you planning to stay here?'

'That's up to you. I don't particularly like these huts myself, but I thought you might prefer it to the tent.'

'Prefer it to the tent?' She looked around at the bare walls, the dirty tables and floor. 'The tent is warm and cheerful. This place is like ...' She searched for words: '... is like some proto-gothic outhouse.' She stepped back outside and spoke through the doorway. 'And just when it's starting to clear up, I'm not going to close myself off inside there.'

Alex joined her outside and looked at the sky. It *was* starting to clear. The ceiling had lifted noticeably since they left the summit of the pass and the cloud layer seemed to be thinning to the southwest. He couldn't actually see blue sky, but he could sense hints of blue through the grey veil.

He looked at his watch.

'How do you feel?'

'Fine. Why?'

'No, I mean physically. Are you tired or do you still have some energy left?'

She looked at him questioningly. 'I feel pretty good. I'll probably sleep like a baby tonight, but I've got lots of strength left for the rest of the day. What are you planning?'

'A little surprise. Bring your pack inside.' He picked up his own pack from where he had dropped it by the door and carried it into the hut.

Inside, she found him emptying his pack onto the main sleeping platform. When she put her pack on the floor beside him, he picked it up and began emptying that as well.

'So?' she asked.

'So this may be hard to believe, but we are in the middle of a spectacular mountain range.' He began sorting the contents of the packs into two piles. 'Right above this hut is a mountain called Mt. Whirlwind. You and I are going to climb it and bivouac on the summit tonight. Tomorrow morning, if the weather has cleared, you'll have the view of your life. You'll begin to understand why Gord was always talking about getting into the mountains to do some real climbing, and you'll want to shoot every roll of film that you have.'

He finished his sorting and began to put the contents of one of the piles back into their packs. 'I'm going to leave behind everything that isn't absolutely necessary so that our packs are as light as possible. I'll just leave the extra stuff here until we ...'

'You *do* realize ...' she interrupted him '... that I've never climbed a mountain before?'

'No problem. A summit bivvy in the winter is the perfect way to start.' He cinched the lid of her pack and handed it to her. 'This won't be a technical climb. It looks impressive as hell but in fact we can ski right to the summit, so don't worry about anything.'

Outside the hut, as they were sticking skins back on to their skis, Alex pointed to the east and said, 'The mountain that's just starting to loom out of the cloud right above us is Mt. Fissile. It's the ugliest pile of dirt and loose rock you ever saw, but it looks pretty good in winter.'

To Linda it looked huge and forbidding, a monstrous white pyramid whose base dominated the scene round them and whose apex was lost in the cloud.

'We're going to climb that?' She was incredulous.

'No, it's hardly worth climbing. We're going to climb Mt. Whirlwind which is just visible to the right.' He pointed, and Linda could distinguish, barely, a ghostly shape in the clouds behind Fissile.

Twenty minutes later they were well on their way, traversing the broad base of Mt. Fissile as the dissipating clouds alternately veiled and unveiled their goal. Where Fissile was broadbased and squat, Mt. Whirlwind appeared tall and slender; a perfectly proportioned and beautiful lady beside a grotesque, misshapen hulk.

Slowly they gained altitude, zigzagging up the lady's skirts and then on to her shoulder where they stopped to look up at her crown, now crystalline, sparkling white against a cobalt blue sky.

Finally, two and a half hours after leaving the hut, they reached the summit. Around them, in the clear light of the late afternoon sun, was a new world; a trichrome world of blue, white and grey. Intense blue for the now cloudless sky: shining, radiant white for the snow-covered mountains that jutted and strutted in proud disarray from horizon to horizon; and here and there a streak or patch of brownish grey for the walls and rockfaces too steep for the snow to cling.

Linda could not speak. She stepped her skis slowly around through a full circle on the small flat space that was the summit of Mt. Whirlwind.

Below her, somewhere, roads ran through forested valleys, became highways that were the arteries of a civilization filling towns and cities; but the roads, and the cities, and the sweating, scheming millions that filled them were invisible, the fact of their existence tenuous and insubstantial in this much vaster world of rock and snow and sky.

'Alex.'

'Yes.'

'We could be the only people in the universe.'

He stood beside her, put his arm around her waist and said, 'When we're up here like this, we *are* the only people in the universe.'

Alex cooked a thick bouillabaisse of canned fish and rice in the one pot he had brought up with him, and as they ate they watched the sun go down and the mountains around them change from white through orangey-pink to magenta, and finally darken to silhouettes against a clear, star-filled sky.

The temperature fell rapidly but, covered in layers of pile and Gore-tex, Linda was snug and warm. She was awed by the scale of the alpine world around her, and by the number and intensity of the stars; and later, as she lay in the double cocoon of her sleeping bag and bivouac sack, with the glory of the universe blazing in the sky above her and the warmth of Alex's body along her left side where their bivvy sacks nestled together, she felt, for the first time in her life, complete and at absolute peace.

They breakfasted on tea and a mixture of nuts, raisins and chocolate that Alex called gorp, and then made the two thousand foot run down to the hut in perfect powder.

Linda fell what seemed like hundreds of times, but the snow was soft and forgiving and the day was beautiful and she did not mind. She marvelled at the grace with which Alex carved turn after turn, seemingly without effort, and laughed with pleasure the few times that he ploughed the snow with his face.

It was still early when they reached the hut, and Alex began preparing a second breakfast for them.

'Today is Saturday,' he said as he ate his porridge, 'and with weather like this there will be people coming up here for sure, and I'd just rather not see anybody else. How do you feel about that?'

'I think I'd like another day of being the only people in the universe.'

'Okay, let's go back to where we camped the first night and then up the other side of that valley a bit. We can camp in the trees and no one will see us and we won't see them.' He put down his empty bowl. 'We can head back out on Sunday morning and be back in Seattle by mid afternoon.'

'And you can start your new job Monday morning and come home with greasy hands Monday night.' She put her empty bowl beside his. 'Maybe I should just stay up here and you can visit me on weekends.'

That night they used the tent again, and made long, slow love in their zipped-together bags. Afterwards as they lay, still entwined, Linda said, 'You know Alex, you really don't have to go back to work if you don't want to. We must have almost a hundred thousand dollars between us . . .' She rolled over so that she could look at him in the light of the little candle lantern that hung from the dome of the tent. 'I've got well over thirty, and you said you had about ten thousand that you had saved, plus the fifty that you and Gordon made. It won't last forever, but you certainly don't have to take a job right away.'

At first Alex said nothing, didn't move or give any sign that he had heard. When he finally spoke he kept his eyes shut.

'I don't know what to do about the money. Maybe I should just give it all to the Salvation Army.'

He lay silent again and Linda didn't disturb him. Eventually he spoke again. 'All the money that Gord and I got paid was in the package you sent to your friend in New York. Neither of us had actually used any of it before Gord was killed, and now I'm not sure that I should spend it.'

He snuggled closer against her.

'But I think that the reason I feel that way is because Gord was killed, not because of what we did to earn it.'

He opened his eyes and turned his head so that he could see her. 'Do you understand what I'm saying?'

'I think so. If nothing had happened, if you and Gordon had had fun in the valley and then come home for the winter that you would have spent it and enjoyed it; but now after what happened to Gordon, you can't bring yourself to touch it.'

'That's right.' He closed his eyes and let his head roll back. 'But that's really a hypocritical attitude isn't it?'

'Yes.'

'But you know', he opened his eyes again, 'even if I decided to keep it and spend it, I'd still go back to work.'

He raised himself up on one elbow and looked down at her. 'Do you think that's silly?'

'No, it's probably something you can't help. I know that even if I had more money than I could ever spend I'd still be trying to sell pictures one way or another.'

'That's how I feel. I like working on engines and the money doesn't really matter that much.' He paused. 'There's only two things I really like, climbing and engines.'

He tangled his fingers in her hair and kissed her gently. 'Or, there *were* only two things. Now there's three.'

She ran a fingertip down his chest and trailed it over his thigh. 'There's no engines or rock faces here, but we can practice number three again if you like.'

She lay on her back with one leg bent and he entered her lying on his side with his top leg across her bottom one. They didn't move much, just lay like that, rocking a little from time to time until sleep claimed them.

CHAPTER THIRTY-EIGHT

Tacoma

'DO YOU KNOW anything about cocaine?'

They were on their way south, about halfway to Vancouver. Alex was driving and Linda was nodding, half asleep, on the seat beside him. 'What?'

'I asked if you knew anything about cocaine.' He looked across the seat at her and then quickly back to the twisting road.

'Your conscience eating at you?'

'Yeah, kind of.'

She sat up straighter and stared out the window. The good weather had ended sometime during the previous night and on the highway it was as grey and wet as it had been on the way up.

'For a while, about a year after Michael and I set up our studio and the work was starting to come in, we did a lot of it. He hung out with a bunch of rich gays and there was never any problem getting it, and then we started to make good money and I could afford a fair bit myself.'

She turned so that she was sitting sideways on the seat, leaning against his right shoulder with her knees drawn up in front of her.

'I did enough of it to realize that if I did any more I'd be locked into it, so I quit entirely. I'm not strong enough to mess with anything that good.'

'That's strange. Gord said just the opposite. He said he'd done enough to know he'd never get hooked. He said it was okay, that he liked to treat himself to a toot now and then, but that it wasn't addictive like booze or heroin.'

'And you,' she asked, 'you never tried it yourself?'

'Once. I didn't get anything out of it, though.'

'Nothing?'

'Not really. It made my nose itch, and I sneezed a lot, but that's all.'

'You probably had something that was about one per cent cocaine and ninety-nine per cent god knows what. Same with Gordon. Vancouver's hardly the cocaine capital of the world and what Gordon was buying was probably cut pretty much to nothing. You could snort that kind of stuff forever and all you'd get is poor.'

She wriggled against him, trying for a more comfortable position.

'In New York we could get anything from street sweepings to nearly pure cocaine, and anyone who's freebased really good coke knows how fast the hook can go in. There may not be a physiological dependence the way there is with pills or booze or junk, but that doesn't mean you don't need it. But Alex ...' She turned so that she could see him and her voice was serious '... giving the money to the Sally Ann or throwing it away isn't going to bring Gordon back to life and it isn't going to take that cocaine out of circulation. If you don't want to keep it, that's fine with me, I've got lots of money right now and you said you had over ten thousand yourself, not to mention a pretty good job coming up, so we can live without the money; just remember that everything that happened will still have happened after you give the money away.'

She fell silent and several miles of wet highway unwound beneath the van before she spoke again.

'Just do one thing for me though.'

'What?' he asked.

'Wait for a month or so. Let's leave the money wherever Michael's hidden it for a few weeks, and then if you still feel like giving it away, fine, you can give it away.'

She turned away from him again, and rested her back against his right side. 'Christmas is only a few weeks away. Let's think about that, and get you settled in your new job, and then sometime in January you can decide what to do with the money, okay?'

'Okay.'

CHAPTER THIRTY-NINE

Vancouver

ANDY CUTLER had never hosted a real Christmas party before, and he was smart enough not to try anything fancy himself. He simply laid in half a dozen bottles of rye whiskey, two bottles each of white rum, gin and vodka, gallons of mix, a few cases of beer, and hired a caterer to do several hundred dollars worth of turkey and hot and cold snacks.

Only about twenty people had been invited but word of his promotion had spread and considerably more than twenty showed up to offer congratulations and press the flesh. Nobody got sick or obnoxious and there were enough civilians to keep it from degenerating into a police bull session.

By 2:00 a.m. only the Hofstadters and Valerie MacGregor were left. All the windows were open and the polluted air of the apartment was gradually being exchanged for fresh. The caterer had removed all of her equipment and taken away a Glad bag full of disposable plates, glasses and cutlery. Cutler and his three remaining guests put the empty bottles out of sight in the kitchen and then sat in the living room with their shoes off to share a final Christmas drink.

Angela Hofstadter was taller than her husband and as

fair as he was dark. Her feet were up on the coffee table
and from where Cutler sat, directly opposite, her legs
seemed to go on forever. She looked at him over nylon-
shrouded toes and said, 'Are you pretty happy to be out of
Drugs?'

He thought about it for a while and finally answered,
'Yes and no. Mostly yes I think. I'm going to miss working
with your old man, and with a couple of the other guys,
but I sure won't miss the kind of people we had to deal
with. I'll definitely be dealing with a better class of scum in
Major Crimes than I dealt with in Drugs.'

He finished his drink and chewed the ice cube, then
went on. 'Her job . . .', he nodded toward Valerie, returning from the kitchen with a tray of coffee, '. . . is a lot
better in that respect than mine was. At least the cop on
patrol meets a cross section of society. It's maybe not the
same cross section that most people meet – it's definitely
weighted toward the asshole end of the population curve –
but it's not too bad. But a detective, and especially a
detective in Drugs, spends most of his time with people
who . . . Well, you've been married to a cop long enough
that I don't have to tell you stories about that.'

They all took coffee and after her first sip Angela said,
'But surely you must meet *some* nice people. Even the
drug world can't be totally populated with ani can it?'

'Ani?' asked Cutler.

'Plural of anus.'

'Oh. I see.' Cutler drank some coffee and thought about
his reply. 'On the whole I'd have to disagree. I think the
world would be a better place if ninety-nine percent of the
people I've had to deal with over the past few years had
never been born.'

'I've never heard you talk that way.'

'I hardly ever do talk this way, Angie, but I've been
thinking back over the four years I spent in Drugs and the
only people I've met that I'd spend time with by choice
have either been victims of, or witnesses to, drug related
crimes.' He took some more coffee and continued. 'And

even most of those have been pretty sleazy; so yes, I guess I am pretty happy about leaving Drugs.'

Valerie MacGregor, sitting sideways in a big armchair with her legs over one of the arms, said, 'Oh come on Andy, it can't have been that bad. Somewhere amongst all those jerks there must be a few nice ones. Surely you don't believe that everyone who uses drugs is an asshole?'

'That's true, lots of decent people use all kinds of drugs, but they aren't the people we were dealing with. We got the dealers, the fixers, the organization guys, and the hard guys, guys who would break your arm if they thought you were standing between them and a ten dollar bill.' He paused for a moment and then said, 'Although, to be fair, I did meet one guy who wasn't too bad.'

He turned back to Angela Hofstadter. 'I don't know if Rick ever mentioned this to you or not, but over the last few months I've been peripherally involved in a case where a couple of guys, basically really nice people, helped smuggle a bunch of cocaine from Peru into the San Francisco area. I think they got involved more or less by chance and I don't even know if they got paid, maybe they just did it for the excitement. But the one I've talked to was as pleasant a guy as you could hope to meet. Good looking, lives with a nice woman, educated, good family background, the whole thing; just like the movies.'

'So there you are,' said Angela. 'It really isn't as bad as you made it sound. You *do* meet some nice people.'

'Yeah. Except that the other guy, the one who helped him with the smuggling, has already been murdered, and this guy is going to be killed soon himself. He thinks he won't be, but he's wrong.'

Angela looked at him in surprise. 'That's horrible. Can't you do something to warn him?'

'I did warn him, but he thinks he's bulletproof. And anyway, now that I'm finished in Drugs it's not my case anymore.' Cutler finished his coffee and stood up. He walked to the open window and looked at the lights of the city spread out below him and said over his shoulder, 'It never really was my case, Angie, and the last I heard it was soon going to be nobody's case at all. As long as the people involved, the two that are still alive, that is, keep their mouths shut there's nothing anyone can do except stand out of the way and let them die.'

Angela Hofstadter shuddered: 'Ugh. This is too depressing for a Christmas party. Who started this talk anyway?'

CHAPTER FORTY

Tacoma

'MERRY CHRISTMAS, TOWNSEND.'

'Nnn?' Alex woke slowly to a vision of beauty. Weak winter sunlight filled the bedroom and as his eyes cleared he saw Linda standing by the bed. She was wearing a lounge robe he had not seen before, a high-collared robe of raw apricot silk. Delicate apricot, the colour of sunrise over a misty lake.

He sat up. 'Merry Christmas to you too.' He rubbed his eyes and then stretched, twisting first one way and then the other with his hands clasped behind his head.

She had been carrying a tray and now she bent and placed it on the night table. On it was a Christmas package, medium large and soft looking. She leaned over and kissed him. 'Open this package now and then go and shave. I'll go to the kitchen and start a proper Christmas breakfast, but you don't get any until you've shaved and washed.' She slapped his wandering hand from the fold of her robe, 'Or any of that either.'

In the package was a pair of leather slippers, pyjama-style shirt and pants in rich burgundy silk, and a dressing gown, also silk, but of a green so deep as to be almost black.

Her 'proper Christmas breakfast' was fresh grapefruits, freshly ground coffee and a lot of Remy Martin. It was the start of the best Christmas he had ever had.

They spent the day drinking brandy and making love. And once in a while opening presents in front of the fire, which they both felt was better than a tree. The presents were small things mostly – books, records, a bit of climbing gear, odds and ends for the kitchen and house, and some clothing.

At the end of the day, after a supper of cold meats and homemade buns and a selection of pickles and chutneys, they went to bed early and recaptured, for the half hour that they stayed awake, the feeling of being the only two people in the universe.

CHAPTER FORTY-ONE

Tacoma

HE CRUISED past the house in the early afternoon but there were two black women standing on the sidewalk about half a block away and he decided against stopping. Were they police spies? He didn't know, but he knew that if a private individual with a few hundred dollars to spend could trace Townsend to his new home, then so could the police.

Why take chances?

He drove on several blocks and then parked and tried to decide what to do. He didn't want to spend more than the weekend away from San Francisco, and he obviously couldn't park in front of Townsend's place in broad daylight.

What to do? Rent a hotel room? Not in a grotty town like this. And besides, with the number of blacks that worked in hotels word would spread on their grapevine in no time. He had taken a big enough chance with the flight up here and the car rental; no sense in taking any more chances.

Same for the telephone. Talking on the telephone would be crazy.

He couldn't think. There was danger everywhere and the pounding in his head was like a sledgehammer. He took two Tylenols from the bottle in his pocket and washed them down with a long pull from the fifth of Scotch on the seat beside him. The whisky burned its way down into his stomach and almost immediately he felt better. Everything snapped into focus and he felt clear-headed and decisive.

He looked at his watch. 2:30 p.m. No problem. He would go back to Seattle and catch a movie somewhere, or maybe find a woman. Then have a quiet supper and come back to Tacoma in the evening. He'd park a few blocks away and in the dark he'd be able to walk up to Townsend's house just like somebody from the neighbourhood.

He took another hit on the Scotchman and pulled back out onto the road.

CHAPTER FORTY-TWO

Tacoma

'LOOK, I really don't care if you impress them or not.' Alex was exasperated. 'It would be great if you liked them and they liked you, but it really doesn't matter that much. I don't even know how much *I* like them; if they weren't my parents I probably wouldn't cross the street to see them.'

'That's easy for you to say, but they *are* your parents, and what do I know about rich lawyers?'

They were in their bedroom, packing clothes into a small suitcase. Linda continued, 'What if I do something really dumb?'

'You mean like fart at the dinner table? Or say shit in front of my mother? Come on Linda, they're human too. And anyway it's only for tomorrow and Monday, it's not as if we were going to be moving in with them.'

He closed the suitcase and said, 'There. We can throw our toothbrushes in when we're finished with them tomorrow morning and we'll be ready to go.'

'Have you got the tickets?'

'I put them in the front pocket of your camera bag along with a couple of magazines to take on the plane with us.'

'Some money?'

'Yes, I went to the bank this morning and . . .'

The doorbell rang and Linda said, 'I'll get it. It's probably Mr. Olsen coming up from downstairs. I told him that I wanted to put a darkroom in the spare room and he said he'd have to see exactly what I was going to do before he'd okay it. He said he might come up and check tonight.'

But it was not Olsen who walked into the living room with her, it was Walter Matheson, and Alex felt the world that he had built in the last two months begin to slide out from underneath him. He looked desperately round the room for some weapon, for an escape, but there was nothing; only Linda, still behind Matheson, offered any chance. He cleared his throat loudly and spoke, hoping that his voice would not crack.

'Mister Matheson.' Pause. Surely Linda would realize. 'I didn't expect to see you again.'

Walter Matheson was dressed in a brown suit and wore a three-quarter length cashmere overcoat over that. The coat glistened with water droplets and Alex briefly wondered when the rain had started.

'Yes. But things have changed and I decided I'd better look you up.'

He took off his coat and handed it to Linda as though to

a servant and turned back to Alex. 'I've got a business proposition to discuss with you, but I think we should do it in private ...,' he hooked a surreptitious thumb at Linda, who had not moved, '... don't you?'

What was going on? How had he found them? Alex could smell the alcohol on the man's breath from where he stood eight feet away, but he wasn't acting drunk or aggressive and with sudden relief Alex realized that he was not about to be killed.

He looked to Linda, still holding the wet coat. 'Mister Matheson and I have some business to discuss. Would you mind leaving for a while? Maybe go to your studio or something?'

He walked to her and took the coat from her hand and guided her toward the front door. He hung the coat in the closet and removed a coat and sweater for Linda. As he helped her on with the sweater he whispered, 'That's Walter Matheson, the guy we carried the cocaine for. He probably wants to get me to carry some more. I don't think he's got a gun or anything, and I'll just try to convince him that I'm out of it for good. Okay?'

She let him help her with the coat and whispered back fiercely. 'I'm not going anywhere. Just because you didn't see a gun doesn't mean he doesn't have one, do you understand?' Her voice was harsh, commanding.

'Yes, I understand, but I really think he just wants to talk.'

'Maybe so, but I'm going to be right outside this door. If he does anything you don't like, you just yell and I'll come through the doorway with as much noise as I can, and maybe we can jump him. Okay?'

'All right.'

He closed the door behind her and returned to the living room where Walter Matheson was standing, looking around at the furniture and the prints that Linda had framed and hung on the walls. Alex expected him to say something like 'Nice place you've got here' or, 'Nice to see you again' but instead Matheson just planted both hands deeply into his pant pockets as if to keep them under control, and said:

'Have you got any whiskey?'

Alex looked at the man closely, then said, 'Just a minute.'

He went to a glass-fronted cabinet that Linda had found in a second-hand shop and removed two shot glasses and a bottle of Seagram's V.O. rye. He poured the two drinks on a side table by the cabinet and carried them to the low coffee table in front of the fireplace and said, 'Why don't you sit down?'

But Matheson didn't sit down immediately. He brought a bottle of Extra Strength Tylenol from his pocket and shook two tablets from it, chewed them hard and then picked up the whiskey and chased them down, killing the drink in one long swallow.

He didn't look good. When Alex had last seen him in the bar in San Francisco he had been surprised at how well he had recovered from the crash, but now, two months later, he looked far worse. His face had lost its firmness and was beginning to sag. There were dark bags under his eyes and the spring had gone from his spine. Two months ago he had looked healthy, successful and in control. Now he looked thin and pale and nervous. Alex wondered what had happened.

'Is it safe to talk here?'

What did that mean? 'Do you mean is the house bugged?'

'Exactly. Do the police know you're here? Have they talked to you?'

'No.' Lie. 'I moved here after I saw you in San Francisco and the police don't know where I am.'

'Good, good.' Matheson walked to the sideboard and poured himself another drink, then returned to the coffee table bringing the bottle with him. He sat down in one of the chairs flanking the fireplace. Alex sat across from him and took a small sip from his glass.

'How did you find me?' He was feeling much more

confident. Matheson had obviously been drinking earlier, and with a couple of stiff ones here he was not going to be able to do anything fast enough to take Alex by surprise.

'Easy. Same way the police will find you if they bother looking. Your name and your girlfriend's name were in the paper with that business in Yosemite. You didn't change your names or leave the Seattle area so it wasn't hard to find you. And there's something else . . .' his voice dropped and he leaned forward, '. . . I noticed a lot of blacks around this area.'

'It's a mostly black district. Our landlord is black.' Was Matheson all there?

'That's not good. There's a cop in San Francisco who wants to get me. He's black, and you know about blacks.'

He *isn't* all there, Alex thought. 'What about them?'

'Just think about it. That cop can put his ear to the ground and pick up all kinds of things. Bellhops, cab drivers, musicians, they're everywhere. You don't notice them, but they see everything we do, and they can pass information about us back and forth across the country as fast as we could by using a telephone.'

Matheson was cruising in the Asteroid belt and Alex was not sure what to say. He settled for, 'Okay, I'll be real careful.'

He tasted his drink again and the taste of the rye brought with it thoughts of Gordon. He put the glass down and asked, 'Just what was it you wanted to see me about.'

'Things have changed in the last little while and I need you to bring in another load for me. I know you said you weren't interested but when you hear what I have to say that's going to change.'

Off the subject of blacks and police Matheson seemed rational. The drink had steadied him and he appeared to be gaining some control over his mind.

'I know you're probably worried that what happened to your friend could happen to you, but you can forget about that. Carl Adams is dead, so you can stop worrying about him.'

Walter Matheson stopped talking and looked at his second drink as if noticing it for the first time. He picked it up, sniffed at it and then threw it back just as he had the first one.

'That's nice whiskey.' He poured himself a third glass, about half the size of the first two, and said, 'You also don't have to worry about anyone else doing the same thing, because this time there isn't going to be anyone else.'

Alex just wanted out. Wanted to tell Matheson to find somebody else, or bring in his own cocaine, but he was afraid to say anything. If Matheson was as crazy as he seemed then best to tell him whatever he wanted to hear, whatever would make him leave happy; and then figure out what to do about it after he'd gone.

'This time I'm going to handle it myself. You can bring it in from Canada through the mountains just like you did last time and I'll take delivery personally. No one but you and me will know about it, and you can walk away in complete safety. How does that suit you?'

'I don't know. I'm not sure that this is a good time. Going through the mountains at this time of year wouldn't be very easy.' But even as he said the words Alex realized that it *would* be easy. As easy as doing it in the summer, and a lot safer.

'I understand what you're saying, but don't worry, this is going to be worth your while.' He reached into his breast pocket and brought out a very fat envelope. 'Here's your down payment.' He handed it across the table. 'Count that.'

The envelope was about two inches thick, and inside were hundred-dollar bills in three separate packets, each held together with elastic bands. Two of the packets were of similar size and the other was smaller. Alex picked one of the large bundles and began counting. Matheson sat and watched, saying nothing until he finished.

'Ten thousand, right?' He pointed to the other two packets. 'And another ten thousand there and five thousand in that one.' He drank his third drink. 'That's twenty-five thousand. And you get another seventy-five when you deliver. One–hundred–thousand–dollars.' Matheson enunciated each word carefully. 'That should go a long way toward making it seem easier. *And* ...' he tapped the table for emphasis, '. . . And, you'll be absolutely safe. You see, this is going to be my last operation and I'm going for the fence on this one. It's going to be big, and I'm going to handle it all myself and then get out of the country. I'm the only one who'll see you, and I'm the only one who'll know you're coming.'

He stopped speaking suddenly and looked at Alex as though waiting for an answer, but all Alex could think of to say was, 'I see.'

That seemed to be satisfactory, for Matheson went on, 'Good. I'm glad you agree. Now, here's what will happen ...'

Alex wondered what Matheson would have done if he'd said 'I don't see' or 'That's crazy' or 'Peter Piper picked a peck of pickled peppers.' Probably nothing. He seemed to be conducting both sides of the conversation himself.

Alex tuned back in: '. . . on the west coast of Vancouver Island at a small fishing village called Tofino. There's one hotel there and one motel. You go to the *motel* on the seventeenth of February, that's a Friday, and stay there until someone contacts you. It will probably be that night, but it might be the next night or the night after. Anyway, stay in your room after seven o'clock every night until someone brings you thirty kilos of cocaine. After that you bring it across the mountains and deliver it to me in San Francisco and pick up your seventy-five thousand. Okay? You know where Vancouver Island is?'

Thirty kilos. That was sixty-six pounds of cocaine. *Sixty-six pounds*!

'Yes, I know where it is.'

'Good. To get to Tofino all you have to do is take the ferry from Vancouver to the town of Nanaimo, and then it's a couple of hours' drive from there to Tofino. How

long is it going to take you to get it across the border and
down to San Francisco?'

'It depends on the weather. If the weather's good, it'll
take about two or three days to cross the border and then
another day at least to get to San Francisco. Say five days.
Maybe seven or eight if I run into bad weather.'

Alex couldn't believe what was happening. How could
he be sitting here talking calmly about the effect of the
weather on the delivery of thirty kilos of cocaine. This was
what had killed Gordon.

'All right. I'll expect to hear from you by the twenty-
second or twenty-third. Or a few days later if the weather
is bad up here.' Matheson poured a fourth drink and took
it all at one swallow, as he had the first three. 'When you
get to San Francisco take a room in one of the downtown
hotels and call me at my office any time betwen 8:30 a.m.
and 3:00 p.m. Just tell the receptionist that you're . . .' He
thought for a few seconds, '. . . what was your friend's
name again? Wilson? Right, just tell her that your name is
Wilson and I'll make sure she puts you through to me, and
we can arrange someplace to meet.'

'On the telephone?'

'Sure. All you're going to say is "Hello, this is Bill, or
Fred or whatever his name was, Wilson, and I'd like to see
you"; and I'll say "fine, let's have a drink at Joe's Bar".
No problem. We go to the bar and make our arrangements there.'

Matheson picked up the whiskey bottle and studied the
label. 'Seagram's V.O., huh? I'll have to remember that.'
He put the bottle back on the table and stood up. 'I'm glad
you're cooperating on this. It saves me a lot of trouble and
as you can see . . .', he pointed to the money on the table,
'. . . you're going to do pretty well for yourself. A potful of
money for not much work and no risk. Not a bad deal at
all.'

He started for the front door. He was unsteady after the
four drinks, and his speech was beginning to slur. 'You
remember everything I said? Go to the motel, not the

hotel, on the seventeenth of February. Stay in your room in the evenings and someone will get in touch with you.'

Alex handed him his overcoat.

'When you get to San Francisco call me and say that your name is Wilson and we'll arrange things from there.'

He opened the door and started down the stairs, hanging on to the handrail, then stopped and said, 'If anything changes I'll get in touch with you, otherwise I'll expect to hear from you around the twenty-second or third.' He carried on down the stairs and out the front door.

Alex was in a trance. He walked slowly back to his chair and sat down again. He picked up his whiskey but didn't drink, just held it in his hand and stared at the money on the table. He heard the door open and looked up as Linda crossed the room and took the chair opposite.

'So what happened? What's this all about?' She stirred the pile of hundreds with a finger, knocking several of them onto the floor.

'I think he's crazy.' Alex's voice was flat and emotionless. 'I didn't say ten words the whole time he was here. It was like I'd already agreed to do it for him and he was just giving me a briefing on the when and how.'

He put his glass back on the table and continued in the same toneless voice. 'He wants me to go up to Canada and pick up thirty kilos of cocaine, carry it across the border and deliver it to him in San Francisco. This ...', he pointed to the money, '... is his down payment. It's twenty-five thousand dollars. I get another seventy-five thousand when I make the delivery.'

'And you agreed to all this? Are you fucking crazy?'

'I didn't agree or disagree. I didn't say one word. *He's* crazy. What was I supposed to do? Tell him to get lost? What if he has a car full of heavies downstairs? What if he comes down on you? No thank you.'

Alex was coming out of his trance. He stood up and said, 'I think I'd like to be out of his reach when I tell him I'm not going to do it.'

He stared agitatedly around the room. 'I've got to get out of here. Let's drive in to Seattle and walk around downtown or something.'

CHAPTER FORTY-THREE

Seattle

IT WAS SATURDAY NIGHT in Seattle. Cold rain was falling and people were scurrying from car to restaurant, from restaurant to theatre, from bar to bar. Lights reflected in the wet streets, and buses and cars hurtled by, their occupants cocooned from the evil weather and barely visible behind misted windows and flashing wipers.

Alex and Linda were oblivious to it all. They walked up one street and down the next, turning left or right without conscious thought, staying in the approximately ten by ten block area that constitutes downtown in a city that isn't quite big enough to have an uptown. They had been walking for an hour, but were no nearer to a solution to their problem than they had been at the start of their walk when Linda had said, 'If he really is leaving the country after this shipment, then it probably doesn't make any difference to him what the police find out. The sensible thing for him to do is to kill you when you make the delivery. That saves him seventy-five thousand and leaves one less person behind who knows anything.'

'But what about the money he gave me? Why would he give me that much if he was just going to shoot me?'

'Twenty-five thousand? That's nothing. If twenty-five thousand will keep you happy until you make the delivery then he's made a hell of a bargain.' She stopped and looked up at him, oblivious to the rain hitting her face.

'Do you have any idea how much he can make with thirty keys of coke?'

'No.'

'Do you know anything about cocaine at all?'

'Just what Gord told me, and what you've told me. Other than what I've read in magazines and newspapers, that is.'

They turned a corner and walked on through the rain and Linda said, 'Basically he's got two choices. Depending on how greedy he is, how much risk he's willing to take and how much time he's willing to put into it; he can either sell the whole lot of it at once to someone who's into full-time dealing, or he can try to sell it off in smaller amounts, a kilo or a pound at a time, to smaller dealers. But if he's really leaving the country right away then he's probably got someone lined up to take the whole thirty kilos.'

'I think that's what he does, because he said that Carl, the one who shot Gord, worked for somebody else, and it was Carl that took the whole shipment last time.'

'So what's happening ...', said Linda, '... is that Matheson has some connection in South America, in Bolivia, or Peru or Columbia, where he can buy cocaine. He has it brought up here and sells it to somebody and never actually gets involved in the distribution business at all.'

'So how much can he sell it for?'

'If it's any good he'll probably be selling it for something like fifty thousand a kilo, whatever that works out to.'

Alex did the multiplication in his head. 'One and a half million.' He stopped walking and said, 'But Gordon said he thought that the load we brought in, which was only fifteen kilos, would be worth about two million.'

'It would have been worth a lot more than that eventually, but Matheson would only be getting somewhere around fifty a key for it unless he was distributing as well as importing.' She took Alex's arm and walked on. 'It gets more and more profitable at each step. Matheson sells it for fifty thousand dollars a kilo, but whoever buys it is going to cut each kilo half and half with something else and then resell the sixty new kilos for about fifty thousand each, which means about three million. If he paid Matheson one and a half that gives him a profit of one and a half million, but he has to make a lot of one and two kilo sales, which ups the risk by quite a bit.'

'And then?'

'And then,' she continued, 'whoever bought a kilo will cut it again – at least half and half – and sell it in ounces or grams, for as much as a hundred and fifty a gram; and if you try and figure the profit there you'll run right off your calculator.' She looked up at him. 'Go ahead, work it out. Just say the average price will be one hundred a gram. That's a hundred thousand a kilo, but for each kilo that he bought he gets two kilos after it's been cut, so that's two hundred thousand dollars for each fifty thousand dollar kilo, and there were sixty of those.'

'*That's twelve million dollars.*' Alex was stunned.

'Plus one and a half million at the first sale and three million at the second sale. Don't forget those.'

'Fifteen, sixteen and a half million.'

'It's hard to say exactly, but it'll be something like that. Somewhere around fifteen million by the time it's all over, but Matheson's share is only one and a half million.' She paused. 'So even if it's costing him a few hundred thousand to buy it and have it shipped up here he can still afford to lay twenty-five thousand on you to keep you happy for a while.'

Alex did not want to be involved. He wanted only to return the twenty-five thousand and tell Walter Matheson to find somebody else, to leave him to live his life in peace. But what could he do? If he refused to help, there was a chance that both he and Linda would be killed immediately. If he went through with it then he might well be killed on delivery. If he went to the police he would probably be killed before he could testify at any trial.

They walked and talked, but they could think of no safe

way to make the delivery or to protect themselves afterward, and finally they gave up trying.

It almost seemed the best chance they had was to go through with the smuggling and hope that Matheson was telling the truth. That he *would* pay the seventy-five thousand and leave the country, leave them in peace.

Cold, wet and depressed they returned to the van and drove home. They shared a long hot shower and went to bed, wondering if a normal life would ever be possible for them; wondering how long life could last for two caterpillars in the middle of a freeway.

Linda half-woke and rolled over to snuggle against Alex, but he wasn't there. She sat up. It was dark and felt like the middle of the night. Where was he? Still not fully awake she stood and stumbled out of the bedroom to find him in the living room. There were maps spread out all over the floor and Alex was kneeling in the middle, measuring distances and making notes on a sheet of paper.

'What are you doing?'

He stood up and stretched. 'I couldn't sleep.' He said, 'I kept thinking about a way out of all this, and I think I've found it.'

They had turned the heat down in the house when they went to bed and Linda was hugging herself against the cold. 'How?'

'Put some clothes on and I'll show you.'

Soon they were both kneeling in front of three small maps. 'These things show the area along the border where Gord and I came across last time. That's Mt. Redoubt on the far right and you can see all the trails marked in green. Now, what we do, you and I, is to pick up the cocaine in Canada and bring it across here . . .' he pointed to a bright green line just to the west of Mt. Redoubt. 'We can drive to within half a mile or so of this trail on the Canadian side and then just ski the length of the trail till it ends here at the Hannegan Campground where we'll have a car stashed.'

His finger traced the route across two of the maps. 'That's what Gord and I did, except that we went up and over the west ridge of Mt. Redoubt and missed a section of the trail. Now,' he pointed to the third, westernmost map, '... the road from Hannegan Campground joins the main road not far from a little town called Glacier. And here ...', he pointed to a spot halfway between Glacier and Hannegan Campground, '... there's a trail that comes right down to the main road, called the Excelsior Pass Trail.'

'That green line with all the zigzags?'

'That's right. The zigzags mean that the trail climbs very steeply – see how close together the contour lines are?'

'Yes. So?'

'So what we can do is this: We tell Matheson that we are going to meet him in the town of Glacier and that he should take a room in the motel there. Then, when we've brought the load across we take it to the Excelsior Pass Trail and stash it just a little way off the road, and I'll wait there. You go to a telephone – there's a couple of bars and gas stations along the road that you could call from – and call Matheson and tell him where the cocaine is and that he should go there and pick it up and leave the money.'

Linda was not impressed. 'So how does that protect you? If anything, he can shoot you more easily there than in San Francisco.'

'No, that's the beauty of it. He's never going to see me. He can bring along ten carloads of goons and it won't make any difference. The *only* thing we need to make this work perfectly is a pair of portable transceivers.'

Alex stood up and went to the liquor cupboard and returned with a bottle of Remy and two snifters. 'Here's how it works.' He poured them each a drink. 'You call him from the gas station or wherever and then drive back and hide the car somewhere near this Excelsior trail. Then you pick a spot nearby, on the other side of the highway where you can hide in the trees and wait. When he arrives you call me on the transceiver and I go up the trail a bit

until I'm out of sight. You can tell me if there's anybody
with him and you can tell me when they've gone that it's
safe for me to come down.'

He drank half his cognac and continued. 'If he's left the
money for us, then fine, I'll pick it up and come down to
the road and we can drive away. If he hasn't left the
money, if he decides to rip us off, well there's nothing we
can do about it, but at least he won't have been able to kill
me. If he brings people like Carl and his friend you'll be
able to see how many go up the trail and how many come
back out, and even if they know I'm hiding up the trail
they won't be able to catch me. I can get up a steep trail a
lot faster than any of them are going to be able to, and
there's a good chance that there'll be enough snow that
they won't be able to chase me without skis anyway.'

Linda sipped her drink and studied the map, but said
nothing. Finally she spoke. 'Assuming that Matheson will
come up to this Glacier place, it would probably work, in
fact it's probably a good idea; but what I don't understand
is why you want to do it up there in the first place. Why
make things complicated with a bunch of screwing around
in the snow with walky-talkies when we could do the same
thing in San Francisco? We could stash the coke someplace, tell him where it is and then watch while he picks it
up.'

'I thought of that. In fact I'd rather do it in San
Francisco if we could because I don't think he's going to
be very happy about coming up here, but there are two
problems that I just can't see any way around.'

He finished his drink and started to pour another, but
changed his mind and put the bottle down. 'The first is
that anyplace we leave a suitcase in San Francisco, it could
be stolen before Matheson gets to it; and the other thing
is, even if we could find a safe spot to leave it, how are we
going to know it's safe to pick up the money? All he has to
do, if he wants to kill me, is to leave somebody watching
the place he's put the money and whenever I come to pick
it up, bang.'

He picked the bottle up again and poured them each a second drink. 'No, if we do it up in the mountains then I can sit on top of the cocaine until you radio me that he's on his way up the trail, and we'll know with absolute certainty whether or not it's safe to pick up the money.'

'If he pays.'

'Yeah, if.'

They both sat silent after that. Finally Alex said, 'I'm not suggesting this because I want to do it. If there is some way to get out of the whole business then I'll take it, but the only way I can think of is to mail the twenty-five thousand back to Matheson and then disappear. Move to New York or someplace like that.' He sounded desperately unhappy. 'And if we have to do that anyway, I'd rather do it with an extra hundred thousand dollars.'

CHAPTER FORTY-FOUR

Vancouver

ANDY CUTLER left the elevator and walked gingerly across the room where he had spent so much of the last four years.

'Hey, look who's here.'

'Howyadoon, Andy?'

''Samatter, Andy, can't stay away from Drugs?'

'He's hooked. He's a Drugs addict.'

Cutler fended off the humour and limped into Sergeant Hofstadter's office.

'Got a coffee for me, Rico?'

'Sure, help yourself. How's it going upstairs?'

Cutler poured a cup and settled very carefully into a chair. 'Upstairs is fine, but I think my body's been run over by a truck.'

Hofstadter shoved aside the report he had been reading and picked up his cigarettes. 'Smoke?'

'Thanks.'

They lit up and Hofstadter asked, 'So what happened to your body?'

'You know how Val's into fitness – all those dance classes and racquetball? Well I decided I should maybe try to get into a little better shape myself, but I think I overdid it.'

Hofstadter laughed, then said, 'But you've always run haven't you?'

'Yeah, but not very hard. Couple of miles every other day.' He shifted in his chair and grimaced with pain. 'What actually happened was that Val came out with me for a run on Friday and cleaned my clock.' He sounded bitter. 'She doesn't even run, right? Just plays racquetball and does those stupid aerobics, and I couldn't come close to keeping up to her; so I figured I'd better shape up.'

Hofstadter was laughing again. 'So what did you do? Try to do it all in one day? Try to run a marathon or something?'

'Kind of. I came down to the club on Saturday and got Willy, the trainer, to show me around the weights. It felt okay, so yesterday I came down again, went for a run and then gave myself a real workout in the weight room.'

'Found out you're not seventeen anymore huh?'

'Seventeen? Christ! I feel like a hundred and seventeen. There isn't one part of my body that doesn't hurt. Not one! And that's not the worst of it either.' Cutler lowered his voice and leaned across the desk. 'She stayed at my place last night, and this morning we woke up and we're both feeling a little horny, so we start playing around a bit and pretty soon I roll over on top of her but my stomach muscles were so sore from the situps yesterday that I couldn't get up on my elbows and knees. It hurt so much I couldn't keep a hard on.'

He sounded disgusted. 'And she laughed at me. Laughed! As soon as I stop hurting I'll teach her something.'

'Poor Andy. Poor pussy-whipped Andy. Wait till I tell Angie. She'll never let you hear the end of this one. She'll . . .' The telephone rang and he picked it up. 'Hofstadter . . . Sure, just a minute.' He pushed the phone across the desk. 'It's for you. You want to take it here or in your office?'

Cutler stubbed out his cigarette and said, 'Here's fine if I can borrow some paper.' He took the receiver. 'Cutler . . . Fine, put him through.'

Five minutes later he hung up the phone. Hofstadter looked up from his paperwork and raised thick eyebrows inquiringly.

'That was Holley,' said Cutler. 'Lieutenant Holley, the narcotics guy in San Francisco. You remember I was telling Angie the other night that everyone involved was either dead or sitting tight and that Holley was pretty much back at square zero?'

'And now?'

'Now he's finally had a bit of luck. Someone that he caught with his pants down is trying to talk his way out of ten years in the pen with news about a big shipment of coke that's going to be handled by the people that Holley's been after for so long.'

Hofstadter stood up and walked over to his coffee pot and poured himself a cup, then said, 'From what I remember, he had his share of bad luck on this, so I guess he was about due for a break. But how does it affect you?'

'Actually Rico, now that I'm out of Drugs it probably affects you more than me, but I wouldn't mind handling it if it's okay with you.'

'What is it?'

'Nothing much. It's just that this guy, the promoter that Holley's fixated on, doesn't normally deal in cocaine, so he figures that there's a reasonable chance that Matheson is involved again. He's got him under loose surveillance and he's asked all the airlines and car rental people, and the U.S. Customs to put a flag in their computers for the name Matheson, and he's asking if we'll do the same up here.

'It would probably take me longer to explain it to one of your people than it would to do it myself.'

Hofstadter scratched his chin with his thumb and said, 'Sure, go ahead, just file a copy of your report with me and if anything comes of it let me know.'

'Not likely that much will come of it. Matheson's been burned pretty good up here, so he's probably bringing this one in through Miami or Portland. If it is Matheson. Still, we can but try.'

He stood up slowly and carefully. 'Thanks for the tea and sympathy, Rico. If I survive this fitness thing I'll give you a call in a couple of days to see if you and Angie want to come over for supper on the weekend.'

CHAPTER FORTY-FIVE

San Francisco

HOLLEY DRUMMED his long fingers slowly on his desk and wondered why, if Matheson was bringing in another load, he wasn't moving. All he had done for the last week was to go to his office in the morning and come home at night. Big deal. Big dealer.

Still, there was no choice. It fit the pattern of Matheson's previous shipments, so he had to be watched. But it was so fucking frustrating. The tempo of his fingers on the desk slowed even further. Half an hour in private with Walter Frederick Matheson and Holley would know everything there was to know about the man, and there would be no more guessing games about who was supplying what, and for how much, to whom.

He sighed. Money. It all came down to money. He could walk into any of fifty nearby bars, pick virtually anyone there, take him into the washroom and slap him senseless in his search for information. It didn't matter whether the man knew anything at all as long as he was poor. Nobody gave a shit one way or the other what Holley, or any cop, did to a nameless junkie, but let him so much as raise his voice to someone with money and he could kiss the case right off.

His fist crashed on his desk. Fuck it. He could play the game as well as anyone, and if Tomlinson was dealing massive amounts of smack, then he, William Holley, would deal with him massively.

He leaned back in his chair and rolled a few fantasies through his mind, and soon felt much better. The frustration was gone, his head was clear and he saw what he had been missing. If Matheson wasn't moving that didn't have to mean he wasn't involved. Maybe he had just been scared enough by the close call last time to run this one by remote control.

Five minutes later he was on the telephone explaining what he wanted to a Sergeant Hemslo in Seattle P.D. Narcotics.

'What I want is for you people to wire this Townsend down so tight that he can't scratch his ass without me knowing about it before he's finished doing it; but since you probably have a few other things going, and since this is kind of a long shot anyway, I'll take whatever you can give me and be happy with it.'

'Well sir, I'll tell you, normally what you would have got would have been the next thing to nothing at all, but as it happens I just might be able to help you.'

Hemslo was a slow talker and Holley gussed that he had come from somewhere a long way south and east of Seattle.

'We have some of our people doing a course at the academy right now. Some of our officers that is, not recruits. They're doing a course on surveillance technique and I don't see why they should be given an artificial problem if we can give them a real one and help you folks out at the same time. So why don't you just give me all the names and addresses again to make sure I copied it all, and we'll get on it for you.'

CHAPTER FORTY-SIX

Tofino (Canada)

7:30. HE TURNED ON the TV. There were only two channels and after an hour he had no idea what he had watched.

9:30. He had read every piece of printed material in the room but couldn't remember one word. He tried the crossword puzzle in the newspaper he had bought in the lobby but couldn't focus on it. He poured a drink. And another.

10:30. He finished his fourth drink and turned off the lights. He lay on the bed, fully clothed, and soon fell into unhappy, restless sleep.

At 11:15 he woke to the ringing telephone.

'Hello.'

'Mister Townsend?' A man's voice – nothing special about it.

'Yes. Who is this?'

'I want to meet you, Mister Townsend. I'm at the hotel, just down the road. I want you to wait for ten minutes then get in your van and drive down there. I'll be waiting in the bar.'

'Who are you?'

'Don't worry about that, I'll recognize you, just don't leave your room for ten minutes and don't forget to bring your van.'

'Are you . . .' But the line was dead. Alex hung up the phone and looked around the room. Nothing. A nothing motel room in a nothing town. He wished Linda was here

with him instead of in a hotel in Vancouver. He picked up
the brandy and walked to the bathroom where he took a
hit straight from the bottle and rinsed it round his mouth
then spat it into the sink.

He left the bottle uncapped on the counter top, put on
his jacket and, in a state of equal parts fear and anticipation, left the room and walked to his van.

He started it up and was about to release the handbrake
when a voice from behind froze him solid.

'Don't move.'

The muscles of his back and abdomen went rigid and his
sphincter clamped down hard. He was paralysed with fear
and couldn't have moved if he'd wanted to.

'Okay, now listen.' A man's voice, the same one he had
heard on the telephone, 'I want you to drive out of town
on the main road. There'll be a turn off, a dirt road on the
right, in about three miles. I'll let you know in plenty of
time. Just drive normally and don't try to turn around and
look at me.'

Alex tried to relax, tried to tell himself that he was in no
danger, that these people *needed* him; but the terrible ride
on the night Gordon was killed came back and shook him
and he could barely keep his hands on the wheel.

He drove, and gradually gained control. The fear was
still there, the memory of the drive with Carl would not go
away, but there had been no particular menace in the
voice behind him, and they really did need him alive to
make the delivery. Some of the adrenalin drained away
and he began to feel better.

'All right, slow down. In a minute or so you'll come to
the turn off ... Okay, there it is. Slow down and turn in
... Now just a couple of hundred yards down this road
you'll come to a spot where you can turn around.'

Branches slapped the windshield and scraped the side of
the van, then came the wide spot and Alex made a three
point turn and stopped.

'Kill the lights.'

He did as he was told.

SAN FRANCISCO   273

'Okay, pal, this is where I get off. The shit's here in the back in a suitcase, just give me a couple of minutes to get clear and then go back to the motel and get some sleep.'

Whoever it was opened the side door and stepped out into the darkness. The door slammed shut and Alex was left alone with the clatter of the engine.

He was on the first ferry the next morning and parking the car in the lot beside Linda's hotel at 10:20 a.m. Ten minutes later he was in the shower in her room washing away the sweat and smell and memory of the night. He called out to her to join him and they made soapy, slippery love, sitting in the bottom of the shower stall with the hot spray beating down on them.

When they were dried and dressed Alex said, 'It's going to take at least four hours to drive to the trailhead, so I guess we better get going. I'd rather stay here in Vancouver for a day or two, but I don't know how long this good weather will last, so . . .'

'I understand.'

CHAPTER FORTY-SEVEN

San Francisco

HE WOKE UP feeling better than he had in weeks. He took only one Extra Strength Tylenol before breakfast instead of the usual three, and was almost cheerful as he sat at the table and listened to his wife chatter.

As he sipped his coffee he wondered idly what she would do if he interrupted her and said, 'Marion, you old gasbag you, do you realize that this is the last time I'll ever have to look at your bloated body across the breakfast table?' On reflection he decided that she probably

wouldn't do anything; just say 'That's nice dear' and carry
on telling him what Sue Ann somebody-or-other had said
yesterday.

Thank God for prostitution.

And he wondered what she would do when he didn't
come home from the 'meetings in Atlanta' next week. Call
the police? That would be pretty funny, and he smiled at
the thought. Then, suddenly, it wasn't funny anymore. He
didn't care what she did or didn't do. He just wanted to be
finished with her. He stood up, said goodbye, got through
her fat embrace by thinking about what he would be
looking at across the breakfast table in Lima next week,
picked up his coat, attaché case and suitcase, and left the
house forever.

As he drove toward the centre of the city his mood
lightened. Walter Matheson had left his house at 7:30
a.m., as usual, and would leave his office at 9:00 a.m. to
attend a meeting on the other side of the country. And
that is the last that would be known of him. Somewhere
between his office and the airport Walter Matheson would
drop from the sight of the world.

He smiled. No matter how deep you probed he was
solid gold all the way through. He was tough – he had
shown that in Korea. He was smart – he had shown that at
M.I.T.. He was successful – he had shown that every day
since he opened his office. His studies were the ones they
based their forecasts on, built their hydroelectric mega-
projects on. His house showed how successful he was. His
cars, his clothes, his holidays. Everything about him
showed that. He was what all the little people in the world
wanted to be.

He laughed out loud. Stupid bastards. Anybody who
would work his ass off for forty-five years just to be able to
afford to play golf in Hawaii for two weeks every winter
until his heart exploded had to be an idiot.

Not him. He had seen the maggots in that chocolate bar
a long time ago, and he had other plans. He was retiring
now, in the prime of his life, and not with the kind of bank

account that would limit him to some condo full of geriatrics in Florida or Hawaii or Puerto Rico either.

He would spend his retirement fucking the most beautiful women in South America in his own villas in cities like Lima and Buenos Aires, and he had more money waiting for him down there than any doctor or engineer or corporation man could get if he lived to be a thousand. He had more money *in cash* in the attaché case on the seat beside him than most so-called successful people had in total when they retired.

He reached out and patted the case, and felt a thrill go through him at the touch.

Inside the case was everything he needed to get out of the country. There was cash: a chamois leather money belt with compartments all the way round holding 250 one-thousand-dollar bills, 50 one-hundred-dollar bills, and three small vials of baguette-cut emeralds – worth as much as the cash in any large city in North America or Europe. Twice as much if he wasn't in a hurry.

And there was a complete new identity: passport, credit cards and driver's licence in the name of Leonard Charles Findlay. All current and all indistinguishable from the real thing. The very best Japanese forgeries, arranged by his brother and shipped up only weeks ago.

And finally there was his protection and insurance: a Smith and Wesson .38 Police Special and a box of shells. He knew he couldn't risk trying to take it onto the airplane with him, but that didn't matter, there were plenty more like it in Lima.

As he got closer to his office his head started to hurt again and he took two more Tylenols from the bottle in his pocket. The headaches had been worse than ever lately, but the knowledge that they would be stopping within a week made it a little easier to take. That, and the decision he had made to leave no one behind who could connect him to anything illegal. After all, he might want to come back some day. He doubted it, but there was no sense in burning bridges if he didn't have to.

Tomlinson, the dealer, and whatever partners he might have were one thing; none of them had actually seen him with the cocaine in his hands, and they weren't going to be talking about it anyway; but this mountain climber was another matter. He had seemed nice enough, and he had saved Walter's life, but ever since he had phoned with his crazy plan about making the exchange up in the mountains Walter had been suspicious.

He would go up there and make the exchange all right, but what Townsend got in exchange for the cocaine was going to be half an ounce of lead.

CHAPTER FORTY-EIGHT

Vancouver

EVER SINCE his promotion and transfer, Andy Cutler's eating habits had gone downhill. For the two months he had either grabbed something from the cafeteria and brought it back upstairs to eat at his desk, or skipped lunch entirely. But sitting in his kitchen with coffee and the morning paper he decided that today, finally, he felt on top of the new job. Today he would only work till eleven-thirty or twelve and then take the rest of the day off. Start the weekend early with a good lunch at a good restaurant, maybe at one of the big hotels; and then maybe just walk around downtown a bit and do some window shopping. He needed a new suit and had noticed in the paper that some of the department stores still had sales on.

Driving to work he decided that some new shirts and pants wouldn't be a bad idea either, and that ten or ten-thirty would be a better time to knock off. There was nothing that needed his immediate attention, and he had worked most of the last three weekends so he was due for some extra time. Ten o'clock it would be.

When he reached his office there was a message on his desk from the switchboard requesting that he call Lieutenant Holley of the San Francisco P.D. as soon as possible. It was marked only ten minutes ago.

He cleared some space on his desk, emptied his ashtrays, made sure that pen and paper were handy, lit a cigarette and picked up the phone.

'Lieutenant, it's Andy Cutler in Vancouver, I've got a message here that you wanted me to call you.'

'I think Matheson is making his move and I wanted to let you know and to ask you to do a couple of things for me.'

No hello, no how are you doing, just straight to it. Well, that was Holley.

'Sure, whatever I can.'

'Good. Here's what's happened. I've had teams of three guys on Matheson for the last week and yesterday morning he just walked away from them. He went to his office in the morning and that was the last they saw of him. His car's still in his parking lot and his office says that he's gone to Atlanta for a series of meetings and won't be back for a week.'

'You must be a bit unhappy about that.'

'I am, Mister Cutler, but nowhere near as unhappy as the guys who said they were watching him. If they'd lost him in heavy traffic, or walking in a crowded shopping area I could understand it, but that building he's in is square, and if he slipped out of it while three of my detectives were watching then either he's Houdini, or two of them were having coffee somewhere.' He paused, then said, 'But it happened and there's nothing I can do about it now.'

'You don't think he went to Atlanta?'

'I've checked every airline that flies out of the entire Bay Area. Walter Matheson didn't fly to Atlanta or anyplace else. No one of that name flew anywhere or has a

reservation to fly anywhere in the next two months.' He
snorted. 'Not that that means dick-all. He could have
flown anywhere he wanted using another name. I've got
people checking out lists of all airline passengers who
bought tickets for cash, but that's going to take too long to
be of much use, so what I'd like to ask you to do is to
notify the RCMP in Prince Rupert that he might be
showing up again and ask them to watch for him, and for
anything on the docks that might be there to meet him.'

Cutler made a note and said, 'Sure, no problem there.
And I'll remind Customs and the airlines as well. Anything else?'

'There's one other thing. I'm not sure what it means,
but it could be important. You remember Townsend in
Seattle?'

'Yes, why? Has he vanished too?'

'You got it, Pontiac. I asked Seattle P.D. to put a watch
on him. They called early this morning and told me a
couple of things. The first is that he's moved. He and that
Cunningham woman have rented a place in Tacoma, just
south of Seattle. It was lucky I told them about her
because the new place is rented in her name, and so is the
telephone.'

Cutler dragged on the cigarette and said, 'I thought
Townsend was supposed to notify you of any change of
address.'

'I guess he forgot. Anyway Tacoma police found the
place and talked to the owner and found out where
Townsend is working, which is as a mechanic for some
lumber company. They talked to his boss this morning and
it turns out he's taken a couple of extra days off, starting
yesterday, and has gone skiing, but they don't know
where.'

Cutler said 'Hmmmm,' and Holley continued:

'Now let me put all this in perspective for you. You
remember that I told you that I heard that there was some
coke on the way?'

'Yes.'

'Well I've had that confirmed by a couple of other people. It's still a bit vague, and I haven't got any names or exact dates, but it looks like a fairly big shipment of coke is expected to hit town some time in the next week or so. Word hasn't reached the street, so I'm pretty sure it hasn't actually arrived yet, but if the middle-level dealers know about it, it can't be far off, so what I suspect is that Matheson is on his way to pick it up, and that maybe Townsend is going to help him again.'

'You could be right, Lieutenant.'

'I could be wrong, too, but what the fuck else have I got to work on? Which brings me to the other thing I need your help on . . .'

'What's that?'

'Assuming that they are bringing it into Canada first, and I've got people working on the other assumption, how are they going to get it down here from there?'

Where was Holley headed? 'I'm not sure I know what you mean. They could take it any number of ways. Car, bus, boat, airplane . . .'

Holley cut him off: 'The problem, Mister Cutler, is that they know that they're under suspicion. I just can't see either of them throwing a suitcase full of blow into the back seat and driving across the border with his fingers crossed. The same goes for flying. They've got to believe that wherever they clear Customs they're going to get the deluxe treatment – fluouroscopes, x-rays, ultrasound, the works – and it's still the middle of winter so I don't see them hiking through the mountains, so what are they going to do?'

The tone of the question was rhetorical and Cutler waited for the answer.

'The only thing I can think of', said Holley, 'is to hire a small plane again. That wouldn't be very smart either, because we've got to be looking for it, but . . .'

'But you'd like to ask me to keep an eye on the charter services anyway, right?'

'If you would. I don't think it's necessary, but I

wouldn't be doing my job if I didn't ask. Can you do that?'

Cutler thought about it for a few seconds. 'What I'll do is give the names and descriptions of Matheson, Townsend and the woman to the RCMP and ask them to circulate them to every charter service they can in B.C. and Alberta. It's not going to be anywhere near one hundred per cent effective, there's a lot of hungry pilots around, and the RCMP aren't going to be giving it top priority, but it's something. And I'll do the same with all the city police forces I can think of.'

He stubbed out his cigarette and wished he had some coffee. 'Like you say, it's probably not necessary, but it won't hurt.'

Holley said, 'Thanks a lot. I imagine that Matheson is bringing this one in through Miami or Mexico, or even through Atlanta, where he said he was going. But I know he's used the Canadian route before, so I've got to go through the motions.'

Cutler sympathized. Car chases and gunfights might sell movie tickets, but going through the motions was what ninety-nine per cent of police work was about.

'You're right, Lieutenant. Matheson is probably in Miami or San Diego and Townsend is probably skiing with his girlfriend at Aspen, but I guess we have to go through the motions and ...' He broke of in mid sentence and groaned aloud, then said, 'Oh shit!'

'What?'

'So much for my weekend.'

'What are you talking about?'

'Lieutenant, I was planning to take most of today off, start the weekend early. Spend some time with my girl-friend, maybe do some shopping today and then head out of the city for a day or two. It would have been my first time off in twenty-six days.'

'But?'

'But I just remembered something.' Cutler was weary. Sometimes he wished that he could turn his mind off, stop it from applying itself to problems that weren't really his. 'I spent some time with some climbers a few months ago, when we were looking into the Wilson murder, and one of the things they talked about all the time was skiing in places like Alaska and the Yukon. I'd never heard of any ski resorts up there so I asked one of them about it and he told me that what they all do is something called ski-mountaineering. It's sort of a cross between cross-country and downhill and apparently they can ski just about anywhere. Uphill, downhill, even right up to the tops of mountains ...'

Holley said 'And so?'

'So what this guy said was that anywhere you could go in the summer, you could go in the winter if you knew what you were doing ...'

'Yeah, so?' Holley still didn't see.

'So one thing they all agreed on was that Wilson and Townsend knew what they were doing.'

'Shit.'

'That's right, Lieutenant. I don't know what you're planning for your weekend, but it looks like I'll be spending mine talking to climbers and helicopter pilots.' He lit another cigarette and continued, 'I'll do some checking and try to find out whether it's possible for someone to hike or ski across the border at this time of year, and if it is I'll get back to you and we can start talking about organizing air searches.'

Holley didn't reply immediately. Then he said, 'Mister Cutler, don't think that I don't appreciate what you're doing for me. If it turns out that it would be possible for Townsend to bring the shit in on skis and you wind up spending your weekend in a radio room somewhere, I'll personally guarantee that there will be two tickets to San Francisco on your desk on Monday morning. You bring your ladyfriend down here next Friday and I'll treat you to the best weekend this city can offer.'

CHAPTER FORTY-NINE

North Cascade Mountains

HIS LOAD was uncomfortably heavy. Thirty kilos of cocaine was sixty-six pounds, the tent and their sleeping bags and ground pads added just under eighteen more; stove, food, fuel, pots and eating utensils was about ten; extra clothing maybe eight or nine; maps, compass, first aid, toilet paper, et cetera, came to another four or five; and the skis and poles which were strapped to their packs added about fifteen.

He tried to add it all up in his head as he walked but he kept losing track. Finally he got it right. Sixty-six plus eighteen plus ten plus nine plus five plus fifteen. One hundred and twenty-three pounds. And then the packs themselves were another four or five each, so that meant a total of a little over one hundred and thirty, and he was carrying a good bit more than half. He did some more arithmetic and finally decided that he must have about eighty pounds on his back. No fun at all. Especially not the first hour.

They left the van at 8:00 and crossed the border slash fifteen minutes later, but they couldn't find the start of the trail, and wasted a lot of time crashing around in spooky forest looking for it. Long beards of Spanish moss hung from the trees and it was easy to imagine trolls and goblins behind the huge trunks in the dim light.

Once they found the trail though it hadn't been too bad. The track was in decent shape and none of the creeks they had to cross presented any serious problem.

About an hour and a half after picking up the trail they stopped for a break beside the largest stream they had seen so far. Alex dropped his pack and collapsed on top of it.

'Thank God this trail isn't steep.' He sat for a few

minutes, breathing heavily, then dug his water bottle out of his pack and went down to the stream and filled it. 'Here, have some water.'

Linda took the bottle and drank slowly, passing it back when it was half gone. Alex took it and drank, then refilled it and drank some more.

'This is Bear Creek. This is where Gord and I joined the trail when we carried the last lot over.'

Linda was puzzled. 'But we've only just started. I thought you went over Mt. Redoubt so that you could avoid this trail. Why did you go a whole day out of the way just to miss three miles, when there's twenty more miles to go?'

'It was summer then. The three miles we missed were the three miles leading from the Canadian border. These trails are crawling with hikers in the summer and there are quite a few Rangers around to make sure that everybody camps in the designated places and carries out their garbage. We thought that there would probably be a couple of them watching the area right around the border, and we just didn't want to take any chances.'

Linda thought about that and then said, 'So why didn't *we* go that way?'

'No need to at this time of year. There won't be anybody on these trails, campers or rangers. We won't see a soul until we get to the other end where we left the rental car. Besides, I don't even know if we *could* have gone that way. At this time of year it would probably have taken two or three extra days, and exposed us to some severe avalanche danger.

They rested a few minutes longer, neither saying much until Alex stood and said, 'Better get going.'

They struggled into their packs and began the slow march along the valley bottom. The sun came and went with the vagaries of the cloud cover, and the temperature in the dripping, silent forest hovered just around freezing.

'How's your load?' he asked.

'Heavy. Not as bad as yours must be though. How are you doing?'

'The load's heavy, but I'll manage. The load in my head is heavier. I wish we didn't have to do this.'

He walked a few steps in silence then said, 'We *could* still back out you know.'

'What do you mean?'

'We could drop the loads right here and just not go through with it. Go back to the van and drive to Seattle to pick up what we need and then go to New York or wherever.'

Linda stopped and turned to face him. 'Alex, if we had just disappeared with the twenty-five thousand dollars we might have pulled it off, they might have figured it wasn't worth the effort to find us. But if we disappear while we've got thirty kilograms of their coke ... Well, they'd never stop looking. All the money in the world wouldn't be enough to keep us hidden if we did that.'

She stood, hands on hips, staring up at him until he said, 'You're right. I know you're right. I just wish there was some way out of this, some way we could just go back to Seattle and live like normal people.'

'Well, there isn't. But we're safe as long as we stick to your plan and as long as we disappear afterward. If we deliver on schedule, and with no hassles, then nobody is going to go to a lot of trouble about us. If we sit still and make it easy, then sure, someone might decide to kill us; but if we disappear, then nobody is going to work up a big sweat looking for us. And probably ...' she relaxed a little, '... probably they *will* pay us, to keep us from coming after them.'

'Us go after them? Are you crazy?'

'Nope.' She smiled, but there was no humour in her voice. 'You went up against two guys with guns and killed one, got both their guns and chased the other one away.' She reached up and touched his cheek. 'You and I know that you're just a frightened little mouse, playing in a game with a bunch of big, hungry cats, but to this

Matheson, and to whoever sent those creeps after you, you must look pretty deadly. They probably feel like pussycats playing with a panther.'

They hit skiable snow in the early afternoon at about thirty-two-hundred feet. They had already eaten lunch but they were still hungry, so they snacked while they stopped to put on skis and skins.

'We're almost there. Only four miles to go, but the pass is near five thousand feet and I think we're just over three thousand here so it's going to be a real grunt,' said Alex. 'It'll take two hours anyway with these loads. How are you doing?'

'I'll be fine. I'm not saying that it's fun, but I'm doing okay, you're the one with the big load.'

'At least getting the skis off our backs and onto our feet will help.' He shrugged into his pack and said, 'Ready?'

'Lead on, bwana.'

The last half mile up to the pass was the worst. They were tired, the snow was soft, and the hill seemed to go on endlessly. It was a broad open slope with high avalanche danger; but there was no other way and by four o'clock they were just below the saddle. Alex dropped back slightly and let Linda go ahead, breaking trail; and waited for the words he knew she would say when she reached the crest and saw the magnificent crags and spires of Mt. Shuksan silhouetted across the valley against the afternoon sky.

'Oh God, Alex, hurry up and look at this, it's beautiful!'

He came up beside her and dropped his pack. 'Quite a sight isn't it?'

'Let's camp right here.'

Alex looked around. They were in an exaggerated saddle with open slopes dropping away in front and behind and sketchily forested hills rising to the left and right.

Immediately on their right was a clump of gnarled old spruce, big around at the base but kept disproportionately short by the altitude. There was a nice flat spot behind them and he was tempted to say yes.

'No. Not quite right here.' He struggled to pick up his pack one last time. 'I think we'd better climb up to the left there, just a couple of hundred feet, so that we're well off the trail.' He pointed. 'See, just below the skyline there's two groups of trees. If we camp behind them we'll be out of sight of anyone who happens by, and we'll still have a view.'

He looked up thoughtfully, as if trying to see through the hill. 'In fact, we'll have a view out over the whole of the North Cascades. C'mon, it'll only take another twenty minutes or so, and the view will be worth it.'

CHAPTER FIFTY

North Cascade Mountains

FOR THE FIRST TIME in seven months Walter Matheson woke without any trace of a headache. The alarm in his watch chirped at 4:30 and he was up and out of bed almost before he realized he was awake. He put on the outdoor-type clothing he had bought in Seattle, strapped the revolver in its shoulder harness over the checked wool shirt and put some water on to boil in the kitchenette.

Goddamn, but he felt good. He hadn't felt this good since Korea. In fact he felt even better than he had in Korea. Korea had been pretty good, but here *he* was in charge. There was nobody to give him any orders, nobody to yessir, no sir. He was it. He had planned this whole operation, he had pulled it off, and in about seventy-two hours he would begin twenty or thirty years of enjoying the rewards.

He checked the mirror in the bathroom. It was a

three-way and came right down to the counter top. He
could see himself from the waist up and from all sides. He
looked good. The day-old beard, the lumberjack shirt and
the gun under his arm gave him a real don't-mess-with-me
look that he knew would cool out anybody who got in his
way. And underneath the shirt, invisible to the world, was
a quarter of a million in cash and that much again in
beautiful green stones. Enough to buy his way into or out
of anything he wanted.

He returned to the kitchenette and made coffee. As he
drank it he recalled last night when he had first looked
carefully at the maps he had bought, trying to decide what
route Townsend would use. There was a road across the
border that led to this area and it was possible that
Townsend would try that. The crossing was at a town
called Sumas and from the look of the road map it would
be a fairly popular crossing for any Canadian coming to
the Mt. Baker ski area. Townsend could just throw a ski
rack onto any car with Canadian plates and come across
like a hundred other people for a day's skiing.

But that meant telling the U.S. Customs that he was a
Canadian, and risking them tearing the car apart if they
found out he wasn't.

A look at the topographical maps showed that east of
the Sumas crossing the border went through a range of
steep, glaciated mountains, with several passes crossing
north to south and a few trails marked on the map that
went almost to the border. To Walter Matheson it didn't
look very promising, but to a mountain climber like this
Townsend it would probably be a piece of cake.

He knew that Townsend would have some complicated
plan for the delivery – why else would he have insisted on
meeting in this stupid motel – so he would just have to
figure that plan out and get to Townsend before Townsend
could put it into operation. It was Korea all over again. 'If
they think we're going to move through *here*, then they'll
probably try to ambush us *there*, so we have to figure out
how they'll get to there and set up an ambush of our own.'

But there were so many possibilities, and his head was hurting worse than it ever had. He looked at one route after another, but he just couldn't concentrate. It was like someone was inside his skull trying to bore his way out with a red hot poker.

And then he had seen it. He had been looking at a pass about twenty miles east when the words 'Mt. Redoubt' came blazing up off the page. The memory of the plane crash exploded in his mind and the man with the poker finally broke through his skull to the outside.

He had passed out at that point and awoken half an hour later sprawled on the floor beside the kitchenette table. As he clawed himself upright he realized that the pain was gone. Completely and utterly. Gone as if it had never been. And at the same time he knew with absolute certainty that Townsend would be coming up the valley below Mt. Redoubt. It was no longer a matter of weighing possibilities, of one route being more probable than another. There was now *only* one route. His life had changed when Townsend found him on Mt. Redoubt and now it would change again when he found Townsend there.

Fate? Karma? Kismet? Whatever, the game would be played to its end on the same ground where it had started.

He finished his coffee, and was soon driving through the pre-dawn darkness, humming tunelessly and smiling the secret smile of a man who knows all the answers.

It was really all so obvious and so easy. He would walk in to a good ambush point, kill Townsend as he came by, carry the cocaine out himself and be in San Francisco again tomorrow. He would make the sale tomorrow night and fly to wherever his fancy took him. Maybe a few days in Rome would be a good way to start his new life. He liked that. San Francisco to Lima. Via Rome.

There was one other car in the parking lot at the trailhead, a newish Citation that would be Townsend's getaway car. He laughed out loud, then grabbed his rented snowshoes from the back seat and set off up the trail.

He was wearing streetshoes and no jacket, but he didn't feel uncomfortable or cold. He was surrounded by some of the finest mountain scenery in the forty-eight states, but he didn't see it. His intention was to carry thirty kilograms of cocaine back down this trail and he didn't have a backpack; but he had tapped into the energy source of the universe and he knew that he could carry twice that, ten times that, if he wanted to.

By 7:40, when he reached the crest of Hannegan Pass and hid himself behind some big trees all of his toes had frozen and his left foot was solid almost to the proximal end of the metatarsals, but he didn't know or care. He was in the pilot seat where he belonged. He could see forever. He was Superman. He was God.

He was Walter Matheson and seven months after his accident an intracranial aneurism was spiralling him ever more swiftly into madness and inevitable death.

3

LINDA

CHAPTER FIFTY-ONE

North Cascade Mountains

THEY WERE ALREADY awake when the sun turned the top of their small tent into a translucent golden dome. Carrying the heavy loads had left them both exhausted at the end of the day and they had slept from sunset almost to sunrise, over twelve hours. But neither felt rested or refreshed and neither had much to say as they wriggled into their clothes.

Alex unzipped the door and stepped out, saying that he would get the stove going for tea, then poked his head back through the door and said, 'The food bag is tucked between the sleeping bags. I think there's a couple of cans of salmon in it for breakfast.'

She cringed. Canned salmon for breakfast? Then she realized with surprise that the thought of oily, salty salmon had her salivating in a way that bacon and eggs or granola could never have.

Fifteen minutes later breakfast was finished and they were on their second mug of tea. Alex looked at his watch.

'Ten to eight. Hmm.'

He stretched as best he could in the small tent then said, 'It's about an hour to the car and then maybe another hour to get set up on the Excelsior Pass Trail; even if it takes Matheson a couple of hours to get there, that's still only four hours.'

He drank off the last of his tea and began pulling on his boots. 'So I'll have five or six hours of daylight to get back down to the car and even if Matheson has some heavies along and I have to screw around in the bush for a while

to get away from them I'll still make it back before
dark.'

Linda said nothing. She was lacing her boots and trying
to think of some way their plan could go wrong, but she
could see nothing worse than inconvenience. Matheson
might not come until later in the day, in which case Alex
might spend a few chilly hours waiting; or Matheson might
have been delayed and not show up until tomorrow, in
which case they would simply rerun the whole show
tomorrow. But in any case they would be safe, and no
matter what Matheson tried in the way of a double-cross,
the worst that could happen was that she and Alex would
have to move east with a hundred thousand instead of a
hundred and seventy-five thousand.

No, this time they were covered. There would be no
careless slip-ups and no one catching up with them a
month from now. She finished tying her bootlaces and
followed Alex out the door, zipping it shut behind her.

The sun was well up and the whole world sparkled. To
the south and east the glaciated spires of the North
Cascades stood on proud parade, and to the west, shining
in the morning sun, were the jagged rock towers and
tumbling icefalls of Mt. Shuksan. The air had the clarity
that comes only with icy, bone chilling cold, but it was
beautiful, and for a minute Linda gave herself a holiday,
to a world in which Walter Matheson did not exist and she
and Alex were here in the mountains to enjoy a few days
of skiing and sunshine.

When she came back to reality Alex had struck the tent
and was putting the last of their loads into the packs.

'Alex.'

'Uhuh?'

'We don't have to move to the east you know.'

'What?'

'Afterward, after today, we could move somewhere
that would be far enough away to be safe without leaving
the mountains couldn't we? Like Colorado? Or Alaska?'

'We can move anywhere we want to.' He stood up and

looked around him. 'I don't want to leave the Seattle area.
I like my job, and I like this part of the world; but I don't
want to be killed, and there'll be good jobs in other
places.' He clamped on his skis. 'But we don't have to
decide now. When we're finished here we can go to New
York and stay with your friend Michael for a little while.
Maybe I'll like it there.' He shouldered his pack and
picked up his poles. 'Or we can go skiing or climbing
somewhere for a while and think it all over. Don't worry.
We may have problems, but we've also got a fair bit of
money stashed away, and we've got each other.'

That thought comforted her. They would be able to
take a room in a quiet hotel somewhere at the end of the
day, probably seventy-five thousand dollars richer, and
plan the rest of their lives.

She started to put on her skis but suddenly felt the
familiar early-morning message from her lower intestine,
more urgent than usual after two huge mugs of tea.

'Can you wait a few minutes, Alex? I've got to go to the
john.'

'Sure.' He said. 'Or better still, I'll take off now and
check out the trail down from the pass.'

'Whatever you like.' She kissed him on the tip of his
nose and hugged him clumsily through all the layers of
clothing they were wearing, and then stood back as he
kick-turned a hundred and eighty degrees and shuffled
through the trees to the edge of the hill. She plodded
through the deep snow behind him and watched as he flew
down the slope below, cranking smooth turns despite the
heavy pack on his back, heading toward the pass and then
banking right and going further down the slope the way
they had come up yesterday, finally coming to a stop
about two hundred and fifty feet below the pass.

She smiled to herself. He hadn't been the least bit
interested in 'checking out the trail', he had just wanted to
get in a few extra turns.

Which was fine. It would take him ten or fifteen minutes
to climb back up to the saddle so she could have a leisurely

shit and get a few pictures of Mt. Shuksan, and maybe a few of the campsite, before the sun got too high.

'First things first though,' she said aloud, and went looking for the toilet paper.

She was on her knees in the snow trying to sort out the best shot of a section of a wind-gnarled pine. The tree was in the right of the frame, her pack and skis in the centre but further back and slightly out of focus, and the blurred mass of Mt. Shuksan was in the background just as she wanted it. But something was bothering her and she wouldn't make the exposure until she found out what it was.

She checked the frame from left to right. Mountain, sky, pack and skis, tree. Nothing lying around on the snow to distract the eye, light at the right angle, aperture set for just the right blur – mountain out of focus completely and pack and skis out of focus just enough to leave the tree as the main attraction. What was wrong?

Angrily, she lifted her head, hoping to see bare-eye what she was missing through the finder.

Then she knew. Voices. The picture was fine but she could hear voices where there should only be silence. She couldn't hear the words, but she could hear the anger and all thought of photography vanished as she ran frantically toward her skis.

ALEX! Someone had found Alex!

She clamped her mouth shut and screamed soundlessly as she floundered through the snow, each step taking forever while her mind raced at lightspeed through a hundred nightmares. She pulled her skis from where they were standing and threw them flat on the snow, then fumbled with desperate, clumsy hands to clamp the bindings down on the toes of her boots. But her fingers belonged to somebody else and her feet wouldn't obey her mind.

Finally both skis were on and she stood up and grabbed for her poles, but haste tangled her feet and she collapsed face first in the snow.

On the verge of hysteria she rolled over and levered herself back upright, spitting snow and swearing and crying incoherently. She grabbed the poles and raced clumsily to the brow of the hill and without stopping to think, beyond being *able* to think, she planted both poles and shoved off with fear-amplified strength.

Below her, hobbled by his skis and pack, Alex was struggling desperately with a man in a red shirt. She locked into the sight and pointed her skis downhill. She had never gone this fast before, but in her tormented mind she seemed to be making no progress at all, skiing in snow that was glue and in air so thick she could feel it holding her, pushing back against her.

Then the man in red broke free and smashed Alex across the face with something in his hand. A gun! Fear lashed her and she bit down hard to remain silent while in her mind she was screaming 'No, don't do it you bastard, don't shoot him or I'll kill you. I'LL KILL YOU. I'LL KILL YOU I'LLKILLYOUKILLYOU.'

Alex swayed, blood streaming from his face and the man stepped back and raised the gun.

She wasn't close enough. She would never get there in time.

'Aaaiiieeeeee ...'

Her scream was louder than a thousand sirens. The man jerked as the gun fired, and tried to turn, tried to bring his weapon to bear on her, and died in instant pain as the tip of her ski pole came through his left eye and into his brain with her full weight behind it.

CHAPTER FIFTY-TWO

Vancouver

THERE WERE TOO many people. To get the job done really only required the pilots and a couple of climbers who were familiar with the mountains along the border. Everybody else could be briefed later and it wouldn't make the slightest difference to the operation, in fact everything would run more quickly and smoothly that way. But since this involved several different agencies from two countries the name of the game had become protocol, and Andy Cutler was rapidly losing interest.

The RCMP would be doing the flying on the Canadian side and in addition to their pilots they had sent along Inspector Mandell to oversee their interest in the case. Mandell had jughandle ears, a bald head and no sense of humour at all. He didn't like the idea of using his people on an American operation that was unlikely to produce any result, he didn't seem to like Cutler, and he definitely didn't like the long-haired climber in the corner.

The American DEA would be making the arrest and had sent two field agents up from Portland. One of them was a woman and Inspector Mandell didn't like that very much either.

The U.S. Air Force, which was going to handle the flying on the American side, had sent two pilots and an observer, a Colonel who wasn't too happy about the idea of having the RCMP involved at all. He remembered what had happened the last time RCMP pilots had tried to help on this particular case, and had made it clear to Mandell that the success probability of the mission would go up sharply if USAF did the flying on both sides of the border.

And the Vancouver Police Department had decided to send one of its own brass along. To do what, wondered Cutler. Observe all the other observers? It turned out to

be a tall, impressive looking captain named Sutherland
who took one fast glance around the room and called
Cutler aside.

'Sergeant, who really matters here?'

Cutler wasn't sure what that meant until Sutherland
added, 'In terms of the air search that is.'

'Only the pilots, sir, and those two guys in the corner
with the maps.'

'Okay, sergeant, watch this.'

Captain Sutherland moved to the front of the room, and
without seeming to raise his voice, caught everyone's
attention with his first word.

'Gentlemen, Madam, as you all know we're here to
finish a job that should have been finished almost a year
ago ...' Cutler could see Mandell glaring, and the Air
Force Colonel smiling, '... I believe that the reason for
the failure on that occasion was inadequate preparation
and inadequate communication and coordination between
the various agencies involved ...' Mandell lightened up a
bit and the DEA types keyed in on 'communication and
coordination': '... so I'm pleased to see this many senior
people here today ...' Sutherland looked like the kind of
lawyer who sat on a lot of boards and all the 'senior
people' were quite happy to suck up to him. 'Now, since
there isn't much time I suggest that we get started right
away. I've reserved a more comfortable conference room
for us upstairs and lunch will be available for anyone who
wants it.'

Cutler doubted that he had reserved any room or
ordered any lunches. But there would be plenty of empty
rooms upstairs at noon on a Saturday, and a call to the
cafeteria would have lunch available quickly enough.

'Sergeant Cutler,' Sutherland made it sound like an
afterthought, 'if you could see to the others, we should be
done in an hour or so ...'

He opened the door and somehow, without seeming to
do anything, separated Mandell, the DEA agents and the
Air Force Colonel from the group and led them out of the

room. Less than a minute later he was back, and in a voice just loud enough for everyone still in the room to hear, he spoke to Cutler.

'Okay, sergeant, I've cleared the deadwood out of the way for you. I'll keep them amused upstairs until you're finished here and then try to get them to buy whatever you've planned. How long is it going to take you?'

'Probably about an hour, sir.'

'Fine. We'll be in Room 502, just call me there when you're done.' And he was gone, leaving Cutler feeling awed, and everyone else feeling important and ready to work.

Soon there were maps spread everywhere and the two climbers, Paul Goossens and a friend of his named Henderson, were going over all the routes they felt possible for a man on foot or on skis at this time of year, and the pilots were making notes and putting marks on their own maps.

Cutler didn't contribute much himself, except to make sure that there was plenty of coffee and sandwiches.

CHAPTER FIFTY-THREE

North Cascade Mountains

SHE WAS FACE DOWN in the snow and her legs and skis were tangled beneath the corpse of Walter Matheson. She made no move to extricate herself or to clear the snow away from her nose and mouth. Her mind was numb and she floated in a timeless trance, drifting slowly over the glowing red embers of Hell.

But when her first inhalation brought a lungful of snow, her body jerked into action without guidance, and as she twisted onto her side her mind returned.

ALEX! Oh God ... *He had shot Alex.* Frantically she tried to pull free, to run to where Alex lay only a dozen feet away, but her legs were trapped and she couldn't move.

She grabbed Matheson's body and rolled it off her legs. She stared for one brief instant of madness into the bloody eye socket and then drew her knees up so that she could reach her feet and unlatch her bindings. It was then, lying in the snow on her side, groping for her feet, that she heard the sweetest sound of her life.

'Linda?'

The last binding came free and she rolled onto her feet and ran to him.

'Alex, oh Jesus, Alex, are you all right?'

Sobbing with joy and sorrow she fell to her knees in the snow beside him. He was lying on his back, still strapped into his pack, pressing his right shoulder with his left hand and staring at her in pain and bewilderment.

'What happened? How did you get here?'

She said nothing, just took his face between her two hands and kissed him as gently as she could, then began unfastening his pack straps.

'What happened? Matheson was here and he shot me ... Has he gone? ... Where is he? ... I think he's crazy ...'

He lay still, speaking slowly, confused.

'Shut up. He's not coming back. He's dead so don't worry about him.'

The straps were all loose but she left him lying against the pack and moved to undo his ski bindings.

'Can you move your right arm?'

He lifted the arm an inch or two and gasped with pain. 'It hurts, God how it hurts.'

She finished with the skis and then said, 'I'm going to have to take your jacket and shirt off. Even if it does hurt, I've got to do it, Alex, okay?'

'Okay.'

Alex was able to sit up, and the jacket and zip-front pile

shirt came off easily, but underneath he was wearing a
body-hugging long sleeve undershirt and he groaned with
pain and almost passed out when she raised his arm to get
it off over his head.

The shoulder was a mess, especially at the back where
the bullet had exited, but there was no arterial blood
spurting out and he had been able to move the arm, so she
hoped that the damage was less serious than it appeared.
At least the front, the part Alex could see, didn't look too
bad.

He sounded fairly calm and rational and she wondered
if she would have been able to hold herself together as
well if it had been her who had been shot.

She took off her own jacket and light pile sweater. The
sweater was made of a fleecy material called bunting and
was the softest garment available. She draped it over his
shoulder and tied it in place as well as she could with his
undershirt, then helped him into his pile shirt and outer
jacket. She could feel the cold through her own underwear and was glad for Alex's sake that there was no
wind.

She looked at him. He seemed all right, didn't appear to
be going into shock. 'Do you think you can ski, or should I
set up the tent so you can wait while I go for help?'

'I don't know. Help me up.'

She put her jacket back on and then, as gently as she
could, she helped him stand and watched as he took a
tentative step, watched him stare in fascination when he
saw Matheson's strangely mutilated face.

'What happened to him?'

Alex stepped slowly through the snow until he was
looking straight down at the dead man.

'Did someone shoot him too? I don't remember anything after he shot me.'

'We were lucky Alex, that's all,' she said quietly. 'He
didn't hear me coming and I just managed a lucky stab
with my pole.' She came to stand beside him. 'I wonder
how he knew to come here?'

Alex put his uninjured arm around her and leaned on her for support.

'He said that he knew everything, that he could figure out my route because he had unlocked the secret power of his mind. He was crazy, Linda, completely insane.'

They stood like that, she supporting him, and neither able to look away from the strange face for almost a full minute. Finally Alex said, 'If you can help me put on his snowshoes and rig some kind of sling for my arm I'll try to make it down to the car.'

He shuffled back along his own footsteps and sat on the pack while she untied the snowshoes from Matheson's frozen feet, and transferred them to his. When she finished that she took off her jacket again and then her undershirt. Despite the sunshine it was cold, and goose-flesh rose on her skin and her nipples puckered before she could get the jacket back on. Her undershirt was the same stretchy, long sleeved kind that Alex had been wearing and using the two of them she was able to fashion a fairly comfortable sling for him.

'Just sit there for a minute, Alex.' She walked toward the body. 'I'm going to drag him behind those trees, and the pack too.'

She took a strong grip on the collar of the red shirt and began to pull. It was hard work, made harder by the deep snow, and it took several minutes to make the fifteen feet to the shelter of the trees. She was sweating hard when she finally got there and she squatted down beside the corpse to catch her breath. She wiped her forehead and was about to stand up and return for the pack when she saw the light tan of some kind of leather belt or pouch where Matheson's wool shirt had pulled clear of his pants.

At first with idle curiosity and some revulsion, but then with growing excitement she pulled the shirt out all the way around and unbuckled the belt, knowing by its weight and feel what she would find inside . . .

CHAPTER FIFTY-FOUR

Vancouver

THE MEETING was going well enough, but Cutler was unhappy. He liked Paul Goossens and truly regretted having had to lie to him, but he was sure that the young climber would not have agreed to help otherwise.

On the other hand, Cutler thought, maybe I told him the truth. For all I know Townsend *is* being forced to do this against his will. But he doubted it. If Townsend was carrying another shipment across for Matheson it was probably for one of the usual reasons. Money or adventure. Probably both.

It was too bad. Townsend had seemed like a nice guy and Cutler almost felt sorry for him. He had fallen into this by accident, but soon, if the pilots got lucky, he would be in the slammer.

Fuck it. Cutler stubbed out a cigarette with more force than he needed. Just fuck it. If Townsend got sent up it would serve him right. He had had every chance. Holley had bent over backward to treat him well but he had lied from start to finish and refused every offer of help.

Cutler lit another cigarette and calmed down. Townsend was probably skiing at Lake Tahoe or Aspen, and Matheson was probably having the shipment brought in through Miami, and the whole thing would go the same route that ninety per cent of all drug cases went. Down the fucking tube.

He poured a cup of coffee and leaned back against the wall and tuned out the talk of passes and trails and altitudes and search quadrants; thought of Valerie, and what they should do next weekend.

'Sergeant Cutler?'

Someone was calling his name and he snapped back out of dreamland.

'Sergeant Cutler?'

It was a very young constable looking at him from the doorway.

'Yes?'

'Sorry to interrupt, sir, but there's no telephone in this room and there's a call for you. A long distance call. You can take it in 213 if you like. I'll have them switch it through.'

Cutler was grumpy and unhappy and didn't want to talk to anybody on the telephone. But he didn't want to hang around this room either, and it was probably Holley so he could hardly refuse to answer.

'Sure, lead on.'

He was gone for more than fifteen minutes and when he returned he walked into the room and said nothing for another minute. He just stood and listened to the talk at the table, watched fingers pointing to maps and pencils making notes.

Finally he spoke.

'Party's over, folks.'

They all looked up at him.

'It looks like we're not going to need an air search after all.' He looked at the two RCMP pilots. 'You guys can go home, and you guys ...', he turned to the USAF pilots, '... are to wait here. It looks like one of you is going to get to take the DEA people into the hills. The bigshots are on their way downstairs and they'll tell you all about it.'

He turned to the two climbers and said, 'You guys come with me.'

He took them to the next room. 'Paul, your friend Alex Townsend is on his way to a hospital in Seattle. I've just spoken to his girlfriend on the telephone. She says he's been shot, but it looks like he's going to be okay. I'm sorry I can't tell you anything more than that right now, except that it looks like I was right, that he was doing this under threat and I doubt that he'll be charged with anything.'

He looked at them in silence for a few seconds then said, 'Do you know where Hannegan Pass is?'

They both nodded.

'And you can get around on skis okay?'

They nodded again.

'Well, if you go back to the other room and make those two facts known you'll probably be asked to shepherd a couple of American narcs on an investigation. You'll get to see a fairly fresh corpse and sixty-six pounds of cocaine.'

The two climbers started for the door but Goossens stopped halfway there and said, 'Do you want me to call you when we get back to let you know what happened?'

Cutler took a deep drag on his cigarette and spoke through the smoke as he exhaled. 'You can call if you want to,' he walked past them and out of the room, 'but nobody's going to be answering my telephone this weekend.'

CHAPTER FIFTY-FIVE

Seattle

THE SUN WAS STREAMING in through the window and the room looked as cheerful as a hospital room ever can. Linda had bought the biggest, most colourful fuchsia she could find and put it on a table by the window, and brought a stack of books and magazines, which now lay in disarray on the floor beside Alex's bed.

They had told the same story over and over. On Saturday night to the Seattle Police and on Sunday morning first to the DEA and then to Lieutenant Holley who had flown up from San Francisco. The story hadn't varied, and it had been easy to tell because it was almost true.

Almost. There had been one addition and one omission. The addition was death threats from Walter Matheson:

Alex and Gordon had saved his life after the crash and he
had responded by threatening to end theirs if they did not
carry his cocaine. The omission was the matter of money:
they said nothing of the fifty thousand dollars.

The same for Gordon's death. They told it almost as it
had happened, adding only that Matheson had ordered
the deaths.

And finally they told of trying to disappear by moving to
a house under Linda's name, and of Matheson finding
them and once more ordering them to carry for him or
die. And again they failed to mention money. Or rather,
Alex failed to mention the twenty-five thousand he knew
about, and Linda failed to mention the vastly larger sum
he didn't know about. She had put the money belt on
under her jacket when she was out of Alex's sight and had
not mentioned it to him on the walk out or the drive to
Seattle. She had known that he would be hospitalized and
probably heavily drugged, that there was a risk that he
might be unable to maintain the lie under police interrogation. If that happened ... well, what he didn't know he
couldn't talk about, and the contents of that belt would be
waiting at the end of whatever the courts did to them.

But it hadn't happened. The cathartic effect of being
able to tell most of the truth for the first time in six
months, and the emotion-blunting effect of the demerol,
had made it easier; letting him tell his small lies without
guilt, letting him face Lieutenant Holley without fear.

A week after Alex had been carried into the emergency
ward of Harborview hospital the attending physician in
charge of his case told him that he was going to heal just as
well at home as at the hospital.

'Stay in tonight, and I'll have another look at you in the
morning, but I don't think that there's anything that we
can do for you here that can't be done at home. You may
or may not regain 100% of the motion in your shoulder
joint, but it'll be close. You'll lose some of your strength,
but all things considered you're lucky to be alive at all.'

He started for the door. 'Have your ladyfriend change the dressings twice a day and come and see me in my office in a week.'

When the doctor was gone Linda said, 'Do you feel up to a short walk?'

'Sure, there's nothing wrong with my legs.'

Alex struggled into jeans and a sweatshirt and Linda helped him with his socks and shoes.

'There's a park just a block from the hospital, let's go and get some fresh air while the sun is still shining.'

The day was warm for the first of March and they sat together on a bench in the little park letting the afternoon sun melt the winter from their bodies.

'How do you feel?'

'My shoulder hurts like hell every time I move, and I'm worried about whether I'll get my strength back, but I just feel so good about being clear of Walter Matheson that I think you could cut off my other arm and I wouldn't mind.' He dropped his good hand into her lap and she took it in both of hers. 'You have no idea how good it felt to be able finally to tell the truth, and to be able to lie down at night without worrying about who might be knocking on the door in the morning.'

He stood up and stretched in the sun, rotating his upper body one way and then the other. 'Just to be standing here in the sunshine with you seems to be almost a miracle.' He looked down at her. 'Do you understand what I'm saying? For the first time in six months we can make plans for tomorrow without having to wonder if we'll still be alive tomorrow.'

She tugged him gently back onto the bench. 'I've got something for you.' She reached into her purse. 'If you're making plans for tomorrow you might like to have a look at this.'

It was an envelope addressed to Linda. Inside was a brief handwritten note on a single sheet of paper:

'Thanks for your letter. Why don't you drag your new

man out here for a visit sometime soon? Everybody misses you. Especially me.'

It was signed 'Love, Michael'.

'Michael?' said Alex. 'Oh, the photographer. Your partner.'

'Ex-partner.'

'You want to take a holiday in New York?'

'Someday. The important thing is that he says he got my letter.'

'Your letter?'

'Actually, it wasn't a letter, it was a package with a letter inside.' She turned on the bench so that she was facing him. 'I didn't know how it would go at the hospital Alex. You aren't much of a liar, and if the police got rough with you, especially if you were groggy and weak, I thought that there was a chance you might not be able to hold it all together.'

Alex started to interrupt, hesitated, then said, 'I understand.'

'Anyway, it looks like it's all over and the police are finished with us, so . . .'

She told him of finding the money belt on Walter Matheson's corpse, and of her decision not to tell him. 'There was two hundred and fifty-five thousand dollars in there Alex. And three little bottles full of what are probably emeralds. So I just put it all in a package and sent it off to Michael for safekeeping. This letter is just him telling me that he received it and that everything's okay.'

'Two hundred and fifty thousand dollars?'

'Two hundred and fifty-five. Plus a bunch of emeralds. Plus the fifty thousand from last summer, plus the twenty-five thousand from this winter. All together Michael has three hundred and thirty thousand dollars and three bottles of emeralds hidden away for us somewhere in New York.'

'Three hundred and thirty thousand dollars?'

'Plus a bunch of emeralds.' She stood up. 'If you're

coming home tomorrow I'm going to have to get going. If I don't clean up the house and do some grocery shopping tonight you're going to take one look at the place and go straight back to the hospital.'

She helped Alex to his feet and continued, 'Anyway, I hope that two hundred and fifty-five thousand dollars and three jars of emeralds makes your last night in hospital a little more tolerable.'

Money had never been important to Alex. He had grown up in a family that had had enough never to worry about it, and as a young graduate he had landed a job which allowed him to carry on not worrying. When he quit that job and began to live on the wages of a junior mechanic he had had no trouble adjusting – he had been unhappy with money and he was now happy without, *ergo* money was not relevant. But that evening, lying on his hospital bed in the spring twilight, he began to realize something that anyone who grows up poor knows almost from birth: money that you have suffered for is always important.

Three hundred and thirty thousand dollars. And the emeralds. Four hundred thousand? Half a million? A million? What would they do with it?

The last thought in his mind as he fell asleep was that it really didn't matter what they did with it. They had each other and they had their freedom. No amount of money was as important as that.

CHAPTER FIFTY-SIX

Seattle

SHE SAW HIM sitting on the front steps as she pulled Alex's van in to the kerb and almost drove away again, but decided that it would be pointless. There was something inevitable about the man and she felt that wherever she might drive away to, he would be waiting for her when she arrived, so she shut off the engine and stepped out.

He stood up and approached the van. 'Miss Cunningham, I'd like to talk to you for a few minutes.'

'Does it matter if I want to talk to you, Lieutenant?'

'Not particularly. I'd rather we sat down with a drink somewhere and talked peaceably, but I can probably get the Tacoma Police to book you for something and we can go down to the station and do it the hard way if you'd rather. It's really up to you.'

For a moment she debated telling him to fuck himself, then shrugged her shoulders and said, 'Come on upstairs. You can help me carry the groceries.'

'Miss Cunningham,' Holley was sitting in the living room in a chair to the right of the fireplace, 'before I say anything else there's two things I want to make clear. The first is that as long as you and your friend Townsend stick to your stories there's not a court in the country that would convict you of anything. In fact, if I were stupid enough to charge either of you with anything I'd probably get reprimanded.'

Linda didn't say anything. She was half standing, half sitting on the edge of the sideboard on the other side of the room.

'That's the first thing. The second is that I personally don't think that you've been telling the truth.' He paused for her reaction, but she continued to lean against the sideboard saying nothing, so he continued. 'Alex may be a pretty nice guy, but he's not much of a liar and it's pretty clear that he wasn't pushed into this business by any threats from Walter Matheson. He *chose* to get involved. I don't know why, maybe money, maybe for the adventure, maybe because his friend was involved, but it was his choice.'

He paused again but Linda remained silent.

'What do you know about Walter Matheson?'

'Just what I said I knew about him in the statements I made to you, to the Seattle Police and to the DEA.' She walked across the room and sat down in a chair facing him. 'Look, you're here because you want something, so why don't you stop screwing around and just tell me what it is, okay?'

He kept himself under tight control. 'Very well, what I want is to put a man named John Tomlinson in prison for the rest of his life, and in order for me to do that, now that Walter Matheson is dead, Alex is going to have to go back into the cocaine business.'

She looked at him without saying anything for almost thirty seconds, long enough for him to decide that she was not going to say anything at all. Then she spoke quietly: 'Tiger bait doesn't have a very high survival potential, Lieutenant, and Alex has already paid a pretty high price. What makes you think that he'll be willing to get involved again? And why are you telling me about this? If you want Alex to help you why don't you go to the hospital and ask him?'

'I don't think Alex likes me very much.'

'And you think *I* do?'

'No, but you're a little more sensible than he is. You're not going to fall apart or run for a lawyer if I say something that upsets you. And as to the price he's paid, let's not get the violins out yet. He's still alive, which is maybe more than he deserves, and I get the feeling that he didn't come out of this broke either.

'I'm not an idiot, Linda.' It was the first time he had used her name and it startled her. 'And I've spent more than twenty years dealing with every kind of lie that can be told. When he made that first carry with Wilson, money changed hands. So let's not cry too much about poor Alex.'

Linda stood up. 'I think this meeting is over, Mr. Holley. You've read all the statements, and you just said yourself that there's nothing anyone can do to us, so why don't you leave. If you want to talk to Alex I can't stop you, but if you push him you *will* be talking to his lawyer.'

Holley made no move to go, just smiled and said, 'Sit down, sit down. I have absolutely no intention of talking to Alex. If I can't convince you then I'll walk out the door and you'll never see or hear from me again.'

Linda sat down. 'So what are you going to do, tell me that this guy you want to put in prison is some kind of monster, that it's our moral duty to help you?'

Holley replied with quiet intensity, 'I happen to think that he is a monster. Personally I'd like to see him in the gas chamber and not in jail, but I also think that one of the things that makes this country a good place to live is that cops like me don't get to make those decisions. And I think it's the moral duty of every decent human being to help put a stop to people like him.

'If I were talking to Alex that's exactly what I'd say, and he would probably buy it, because I think he is a pretty decent guy. But I also know that you'd be the one who made the decision, and I'm pretty sure that you'd let half the human race go down the drain before you let him get involved in this again. You may have a soft spot for Alex Townsend, but it's the only soft spot you've got.'

She started to speak, but he cut her off. 'John Tomlinson is one of the biggest smackmen on the west coast, and I think that you lived in the gutter long enough – yes, I do my homework – long enough to know what that means in terms of human misery. Matheson was selling coke to him, and he's waiting for the thirty kilos you were carrying.'

'So?'

'Have you read any newspapers this week? Watched any news?'

'Why?'

'You haven't seen your name have you?'

'What are you trying to say?'

'The body of an unidentified white male was found in the North Cascades last weekend. He had obviously been murdered but that was all that anyone knew. There was nothing about thirty kilos of cocaine, and no mention of you or Alex, just one unidentified body. Page one for a day and then page nineteen and then nothing. Sometime soon we'll identify the body from its fingerprints and that'll make headlines for another day or so and that's going to be it, no one will ever know what happened and in two weeks the whole thing will be forgotten. But Tomlinson will know what happened, and he'll probably be just as happy to buy from Alex as from Matheson.'

'And you'll be there when he does. Right?'

'That's right.'

Linda didn't buy it. 'And while you're shooting the tiger who's looking after the bait? No thanks Lieutenant; get some undercover hotshot from the DEA to do it for you, or do it yourself, but leave us out of it.'

She stood up again. 'You said that if I said no, you'd never bother us again. Well I'm saying no. Do you understand?' She crossed the room and waited by the door of the entryway.

Holley followed her across the room, walked through the entryway and stopped at the top of the stairs. 'The reason I want Alex is that Tomlinson may already know about him.' The sympathy had gone out of his voice, and he looked down at Linda with no apparent emotion. 'I won't be calling you again. If you won't cooperate, you won't cooperate, and I'm going to have to try something else. It probably won't work but it's the only thing I can think of.'

He stepped down one step, but was still far taller than Linda. 'When I get back to California tomorrow I'm going to get the word out that you and Alex hijacked that coke.' He was implacable, immutable, a black stone-man, and as he spoke Linda could feel herself growing old. 'Nobody is likely to care much about Matheson, but like I said, Tomlinson is expecting his thirty kilos.'

He started down the stairs, but stopped halfway and turned to face her one last time. 'That shipment is worth a few million to him. I expect that he'll take time out of his busy schedule to come and pick it up.' He turned and descended the remaining stairs, speaking over his shoulder as he went. 'Nothing's free, Linda. Nothing at all.'

Author's Note

I would like to thank Robb MacLaren of the Vancouver Police Department for the considerable time and effort he spent demonstrating the inner workings of a modern police force. The credit for whatever authenticity I have achieved regarding police matters is largely his.

UNDERCURRENTS

Ridley Pearson

Driven by guilt, Sergeant Lou Boldt heads a special task
force within Seattle's homicide bureau. Their job: to find
the 'Cross Killer', the twisted, perverse murderer who has
paralysed Seattle for six months; the crazed psychopath
whose grisly trademark is a crucifix carved in the flesh of
his victims . . .

With the help of Daphne Matthews, a police
psychologist, Boldt begins to discover the missing links in
a terrifying, complex puzzle. But when the killer's pattern
changes, he comes to the chilling realization that they are
looking for not one, but two killers. And the second one is
prowling among them . . .

0 7474 0389 9
ADVENTURE/THRILLER

CRUX

Richard Aellen

Years ago, in the jungles of Vietnam, Keith Johnson
witnessed something he wasn't meant to see . . .

So they framed him, disgraced him, and left him for
dead. Then they stole his wife, his child, and his future.
But rage kept Johnson alive in a North Vietnamese
hellhole for twenty years.

And now he's coming home . . .

He's coming to seek revenge on the three who destroyed
his life: the head of a Los Angeles security firm, a
powerful international arms dealer, and the man who
could be the next President of the United States . . .

0 7474 0692 8
GENERAL FICTION

Sphere now offers an exciting range of quality titles by both established and new authors. All of the books in this series are available from:

Sphere Books,
Cash Sales Department,
P.O. Box 11,
Falmouth,
Cornwall TR10 9EN.

Alternatively you may fax your order to the above address. Fax No. 0326 376423.

Payments can be made as follows: Cheque, postal order (payable to Macdonald & Co (Publishers) Ltd) or by credit cards, Visa/Access. Do not send cash or currency. UK customers and B.F.P.O.: please send a cheque or postal order (no currency) and allow £1.00 for postage and packing for the first book, plus 50p for the second book, plus 30p for each additional book up to a maximum charge of £3.00 (7 books plus).

Overseas customers including Ireland, please allow £2.00 for postage and packing for the first book, plus £1.00 for the second book, plus 50p for each additional book.

NAME (Block Letters) ....

ADDRESS ....

....

☐ I enclose my remittance for _____

☐ I wish to pay by Access/Visa Card

Number ☐☐☐☐☐☐☐☐☐☐☐☐☐☐☐☐☐

Card Expiry Date ☐☐☐☐